Praise for *Un...*

Historically vibrant and sadly exquisite, *Until We're Fish*
renders a poetic and cinematic view of Cuba through the lens of
loves—familial love, romantic love, patriotic love—and their complex
intersections, all beautifully and uniquely told through this compelling
story centered on lives that make history come alive.
— RICHARD BLANCO, Presidential Inaugural Poet,
author of *How to Love a Country*

"In her soulful debut novel, Susannah R. Drissi offers a meditation on
what it means to be Cuban, living between unfulfilled revolutionary
ideals, lost illusions of love, and the sea, always the sea."
— RUTH BEHAR, Pura Belpré Award-winning author of
Lucky Broken Girl, and *Letters from Cuba*

"Stunning. As full of poetry and verve as a drop of water,
Until We're Fish is an unforgettable portrait of a man trapped by
his obsessions. A remarkable debut by a writer preened and primed
by the helter-skelter world of the 1959 Cuban Revolution.
Susannah R. Drissi is a master prose stylist,
and this novel is a masterpiece."
— EMILIO BEJEL, *The Write Way Home: A Cuban-American Story*

"Riveting...Beautifully written and thought provoking...
about unconditional love, misfortunes, grief,
disillusionment, and survival. A fascinating tale of
'fish in a barrel' trying to find a way out."
— ASELA R. LAGUNA, Professor Emerita of Women and
Gender Studies, Rutgers University, *Goodreads*

"A deeply immersive experience. A novel of unrelenting loss
and inescapable despair, yet punctuated with humor and philosophical
observations, sometimes cultural, sometimes whimsical. The geography
and the characters are vivid, genuine, and transformative; and mundane
events are so evocative that a smile of recognition was never far
from my lips. I think this novel is wonderful."
— ADRIANA BOSCH, Emmy Award-winning director of
PBS American Experience: Fidel Castro

Until
We're
Fish

A NOVEL BY

Susannah R. Drissi

PROPERTIUS
PRESS

Printed in the United States of America
Edited by Nick O'Hara
Cover design by Lance Buckley
Interior design by Raven van den Bosch

PROPERTIUS
PRESS

ISBN Print: 978-1-67810-739-0
ISBN eBook: 978-0-46360-646-9

NATIONAL AUTHOR ENGAGEMENTS
For interviews with the author and to set up an event, please contact:
Kim Dower
Kim-from-L.A. Literary & Media Services
kimfromla@earthlink.net
323-655-6023

For my family, always

In my book of memory, in the early part where there is little to be read, there comes a chapter with the rubric: 'Here begins a new life.'

–Dante Alighieri, Vita Nuova
Translated by Mark Musa

PROLOGUE

Fish Eyes

HE ROUNDS THE westernmost tip of the island. Nearing the reefs
he jumps up, and falls back in. Sunlight bends against the waves, then
spreads into blue glow. The entire hemisphere of the sky compresses into
a circle over him. Coral heads stretch up to the surface like underwater
skyscrapers. Multicolored scales rush by.

This is life, Elio thinks, and why it simply goes on. This kept him
from succumbing to the small failures he'd endured one after another—
the meaning of which he now understood. Had he stayed any longer,
long enough to outlive his obsessions, he would have lost something
precious. Something that had been in him, perhaps always. Something
not belonging to him, but to life itself.

Ordinary as his days had been, they formed a pattern—how life
works, how life really works. Spread them out on a table like puzzle
pieces, fit them all together by color, timbre, and shape, and an image
eventually appears. Because it isn't enough to identify the pattern. One
has to get close enough or far back enough to see the image.

Part 1

Three Kings' Day

Bauta, 1959–1964

CHAPTER 1

ALONG A BLOCK of mostly abandoned shops near Galiano, a young man in suit and tie turned his storefront sign to "CLOSED" and tore off the red plastic arrow at 2:00 p.m. Elio stared at him from a few feet away. Kicked a Coke bottle into the street, avoiding eye contact.

"Dream on," the man shouted to Elio and disappeared behind a door. Elio glowered at the window display. He thought about walking away. Instead, he found the Coke bottle and hurled it at the storefront. Shattered glass flew in all directions.

"Take that," Elio shouted at the gaping hole in the window, "hijo de puta, see if I care about your stupid bicycle." He took off running down the sidewalk, turning around only once to stick out his middle finger at the store clerk, who had run outside and was now, hands on his hips, cussing and spitting into Havana's hot afternoon air.

Not stopping, Elio made his way through the last of the rioting crowds that shouted, laughed, and cursed even as they sprawled toward every place at once. He followed the path of broken glass and shattered storefront windows, torn awnings, and rows of abandoned cars. Nearly a week earlier, on January 1, upon the news that Batista had fled the island, parades had broken out in Havana, turning quickly into bloody riots.

Throngs had wrecked casinos, sacked hotels, and set the offices of the newspaper *Tiempo* on fire. They broke into credit and investment banks, smashing windows and destroying everything in their path. But most of the crowds dispersed after the Batista flag was lowered. The big event was yet to come, though.

When Elio finally stopped to catch his breath, the store and the clerk were almost half a mile away. But, with the storm-tossed chaos that was life in La Habana those days—cops, mobs, tearaways, and hoodlums—he needed to keep going. He ran north, across Galiano, pumping his legs as hard as he could, until he reached the Malecón. The seawall wasn't more than four feet high. He scaled it in a matter of seconds, panting. As he waited for his heart to slow, he surveyed his surroundings.

To one side, old men in guayaberas as starched and pristine as their daughters, puckered mouths around habanos; to the other, university students huddled, whispered, and strummed guitars. Beyond them, the waves of the incoming tide lashed themselves into frenzied foam against the rocks. Spray drenched Elio's face. Yes, on the other side was the sea. His legs had taken him toward a place that could one day prove very useful. Someday, he thought, he might need to escape again. And, if that day ever came, the Malecón would be the first place he'd think of.

The landing would be no picnic, but he'd find a way. He considered the matter so intently that soon the rocks on the other side of the wall seemed to disappear completely. And when they were nothing but a cushion of white powder at the bottom of the ocean, Elio got ready to dive in. He stretched his arms out, like a bird, then straightened his legs, bent his body forward at the waist, and pointed his toes toward the crashing waves.

"What the hell do you think you're doing?" a raspy voice said. Someone tugged on Elio's pant leg.

Elio tried to catch his balance, but tumbled back off the seawall, falling butt first on the sidewalk, hands hitting the ground. Embarrassed, he quickly pulled himself back up, groaning under his breath, to the Malecón's glittering afternoon light.

"You think you're a bird, or what? It's all jagged rock down there—" the man with the raspy voice said, dusting Elio off.

"Yeah, I know," Elio said, flicking the man's hand away, then turning to look up at him. It was a fisherman—tall and thin, with long, greasy dark hair, and a scraggly beard. Elio gave him an irritated look. "What did you think I was doing? Trying to kill myself?"

"Well, I don't know," the fisherman said, sucking on a wad of tobacco in his cheek. "It sure looked like something."

"Nah, just messing around—" Elio said.

"Messing around? Don't you have something better to do?"

"Like what? Like getting off the island?"

"Listen, kid," the man laughed, "there's no such thing. On this island, we've always been fish in a barrel. You know, you can't escape. We got just enough water to remember we're fish. But if they want us gone, all they gotta do is drain the water out."

"Water? What water?" Elio smirked. "I don't see any water. I see Centro Habana to my left and Vedado to my right," he said, pointing left and right toward the cityscape. "I see royal palm trees, and sun, and clouds. But water? Never heard of it," he said, continuing to smirk.

"Look," the old man said, flapping his arms, "these hands were once fins. Your blood is as salty as the sea it came from. We're fish, little man, fish. They say the sea levels are rising. But in the meantime, we're stuck in a goddamn barrel."

"Well, you're a barrel of laughs. Are you drunk or something?" Elio said, pulling himself up to sit on the seawall.

"Or something." The man leaned over on the wall to spit onto the rocks. "All I know is that if I was a fish, I'd be on my way somewhere."

"Sounds like a plan to me." It was clear from the man's voice that he was as amused as Elio. Elio hoped they'd become friends.

"You live around here or something?" Elio asked.

The old man squinted up at Elio. "Goodbye, kid," he said. "If the fish are smart enough to avoid the Malecón today, we should too. Not one fish today, not a single one," he said, gathering his fishing gear.

Elio returned the squint with a distrustful squint of his own. It's his loss, he thought. "Goodbye! Until…you know!" Elio waved down at him.

Watching the old man drift further and further away from the seafront, Elio's mind went back to the bicycle. It had been a Schwinn, but not just any Schwinn: the Panther II. Just like the one he'd seen at the Sears window almost a month ago, with a big red bow and green streamers coiled around handlebars. Behind it, a vinyl panel: an American couple in matching bathrobes leaning against a garlanded front door. Five children—mittens and winter hats—goggled at the lustrous red Schwinn parked on the snow. Below it, the only English Elio really ever managed to learn: "New for Christmas!"

He was thirteen then and, besides Maria, this was his second obsession. The thing he couldn't have no matter how many times he stood in front of that shop window.

The 1959 Panther II was a beauty, he thought, leaping off the wall. He veered to walk around the students, but when he tried, he tripped. Suddenly, he found himself surrounded.

"Terribly sorry," one of the students said. Elio ducked, meaning to slink past him, but found himself, to his horror, in his grip. The student— taller and at least five years older than Elio, with high cheekbones and a thin dark mustache—clutched him by a forearm.

"Oh my goodness!" he said, whipping Elio around. "Take a look at this little top from the province—Bejucal? Punta Brava? Bauta?" He looked down at Elio's shoes, which were tattered and white around the edges where the leather was scuffed and more overworn.

"Bauta," Elio tensed his face. "Get your hands off me."

"Let the kid go, Raulito," one of the students said. He was about Elio's height, a foot shorter than the others.

"Wait, look at his shoes. Don't they make shoes your size in Bauta, papito?"

"Nope. Your mother shoved them all up her ass." Elio grinned, wiggling his toes—stuffed inside his shoes like sardines.

"How old are you, you little shit? I didn't realize your balls had dropped yet. Good for you!" The guy's laugh was more of a whoop.

"Thirteen," Elio said.

Still laughing, the guy leaned back and clapped. "In that case, go ahead." He curtsied, bending one foot behind him, "the Malecón is all yours."

"Terribly sorry," one student smirked, bowing and lifting his guitar in the air by the neck. He was tall and muscular, with ropey locks that reached his shoulders. The guy looked like he could break Elio's jaw with a single punch. It was clear to Elio they'd come to a standstill.

Except for Elio and the students, only the old men in guayaberas remained on the Malecón. They watched silently from far away, as though Elio's scuffle was the first in a series of surprising, but inevitable, events. The fishermen, who stood along the seawall casting their bait into the surf, had packed and gone. The dark-skinned men trolling the waters opposite El Morro had left too. And the couples who normally leaned against the wall, chattering and kissing against the shadow and light of old Havana, had stayed home that afternoon, and so had the children, with their makeshift fishing poles and cans full of red worms. A revolution was coming and, for better or for worse, Cubans were elsewhere, Elio thought.

"Eh!" finally, one of the old men in guayaberas shouted. "Eh!"

The student let go of Elio, who quickly brushed himself off and straightened out his shirt. "Tu madre!" Elio bellowed, pushing the student and sending him reeling. The guitar dropped onto the pavement with a thud. But instead of picking it up or grabbing Elio, the student took a quick step away, his hands behind his back.

"Would you look at that?!—that's the kind of shit you get in the province," the student said.

"Eh, relax. It wasn't a gunshot, man. Relax." The short one patted him on the back.

Elio hesitated for a moment, then took off running across the avenue toward the Hotel Nacional. On the off chance they decided to come after him, he'd be halfway to the Río Almendares by the time they reached Línea.

Nearing the hotel's entrance, he blinked at the sun reflected off the palm tree trunks lining his grand view of the driveway. He thought about going inside, but he'd never make it past the front door—not with the provincial pinta he carried around like a goddamn birthmark.

A small crowd of American tourists—on their way to the port— waited for taxis on the lawn. They'd been sent packing. They knew what was good for them, and they took off in fancy yachts with leather-bound interiors and names like *The Bubble Gum* and *Kittyland*. They loved the island, though. For years they'd come in droves, filling casinos and brothels with clouds of Yankee cigarettes, sauntering up and down the Malecón and framing it all in black and white Polaroids. They gave Cubans gin rummy, bridge, bingo, and those goddamn crossword puzzles Maria bent over for hours, pencil poised and cross-legged on her front porch.

Elio stared at the hotel for a while and, when the heat in his shoes
made his toes curl, his mind went back to the university students. They
were just like him, he told himself; same big dreams and resolute gestures.
There was one small distinction, though. The students might end up in
Bauta cutting sugarcane one day. He, on the other hand, would never be
a student in Havana—or, as his dad would say, "on the notable hill that
was occupied by the University of Havana." After all, rolling downhill was
always easier than scaling up the side of a mountain.

He took off walking. And his thoughts once again settled on the
bicycle. What a gem! A two-tone seat with a big "S" on it, dual lights,
rear racks with little reflectors on them and a new trimline tank. If he had
a bike, he wouldn't have to put up with those lowlifes. He could speed
away, with Maria sideways on the rear rack all the way to Baracoa. With
Maria on the handlebars, arms outstretched down the Loma de Pita. With
Maria pedaling the hell out of the bike to Rosa Marina and him standing
on the back.

Shit, with a bike like that he could go from one end of the island
and back in a day's time. But who the hell had $39? His life was nothing
like the vinyl panel. Christmas now a month behind them, no possibility
of snow ever, and the only American parent he could think of was not
American at all, but a Cuban from Vueltabajo who'd gone up and left
them. Last he heard, that bastard was an actor in Chicago, sweeping floors
on the side. No, there'd be no Panther II for Elio. Not now, not ever. Not
unless he still believed in miracles. And he didn't.

Once he decided that he was free of the students for good, he walked
down Calle L, toward Avenida 23. In less than ten minutes, he was
standing in front of Cine Radiocentro. At about fifteen years old, the
Radiocentro movie theater was only a few years older than Elio, and a
real beauty. The screen was 180 degrees, the ceilings were high, and the

seats were red velvet and so soft Elio loved to cushion himself on them to gobble up popcorn and watch the show.

Elio remembered going there with his dad once or twice to watch American Westerns in 3-D. "There's a whole lot of dreaming at the movies," his dad had told him then, "and you don't even have to close your eyes." Elio had enough reasons to want to dream: his father, the movie lover, was a thousand miles away; his mother was a train wreck; and his life was going nowhere he could foresee.

He paid fifty cents, and went into the theater. The place smelled like popcorn and cigars, and the floors were sticky with spilled cola and chewing gum. In the dark, Elio scanned the best available seats. There were about thirty people in the theater already. They were talking and laughing. These were the real movie goers of Havana, Elio thought: people who knew movies and movie theaters like the palm of their hand; who could tell the difference between Gary Cooper and Gregory Peck; who watched the latest films and spent their Sundays at matinées, watching Woody Woodpecker and Mr. Magoo on the big screen. These were the *real* dreamers.

The theater had three seating areas, with two aisles dividing the side rows from the wider center rows, which held more seats. It also had a balcony. Elio liked the middle row—not too close and not too far from the screen. There were two people already sitting almost in the middle. The two seats *exactly* in the middle were vacant, though. Elio took the one on the left, leaving the right one open.

He'd arrived very early, but the theater filled up in about a half hour. In less than an hour, the lights dimmed. The news came first: "The rebels are getting closer to Havana," the news anchor confirmed, receiving a unanimous cheer and flying popcorn from the audience. Then, about half an hour later, what everyone had been waiting for: *Cinerama Holiday,* the much anticipated sequel to *This Is Cinerama.*

"Prepare yourself for the most beautiful and impressive trip of your life,"
the voice on screen said. Just as Elio was about to sink into his velvety
seat, a guy climbed into the vacant seat next to him. For a moment, Elio
froze, thinking it was one of the university students. But he was wrong.
The guy who'd landed next to him and proceeded to fidget incessantly was
taller and thinner than any of the losers he'd left behind in the Malecón.
Elio glared. The guy searched his pockets and continued to squirm, as
the *Cinerama* promotional reel went on: *"…without luggage, passports, or
visas…just take your seat at Cine Radiocentro and…you're on board!"*

The screen showed a young couple rising out of the snow. *"You will
enter Switzerland flying on ice… You will go down on a bobsled at 118 miles
per hour through the steep slopes of the Alps…"* The guy was still making
a ruckus. Elio glared at him again. This time, the fellow settled into his
seat and Elio didn't hear from him the rest of the night, except for the
occasional snore.

When Elio walked out of the theater two hours later, he could still
hear the voice from the screen: *"You will know the excitement of the famous
Las Vegas Casinos… You will experience springtime in Paris… You will
stroll Paris by day and Paris by night… You will be charmed by the streets of
Montmartre… You will discover the most interesting and beautiful places on a
trip full of adventures! **YOU are the real star of Cinerama Holiday!**"* Sure,
Elio thought.

Only the lesser part of the night still remained by the time he left
Havana and headed for the two-hour bus ride back home. The scent of
jasmine clung to his face as he crossed Avenida José Martí. Bauta was,
as usual, silent at this hour of the night, except for the purring of the
water tank, the occasional barking of a dog, and the crowing of a lone
cock who, having nothing better to do, had rushed the dawn hour. Elio

knew this town. Street by street, house by house, and porch by porch. Its rivers and sea endlessly linked in one great cycle. With waters that flowed nowhere.

The town could go on forever. On and on. If he ever tried to escape it, leave it behind like his dad had done, he would need to climb out of it, or wait for the tide to rise.

It was almost noon by the time he woke up. Long slants of sunlight fell across his face. He sat up and looked through half-opened shutters toward Maria's yard. She stood halfway up a wooden ladder that leaned against a concrete fence. White organza dress and tense calves. Blonde mane billowing. Blonde hair on arms and legs glistening like gold filament. Beyond her, Bauta's lagoon. Mute, still, and dismal, it sprawled its swampy shores into people's yards, heralding droughts and floods.

"Mima," Maria shouted toward the house. "Come quickly! *Men's suits for all occasions,*" she said in English.

Elio knew exactly what she was doing. He'd heard her spewing English phrases from the Sears catalogue enough times to know. "Americana," he said aloud, jumping out of bed.

"What's happening out there?" her grandmother asked from somewhere inside the house.

"*Children's pajamas,*" Maria responded. She bent over the concrete fence that separated her house from Bauta's lagoon. "Come look!"

Elio got closer to his bedroom window. It was perfectly reasonable, he thought, to want to stare at Maria's legs without being seen.

"Get ready," her grandmother said. "We're leaving for Cabañas on the

4:00 p.m. bus. In case the madness spreads, I don't want to be here when the rebels reach Havana."

"But…*Christmas discounts,*" Maria responded. Leaned over the wall even further.

"Oye, Americana, you're gonna fall head first into the lagoon!" Elio shouted. He laughed when Maria's legs rocked the ladder, a sure signal she'd heard him loud and clear.

"Stop the nonsense, muchacha!" her grandmother shouted.

"Women's shoes," Maria finally said. And came down the ladder, sauntering away from Elio's view.

Cabañas? What the hell? Elio thought. It was now or never. He closed the shutters and walked toward his bed. When he'd made his sheets into one big ball at the center of his mattress, he shouted at his mother. "Aurelia, the beach is waiting for me!"

"Not now, Elio. Forget the beach. You don't want to miss the rebels."

But he couldn't forget the beach—not today. Today Maria was going to Cabañas, and there was no way he'd let her leave without a Three Kings' Day gift: a pail of gobies. As long as he made it back with the fish by 3:30 p.m., he would see Maria before she boarded the bus. It was that, or wait for Pepe to make his move, and he wasn't about to let *that* happen.

Not that Pepe would ever end up with Maria. *That* was as farfetched an idea as he'd ever heard. Pepe was a player—not that his girlfriends minded. He was a kid from Belica, a nearby neighborhood, who happened to be Maria's friend. He was about Elio's age, but taller, more muscular, and, according to Maria, a much better swimmer too. Maria had told Elio once that Pepe could have been a star swimmer, if he'd wanted to. Elio remembered watching Maria's face when she told him. She'd transformed into one big flurry of smiles and batting eyes. It was pathetic the way she'd flipped her hair and said that if *she* wanted to, Pepe could be her boyfriend *any* time. Right then and there, Elio developed a certain deep dislike for the kid. He knew what Pepe was up to, so that was all it took: Elio might never get the Schwinn, but he would get Maria.

"I'm in the middle of something, woman!" he said to his mother.

He took off his boxers and crumpled them into the ball he'd made with the sheets; then he ran to the shower. Carajo! He kicked the wall. A drop of copper-colored water from the rusted showerhead fell on his pito, still at half-mast. Just as he was about to call out to his mother, a gush hit him full force. "Shit," he said out loud. "This has got to be shit." He stepped aside, waiting until the water ran clear to redeploy under it. Taking his time, he lathered up. He had a few hours and the gobies weren't going anywhere. Hoping he wouldn't go blind, he closed his eyes.

"What the hell are you doing in there?" his mother called out. "The revolution's coming, Elio! It's on TV!"

He was a fish, a big one. Swimming through Bauta underwater, all of it. Bodega Los Cubanitos, the park, the church, and La Glorieta submerged in blue water, with schools of yellow, orange, and red fish. All the way down the Carretera Central to Havana. All that water making its way to the bay. Like in one of those vivid dreams he'd had before, everyone was gone. Poof, disappeared. His breathing quickening, his heart pounding, his legs shaking. And all that water.

"Fidel's making his way to Havana!" his mother shouted.

Elio guessed she'd been glued to the television since daylight broke, following the rebels' every move until they'd reached the capital.

"They're close! Elio, come watch! Get out of that shower, muchacho!" She called again.

Now dressed, he slid into the squalid living room. A colander and
old pantyhose swung from a belt loop in his shorts. His mother stared at
her pantyhose and laughed. Since his father had left, she'd lost interest in
most things. Letting the house sink lower and lower into some dark hole,
where coming up for air involved making way through old newspapers,
dirty dishes, and unwashed clothes. Elio's room was the only truly clean
place in the house. The only part of his life he could control, and where
he hid his precious glass marbles, and his sketches of Maria's legs and of
American bikes. He'd learned to fend for himself. He even began to look
forward to surviving, to tidying things up, to mending, and washing,
and polishing.

That morning she seemed more excited about the rebels than she'd
been about most things in the last few months. But it didn't last. As
soon as she saw the beards, her shoulders drooped. "Facial hair like that
reminds me of your father," she'd said. "Anyone with hair like that can't be
trusted. Too much blah, blah, blah behind the curtain, and not enough
action. You want to be a man of action, Elio. A man of arms and letters,
like Martí or Don Quixote. Not some lazy, no-good dreamer like your
father or those lazy, no-good dreamers on TV."

"The rebels are heroes, Mom. Tell me all about it when I get back,"
Elio said, lightly kissing his mother's head. "Someone's gotta dream."

"Are you skipping school, Elio Perez?"

"Today's a holiday, Mom. You know, Three Kings' Day? Presents?"

"Verdad que sí," she said. She looked confused. "Deja eso, niño.
Come sit with me, c'mon!" Her head cocked to sidestep his lips. "I called
in sick today."

"Again?" Elio said.

"Not again, just this once…Plus, like you said, it's a holiday…so you
and I can watch los rebeldes on TV."

"Who's supposed to open the pharmacy, if you're not there, Mom?"

"We open only until noon today, Eli. Plus, no one's gonna die, if they don't get their diazepam or their tetracycline for one day... This is big, real big—your father would've…"

"I gotta go, Mom."

"And the mangoes?"

"Tomorrow."

By the time she turned around, he was out the door.

The sun beat down, hotter that day than any other day that January. It was more humid than usual too. Elio's pit hairs swashed whenever his arms moved, and his boxers stuck to his ass like Chiclet. He hitchhiked all the way to the beach, starting in Yumurí, then passing by Villa Paz Farm, and riding down the Loma de Pita on the grille of someone's old Schwinn, hairy brown legs dangling on the sides. Then rode in the back seat of a green '57 Chevy on its way to Baracoa.

The smell of sea salt danced in the breeze as soon as they passed Rosa Marina. The car shook and quivered over uneven asphalt as the voice on the radio announced: "Rebel leaders prepare for triumphal entry into Havana. We should *all* buck up."

All the tittle-tattle about the revolution made Elio nervous. He wriggled so much, a tear on the vinyl cut into his right calf. When the driver complained about all the fussing, he was left to walk the rest of the way, some quarter of a mile to the sand. According to the clock in the car, though, it was only 1:30 p.m., so Elio had plenty of time.

He trudged past pairs of lovers, their tangled limbs like vines under the uvas caletas. Bodies pressed against the sand in some Creole version of *From Here to Eternity.* Naked pot-bellied children flying kites or digging tunnels in the sand. Carrying water in blue plastic buckets to and from the shore. Filling the tunnels with water. Crying. Starting anew. "What did you expect?" he hears somebody ask, "to reach China?"

Elio looked ahead. He adjusted the pantyhose on the loop. He turned the opening for the panty leg outward and pulled on the little bag for the foot. It was his old makeshift goby catcher, and it would do.

He dug his shoes in the hot sand, leaving deep tracks behind him. He wrestled with mangroves on the way to the pier. Snarled roots blockading his way. It was a Tuesday and the beach was nearly empty. Radios and televisions, from Guanahacabibes to Baitiquirí, held the good island people captive like nothing ever had. Even the ones who'd managed to reach the beach had Havana on their mind. There were "rebels this" and "rebels that" and "Batista fled the coop." Though in small numbers, there were enough people in the water that day—any one of them could have spotted the shark. But only Pepe saw it coming for him.

Elio hid his shoes among dientes de perro surrounding the pier. Ran back to the sand until he reached the shore. Had he been looking for signs, he would have noticed one or two. Nothing like a ladder or a black cat crossing the road or a broken mirror. Something more like slivers of glass shimmering sunlight against his eyes, and Pepe—cigarette hanging from his mouth, bucket of jaivas in hand—crossing the road somewhere between Rosa Marina and Baracoa. "Hey!" Elio'd shouted at Pepe that afternoon. But the boy had been too far ahead to hear him.

Feeling the mushy sand underfoot, Elio waded in the water until he was about waist deep. He was looking for gobies. He found blennies instead. Both were only half an inch long or less. Small bastards, so they made great bait. Divers always missed them. Blennies had one single continuous dorsal fin. Gobies had two and were a little high strung as well. Blennies seemed to take it as it came; they were cooler that way. Way too cool to eat or want to sell. They were like the James Dean of Cuban fish under one inch.

Though the sun was high over the beach now, water reflecting like a mirror, Elio could still make out thousands of tiny fish gleaming like blades in the water below. He was mesmerized. By the time he looked up and spotted the fin, it was too late. He couldn't scream. He was too busy gasping for air. Mouth sinking below blue water. Coming up long enough to exhale-inhale only to sink again. His arms flailing, pushing water down, fighting for his life. Fuck, I'm gonna die, he thought. And all for some dumbass gobies. Some afternoon. He went in looking for gobies and found a shark. It came out of nowhere. They always did.

He could hear the rapid thuds of his heart against his rib cage. And the splashing of water, broken by voices in the distance:

"Swim, coño! Swim!"

He had wanted to scream, "Tiburón!" but couldn't keep his mouth above water long enough to make a sound, let alone a word. The sun was a mass of blinking yellow against his eyes each time he managed to pull up for air. The shark had him by his right leg. No pain, just heat that went up from his thigh to his ass and up into his spine.

Near the shore, some twenty feet away, Pepe took one quick puff of his cigarette, then flicked it into the air. He dropped his bucket of jaivas on the sand and strode through the water fully dressed.

"Tiburón!" someone shouted, prompting a small crowd of tourists in black Speedos and yellow string bikinis to gather near the abandoned bucket and look out to the water.

As Elio flailed in the waves, his mind leaped back in time to a mass of blonde curls, a Cuban Shirley Temple in a red and white romper jumping over the half wall between his front porch and hers.

"Get out of here!" he'd shouted, scooping up his marbles. "Shush, shush! This is for boys!"

"Ugly," she said, kicking the bag of glass marbles. "Let me play, you big ninny." Elio's eyes turned in all directions. Even his green cat's eye ended up in some distant corner.

"Fat chance."

"Ugly and flaco like a twig," she said. He froze. Watched her saunter off of his porch and back to hers. Hand on the door, she turned. Stuck her pink tongue out so far he'd thought it unnatural.

Ugly and flaco like a twig? He'd show her.

"I'm gonna tell on you! Wait till I catch you out here again. Albino rat. Get outta here, before I beat you with a stick!" He stomped his foot twice on the tile. No sound. She didn't wince. Gave him her back, and went inside. The door slammed behind her, and he loved her then. What balls! A decade later, on January 6, 1959, there he was. Gobies for Maria on Three Kings' Day.

Snap. Snap, again. Pain rushed into his hip, his groin, and up his spine. Something was torn. Everything went black.

CHAPTER 2

THE BUS LEFT La Calzada, heading for the neighboring town of Caimito. Maria sat by the window, next to her grandmother. An open book wobbled on one knee as the bus rocked over uneven asphalt. She glanced at the little note from Pepe she'd been holding in her hand since they left Bauta, then slipped it somewhere between Charles's first encounter with Emma and Heloise's unfortunate death. Flipping the pages one by one, she arrived at where she'd left off.

Right at Emma Bovary's wedding party, with the ladies in bonnets wearing dresses in the latest fashion, gold watch chains, pelerines with the ends tucked into belts, and little colored fichus fastened down behind with a pin, leaving the back of the neck bare. Maria touched the back of her own neck. She would have loved to have been one of those ladies, surrounded by boys in fine tailcoats, overcoats, and shooting jackets— if she reimagined the cuts, adding trimmings and reshaping the more outdated parts, they were just like the ones in the Sears catalogue. All so *very* darling.

She didn't care much for some of the more discomforting moments of the novel. She sided with Emma, finding Charles as unimaginative as the protagonist did. Emma's frustrations couldn't pass unnoticed. Of those, Maria herself had plenty. To begin with, there was the heat, and the mosquitoes, and the potholes, and everything else that was unpleasant about living in a small town. Maria, too, despised ordinary life and, were it not for books, she'd drop dead of boredom. If she could, she'd go right on reading all the way to Cabañas.

But the thrumming of the bus engine and the fade-in and fade-out of voices behind her made it impossible to fully remove herself from her surroundings and join Emma's celebration. She gave up temporarily, closing her book and smiling at her grandmother. Her grandmother didn't smile back. Instead, she looked down at the book. "You know," she said, "With your head stuck in a book, you'll never see where you're going."

"We're going to Cabañas, aren't we?" Maria said. Looking straight at her grandmother, she discreetly slipped the book under one thigh. The last thing she needed right now was for her grandmother to discover Pepe's note inside the book, or to question just how appropriate a choice in books was *Madame Bovary* for a girl Maria's age. She shuffled in her seat, then threw a furtive look to the road through her window glass. Güajiros, their leathery faces under straw hats, sold catauris filled with giant mangoes by the side of the road. They also sold pirulí, and cariocas, and even those refreshing snow cones Maria loved *nearly* more than reading.

"Open the window, anda," Mima said. "Maybe if you weren't always dreaming about this or that place, you'd enjoy where you are a little more."

Maria clicked her tongue and pushed the window open. A cloud of exhaust made her stomach turn and she gagged. *"Terrible,"* she said in English, pinching her nose. A group of farmers in the last seat shouted, catching Maria's attention. She looked over her shoulder. The farmers laughed, and made vigorous gestures. As hard as she tried, Maria couldn't make out their words over a curtain of beards and a roaring engine.

Beyond her window, and past the fruit and snow cone vendors by the side of the road, a rolling sea of green pastures. White and brown cows bowed heads against round bellies, appearing and disappearing in the window frame. Alongside the bus, oxen pulling carretas of hay claimed their own journey, along with Plymouths, and arañas, and Ford pickup trucks—city and country folk on the way to Havana. After all, a revolution was coming and Havana was the place to be.

The bus sped up, zigzagged, and made good time, lifting pebbles and the smell of fresh manure into the air and leaving tire marks on day-old tar.

"It's twenty-three miles from Bauta to Cabañas," her grandmother reminded her.

"Are we almost there?" Maria asked.

Her grandmother laughed and shifted in her seat to face her. She pulled her box-pleated skirt over her bony knees to hide a white slip. "No, not yet. We have about an hour to go. You'll know we're very close when we reach La Mercedita."

"Yes, I know. How long will that take?"

"About an hour. You're very impatient."

"Cabañas is boring."

"Who told you that?"

"I just know." Maria said.

"Never mind what you think you know. Wait till you see my sister's house…you won't believe your eyes."

"I've seen big houses before."

"Not as big as this one."

Maria held her grandmother's hand, which was small and soft, like a child's. Her tan skin, flat little nose, and elongated eyes made her look

Vietnamese. Maria thought so, at least—she'd seen one too many pictures of Ho Chi Minh and young Vietnamese women in military uniform not to notice a remote resemblance. But, more likely, and given Mima's weakness for heaping bowls of gofio, and quimbombó, African blood flowed through her grandmother's veins. Blood of Berbers who'd settled in the Canary Islands where her mother and father came from, and that mixed with the blood of Congos or Carabalís of West Africa. As her grandmother would often recite, "In Cuba, whoever didn't come from Congo, came from Carabalís."

Her grandmother wouldn't have it though. She was 100 percent Spanish blood, she swore, attributing her tan skin to her daily walks to Bodega Los Cubanitos without a parasol. And her slanted eyes to old age and her 1955 Singer featherweight. Her nose…well, she just got lucky, she'd say. Severity and widowhood conspired against her at the age of thirty-five, and she never remarried. Never looked at another man, as long as she lived.

An hour or so passed. Maria sat closer to her grandmother to avoid the sun. Finally, she gave up, and laid her head on her grandmother's lap while her grandmother knitted a daisy-stitch bolero and told stories. She told her about the bembé celebrations behind her house, where the souls of dead African slaves were called to join the living, and where people danced so fast you couldn't see their feet.

"Tiki-tiki-tiki," her grandmother said, tapping her feet on the floor of the bus as fast as she could. Maria had never been to a bembé, but she sure wished she had. She let her grandmother's voice go on, lulling her to sleep.

Enough time passed that, finally, the bus came to a halt. "Cabañas," the bus driver called. "Come on, Maria," her grandmother said, tucking her knitting inside her bag.

"I'm tired," Maria moaned, standing up and stretching her arms out. "You'll be fine."

They waited their turn to descend the bus. Outside, the fresh air and the cloudless blue skies made Maria thankful for the end of the journey.

Side by side, they walked up a steep hill. Twigs cut into Maria's ankles and shins as they climbed the road, but she pressed on, negotiating rocks under her feet, and pebbles wedging into her sandals. Soon, the rough terrain gave way to smoother pavement.

"Thank God for sidewalks," she told her grandmother.

Finally, a two-story corner house came into view. With black and white checkered marble on the porch, the house was a real beauty. Iron rail like black lace on the veranda. Sunlight tracing arabesques against the marble, refracting into a thousand pieces. Yes, light—lots of it.

"This is Tía Victoria's house?" Maria asked, taking the first steps up toward a large front door. As Maria took in the house in all its splendor, everything around her receded into the background. It was just the house and her, as if they'd been made for each other.

"I told you you'd like it," her grandmother said, pulling down on her skirt, yet again.

"It's *dazzling,"* Maria laughed, her mood changing for the time being. *"All nylon and lace elastics, just like Fina's,"* she said in English.

Fina Carreira, who at the end of their block, had the biggest house in the neighborhood. So big that Maria couldn't help but think about it in Sears English. According to her, Fina's house was *exciting, outstanding, and* extra *variety.* It was truly and utterly *satisfaction guaranteed.*

"The size of Fina's house proves absolutely nothing," her grandmother said, clicking her tongue. "I wouldn't want that house if she gave it to me. Too gloomy. Victoria's house, on the other hand, now that's a real *darleen* house."

Her grandmother's attempt at English and her obvious irritation with

Fina's lot in life made Maria shake her head.

"Hello, there!" The woman's voice came from just behind Maria, so close that Maria could almost feel her breath on her neck. A shudder ran up her spine and she turned around, startled. "Victoria Martínez," the woman said, holding out her hand. "But we've met before, *haven't we, darleen?"* She said, fixing her eyes on Maria, as she finished the phrase in English.

It took Maria a moment to react, perhaps because she wasn't used to anyone greeting her so formally, perhaps because she'd never have imagined Victoria could speak English.

"I didn't expect you so soon," Victoria said, kissing her sister Cuca on the cheek.

"The bus made good time, after all. Did we almost miss you?"

"Oh, no. Not at all," Victoria said. "I'd gone down the hill to check on a sick neighbor. Please, come in."

Maria and her grandmother followed Victoria through the front door. The house was as beautiful on the inside as on the outside. The black and white marble tiles extended from the porch all around the house, which wasn't huge, but it was far larger than Fina's. There were mirrors everywhere, and porcelain vases, and crystal lamps. Maria wondered how it was possible for two sisters to end up with such different houses. Her grandmother's house was clean and spare—that was the extent of it.

"Would you like something to drink?" Victoria asked, scanning Maria with what seemed to be a heightened sense of curiosity.

"Yes, thank you," Maria said. She guessed that Victoria was looking for a specific answer, but she wasn't really sure what the question was.

"How's life with Cuca?" Victoria said, gesturing toward her sister.

"My *grandmother?"* Maria managed to answer. Perhaps it was only her imagination, but Maria thought she sensed the trace of a satisfied smile at the corners of Victoria's lips. "It's life," she said, resolving to answer her question.

"Well, it's more than just life," her grandmother chimed in. Her voice, more tense than usual, telegraphed two things: one, that Maria should heed to whatever advice Victoria was about to give her; and, two, that Maria should keep most of the details of life with her grandmother to herself.

"That's wonderful," Victoria said. "I sure wish I'd had a grandmother like Cuca when I was growing up. Instead, I lived with a mean ol' woman whose idea of a compliment was to tell me I was way too fat for my britches." She laughed, winking at Maria as she did so. "Now, you must excuse me while Cuca and I prepare your lemonade."

Victoria and Cuca made their way to the kitchen, leaving Maria to appraise her surroundings. Once alone, Maria concentrated her gaze on the perfection of every little detail of the room. The ornateness of the lamp bases, the expression of joy on the porcelain figurines, and even a brass chandelier's tiny prisms whose colors danced and shimmered in the afternoon light.

By the time Victoria and Cuca came back with the lemonade, Maria felt dizzy with so much *luxurious living.* She waited for Mima to hand her the glass of lemonade, then took a long drink. After such an exhausting trip, *truly,* she was parched.

"What do you think of Cabañas so far?" Victoria asked.

"I think I'm going to like it here," Maria said, finishing off the last of her lemonade.

Cuca laughed. "Good! Tomorrow Victoria and I will show you around town a bit. Today, I'm worn out."

"Sure, sure," Victoria said. "We'll leave it for tomorrow...now, tell me," she turned to Maria. "What sorts of things do you like to do in Bauta?"

Their conversation went on for another half hour, during which time they talked about Maria's bent for algebraic equations, and her *excellent* reading habits, and even Pepe, whom Maria revealed as a friend from Belica, and a *fantastic* swimmer.

"You must be very hungry," Victoria finally said, looking at her watch. "Would you like…? Better yet, come with me. I want to give you something first." She led the way.

Maria followed Victoria into a bedroom. The shutters were closed, and the thick stale smell of tobacco and violet water filled the air. In any case, it was a beautiful room, except for the small table by the window, where Maria noticed an ashtray filled with half-smoked cigars, the remnants of a box of chocolates, and a decent-sized pile of mango rinds and chirimoya seeds. Maria reflected that, for such a pristine house, she would have imagined less overindulgence and less, *how do you say,* less mess.

She sat beside Victoria as the woman sank down on the bed and pulled out a little piece of paper from her bra. The paper was folded several times, and tied with red yarn that came to a lopsided bow right in the middle. "Here," she said. "A message."

"What kind of message?" Maria asked. She was surprised Victoria had brought her into her room for something as banal as a message.

"It's a secret," Victoria said, crossing her lips with an index finger.

Maria responded by smiling bashfully. But, really, she didn't know *how* to respond. Her great-aunt had taken up the reins of the afternoon. She was like a sorceress with a chignon and a penchant for bonbons and tropical fruits. The features of her face were marked with soft lines, a radiant smile, and a bearing so imposing, so decisive, that beside her Maria's poor grandmother looked like a country bumpkin at Madame Bovary's wedding party.

Later that day, as Cuca and Victoria played catch-up and ate fried snapper for dinner, Maria sat cross-legged on Victoria's cool porch tile. She thought about the message scribbled on the piece of paper Victoria had given her. Her eyes roamed beyond the veranda across a motionless sea of light. She wished the message had revealed something entirely different, like the more pressing questions of who she should marry, and when. She'd been in such constant expectation for either Elio or Pepe to declare their love to her, that Cabañas's pleasant quiet felt more like punishment than a last-minute getaway. Elio had committed to *a ton* of gobies, while Pepe had promised her jaivas, *lots of them*. Maria didn't even like jaivas all that much. She didn't like gobies, either. What she really wanted was a chance to see the boys again. She figured that the sooner she saw them, the sooner she could decide who *she* actually liked the most. But she wasn't even sure she would see Pepe again, after all. In fact, at this point, she wasn't even sure he was still on the island.

A few days earlier, Fina had burst into their house blabbing about Panama, from where Pepe's parents had just returned. Mima, whose sunny honeymoon in Panama City had been stolen by three days of non-stop hurricane weather, stood there in their kitchen, holding a stack of sugarcane that she had spent a good part of the afternoon loading into her mouth, staring with doubt at her neighbor for a good ten seconds. The next day Fina came by again with yet more news. This time, she'd learned from someone or other that Pepe's parents would be leaving again, this time for good. Although Maria's grandmother had insisted that Maria shouldn't believe a word Fina ever said, Maria couldn't help but wonder if any of it was true. Did that mean that Pepe was leaving too? Had he lied about the jaivas?

That night in bed, at Victoria's house, at some namelessly late hour, neither Maria nor Mima was able to sleep. While Maria still dwelled on Pepe, her grandmother made her promise that she would never leave the island, no matter the circumstances, no matter the reason, no matter how great the destination. She was not to go. Not to leave. She spoke with such genuine sadness that Maria had no choice but to promise. "Swear it," her grandmother said, turning over to peer through the dark into Maria's eyes. "Swear to God."

"I swear it," Maria whispered instantly. Her voice seemed to emerge broken from her throat, laden with confusion.

CHAPTER 3

IT TOOK ELIO a few moments to register where he was. His body hurt all over and his head felt like he'd slept in for longer than he meant to. He threw off the thin sheet covering him and made to move his leg. The heaviness of the cast, like a slab of lead on his hip and groin—let alone his leg—shocked him momentarily. It was then he remembered the shark; and Pepe swimming toward him; then he, Elio, being hauled into a truck by a couple of strangers.

His eyes wandered over to the window, so close to him he could have climbed out—only he was probably at least twelve feet from the ground outside. Below him lay El Cerro with its clipped gardens where, according to his dad, at least one famous person in Cuba had been born. His mother would not be impressed by the view, neither outside nor inside. He looked around. Not bad, he thought to himself. The room was newly decorated and, on account of the renovations, the smell of paint still lingered in spite of the small jar of fresh flowers near his bed.

Just as he was about to doze off, soft knocking on the door startled him. "Coming in!" a voice called out. Elio grabbed the sheet and pulled it up to his waist. The door inched open. In came a male nurse about his dad's age, but not as tall. Elio didn't know that men could be nurses, just like he didn't know that hospital rooms could sometimes look nicer and cleaner than your whole house.

"Is my mom here?" he said to the nurse.

The nurse's dark face broke into a wide smile. He walked toward Elio and stood right next to the bed. "I'm Emiliano," he said, checking Elio's vitals. "Emiliano Zapata."

Elio couldn't help but notice the resemblance between the nurse and his dad—perhaps it was a combination of the nurse's broad smile and his voice, which was soft and soothing, just like his dad's. In any case, Elio didn't laugh at his joke. Why was this guy, whom he'd just met, ignoring his questions?

"Your mom's on her way," the nurse said finally. "It may be a while, though. The streets are jam-packed all around the Malecón and the presidential palace."

"For what?" Elio said, furrowing his brow.

"The rebels, niño." Emiliano's voice was soft, but a little agitated. "Batista has escaped the country. That piece of…ran away to the Dominican Republic like a goddamn coward."

"That's old news," Elio said. When would the rebels get there and set their world right-side up again? he thought.

"It sure is." Emiliano said, smiling at Elio.

"I need to know something," Elio said.

"What?"

"Do I still have my leg?"

"You poor thing!" the nurse said. "Yes, you have both legs. And, better still," he continued, fixing his eyes on Elio. "Spine, heart, and organs all look fine. Your right ball, not so much. It's gone."

"Gone?" Elio said, looking a bit dazed.

"It's okay," Emiliano said. "You only really need one, you know. Your hip, it's shit, too, but it will heal. And get ready. Because as soon as your leg's kicking again, I bet your mom'll give you an unforgettable beating. I mean, what were you doing at the beach when everyone else was glued to the TV?" The nurse met Elio's gaze. "Mira eso, with those green eyes. Ay, mi madre. Good thing you're as flaco as a rod, or the shark would've chewed you up."

Elio scoffed. "I can go home when I want to, right? There's something I need to do," he said, leaning forward, then grimacing with the pain of his injuries.

The nurse shrugged. "I think they mean for you to stay. Whatever you need to do, it'll have to wait…until tomorrow, at least."

"Tomorrow's too late," Elio said, then paused, as if considering a possibility. "What time is it?"

"Well, let's see." Emiliano pushed up the sleeve of his uniform and squinted at the Mickey Mouse watch on his wrist. "It's a quarter to now, mi vida. Too early to leave. I mean, too late to refuse to stay. Y si el Ratoncito Miguel lo dice, it must be true."

"What do you mean?" Elio asked, then quickly realizing the joke, he smiled. "Very funny," he said. "Three? Er, no, a quarter to three?"

"A quarter to seven," Emiliano said.

Elio gazed at the bright Mickey Mouse on the face of the watch. "It's too late," he muttered, a shimmer of tears in his eyes. He wiped them away, feeling foolish. "How long have I been here?"

"Four hours, at least. And don't worry, like I said, you still got one ball."

Elio slumped back on hearing this. Again with the one ball. He was on the brink of tears. Although he wanted to tear off the bandages and look at his injury, he simply wasn't bold enough.

The anesthetic was beginning to wear off. Pins pricked at the nerves of his groin and thigh muscle. Then there was more generalized pain that came from the inside, from nowhere in particular, it seemed. But painful, just the same. Dampness quite different from sweat appeared on his forehead. "Do you have something for the pain or what?" he asked.

"Sure thing," Emiliano said, walking to a small sink and cabinet beside the window. "Ahí voy."

He proceeded to wash his hands vigorously, then prepared a small syringe. Once done, he walked over to Elio's bed and emptied a three-cc syringe into Elio's IV bag.

"Poof! Pain be gone," Emiliano said. "More later, if you need it, okay?"

The pain seemed to loosen its grip on Elio in a matter of seconds. The muscles on his face relaxed, and he leaned back into his pillow. "This is good," Elio said.

"Of course it's good," Emiliano laughed. "Ready to turn?"

The nurse turned Elio to one side and pulled half of the bedsheet off. "It's okay to be scared, kid," he said, walking around to the opposite side of the bed, then turning Elio again. "Some of the greatest men have been scared, you know that?" Da Vinci? Scared shitless, right before the Mona Lisa. Martí? Freaking out, in the middle of Dos Ríos. And God, well, he's got the world in his hands—how do you think *he* feels?"

Elio gave a semblance of a smile, then clenched his teeth. "My leg still hurts."

"I know, mi lindo, I'm going as gently as I can," the nurse said, lifting Elio away from the bed enough to pull the rest of the sheet off.

"Ow!"

"It's a girl, am I right?" He rocked Elio back and forth, tugging and tucking, until the bed was made again. "It's gotta be a girl...unless it's a boy, of course," he added, standing by Elio's exposed feet, and staring straight at him. He was a little out of breath, sweat beading on his forehead. "Does she or he have a name?" One more tug and Elio's feet were covered.

"It's a she," Elio said, annoyed. "And her name is—" Right as he was about to say *Maria,* his mom and Pepe walked through the half-opened door. The last person Elio wanted to see at that moment was Pepe, his rival, who unlike him had probably seen Maria before she left for Cabañas that afternoon. Elio knew he should be grateful to the boy, but he felt nothing but contempt.

There were tears coming down his mother's chin. Panicking, she ran up to Elio's bedside. "Is he all right?" she asked Emiliano. "Why isn't he walking around?" Then suddenly turning to Pepe, "I think you had something to do with this. I'm not a fool!"

Pepe caught Elio's eyes and raised his brows. "Well…" he started, clearing his throat. "If it hadn't been for me…"

Just like Elio guessed, that kid wasn't going to let up from this point forward. "No, Mom, that's Pepe. You know him. He didn't have anything to do with this. I mean, he did, but not like you think," Elio said. "If it hadn't been for him…I mean, he actually saved my life." Elio reached out for his mother's hand, attempting to calm her down. "He's Maria's friend, Mom. You know, the son of Berto and Rosita."

"It was nothing, really." Pepe said, feigning humility.

"Yes, yes, of course," Elio's mother said. "Thank you."

"My dad worked with your husband at the Farm El Pilar," Pepe said. "He used to come around a lot, with plantains and malangas for my mom and dad. Nice guy."

Elio grimaced. Couldn't Pepe tell that his mom had enough on her mind already without him bringing up his dad too?

Elio's mother didn't respond right away. She took a moment to answer. "Ay, mijo," she finally said. Shaken, but more composed, she turned to Pepe. "I'm so ashamed. So sorry." Not a word about his father—somehow, they'd dodged the bullet, Elio thought.

"You're just nervous," Emiliano told her. He knelt on the floor and began restocking the cabinet with what seemed to be hospital room essentials: bandages, gauze, alcohol bottles, and that stretchy tape Elio's mom brought home from the pharmacy sometimes. "Who wouldn't be?" he said, looking up at her. "But, no need to worry. He's doing just fine. If all's well in the morning, he's going home tomorrow. It's going to take him a while to recover, though. He's lucky—the injuries were mostly superficial. Bruised ribs, broken leg, but no torn tendons. No real permanent damage, except, you know…But he'll need to take it easy for a few months."

Elio was grateful that Emiliano left out the more salient detail about his injuries. In any case, although Pepe took a seat near Elio, he didn't seem to be paying attention to the conversation. He entertained himself by chewing on his cuticles.

"The rebels are close," Aurelia said, as though she hadn't heard a word Emiliano had told her. "Everyone's on the streets." His mother's anxious face told Elio that she was worried about more than just the rebels. She was scared, afraid of what would come next, for him and for her. Elio threaded his fingers through hers. "I'm right here, Mom," he told her, "I'm okay," although he was just as terrified about the future. Somehow, in their hearts, they'd both managed to feel the arrival of the revolution, the trauma of the shark attack, and the heartbreak of an absent father as one single, winded beat.

Emiliano looked at her. "It's a funny thing about Havana," he said. "People are always in the street, whether it's a carnival or a revolution. Everyone shows up to see the chaos firsthand."

Aurelia looked up at him. "I don't need comforting." She said.

"It's okay, Mom," Elio said. "Everything's going to be okay." He wondered when exactly it had turned to him being the one easing her fears.

She slipped her hand away from Elio's and walked toward a chair opposite his bed. She placed her purse on a small tray table and sat down. Outside the room, the staff couldn't keep their voices down. Elio could hear them talking about why Cubans needed a revolution, and why even the hospital would be an instrument of change.

"I'll tell you what I think," Emiliano said, "I'm with whoever is right. The problem is that I only half-believe those do-gooder mountaineers are right. The other half tells me we're in for a long ride. All those beards and battledresses make me cringe, you know what I mean?"

Elio's mom acknowledged the nurse's words with a nod. From her purse, she pulled a compact mirror and a red lipstick. She held the mirror up to her face and started to put on the lipstick.

"Well," Elio said, with a sigh. "If a revolution means that I'll finally get a goddamn bike, then I'm all for it."

"Elio!" his mom said, "Don't talk like that, please."

"Sorry, Mom."

"I, for one, am pro-Yanqui," Pepe said. "They're like a rocket ship to the moon—fast, sleek, and nearly indestructible. Anyway, my dad says this revolution will be done for in less than six months."

"I don't know, kid," Emiliano said. "I think they mean to make history, and history takes a damn long time to make."

Pepe moseyed up to the edge of Elio's bed. "Enough about revolutions, compay. How's life treating you, neighbor?" He said, rapping Elio's head firmly with his knuckles. "You made it, after all. Look at this! Coñó! They got you all set up like a king here. Wish some shark'd gone and bit me, too," he said, a smile from ear to ear.

"Don't go getting your leg chewed just to end up here." Emiliano chuckled.

"No sir," Pepe said.

"Good times." Elio stiffened his spine and puffed up his chest as best he could. "It's not my first shark, you know."

Pepe shook his head. "You know," he laughed. "I got a friend who fell on his head and he talks just like that."

"Oh, yeah?" Elio said. He was starting to feel hot all over. What was this guy doing here, anyway? If it hadn't been for his cast, hip and leg, and the throbbing in his groin, Elio would have sprung off the bed and walloped the guy on the nose. Nonetheless, no cry or groan escaped him while Pepe was in the room.

Pepe grinned. "Yeah, that's right—"

"How much do you remember?" Elio's mom asked as she stood and walked closer to Emiliano who patted her on the back.

Elio shrugged, feeling defeated. "Not a lot. Pepe, the pain, and some bits and pieces from the emergency room…"

"It's a shame to have curtains on the windows, don't you think?" she said, looking around the room. "They block out the view."

"Who can be sane in this damn hot weather, anyway?" Emiliano said, as if reading Elio's mind. "There's enough heat in here to roast a pig."

Pepe moved closer to the windows, pretending to draw the curtains. Elio knew there were no curtains, but he stayed quiet. There was no use pointing out what she couldn't see in all that darkness beyond the windows. She had a way of being tender and insane at the same time. Sometimes Elio understood why his dad had left her. She was difficult, like a knot in your shoelaces, or one of those algebra problems he couldn't figure out. At other times, though, there was no one else he loved more.

"Well, now," the nurse said. "Would you believe it if I told you that you'll be back at the beach in no time at all?"

"Nope." Elio wasn't planning on setting foot at the beach any time soon. In fact, just the thought of it made his heart pound in his throat. He'd lost the chance to give Maria those blennies and now, well…now she was somewhere in Cabañas having the time of her life and she wouldn't be back for another month.

"Tell you what, can I get you two bocaditos from the cafeteria?" he asked Elio and his mom. "You, on the other hand," he turned to Pepe, "You need to get home."

"I'm not in a rush," Pepe said.

Elio nodded. He was injured, not dumb. It was way past dinner time, and Pepe looked so hungry. If he stayed, he'd chew up Elio's bocaditos, plate and all. Was this kid a pain in the ass, or what? Elio thought.

Emiliano waved his hand. "Farewell, now. Shoo!"

Pepe looked disheartened, but he managed to push out a smile.

"Say hi to your mom," Aurelia said, as though something in the air had cemented for her who Pepe was. "And thank you!"

"It was nothing," Pepe said.

"Eh," Elio said to the boy, "Did you get to see Maria today, after all?"

"Nah, didn't make it on time, on account of some crazy kid at the beach." Pepe winked.

"Good one," Elio said.

Pepe laughed. "We should hang out sometime."

"Sure thing," Elio said, watching Pepe leave without a backward glance. He didn't know Pepe well, but he understood that when someone saves your life, you're linked to them forever.

"Looks like you made a friend," Emiliano said.

"Nah."

Thirty minutes later, Elio sipped at the water the nurse had set before him. There was something about almost dying that kept him from glugging the drink.

"That's right," Emiliano said, looking at Elio's cup of water. "Pace yourself. In any case," he continued, handing both mother and son a full aluminum plate, "this will set you up for the rest of the night."

Elio made slurping sounds. There were thick, juicy tomatoes, two fried eggs, and at least five bocaditos on each plate. "Coñó, what a feast, thank you." Elio said, with more tomato than mouth.

"Thank you, Emiliano. Yes, this is too much," Elio's mother said.

"Enjoy it," the nurse beamed, as he backed out of the room, "because...the ways things are going out there," he said, pointing beyond the window, "it's gonna go away so fast, you won't remember its name. For now, we're not about to let you go hungry, are we? Especially when you've traveled so far to see us."

"Not that far," Elio said, wondering what Emiliano had against the rebels...and against Bauta.

The nurse laughed. "Bauta might as well be Oriente. It's not La Habana."

"Actually—" Elio started to say, but the nurse interrupted him.

"Niño, Bauta's a dump. Why kid yourself?"

"I don't think I'll need anything else tonight," Elio said. He figured he could go on a hunger strike, for the simple reason that he didn't like anyone calling Bauta a dump.

The nurse laughed again, leaning against the door. "Tell me," he said, "is this your first time in a hospital?" Elio hesitated before answering. He didn't feel ready to start talking about his mother's medical history, especially with a complete stranger who called Bauta a dump. Let's just say that, when it came to living, Elio's mother hadn't always been convinced it was worth the pain. If he ever saw Emiliano on the street one day, though, he would tell him. Emiliano the nurse, he thought, in spite of his shortcomings, was the kind of guy you could talk to when nobody else would do.

Terrified the shark would come back in a dream, and with pain that seemed to throb everywhere like a pulse, Elio couldn't shut his eyes. Outside, beyond his window, he could hear the crickets, thousands of them drowning out the coughs and grunts of patients across the hall. When he finally closed his eyes, he was awakened by one of the talk shows on the radio they'd kept on for hours in the nurses' station. Somebody assessing the situation on the island. The announcer said something that made Elio listen closely and stay up the rest of the night. "Revolutions," he was saying, "are never what they seem." In his mind, revolutions and shark attacks were one and the same.

But mending his relationship with his mother was like mending an old sock: just as you got rid of one hole, another one opened up. For days after Elio came home from the hospital, they sat in the kitchen listlessly, neither of them brave enough to talk, neither of them decisive enough to leave the table. Their relationship deteriorated even further when one day she brought up his father.

"Go somewhere. It doesn't have to be Chicago. It can be Pennsylvania or New Jersey or Miami. He's not coming back, Eli…he left us. Not a call, not a letter, not a dollar from that son of a bitch. He's a goddamn bastard," she told him. "He doesn't matter, coño." She started to sob.

"What's wrong with here?" Elio said. His mother needed him. Even if he wanted to leave, it was too late.

"It's not el norte, Elio."

He heard in her words the terrible hopelessness of someone who'd lost her compass, a tone Elio detested. "Leaving is not always the right thing to do, Mom."

In a nervous grimace of a smile that showed her beautiful teeth, she said: "Are you playing the know-it-all? You think you know better than me, chiquillo de mierda? What do you intend to do with your life? Tell me, what? You think you can sell stolen mangoes for the rest of your life? Do you think that your mangoes and my job at the pharmacy are going to pay for that fancy bike you want?"

"No."

"Tell the truth, damn it."

He hesitated. "I don't know."

"You've thought about leaving too. Like everyone else. They think, and they plot, and they leave in the middle of the night. You want to leave me behind, just like he did. That, that deceased, that stiff—because he doesn't deserve a name, you know that? He's dead to me. If you want to leave, you should do it now."

"That's not true, Mom. I'm not leaving," he said. "Stop, please."

"I should just disappear."

"People can't just disappear, Mom."

"You think I'm not capable? You think I won't do it?" She had a pitiful expression, and she scrutinized him, her pupils hardly visible, her lips half parted.

Elio wasn't sure what to say. He knew what she was capable of, yes; but he was silent, quite still. And when he made it clear that none of her threats were doing any good, she sat down in a rocking chair, covered her face, and began to cry. Elio told himself she would be fine, but he didn't believe a word of it.

CHAPTER 4

RICKY PEREZ, a slow speaker, was always attentive to whomever he happened to natter away with. Tall and slender, his elegance was derived from an almost imperturbable serenity and a single piece of jewelry, a thin wedding ring. His three-ways-clean Colgate smile and twinkling eyes made him look more like a black-haired Gary Cooper than the Cuban scoundrel he actually was. Ungainly only in matters of the heart, he was a first-class tinkerer with a mind for numbers, for probabilities and risks, for profits and losses.

He could have been an actor, though—a really great actor. In fact, he had left Cuba for two reasons and two reasons only: first, Cuba was bad business and he wasn't about to stick around and see what greater mess those mountaineers made of the country; and second, he was determined to join the theater scene in Chicago. Often, he was unsure which of the two reasons weighed more, especially when he closed his eyes at night and dreamt of *Ricky Perez* on a large marquee. But Americans weren't ready for a Cuban Stanley Kowalski, although Ricky could have sworn that only *he* could have played the role the way it was meant to be played: with gusto. Unfortunately fate—so pretty and so fickle—was a brutish mistress and the only role Ricky ever managed to land was a Willy Loman understudy for a second-rate theater company that never managed to get on its feet. Willy Loman. Willy Low Man. Ricky Low Man. Nah, he'd been miscast, anyway. He'd always been more of a Stanley Kowalski, if you asked him.

Some nights, when Ricky laid his head on his pillow, he wondered if he should have gone to Hollywood instead. After all, if Ricky Ricardo had made it in Hollywood, why couldn't Ricky Perez make it too?

It was raining and the low, gray sky over Chicago made him feel defeated, as if he were surviving a storm on fear alone. Fear that, even now, even in the Windy City, he was still running away. He was engrossed in sweeping under the thousand and three hundred movie seats at 54 West Randolph in the old Woods Theater building. The gig *was not* what he'd dreamed of but, as far as he was concerned, it kept him afloat. He sent small sums of money to Aurelia whenever he could, twenty dollars one time, fifty dollars another, and one hundred dollars every so often— whenever he managed to skip paying for his utilities and his trash bill. He knew it would make a difference, although he never did hear from Elio. He'd never truly known what had happened to the money—if they received it, they'd never even said thank you. It would have been nice to get a letter from Cuba. It was starting to get really lonely in Chicago.

While he swept, he thought about the leggy redhead he'd met that day. He'd gone out earlier to get an olive burger and a piece of apple pie with ice cream at the 17 Restaurant at 17 West Randolph. As soon as he'd walked up to the door and seen Sally hamming it up for Chicago's finest—who sucked in their burgers like fleshy-lipped sturgeons in the back booth—he'd been smitten. Se puso bobo, vaya. Tall and lean, with hair done up into a grand bouffant, Sally was a vision, a midwestern American beauty queen.

In Cuba, he'd have waited for her to get up. Then he'd pass by her, grabbing one of her nalgas as he walked away and he and Sally would have gone off into the sunset. But las Americanas were different. And what mostly had been a hit in Cuba, didn't have the expected effect in Chicago. As soon as she'd felt his hand over her pants, she'd said, "What the fuck are you doing?" She'd thrown her drink, her shoe, and then her purse at him—if there'd been a cat nearby she would have thrown that too. When she was done, she turned to him and said, "Sally Rogers. I'm in the phone book. Next time, grab your own ass." There were way too many people named Sally Rogers in Chicago, he discovered. But he'd found her number, finally, and called her. In any case, he learned very quickly that Sally would sooner cut off her right tit than put up with his bullshit. He loved that. But he missed Aurelia, goddammit. He missed the kid too. Tell anybody in Cuba that. For the time being, though, he was looking to *forget* about Cuba, and Aurelia, *and* the kid. It was just way too hard to remember.

He swept the floors and thought of Sally. When his shift was over, he changed into his street clothes, then went outside to hail a cab. "Take me to the South Side," he told the cab driver. 'Cause I'm meeting with a peliroja with long legs and a sailor's mouth, he added—in his thoughts.

CHAPTER 5

"THESE DARN PINS let the clothes slip out. If you happen to pinch them even slightly off center, they spring apart. Just look at this!" Maria's grandmother said, holding up a wooden clothespin to the sun. Close by, Maria folded towels and pillowcases over the tense clotheslines. She clicked her tongue each time a clothespin snapped loose from the wire.

"Darling grandmother," Maria said in English, examining the wooden specimen in her hand and throwing a furtive glance at Elio's yard. "They're flying fish. See how they leap off and fly over the wall into the lagoon—*lovely, isn't it?"* She threw a pin over the wall.

Her tone was theatrical. But less babyish than before she left, Elio thought, peering through his shutters. It had been a week since she'd returned from Cabañas, and at least a month since his accident at the beach. In only a month's time, she had filled out, and peeling skin still covered her sunburned arms and shoulders like snowflakes. She looked damn pretty, that was certain. But best of all, Elio could tell, she was putting on a show just for him.

"A clothespin is a clothespin, right?" her grandmother said, holding one end of a bedsheet.

The sun was so bright, the white sheets dazzled. It was especially warm too. After days of rain and, even in January, the air appeared thick with the exuberance of hummingbirds and flies, and the aroma of sofrito sizzling on frying pans and pouring in through Elio's window.

"You'd think," Maria said from the opposite end of the sheet. "But watch out for Mima's nylons. These darn pins will snag the toughest undergarments!"

The old woman glared at her granddaughter, snapping down the sheets with a jerk. "Nothing wrong with Sears," she said, raising her voice, "but truth be told, I've had just about enough of these faulty imported products."

"Well, I love Sears. And I'm sorry to see it go," Maria said. *"Undergarments,"* she concluded.

"You're something else, aren't you?" Her grandmother laughed. "It was all that fried snapper in Cabañas," she said. "You're cutting a tongue like you once cut teeth. You know, you've got your head in those damn books day and night. And if it's not a book, it's the Sears catalogue. Nothing good can come of it."

Maria rolled her eyes. "It's books, and fashion, Mima. Not typhoid fever," she said.

A soft breeze brought the sound of a radio from some houses away. "Hola, soledad…" The voice of Rolandito La Serie, "El Guapo," vibrated in the air. Beyond it all, the stagnant waters of Bauta's lagoon. But Elio chose to ignore that.

From behind his bedroom shutters, he registered every word as faithfully as a Dictaphone. His heart was pounding. He wondered what, exactly, Maria would need to read to make her choose him over Pepe.

One morning, a month later and near the end of that winter, he told Maria he wouldn't go back to school. For a while, there was only the sound of pages turning, like blades of a fan in the afternoon heat. The street was quiet, with a bicycle squeaking by every now and then, and a car sputtering around potholes at intervals. The sidewalk was almost deserted. Whenever someone did pass by, Elio nodded briefly, repeatedly glancing down as if he were reading. But who knew what passersby thought when they saw him—Aurelia's son, the kid whose dad had left him holding the bag. He felt himself growing anxious. Perhaps it was because he wasn't fully recovered from the injury yet. But it didn't matter what passersby thought. Only Maria mattered, and she was there now. Right next to him.

She was reading, cross-legged on the tiled porch. He sat straddling the low, cement wall that divided her house from his. His cast leg dangled on one side like a pendulum.

Maria tried to calm her breath, focusing on the words on the page. "Oh, yeah? No school? Why is that?" she frowned.

"Not interested," he said. His index finger in the air accounted for all the potholes on the street. "Plus, I've missed too much already—you know, with the injury and all. Algebra alone makes me dizzy on good days. Imagine what it'd be like after a month away. Anyway, I have a job now."

"Doing what?"

"Importing and exporting, that sort of thing."

"Hmm," she said, seemingly intrigued. "Importing and exporting what?"

"Fruits, vegetables—*that* sort of thing."

"Can you read, at least?" she turned another page.

"What do you think?" his finger pointed at the twenty-ninth pothole.

"I think you stutter." She looked up at him.

"Tra-tra-try me," he said. He was still recovering from his shark injuries and felt a little winded.

"I don't have time, you weirdo." She clicked her tongue.

"I think you're scared."

"Okay," she shut the book and lifted it up to him. "Read the last paragraph on page 112."

"Nah, I don't need to prove myself to you."

There was no way he could read something out loud, he thought. He was already so out of breath, he wouldn't make it past the first sentence.

"Are you scared?"

"What's that book about anyway?"

"It's about a knight errant, bruto," she said, balancing the book on her leg.

Maria's thighs made Elio nervous. He looked at the potholes again. "Yup. I know all about it."

"Sure, you do. Anyway, it's about a guy who wants to be a knight. He gets an armor and a skinny horse, and leaves his house in search of adventure—are you paying attention or what?"

His eyes shifted in her direction. "A skinny horse! I bet it was a burro—why does he want to be a knight, anyway?"

Maria laughed. "He loves swords, just like you, dummy...but he didn't make his from an avocado branch."

Elio's face turned bright red. "Very funny. It wasn't supposed to be a sword," he said. Although annoyed to discover that Maria had caught him messing around with the branch, he couldn't help but smile to himself—after all, he wasn't the only one spying on his neighbor. In any case, he wasn't pretending it was a sword. He was trying to figure out if the stupid thing was strong enough to knock down mangoes—and it wasn't.

"Anyway," Maria continued, "he's a country gentleman who's been *enchanted* by books of chivalry—"

"There you go. That's exactly why I don't want to go to school anymore. They read crazy books about knights and use words like *enchanted.*" He paused to catch his breath. "Schools are full of hypocrites too."

She smiled. "I'm not a hypocrite."

"Really? Well, then why the hell are you talking to Pepe?"

"Pepe's my friend. You should be grateful too. If it wasn't for Pepe you wouldn't be here."

"You mean, your boyfriend. The shark? That was nothing. Plus, I hate to disappoint you, but Pepe's my friend too. Do you know how many times he's come over to play marbles since the accident?

"How many?"

"More than I can say. Just because you weren't invited, *or were stuck in Cabañas for all of eternity,* doesn't mean it didn't happen."

Maria stuck out her tongue at him. "Don't be a clown. It was a month—not una eternidad," she said. They both laughed.

She was right, though. He should be grateful. But there was something odd about his friendship with the boy. It was more than that they were both in love with Maria. Elio remembered thinking soon after the shark accident that something strange happened when people saved your life. You were linked forever. In fact, people who saved your life had a surprising effect on you: permanent humiliation.

"Yeah, yeah—that's why you're still limping…and, just so you know, I'm not allowed to have a boyfriend."

"Well, whatever. Pepe's a weasel."

"He likes me."

"And? Are you gonna marry the first weasel who likes you?"

She looked at him and smirked. "You like me too."

Elio could feel himself blushing bright red again. "Is that right? Tú estás loca."

"Whatever you say—"

"Well, does the guy go alone or what?" Trying to change the conversation.

She laughed. "No, not alone. He has a squire."

"Where did he get him from?"

"He finds him."

"So easy?"

"No, not so easy, stupid. He promises him an island." Maria took a breath, summoning patience.

Elio leaned back on the wall and took a deep breath himself. "As if islands could be given away just like that—sounds like a ridiculous story, if you ask me."

"But I didn't ask you. Anyway, you wouldn't get it and never will because you're not going to school."

"Like I said, I was injured, so I couldn't go to school. And, anyway, I already had enough schooling for one lifetime. I got stuff going on now."

In truth, he had very little going on. Other than knocking down mangoes from trees in the nearby groves, taking care of his mother, and pursuing Maria, he had next to nothing happening in his life. If he could muster the courage to go back to the beach, he wouldn't be so goddamn bored. But he hadn't set foot on the sand since the incident with the shark a month earlier; he was staying away from the water.

"Oh yeah, like what?" She was starting to find him amusing.

"Like stuff. I'm telling you, you wouldn't understand."

At first, Elio was irritated. Maria could be a royal pain in the ass. He could read, he could read just fine. When he thought about it a little longer, however, he couldn't help but love Maria even more. She liked him too. He wasn't sure exactly why, but he made her nervous. Nervousness, everyone knew, was the first sign of love.

Again, there was only the sound of turning pages, now accompanied by the clinking of a spoon beating against a glass from somewhere inside Maria's house. Elio knew it was Maria's grandmother's way of telling her to cut short her chitchat with Elio. "The lemonade must be ready," Maria called, letting her grandmother know she'd registered the signal. "Well, it's good for you that you've made up your mind," she said to Elio. "I, for one, plan to go to school."

"I don't like you, *by the way!*" he shouted at her.

She went inside the house, slamming the front door behind her. "Yeah, like that's true."

Inside the house, Maria leaned into a rocking chair, sipped from a cold glass of lemonade, and weighed her options. At thirteen, both Elio and Pepe were one year older than her. Pepe was tall enough to wear his dad's pants. He was also strong, and a good swimmer. But she didn't know him so well.

Elio, on the other hand, was lacking in muscles. And since the shark, he wouldn't go near water. But, he had a father in Chicago—and wasn't Chicago home to the biggest Sears of all? If she had a father who lived in Chicago, she would have been the happiest girl on the island. In fact, if she had a father anywhere, she would have simply been happy.

Touches of Elegance, Gifts of Luxury, 24-karat gold-plated boudoir beauties for Milady's boudoir. "Charmed, I'm sure," she could hear herself saying in English to someone in a red velvet coat outside the Tribune Tower in Chicago. Elio—as skinny as ever, but handsome in a *100 percent soft*

Acrilon jersey knit shirt, or in a sweater knit in Italian homes—would thrust a clean-shaven face into a winter sun. She, in *homespun wool sportswear imported from Ireland,* would tilt her head back and laugh, take his arm. And oh *the Luxury of the Orient…the Lore of the Orient—Imported from the Royal Town Colony of Hong Kong.* She'd have that, too—just like page twenty of the 1959 Sears Christmas catalogue told her she would. And they'd have children, at least three. One of them she'd name Milady. All smart, clad in *Pagoda print sport shirts.*

Her fantasy ended when she remembered what her grandmother had said. "Those rebels will cause more havoc on this island than sugarcane and the sinking of the USS *Maine.*" Maria only hoped some things would stay the same. What would become of Sears?

Satisfied with the effect she knew she had on Elio, she decided that, for now, Elio was the one. Because she wasn't even sure Pepe liked her. She wasn't pretty like the other girls in the neighborhood. Her waist was nothing like the wasps her grandmother had in mind. She had no hips, and her breasts were slow in rising, like spoiled dough.

While Pepe was a gamble, Elio was a sure thing. And he was funny too. And best of all, he pretended not to like her. Plus, he was the only boy she'd ever seen fencing with an avocado branch, in his underwear—and didn't that make them *almost* married?

CHAPTER 6

EVENTUALLY, Elio's back-and-forth about Pepe became a peaceful routine. And, like Maria, he weighed his options. But his teetered on whether or not he should be Pepe's friend. The whole affair was knotty. He liked the kid. The kid had saved his life. But, the kid was after Maria. And Maria seemed to like the kid too.

Days and weeks passed and he regained his normal state of health. He'd spent several months with a hopeless sense of isolation. He'd been so bored, he'd even started reading, mostly because he wanted to impress Maria, but also because he'd figured that, if he wasn't going to school, then he better know something about something.

He'd tried a few times to speak to Maria, but the answer he got from her was always the same: "I got school work to do." He was so eager to get out of the house and do something that when Pepe showed up at his door wondering if he wanted to *hang out,* Elio felt he'd gotten a second chance at life. Like him, Pepe seemed to be lonely and looking for a friend.

Pepe'd knocked so hard on Elio's front door that he'd nearly brought the house down. When Elio opened the door, the first thing Pepe asked was, "Where should we go?" He was wearing the same gray shirt and navy blue shorts he wore to the hospital. The only difference was that he now had an unlit cigarette hanging from the side of his mouth.

"Let's go to your house," Elio said.

"Why would you get out of your house just to end up in mine?" Pepe said. Elio shrugged.

"You can come to my house tomorrow. Let's do something else today," Pepe said. *"Someone* told me you're in the import-export business…fruits and vegetables, mostly." He laughed.

Elio was annoyed that Maria had shared their conversation with Pepe but he laughed too. "Are you sure you're ready for that?"

"Muchacho, I was born ready," Pepe said.

The sky was a bright blue, with no traces of white clouds or thin streaks of gray promising winter showers. Large jute bags in hand, they walked down Avenida 243, passing Brisas de la Laguna, with Elio leading the way. They then turned right on Avenida Máximo Gómez. They concentrated on walking, with hardly a word between them. Not having indulged in such outdoor activities for some time, Elio found himself short of breath.

"Having a tough time?" Pepe shouted from a few feet away.

"Kind of," Elio said.

Every now and then, he pretended to need to fix his shoe, just so he could stop for a few seconds and catch his breath.

Moving ahead, he thought of nothing but mangoes. Lots of them. On his end, Pepe walked and whistled a tune Elio liked, but couldn't quite place. They continued on for another ten minutes until, a little beyond the town, right before the Loma de Pita, they came to a large iron gate with the name Villa Paz on it; the gate was followed by the big fenced area that was the farm. Elio took a good look over the fence. There were no signs anywhere of Vito, the farm's foreman, which could only mean one thing: all the mangoes in the world were there for the plucking.

They followed the barbed wire fence line all the way to the back of the farm, away from the main road. Walking in waist-high grass for another five minutes, they reached a segment of the fence that appeared to have been tampered with. "It's here," Elio said. Though in most areas the barbed wire pressed against the ground, that part of the fence was slightly bent. Elio slid his hands underneath to lift the wire, trying not to poke himself with the sharp spikes and leaving an opening large enough for Pepe to crawl through. Then it was Elio's turn to go while Pepe lifted the barbed wire.

"Let's do this," Elio said, rubbing the palm of his hand where the sharp tip of a spike had scratched him. At least he'd crawled under the fence without tearing his shirt, he thought.

Every branch of every mango tree had fruit clinging to it. There were mangoes from every variety imaginable. "Do you see that?" Elio said to Pepe, feigning dizziness at the sight of all the ripe fruit. Pepe said very little but his mouth was half open, which suggested to Elio that he was so overwhelmed by what he saw that he simply didn't know what to say.

The weight of the mangoes bent the branches to near-breaking point and their sweet fragrance was so strong that Elio's mouth watered. There were mango jobo, mango filipino, mango francés, mango de chupeta, mango huevo toro, manga blanca, manga rosa, mango mamey, mango bizcochuelo, and mango manzano, which was Elio's favorite and the one they'd be taking home that afternoon.

"Come on now, we can't waste a second," Elio said. Resting one foot in Pepe's linked hands, he pushed himself up until he'd gripped one of the thickest branches. It was nice to have help, and an *accomplice,* for once. Going at it alone was not eventful enough.

"Go fast," Pepe insisted from the ground. "Up you go," he said, boosting Elio up one final time. Elio scaled the tree at record speed, ending high near the top.

"Get ready!" he shouted down at Pepe. "Uno, dos, tres, take cover!" Elio yelled, shaking and bouncing on the branches with such force that dozens of mangoes dropped to the ground with a plop, plop, plop, at different intervals, like some blessed rain. It all happened so fast and with such gravity that Pepe didn't have time to heed Elio's warning and cover his head.

"Coño!" Pepe shouted, rubbing his right temple, where a mango had struck him on its way to the ground. He was looking at the huge red and orange bounty all around him like a hungry orphan. "You're good at this shit! Did your dad teach you that?"

Just as Elio was about to say *maybe,* he heard Vito. The foreman, a huge, light-skinned black man with a baritone voice, shouted, "Stop! Me cago en tu madre! Stop!"

"Vito's coming!" Elio shouted at Pepe, who was already rolling mangoes inside the two large jute bags. "Run!"

"Jump and run!" Pepe yelled.

Elio jumped, and fell, and another rain of mangoes fell after him. He'd barely hit the ground before he grabbed Pepe by his shirt, jute bags and all, and dragged him through the opening in the fence. The last sound Elio heard was Vito's rough voice yelling, "I'll get you next time, sons of bitches!"

They began to run, hauling the jute bags with the mangoes, not knowing if Vito was following them. Pepe lost a shoe, and a few mangoes fell out of Elio's bag, as they finally reached Avenida 243. Neither Elio nor Pepe stopped to retrieve—they just kept running, Pepe half barefoot, and Elio tripping and short of breath. When at last Elio saw the sign, Welcome to Bauta, he knew they'd reached their destination.

"You walk like a girl," Pepe laughed.

"Nah, I'm just out of shape."

"Playing with girls on the porch will do that to ya," Pepe said, running up behind him and pushing him.

Elio laughed. He wanted to answer with an equally teasing remark, but he was too winded to speak.

Half an hour later, they were sprawled on Elio's porch, drinking lemonade and shooting the breeze. Laughing their asses off whenever they brought up Vito. Elio's throat still burned from all that open-mouth breathing he hadn't been able to avoid while running. His groin felt sore too. Perhaps knocking down mangoes had been a bit too much too soon, he thought—but it'd been worth it. He hadn't laughed like that in a long time.

"Well," Pepe said, taking a swig from his glass. "You saved me from the wrath of Vito. Who owes who his life now?"

"I guess so," Elio said, somewhat embarrassed but thankful for Pepe's kindness. Elio knew that Vito was hardly a shark. Unlike Elio's life, Pepe's had never really been on the line.

"Do you do this very often?" Pepe chuckled.

"Once a week," Elio said. "Enough to make a good sale. It's so easy. You wanna try and sell a few?"

"Nah," Pepe said. "I wouldn't be very good at it. Plus, I don't have enough time—I work at the textile factory. You should come work with me. Better pay...and no Vito." He looked at Elio with a half smile, and a bit sideways.

"There's always a Vito," Elio said.

"You ever get the feeling you're all alone in the world?" Pepe said, now with a full smile.

"All the time," Elio said. "Why do you keep looking at me like that?"

"Well, you're not alone. I think I know someone named Maria who wants to keep you company," Pepe said. "Do you want to keep her company too?"

"Could be," Elio said.

The next day, and just as Pepe had promised, Elio visited Pepe's house in Belica. It'd been raining when Elio left his house. So, although the rain had stopped by the time he arrived at Pepe's door, he was soaked. Just as he'd predicted, the house was nothing like his, not in the way that mattered. Pepe's house was hushed, peaceful. The kind of house you wanted to keep going back to.

The smell of rain clung to everything as he followed Pepe up a steel ladder to the roof. Pepe took an extension cord and his Vittorio record player along with some colas and a small bottle of Havana Club he'd hidden under his shirt. The smell of oregano drifted up to them—some kind of meat stew. They sat down on the rough concrete and leaned against an aluminum tank Pepe's parents used to collect rain water, already warm with the heat of the sunlight.

Pepe turned on the record player. "Charlie Parker," he said. He then poured some cola from each bottle and filled the space remaining with Havana Club. "Cuba Libre!" he said, lifting his bottle up toward the clear skies. Charlie Parker's saxophone soared, enveloping everything.

"Cuba libre!" Elio repeated, laughing then taking a swig from the bottle. So much had already changed since the rebels first entered Havana a few months earlier that *Cuba libre* seemed the only appropriate thing to say—what it might mean in the months to come, however, Elio couldn't be sure. For one, red Schwinn bicycles behind storefront windows were now a thing of the past.

"You know my parents are leaving, right?" Pepe said. He tried to seem casual, but his eyes were watery.

"Yeah," Elio said. "Seems like everyone leaves sooner or later."

A dull roar of jumbled sounds—car mufflers, truck engines, blenders, radios, and barking dogs—hung over the neighborhood. Once in a while, though, Elio could make out a child's cry or an argument somewhere or Pepe's mom's calling, "Are you boys alright up there?" Mostly, he could hear Charlie Parker, and that was a lot more music than he'd heard at his own house in the last six months.

They sat in silence for what seemed to be an entire afternoon. Elio felt a little woozy from the alcohol and the sun. But he let each isolated moment melt into the next, as if only the roof, Charlie Parker, and the sky existed.

"If you like her, I can let her go," Pepe finally said. He put a cigarette in his mouth, shielded it with his hand as he lit up, and inhaled.

"Just like that? I thought you liked her too," Elio said, shielding his eyes from the sunlight to take a good look at Pepe's face, in case the kid was messing around.

"Nah," Pepe said, taking another drag from the cigarette. "She likes you—and I'm fine with that."

Elio's heart wanted to jump out of his chest. Maria, he thought, could have chosen to like somebody a little more handsome, someone a little less *damaged*. She could have chosen to like Pepe. But she didn't. She liked him.

By the end of the summer, Pepe's house had become Elio's second home, and they'd knocked down so many mangoes from Vito's grove that, out of pity for Vito, the boys decided to move Elio's export-import business to Farm El Pilar, at least temporarily.

CHAPTER 7

IN THREE YEARS' TIME, the affection between the boys had grown. And by the time Maria's fifteenth birthday came around, Pepe, el Casanova de Bauta, had gone girl rabid, pursuing anything with a chest, long hair, and a mini skirt. His latest conquest, Isabelita, a girl from Oriente, with a chest like manzano mangoes, hair that reached her nalgas, and a skirt so short it had Pepe seeing color on a black and white TV. There was no question Elio'd won the girl—at least for now. So, it was Elio, not Pepe, who glided to "Blue Danube" across checkered tiles on Maria's quinces, his arm wrapped around Maria's cinched waist like satin ribbon.

Convinced more than ever that he needed to make a life for himself and for Maria, Elio had begun to work at the Textilera de Ariguanabo with Pepe, who'd been there since his parents left for Panama a couple of years earlier. Driven by un sueño soviético, Pepe had joined the working class. Pepe had begun as a simple apprentice, doing the most menial tasks and handling dangerous machinery, which he said he liked because it made him feel "on the edge." Along the way, Pepe had been promoted to a more demanding position mixing dye. Elio hoped to follow the same fate.

The textile factory wasn't far from town. In fact, there was even a bus that picked workers up at La Minina and dropped them off right in front of the factory. Although sometimes he and Pepe opted to walk, Elio always enjoyed the bus ride. He loved the chitchat and comradeship and all the jokes cracked, wise cracks, and banter with people on the bus. He missed that about being with his dad. He missed the joshing and fooling around, the kind of roughhousing that often happened between men—and especially between father and son. Sitting in the bus, listening to the men around him, Elio imagined what it would have been like to ride that bus with his father every morning. To sit next to him, elbowing each other, or bumping fists when one of the workers, or even Pepe, said something crude or funny and worthy of a good laugh—like in those American Westerns his father had loved so much.

Whenever he imagined his father, however, Elio quickly busied his mind with clutter, so desperate was he to put distance between himself and that disheartening place he called leaving. Why had his father so cruelly deserted his mother just when she needed him most? What had he, Elio, done not to deserve a father's love? His father wasn't a father to mourn—that was certain. He would think of his mother then, lost and troubled by his father's irreversible choices. Her shifting moods always reminding Elio of unpredictable fires. But he had understood it all wrong. She wouldn't leave by fire.

In the spring of 1964, as Elio's eighteenth birthday neared, his mother drank herself to death. He spent the nights that followed in reflection and in tears muffled by a bed pillow.

Emiliano the nurse, he remembered, had cautioned him to be careful: under the right circumstances, too much water could kill you. And Elio's mother had sought to drink all the water in the world. One glass of water after another, she drowned those regions where memories had made a home.

She didn't leave a note, nor instructions about her funeral. If she had, Elio would have known what color the casket's inner lining should have been, what song to play at the service, how to write her goddamn eulogy, and all those details that would have seemed important, at least to other people. To him, all that mattered was that he didn't know. He didn't know, coño. He didn't know, repinga. He simply didn't fucking know. If it hadn't been for Maria, he, too, would have drowned in all that water.

The year before, his mother had seemed to have achieved a certain level of high spirits, visiting with a friend or two in La Cubalina during the week. And making paper flowers on those rare occasions when papier-mâché became available. Sometimes, at night, she sang to him—she didn't sound like anyone else. "You're a lucky boy," she'd tell him, her eyes shining with love. "You're one lucky boy."

But Elio didn't feel so lucky. Upon news of a neighbor's leave-taking, of another goodbye, Elio'd walk into the house and find her perched, like a wingless bird, on the crest of dirty bed linen. Time slipped and fell around her, unanchored. As if parts of her had already begun to drift away. Where did his mother's story begin, and when? And him—where did *his* story begin? Perhaps it didn't matter.

If he'd looked closer, he would have seen, in those final hours before her death, in her quiet rocking, an early departing—an early clambering up to the bow. But he'd been simply too busy thinking about Maria to notice. In fact, he was so shocked by what he saw when he discovered his mother's limp body that he didn't reach out his hand to touch it.

The day of the funeral, Elio wished for rain—he needed something like hope to sustain him, something like a washing over to start anew. But it was hot as hell and, by the time he took a seat at the front pew, dark circles of sweat pooled under his armpits. He had a terrible toothache, too, in one of his back molars. If he could have, he would have yanked the thing right then and there, if only to feel a void somewhere other than in the pit of his stomach. To make matters worse, the clothes on his back had come off somebody else's: he had on Pepe's polyester suit and shoes, and a crooked tie around his neck—also Pepe's. Although he didn't turn back once to look at her, Elio was aware of Maria sitting in the pew right behind him. He wanted to reach back and touch her soft skin. If he had, perhaps he could have made it all the way to the end.

Everyone was kind to him. Too kind, perhaps. He hated their sympathy, their plastic flowers, and all the good things they had to say about his mother. "Doesn't she look beautiful in the casket" and "Hadn't she been a great mother" and "Who can blame her?" But, although muted by sobs and handkerchiefs, there were also "Who knows what the kid'll do now" and "He's practically an orphan" and "Suicides go to hell." As with leprosy or tuberculosis, there must have been early signs, they said. Like a recurring blister on the skin or a persistent cough, but different. It ran in families, they said that, too. Sooner or later, everyone swore, the gene rose to the surface and a switch went off.

Their theories were so goddamn pathetic they made Elio want to laugh. At least twice during the first fifteen minutes of the service, after overhearing one, he let out a whoop that Pepe, sitting next to him, was quick to muffle with a cough and a hard blow to Elio's back. The truth was that, at least then, laughing for Elio was a way of crying.

Midway through the service, he fixed his eyes on the open casket. His mother's rigid profile rose above a gray velvet lining. A pang in the pit of his stomach reminded him, yet again, that there was more than one parent gone. Gagging, and turning his head downward, as if his head and shoulders were made of lead, he threw up.

At the cemetery, the lingering smell of vomit on his clothes made Elio feel ashamed, and he avoided Maria's eyes. He diverted all of his attention toward his mother's casket, imagining that she was still alive, swallowing soft, red earth each time she gasped for air. Falling deeper into the ground, each time she thrashed. He imagined that he, too, fell deeper and deeper—always descending, with no final resting place in sight. He stared at the fresh mound of earth, unaware of the small crowd of people around him or of Pepe's hand on his shoulder. Absorbed in his mother's task of taking yet another breath, he felt like he was choking and swallowing water.

When the priest walked up to him and whispered, "Go ahead," Elio was drowning. His mother, Elio thought, should never be confused with the words he'd used to describe her. Because he couldn't come up with words different than the ones he had at his disposal, he decided that he wouldn't read his mother's eulogy that day.

"If she didn't leave a note," he said to the priest, "I won't either." It was then he looked up to see Maria, like a lifeline, across from the fresh mound of earth. One small leap over his mother's grave and she could save him.

CHAPTER 8

MARIA, LA VIRGEN del Cobre, de Guadalupe, de Lourdes, del Pilar, de Todos los Angeles. Maria de Leningrado, flor de los siete colores. Ave Maria. Full of Grace, Full of Youth. Bearing Fruit, Good News, Good Graces. Nice legs, blue eyes, blonde hair. At night she comes to him. Knocking first, then pushing the slightly open door all the way until her hologram appears, floating above the threshold. Maria of Bauta, of the Lagoon. Maria, with freshly brewed coffee and buttered bread. Maria, with cumined black beans in a tin can. With tomatoes and eggs. With Russian canned meat. Maria Tovarish, Maria Naparnik. He could kiss her, but won't dare. He could brush his fingers against her bare shoulder, but he'd die first. He wants to lie next to her. With her, in her. Not to fuck. He doesn't even know what that means. But to rest his head against the tide of her bloodstream. Wrap his legs around the curves of her rib cage. Gulp the soft mass of her brain. She's saved his life one soft knock at a time. He is dying to give his life away to something, why not to her?

CHAPTER 9

IT WAS SATURDAY, and only a few weeks had passed since his mother's funeral. A busyness in the air reminded Elio that, when loved ones depart, life moves on without them. Old ladies, with talcum powder on their necks walked from la bodega carrying their allotted loaf of bread. Middle-aged men with furrowed brows leaned against light posts and porches, smoking cigars. Young mothers muscled children out of the house and into the street, making way for soapy mops and buckets of water thrown full force onto dusty tiles.

The children were all at the park now, kicking cans against the fence. Elio sat on a bench near a teeter-totter. He had a handful of his old glass marbles in his hand. He threw a couple into the air, one after the other, letting them drop into his hand with a clink. Raising a closed fist, he waved at Pepe, who was only a short distance away.

"Couldn't you have come up with a more private place? Anybody could hear us here," Pepe said, kicking sand into the air and taking a spot on the bench near his friend. He was starched to the gills in gray pants and a dark green shirt, big circles of sweat under each arm. The sun hit the small acne scars on his face—he looked almost lunar.

"Forget about it," Elio said. "Look, we gotta talk."

"It sounds serious. Should I be worried?" Pepe asked with a smirk.

"Nah, it's not *that* serious." The afternoon sun blazed above Elio, and the air was heavy with moisture.

"Whatever it is," Pepe said, "Don't do it." He took a red marble from Elio's hand and started tossing it up. He must have been out of cigarettes, Elio thought.

"No comas mierda, chico. Look, someone's got one of those black B-112 bikes they give to athletes," Elio said. "Just like new, the guy told me."

"One of those shoddy Soviet deals that go dasvidaña on you, if you as much as brake too fast," Pepe said. "That's a problem, not a bike. What does he want for it, *rubles?*"

"Coño, viejo. No aprietes. They're not that bad. I gotta finally get a bike, mi hermano. You know, to go around with Maria and shoot the breeze and shit."

The last words seemed to catch Pepe's attention. "What does that have to do with me?" he said.

Elio moved in closer. "It's got everything to do with you," he whispered. "I think the guy selling the bike's a friend of yours. Plus, he's looking for dollars…says he got the bike in the USSR for about ninety rubles, something like half of his athlete's monthly stipend."

"What does he want for the bike, a stipend?" Pepe said. "How much is that in dollars, anyway?"

Elio fixed his eyes on his nails. Dyestuff from the textilera had changed their color. They were an indigo blue where brown flesh should have been. He rested elbows on knees and lowered his head closer to the sand to shield his words. Attracted by the marbles, barefoot children ran back and forth near Elio and Pepe. It was easy to imagine that any one of them could overhear what he wasn't supposed to and report it. Children had been taught to nose out whatever they could about their schoolmate, their teacher, or their neighbor.

"I have no idea," Elio said. But you got dollars, don't you? From your mom and pop?" he finally asked.

"Yeah, but..." Pepe fixed his gaze on the children. "Shoo!" he told them.

"I'm good for it," Elio said. "I've been putting aside a little money from my wages at the textilera. Not a lot, but enough for the bike, I think."

Pepe shook his head. "You're gonna lose your shit when the bike breaks down on you. But, sure, why the hell not? It's for a good cause, right?"

"It's for a great cause," Elio said, rounding the palm of his hand over his friend's shoulder. "I love you, man—like a brother. Hell, I don't have any brothers, so you know I mean it."

"Leave the sap for another day, you fucking weirdo," Pepe said. "Who's this friend of mine, anyway?"

"You know, Yusnay. The kid who got kicked out of school for pissing in the courtyard during recess, then became a triple jumper in Moscow."

"I'm not friends with that kid."

One of the children came too close, nearly hitting Elio on the back of the head with his wiry, flailing arms. Elio shooed him away.

"Are you sure you wanna get a Soviet bike?"

"Where else am I gonna find a bike right now?" Elio said. "There won't be another one."

"Do you even know how to ride a bike?"

"Yup."

"And you know you won't find spare parts, right?"

"We won't need 'em. You'll see."

The children were back, and they'd plopped down next to Elio, making a lot of slurping noises and spitting onto the sand.

"Coño, no jodan más," Elio said. "Shoo!"

Two and a half hours later, Elio rode down La Loma de Pita on his just-like-new Soviet bike, with Pepe on the handlebars. "Cuba libre!" Elio shouted. "Cuba libre!" Pepe echoed, as cars and produce trucks alongside them on the road beeped in tune. Jesus Christ, Elio thought. Finally, a bike! And what a gorgeous thing it was. In essence, and where it mattered, in the machinery of the thing, there was no real difference between this bike and his red Panther II—none.

The sun stomped down on them as Elio let go of the pedals downhill. "Me cago en tu madre!" he shouted again. He felt a sudden emancipation, a liberation of body and spirit, as though he were finally free of so many burdens—his father, his mother, and even himself. He felt pure joy on that bike. It all came to heartbreak, however—and much sooner than Elio had anticipated. While hurtling down the hill, one of the axles broke. The front wheel bent, locking the wheel in place. Pepe, then Elio, flew into the air crash-landing feet away, their faces stuck to the pavement. Elio's marbles scattered all over the road. It was a real Homeric spill, in remembrance of which Elio decided to call that piece-of-shit bike the "Soviet Odyssey."

Although they tried to get their money back from Yusnay, the kid refused, claiming that had Elio adhered to one rider per bike, the bicycle's assembly—whether poor or not—wouldn't have succumbed to the pressure. Pepe called Yusnay "a real piece of shit." Elio kicked the bike a few times before leaving it beside the road near Yusnay's house. "They'll be another one, brother." Pepe patted Elio on the back. "I hate to say it, but I told you so." And that was the end of the Soviet Odyssey.

CHAPTER 10

DURING THE MONTHS following his mother's funeral and the fiasco with the Soviet bike, Elio felt paralyzed. He had to keep hold on reality while sidelining a steady flow of images, what ifs, and thoughts that tied his goddamn tongue into knots. Meanwhile, he tried to give himself strength, attempted to goad himself into action, to do the thing he'd been waiting to do all these years: ask Maria to marry him. His mother's sudden death had frightened him—it was yet another uncontrollable twist of fate. But she hadn't taken away his world with her any more than his father had.

He hesitated for a long time, keeping every thought, every doubt to himself. He never told a soul that he was scared shitless—not even Pepe. Especially not Pepe. But in the end, after weeks of obsessive questioning and negotiations, he decided. So one morning he found himself sitting in Maria's living room. He looked around to the dark mahogany coffee table, two armchairs, rocking chairs, and black and white TV. Perhaps because his presence there meant much more than a casual visit, the room was filled with a dense, anxious silence that coated everything.

His gaze rested on Maria's hands. Her fingernails were translucent, clean, and neatly trimmed. He tried to smile, but the stretch of his lips felt strange. Maria rested her head on the back of a rocking chair. Pushing against the tile with her bare feet, she kept the steady to-and-fro of the curved rockers from a full stop. Mima sat quietly beside her.

"I don't know that I can explain. Coming here, it was like—well, I think we all understand that, even though I don't have a great deal to offer right now, I will do whatever it takes to make Maria happy," Elio said.

He was willing to be whatever Maria wanted him to be. He didn't care much about holding on to who he was. He'd never really been sure about what the hell he was supposed to do with his life. How many times in the past had he dreamed of that gleaming red bike? And all the dreaming in the world wouldn't have been enough to fulfill his wish. Dreaming had got him nowhere. He had nothing to show for it. From that point forward, marrying Maria was the only thing that mattered.

"I know that I should be a doctor, or a lawyer, or an engineer...I am none of those things," he added. Maria's rocking chair came to a full stop. She looked at him, shaking her head.

"That doesn't matter to me," Maria said.

Elio was surprised by the conviction in her voice. He was looking at her so intently that she brushed her hand lightly across her face, as though worried that something was there.

"Of course it does," her grandmother spoke finally. Her voice was as taut as the fabric on the embroidery hoop in her lap. She, too, rocked back and forth, smiling at him, then looking down at her needlework. "It has always seemed to me you're a very decent young man who has had a difficult time."

Elio didn't know what to say to that. He wasn't even sure if it was time to leave. Hadn't he said he would only stay an hour? Had he taken too long? He didn't know the time, but surely they hadn't been talking for longer than that.

"You want to marry Maria," the grandmother said, her eyes locked to Elio's. Her voice was calm, reassuring.

"I do," Elio said.

"And a job?" she asked.

Mima fell silent long enough for Elio to sit up straight. She smiled at Maria, who was still rocking, faster now, as if the tide had turned.

"I took a job at the textile factory," Elio was quick to answer.

The grandmother gave a sigh of relief. "And military service?"

"Scoliosis," Elio pointed at his back.

"I see," the old woman said.

A week later, Maria had slipped a note through his shutters. He was back at her door, this time holding a small bouquet of red carnations in one hand and a bag of mangoes in the other. He was more nervous than before, even less sure of himself. She wanted a real proposal, the note had said, a *Will you marry me, Maria?* None of that namby-pamby nonsense he'd barely been able to utter to her grandmother. She wanted to hear him ask, and wanted to hear herself say Yes.

When Maria opened the door, she leaned against the door frame. *"Hello,"* she said in English. *"How are you?* I haven't said yes, have I?"

"No?" He moved closer, just a little. She drew back, looking away. Then she shifted her weight and stretched out her toes. "Do you love me or what?"

He swallowed. "More than words can say." One drop of sweat and then another bubbled up on his upper lip. His shirt was drenched.

Maria stared at him. "Ask me, coño. The sooner you ask me, the sooner we'll get to Chicago."

Somewhere, nearby, Elio heard water crashing against tile. He gripped the bag of mangoes a little tighter. What was she talking about? Living in Chicago? "Marry me," he said.

"Yes," she said in English. *"Yes. Yes. Yes."*

CHAPTER 11

THE RADIO WAS ON, but bad news lingered in the air and Ricky couldn't allow himself to enjoy the music. In Cuba, there would have been no music or singing or TV for weeks out of respect for the dead. But he was in El Norte, where there were wakes, and jazz funerals, and laments, and all sorts of other ways of singing the dead away, and of keeping the grieving from staying silent. Plus, Sally'd insisted that music would help him with the mourning process and would even smooth out his connection with the deceased which, in Aurelia's case, he certainly needed. Although the music Sally'd chosen wasn't exactly his cup of café cubano, at least it wasn't rock, or that hillbilly rhythm her upstairs neighbor had been blasting for the last three hours. It was closer to those weird, metallic tapes she listened to when she started collecting crystals and tirando las cartas. The kind of stuff that puts you in a zombie, meditative state. Whenever he listened to it, he liked to say he might as well be in a coma.

It was Sunday morning. At Sally's table he sipped her version of Cuban coffee, which really meant a small cup of American coffee with a whole lot of sugar, accompanied by a teaspoon. Sally stood on a plastic stool, feeling inside the cupboards for a pack of lighters she'd bought earlier in the week. She was wearing a leotard and tights with a sweatband that pushed her mass of red hair away from her face. "It's for the Ed Allen Show," she'd told him earlier that morning. "This body's not an accident, you know." Ricky was thankful he'd spent the night at her place. Sometimes, he thought, you just don't want to be home.

"How did you sleep?" She looked down at Ricky from the top of the stool.

"Not so well," Ricky said. "I kept waking up." It made him feel a hell of a lot better that, after almost five years together, Sally still cared enough about him to ask.

"Bad dreams?"

Ricky hesitated. "Just restless. Confusing."

He wanted to ask her what kind of man would a son become who is without a father or a mother but the question wouldn't come out. His thoughts felt as clouded as his dreams.

"You're still in shock," Sally said. "It takes time. Did Elsa say how he's holding up?"

"Elsa said he's broken up about it, but alright. What's the kid gonna do now, though? A father in Chicago and a dead mother? Jesus fucking Christ. What shitty luck. Te lo dije. I saw it coming. Aurelia was a fucking train wreck waiting to happen. Me cago en su madre. I should've taken the kid with me when I had the chance." He looked down at the table. He wasn't brave enough to look up at Sally, afraid she'd notice his tears. "But you know, she fucking pleaded, and pleaded. I could never see her cry. She was a really good mother most of the time, you know. She loved that kid. She really did."

"What's done is done," Sally said. "You can't beat yourself up about it." She held out the lighters for Ricky to see.

He managed a smiled. "You're right," he murmured, wiping his eyes. "Te lo juro," he said, "as soon as there's a chance, I'm going back for him."

The hillbilly music from the upstairs flat was so loud, it seemed to drown out his voice.

"Of course I'm fucking right," Sally said and jumped down from the stool. She opened the pack of lighters, took one out, and lit a cigarette with it. "Anyway, if you went back for him, you'd be doing the right thing. But don't think about it anymore right now. Your son's at least alright, and that's a good reason to be glad. So come on," she said. "Write that postcard. It's gonna make you and him feel good. You'll see. I know what I'm talking about."

Ricky stared at the postcard leaning against the little empty vase on the table. It was one of those 5x7 deals they sold at the souvenir shop on Michigan Avenue, where Sally had bought her lighters. Although the lighters were ridiculously overprized, she liked the miniature Chicago skyline on them, the glittery "I Love Chicago" right above it. Ricky examined the card. It was nice, he thought, with one side showing Chicago's skyscrapers rising up from winter slush into dull, gray skies. On the back was the empty rectangle where he'd have to write something. *Hello from Chicago!* he said to himself.

Part 2

The Honeymoon Years

Bauta, 1969–1970

CHAPTER 12

SUMMER OF 1969 came in wet. Rain had been continuous since June. But to trace out the history of the whole summer in terms of rain, Elio thought, to say how it was raining at any given moment, to determine how yesterday's drizzle was different from today's showers, was utterly impossible.

Elio had always loved the rain. Regardless of its type, rain always came with impunity, drenching clotheslines, drumming on rooftops, seeping through crevices, and dropping with a tin-tin-tin into cooking pans in someone's living room. It was the one thing on this island no one could control. In revolutions, everything shifted and nothing changed. Reform after reform replaced the names of things with newer, shinier names, but the things themselves remained the same. Teatro Blanquita in Havana became the Karl Marx Theater, but continued to be what it had always been: the largest movie theater in Havana. The Hilton Hotel in Vedado was renamed Hotel Habana Libre, but its standing as Latin America's tallest and largest hotel was left unaltered. And as far as Elio was concerned, he could no more get his hands on a bicycle now than he could have years earlier. But he could always count on the rain to make him feel—well, hopeful. And there was hope. Ten Million Tons of hope, to be exact.

In only five years, they had become the new men and women of a new world, a different, better world. So new were they that a man might discover that he was meant to teach, and labor in the earth, and commune with his fellow man. So new that the island women—tired of clotheslines and dinners and mops—might run for the hills, alphabets floating behind them like clouds, to teach the unlearned to read and write. So new that children became the wards and the heirs of the Revolution. And all were energized by a new resolve, by the opening up before them of the blinding, flower-strewn meadows that led to justice, finally. To victory, always. And perhaps, because it was only the beginning, they were full of excitement and romance and love. Elio and Maria, too. Especially, Elio and Maria.

For several hours, hand in hand they walked in the Viñales landscape. Known for luminous skies, rust-colored tobacco fields, an emerald green valley, and craggy outcrops known as mogotes, Viñales was a town in the westernmost region of the island. To the people living in its small, wooden houses, rightfully outfitted with rocking chairs on shady porches, it was an agricultural town like many others on the island. To Elio and Maria, alone for the first time, it was paradise.

Rivulets of water pouring off their umbrella, they kept up a slow pace, wanting to possess every moment of their afternoon in the rain. They did not speak. But they were newlyweds; not speaking wasn't yet something to worry about.

Toward midafternoon, the pangs in Elio's belly gradually became stronger. They hadn't eaten anything since leaving Bauta early that morning. He was so famished he could have eaten a whole racimo de platanitos without interruption—not that there were any available. He tried to hold on as long as possible, but when the rain finally subsided around 3:00 p.m., they slopped in through the door of their thatched-roof hotel room. Assuming Maria was hungry, too, he broke his hold of her hand at last.

He began foraging through one of the bags they'd brought along for the trip. His neck and back ached horribly, enough that he wondered how much bending, pouring, and mixing dye at the textilera he'd manage to endure in the future.

Day after day, he'd put up the brave struggle and played his role, only to end up in a honeymoon suite whose walls were irremediably thin, while he tried to ignore the radio broadcast in the room next door. All the laughter, moaning, and bed thumping told him that their next-door neighbors too, were on some kind of honeymoon.

"What are you doing?" Maria plopped herself on the bed, dabbing wet limbs with a corner of the bedcover.

"Cake time," he said, lifting a small can in the air like a trophy.

"Already? I thought we would save it for after—you know?" She leaned back on the bed, a hand fluffing wet tresses, like she was looking into a mirror.

"A person must be prepared to receive nourishment." He laughed, then pulled off the yarn around the paper covering the can's opening. "I'm ready to feast, aren't you?"

Maria laughed. *"Sugar smacks,"* she said in English.

"Did you bring a spoon? Or a fork?"

"I didn't think of that," she said.

"Are you hungry?" Elio asked.

Maria used her finger to point to her mouth, on which remained a smile. "Very," she said.

Elio decided he'd come home, at last. He scooped out a handful of white frosting and yellow cake. "So good," he said. "Don't you want some? I can't eat all this."

The cake, their wedding cake, had been a gift from Fina Carreira, proud owner of the biggest house on the block, and for whom Maria did a bit of dusting here and there whenever the old woman happened to need it. Frosted with meringue and layered with vanilla custard and guava marmalade, the cake was just the way Elio liked it. Maria's grandmother had been furious, though. She hated anyone getting the jump on her in the gift department, especially if *anyone* happened to be Fina. Eventually, however, Mima got over it. She had no choice, she said. She'd never tasted anything quite as good in her life. Maria seemed to agree. Fina's cake, she'd told Elio, was *Plus Value* and *Orlon Blend*.

If they ate the cake now, Elio thought, they could focus on that invisible celestial signature that was the honeymoon business for a while longer. Hunger, he knew, shortened lifespans, and he'd resolved to pull an all-nighter. He wanted every moment of it to be perfect. Flowers, a light breeze, and the moonlight cascading through half-open shutters.

"It's too bad we couldn't get a nicer room, something with a window," he told Maria. "Did you tell them that you wanted the honeymoon suite?"

The hotel room's amenities included a small bar of soap, a stream of water that didn't so much run as crawl, and an alarm clock frozen at 8:30 a.m.

Maria frowned. "This *is* the honeymoon suite. In any case, the mattress is better than ours," she said, bouncing up and down on the bed to make her point.

"Well," he said, reaching out his meringue hand to touch Maria's lips, "at least that. As for the rest, just leave it to me."

"I leave it to you, then," she said.

Elio had himself pegged as an optimist. After all, he'd managed to land a job at the textilera, and he'd found a way to end up in Viñales— plus, he'd married her, hadn't he?

"The whole thing will require some thinking," he said with more cake than mouth.

"Can you get us some chocolates?" she said.

"I wish."

"Mangoes?"

He watched Maria unbutton her shirt, and lean further back on the bed. He looked closely at her face. "I'll be right back."

An hour later, Elio walked through the door, his face hidden behind a large bundle of wild flowers and palm fronds. Hanging from his arm, a bag full of mangoes. The room was a different place in no time. While there was no window, there was no longer the need for one. He'd brought Viñales indoors.

"Elio," Maria put her hand to her mouth, clearly trying not to laugh, "this is the sweetest thing anyone's ever done for me. Conchó, this is beautiful! Where in the world did you get the mangoes? There isn't a bodega or a street vendor in sight."

Elio puffed up his chest. "The island giveth," he said, "but the hotel's out of spoons."

"It's perfect, darling," Maria said, leaning against the bed's headboard. Her cheeks were flushed, her eyes a bright blue. No matter how she shifted, the light in the room seemed to love her face, her shoulders, her thighs, the softness and angles of her body. Her pale skin beneath waves of blonde hair.

Elio stared at her. He could afford to stare. She was his beautiful bride and she was, like a hilltop, above everything else he had ever desired.

"We can leave the mangoes for later," he said, tearing off a piece of cardboard from an old phonebook cover. "We got ourselves a spoon."

"Did you miss your mother at our wedding?" she said, going back to the can of cake, now with Elio's makeshift scooper in her hand.

It took Elio a moment to respond. They'd managed to talk around certain things so far, but it was their honeymoon, so he decided to try at least *some* part of the truth. "Every minute of it," he said. "But it's been nearly five years—I've healed."

Maria held up her finger as she was chewing. After she swallowed, she gave a sad half smile. "Have you ever thought that you could end up like her?"

"Like who?"

"Like your mother?"

"You mean, kill myself? Nah, not as long as I know where I'm going and have a way to get there. Not as long as—"

Maria laughed, then looked at him skeptically. "Let's just hope you find what you're looking for."

"I have," he said, kissing her bare shoulder.

CHAPTER 13

A MONTH AND A DAY after their wedding, the sun was high and the sea was a glittering blue as Elio and Maria walked to the shore at Baracoa Beach. A surge of large, smooth waves came toward them, frothing up around their feet. They held hands and kissed, letting the ground sink beneath them as the waves pulled back into the sea.

"C'mon," Maria said. "We didn't come here for nothing." She was standing on one foot, with her arms outstretched, playing burnt flamingo under the sun. Her skin had turned a bright red and Elio feared she'd had enough sun for one day.

He stared out toward the quiet menace that was all that water, a machine, with machine-like creatures lurking beneath the surface. He didn't have the heart to swim. He simply couldn't do it. His legs wouldn't move. His body wouldn't budge. He was terrified.

"You go," he told her, even as his heart beat fast for her, and for what he knew could happen in the water.

"C'mon, don't be a ninny!" she said, hopping, laughing, and pulling him by the hands.

Elio could do nothing more than hold his ground. "No," he said, lifting her hands to his mouth to kiss them. "I'm not getting in the water."

"Fine," she said, pulling her hands away. "I'll go in alone this time, but you'll have to get over your fear sooner or later."

Elio watched as her body broke the waves and disappeared into the sunlight. He walked back to their towel, and sat down. While he waited impatiently for her to come back, he tried to read but his head was nowhere near Lincoln Island and the Nautilus. It was with Maria, and he hoped, prayed, she'd come back from the water in one piece. He felt sick to his stomach.

They'd spent all afternoon at the beach telling each other stories. He, the one about the guy who found a cave full of gold, and silver, and precious stones. She, the one about the magic lamp and the other one, the one about the sailor. Then she'd said they should start with the greatest book ever written in any language. "Once you read it, you'll never be the same," she said. And she told him about windmills and giants, and about the greatest of friendships between a caballero andante and his squire, and about the caballero's unbounded love for his Dulcinea. Elio was mesmerized by the lull of her voice. "This will be a story long enough to last us all the years we'll spend together," Maria told him. Elio loved the idea, and he loved her.

She told each story with great care, tenderly, quietly, rounding out every word as though each time was the first and the last time she'd pronounce Había una vez. Sitting beside her on the sand, Elio concluded that Maria knew all there was to know about loving him. Perhaps she could guess that as long as there were words, as long as there were stories—that he would want to hear again the next day, and the next, and the next day after that—she would save him. And there would be no other destination than Maria. Because she would be the only place he would ever want to be. His one-and-only story.

And they made so many plans, which they erected before them like sandcastles, as elaborate as the stories they'd told, and just as beautiful. They decided where and how they would live, who their friends would be, and what they would wear, and eat, and watch on TV. And how they would never let anyone dictate their lives, or make choices for them, or make them feel unwelcome or afraid. Because they were young, and this life was new, and like all new things, they were wrapped up in dreams.

Though he tried to remember the finer details of each story—colors, sounds and textures—his mind drew a blank, choosing instead to imagine Maria choking and swallowing water. Absorbed in the one task of getting another breath, her body flailed hopelessly against a force she couldn't see.

Unable to wait any longer, Elio ran to the shore and looked out over the water. Children waded in and out of the surf while a small blue motorboat crawled slowly toward the pier. Elio couldn't see anybody on it, and he couldn't see Maria in the water. His heart beat faster. He pushed into the surf, far enough for the water to reach his calves. But he froze. He couldn't go any further. "Maria!" His voice came out broken. "Swim back!" A beat, then another. And, suddenly, there she was. In the distance, Maria, a small dot in a sea of sunlight, saw him and waved. Elio waved back, squinting. "I think you should get out of the water!" he shouted, his heart pumping in his chest.

"I'm coming!" she yelled back.

CHAPTER 14

A YEAR INTO their marriage, they were quite settled into Elio's house, which became their official residence and to which they both tended with care. Most nights, Elio feared he wouldn't be able to sleep a wink, so unaccustomed was he to folded linens and crisp, white sheets. To dishes and pans that were washed, dried, and put away after each meal. To floors free of dust and dirt.

Like him, Maria, too, had found a job. She was a telephone operator at the telephone company in town. Perhaps the job had never seemed to her a very appealing fate, compared to other *métiers* (fashion came to mind, for example), but she appeared to learn fast that, with his optimism and her tenderness, any job would be enough to secure them a happy life together. After all, they were both stirred by passion and by the certainty that, no matter what life had in store for them, together they would persist, undiscouraged. There were reasons for the excitement they felt, for the euphoria of that first year, the love with which they tended to each other's every need, as though only *their* needs existed. They were in love, and they were beginning. And although the future seemed to Elio a distant dream, anything was possible.

However, it was Maria who, perhaps unwittingly, disrupted their peace. Privately, in some uneventful afternoon, when Bauta's park was nearly empty, she led Elio to one of the nearby granite benches. It was starting to get dark but it was still possible to make out the last glimmers from the sun. The park smelled of greenery and night-blooming jasmine. A light breeze reminded Elio that, on an island, the sea was always close. There was the sound of crickets, too, lightening up the atmosphere with what to Elio had always sounded like music.

The park had a playground, a sandy area separated from Bauta's church by a tall, mesh wire fence. Inside were a few swings, slides, some teeter-totters, a roundabout, and a little train that had been added recently. To the left of the church was the bust of Carlos Valdés Rosa, Bauta's distinguished teacher. Toward the front, a bust of José Martí, poet, essayist, and national hero. Behind it all, there was the Glorieta, a gazebo whose most distinguishing characteristic was its amazing echo.

Gently, Maria pushed Elio onto the bench. "I need to tell you something," she said.

He sat at the edge, looking up at her. He was, as his dad liked to say, decoding storms in the clouds. He felt he should have known; he and Maria weren't exactly strangers who'd met one day at a bus stop. They'd been neighbors first, childhood friends, and that meant something. He was convinced he'd found what he'd been looking for—had she? Elio feared that Maria would want a separation, or worse, a divorce. So many people they knew had divorced only a few years into their marriage; he was afraid their own marriage would fall apart before it truly began. He dreaded the idea of being alone again; but, most of all, he dreaded the idea of being without her. He had found someone with whom to spend the rest of his adult life. He didn't want to think about ever having to wake up to loneliness and void.

"There are other things to do," she said, sitting next to him.

"Like what?"

"Elio," she said, "for a whole year, we've been worried about the day to day. We wake up, we go to work. We come home, then we climb into bed, make love, and go to sleep. How about the future? We're young. We could be building a house, traveling, enjoying *today's modern, today's new,*" she said in English. *"I want to live life every golden minute of it, every golden drop of it. It's light-up time,* Elio. I want to feel like new, don't you? —*It's the chocolate, it's the nougats, it's the nuts.* Do you know what I mean?

"Are children part of that plan?" Elio tried to hide from himself the anxiety he felt, but he couldn't hide it from Maria. By now, she seemed to know him too well. Was it children she wanted? And why not? It'd been a year already and they'd been so careful, so clinical about preventing any and all possible accidents—was it time? Why not children? Did he want to be a father, sleepless nights, and lullabies? He'd seen small children running barefoot in the sand only feet from where they were—they didn't seem a nuisance or mistakes.

"No, not children," she said. "Don't you want me to be happy? I want to live in Chicago, Elio."

Elio had a hard time admitting to himself that once or twice he'd thought about leaving. Pretending he'd made up his mind one way or the other was a lie she didn't deserve, though. And lying to himself was pathetic. He simply didn't think he'd ever be willing to go—besides, even if he wanted to, free travel abroad was a thing of the past.

"I'm sorry, of course I want you to be happy," he said weakly. "But it's just too hard now, you know that."

Maria turned to look at him. She must have seen in his face the sadness with which he'd understood the situation they were in—she wanted to leave, and Elio simply wasn't sure he ever would. He looked away from her. He had an unpleasant sensation of loss. Feeling Maria's warmth escaping him, he was in a bad mood with his thoughts in confusion. He wanted Maria back. He hoped that she would start crying, that he could touch her, comfort her.

She brought him back. "I want things—shiny stoves, and washing machines, and cars, and clothes, and shoes. I'm tired of a grimy kitchen, and of washing clothes by hand until my knuckles are raw, and tired of walking. Tired of old blouses, and polyester pants, and tattered shoes. Tired of standing still. I'm young, Elio. Don't you want a better life? If you mean it, then let's leave this place."

This place, of course, meant neither the park nor Bauta. She meant the island. She meant Cuba. Even if he wanted to leave, even if he suddenly changed his heart, there was no way out. No route of escape, no outflow. The ban on leaving the country was, at least until further notice, permanent and continuous. Was there any sense in wanting what you couldn't have? Elio feared that Maria had begun directing her budding frustrations toward him and not toward the very system responsible for them. She avoided blaming the island for her life, he thought, because doing so would only have reminded her that their lives were, even then, at the mercy of a force greater than them.

Elio stared at the pavement for a moment. He pressed his lips together as if to restrain a smile and said affectionately, perhaps a little bitterly, "You've reminded me of the little Americana you always were."

"Home appliances," she said in English.

It occurred to Elio that talking, as long as they didn't talk about that, could be the distraction that made their differences ebb. On the radio and the television, talking was the order of the day. Talking itself would become a way of anticipating everyone's needs, not just Maria's. Everyone talked, either about each other, or about the state of affairs on the island.

On stages, and plazas, and in whispers and murmurs, and through clenched teeth everyone discussed everyone else's fate and the absolute nationalization of the economy. Having already taken over factories and hotels and social clubs, now bodegas, barbershops, beauty salons, shoe and auto repair shops, small restaurants, and snack shops became the new goals. Even Pepe's friend Cho had lost his father's Chinese restaurant in the process and Bodega Los Cubanitos, one of Bauta's first bodegas, was now a thing of the past. The state also went after Catholics like their neighbor Elsa La Gorda and men like Emiliano, and anybody who could be accused of cultural nonconformity—anybody. Most churches closed and, although Bauta's church remained open, many avoided it altogether, afraid of the possible consequences for being found inside—or worse, for attending service.

Talking was one way—or perhaps the only way—of moving ahead. But for Elio, love was there, always. Without love, a most profound love for Maria, he would have found nothing to say.

Part 3

Shifting Tides

Bauta, 1980

CHAPTER 15

BUT A MARRIAGE IS LIKE a revolution—and the honeymoon never lasts. So much had altered over the course of the last ten years. Emiliano the nurse had been right. Life on the island would shift so fast, it'd be hard to keep up with the latest changes. After all, who could have anticipated that on account of a small group of hairy machos—as Elio's mom had liked to call them—such huge transformations could take place on his small island?

Every year the situation seemed to Elio to become worse. Envy, resentment, and frustration had spread like a virus. People harbored, at the very center of their gut, a desire that couldn't get out. The desire erupted, burst in other ways, like cysts or boils, swollen with venom against your neighbor or your lover, against the Soviets and the Americans, against national heroes, churches and their faithful, against writers, poets, artists, film-makers, homosexuals and—perhaps even worse—against themselves. How could anyone not want to disappear from such a place? From such madness?

Elio imagined his dad, wherever he was and to whomever would listen, saying that he, Ricardo Perez, had known it all along. But Ricardo

Perez was too far away to know what was actually happening on the island, much less in Elio's life. Elio, on the other hand, was far too close to understand what in fact was taking place. Somewhere in between would have been the ideal vantage ground.

Bit by bit Elio and Maria had become full adults. While Maria's hips had widened, her face had lost some of its glow and had become narrower. Elio, who had been skinny for most of his childhood—and nearly all of his young adulthood—had begun to see the first signs of a belly. Together, they seemed to stand for a certain kind of truth about the Revolution—in both cases, the romance and excitement of earlier years had started to wane.

At the textile factory, Elio came and went, accustomed by now to a certain routine. He worked long hours for little pay and in dreadful conditions, doing highly monotonous tasks. The factory was poorly lit, very noisy, and lacked adequate ventilation. Without air conditioning and only a few fans to go around, Elio wished he wasn't so goddamned scared of the water so he could go back to the beach, if only to feel the cool, wet sand under his feet.

He had spent the last ten years cleaning and processing the raw material, spinning it, and dyeing it. And, in spite of the long, hot days, he had figured out a way to mitigate his boredom. By paying close attention to the printing and embroidering of the fabrics, Elio had discovered that he had a knack for both. He even had a certain eye for what he called textilerías, a combination of various skills having to do with fabric and clothing manufacturing that involved both legal and illegal means. He was continuing to read too. He read, he sewed, and he passed the time.

While Elio had found a way to live on the island, however, Maria had become more and more impatient. "I want more," she'd tell him. "More out of work, more out of life, and more out of you."

She was right. They barely made ends meet—and, certainly, there was no room for dreaming. It was more than just a matter of finances: more like there was no incentive and nothing to finance. More like there was nothing. Or, almost nothing, which was actually worse. Nothing would have made a statement. On the other hand, *almost nothing* turned life into a series of "nearly there's."

Elio was *nearly* able to trust his neighbors who, adhering to the island's knack for social control, were part of a mutual system of citizens' vigilance, selling each other out for an extra roll of toilet paper or a bar of soap. He was *nearly* able to say what was on his mind without whispering, or closing the shutters, or turning up the radio. Nearly able take a full shower before the water was cut off. Maria was nearly able to trade two eggs for a bar of soap. They were *nearly* able to season food beyond a can of Vita Nuova. If he'd at least developed an ulcer, they could have had, among other state-sponsored perks, extra chicken and milk.

In sum, they were *nearly* able to live with some goddamn dignity, which was what anyone, on any remote corner of the world, would have wanted. But hadn't it always been the same? What was it about islands that conned people into believing that anything would be different? One thing was certain, the honeymoon was over.

But just after three o'clock in the afternoon on April 2 the island's relative, near calm was shattered for what would be several months.

There had been a brief, sudden shower earlier that day. The factory was closed, yet again, until further notice due to repairs. As the downpour began, Elio peered at the street through his shutters. The boys in calzoncillos kept playing ball. Scrawny, snotty, younger ones tantrumed on their porch, wishing they could join the others. And there was the one girl who, defying the rules of her gender, had dropped her book bag somewhere near her door and joined the rowdy brood in underwear.

Everyone else was indoors.

It was as if island life had stopped ticking right before a great, big pop.

Elio turned away from the window and went back to his ironing. He was pressing a small stack of pitusas on the dining room table when the news came in. Not any news, the news: a bus had rammed the fence of the Peruvian embassy in Havana; a mob of people followed.

"Cojones." Pepe barged in. The front door slammed behind him. "The element of chance, repinga," he whispered, rushing toward Elio. "Leave the goddamn jeans and let's get the hell out of here. It's now or never, mi hermano."

Elio pressed down on the hot iron, back and forth over gold seams and hemmed pant legs. He didn't respond. It was as if he'd dived into the deep end of a pool and his ears had popped. He grabbed a thin iron rod at the end of which the letters L-e-e were welded, and sauntered into the kitchen. He opened the box of matches on the counter and took out one. By the time Pepe was standing next to him, Elio was holding the letters to the flame on the burner.

"Did you hear a word I said?" Pepe shouted.

Elio seemed to have lost his ability to speak. His gaze slid away, and he nodded his head. Yes, he'd heard him.

Once the letters turned a glowing red, he walked back to the jeans. He pressed the letters against the small leather rectangle on the pants' back right side for a minute or two. When he lifted the stamper, as if by magic, a word appeared: "Lee."

"I'm making progress here," he finally said. "I'm a bárbaro, brother. Take a look at these pitusas. Factory made. Who the hell's gonna say these aren't real—you tell me that."

"Oye, are you dreaming again? This island is shit," Pepe said. "Your jeans are shit, and they're illegal. If they catch you making jeans, you're

going to jail,—and not because they're fake Lees, but because making
your stupid fake Lees is an act of self-determination. You get it? Life is
elsewhere, mi hermano. But not here. It hasn't been here for a long time."

"Jesus," Elio said, "do you realize that someone we know is probably
trapped in the embassy at this very moment, getting beaten, trampled,
or humiliated in the worst possible way? Hopeful that on that one small
plot—on that island that is and is not Perú, inside another island—
someone'll open the can and set them free."

Suddenly, like someone who had just found his anger, Elio hurled
the rod across the room. It went spin-wheeling into the air, then lost
momentum until it clattered onto the tile, sliding, and coming to rest
between armchair legs. He didn't need to close his eyes to see the shark
coming for him. Feeling the phantom sting of tearing flesh near his groin,
he jumped back.

Pepe's clenched fist banged on the kitchen table. "Qué repinga's going
on with you? Wait, the rain—I got it. It got you all hopeful again…you
actually believe you'll make a life in this goddamn island. Get your head
out of your ass and let's get the fuck outta here. You know what rain is,
right? It's all this heat de pinga rising up, then dropping down because it
couldn't get its freakin' shit together."

"This is how we win," Elio said. His words sputtered saliva. "You
simply invent what you don't have. They don't have a plan against
invention, do they? Nope. Not as far as I know." He had resigned himself
to the absurd state of the island with a mix of despair, invention, and
compliance. Even when he felt that he, too, should leave, he fought
against his feelings, and his fear always won.

Pepe looked around. "Where's Maria? Where in repinga did she go?
She's probably there already, brother! Dale, people are getting through. It's
now or never, recoño!"

Elio shook his head, but didn't answer. These people, all of them, needed a serious fucking clue, he thought. Just what did they think would happen? Did they assume everything would change if they left? Was it really so bad that it was worth putting up with the worst humiliation as long as, sooner or later, they'd find themselves on the other side of the ocean? Wasn't Perú in the middle of a civil war?

Maria was gathering up her things to go home when she heard the news. Or, at least, that's what she told Elio later. In fact, she'd heard while still working. As soon as the bus broke through the fence of the embassy, her phone lines started blinking. "La gente se va por el Perú!" and "Fuera la escoria!" and "Out with the lumpen!" Voices shouted from receivers all around her. Every telephone console at the Bauta telephone company lit up like a field of Christmas trees. At that moment, from the intermittent glow of lights all around her, Chicago's skyscrapers emerged. She could see the city so clearly: Chicago covered in newly fallen snow. On the island, for better or for worse, it was always summer, she thought.

Maria fumbled with her headset before taking a resolute breath and setting it on her console table. She looked down the corridor that spanned the length of a large room. A dozen of her fellow operators sat on high-backed metal stools. They answered calls into the Central Office, either dispensing information or connecting calls by taking the plug from the incoming exchange and placing it in the corresponding jack of the party they wished to call. They also disconnected calls, lots of them, especially the ones that came from abroad. That day, in particular, the switchboard lights flashed incessantly. Cuban exiles hoping to make contact with loved ones on the island were jamming the lines. When they finally got through, the line was suddenly cut, unplugged, in a deliberate, collective effort to thwart communication between Cubans on the island and the outside world.

It wasn't particularly straightforward work. You had to have a knack for deception and a temperament that motivated you to follow the rules at all times. Maria wasn't cut out for it. "Try again later, mi amor," she could hear Yenisleydis saying. "So sorry, there seems to be no one to receive the call." At twenty-eight years old, Yenisleydis would have given an arm for a chance to leave the island; yet, there she was, giving up her soul instead, one cut telephone call at a time. Other operators, young and old, and in various stages of dissension, joked as if isolation, confusion, and miscommunication were something to joke about.

When she finished her shift, Maria walked to the break room and slid the tattered novel she read on breaks inside her handbag. With the uncertain step of someone without a roadmap, she crossed the hall beyond her space at the console and made her way out the door. Walking home she thought about Elio. She tried to keep calm, but the closer she was to home, the angrier she became. Elio's refusal to ever change their lives in any real, permanent way infuriated her. Ultimately she translated his refusal into a lack of caring, a lack of feelings, and an utter lack of love. What would he say about the Peruvian embassy? She wondered.

By the time she opened her own front door, Pepe was gone. Elio was still ironing on the dining table, his T-shirt yellowed by the afternoon's sweat. Short strands of graying hair plastered on a glistening forehead.

She walked straight to the kitchen, slamming her bag down on the counter. Her heart was speeding up. She was torn. She felt like going up to Elio and punching him in the crotch, scratching out his eyes, then going on a rampage, turning over tables and chairs, and breaking plates against the wall. But she was also afraid, afraid of the unknown, afraid of the suffocating heat, and afraid of the passing of years. In a few months, she'd turn thirty-three, and what did she have to show for it? She recalled then the reason they didn't have children. Her reasons, at least, the ones she'd never revealed to Elio. He wouldn't have understood that, if they ever ended up attempting to leave the island, children would make it all that more challenging, all that more difficult to start over wherever they'd end up. Children were cumbersome, obstacles to the kind of life she'd always wanted to live. Last-minute decisions, she knew, were difficult enough without the added considerations that children imposed on their parents.

She thought of looking for Pepe. Over the years, Pepe had often seemed to her a more compatible choice. She didn't want Elio to tell her that it was too late to join the mob at the Peruvian embassy. She wanted to be encouraged. She wanted to know that leaving was on everyone's mind—including Elio's. But what could Pepe do? Once Elio had made up his mind, not even Pepe would prod him into action.

Later that night Elio and Maria sat at their kitchen table, the stack of Elio's clandestine Lee jeans at their side. The lights were out. The glow of a small quinqué spread over their bodies.

"What do you think?" he said, lifting a pair of jeans in the air by the belt loops.

"I don't know. Who did you say's going to buy those pitusas?"

"Anybody who's anybody in Bauta—that's who."

"Why can't you think of something else, coño. If somebody catches you—"

"Who? The same poor bastard who comes for the jeans. Isn't *he* risking his hide too?"

"I wish we'd been there," she finally said, resting her forehead on an open palm.

Elio looked at her, noticing a thin crease on her forehead. Had it always been there? Why hadn't he noticed it before?

"We're surviving, Maria," he said.

"I don't want to just survive, Elio. I want more."

"This is more," he said, lifting the jeans up by the loops. "This can make us some money for the time being."

"And later?"

"And later we'll see." he said.

"At least say you wish we'd been there." Maria said. Her shoulders slouched, looking so heavy they seemed capable of foundering both of them. She was crying, explaining something, pointing toward the street, and then at him, and now at the dark cracks on the walls and the holes in the ceiling.

"I can't say that. Can you imagine what it's like in there? People at the tops of trees, on the roof, getting kicked in the balls, pissing and shitting in corners, like animals. They've turned us into animals, Maria."

She looked away toward the bubbled paint on the walls. Toward the cracks in the ceiling. Toward the stack of jeans on the floor. Her expression remained the same, and she continued to cry. He couldn't blame her. Their house was decorated shabbily in a style that had more to do with scarcity than with a sense of taste or personal comfort. She tried to keep it tidy, clean, but truly nice, as in *See what I got for Christmas? Isn't it good looking?* was nearly impossible. Ugly paper flowers on a mishmash of antique tables flanked a small black and white TV in the living room between two wooden armchairs. In the small kitchen, an old wooden table and two chairs. In their bedroom, a small side table, the only furnishing in the room besides the bed with its old mattress. Maria'd had enough. Where was the formica, and the steel to make things last? Or the paint that gives your home a sunny disposition? Where was the magic?

"I'll get out, Elio Perez. I swear it. Whether they permit us to leave freely, or I have to swim away all the way to Chicago in the middle of the night. Bound, gagged, or blindfolded—I'll leave. Am I to assume that you wouldn't leave with me?"

Elio knew her face, and something about it was different. He remembered the surprising effect foreign photographs, always in color, had on him. Or the smell of Cuban exiles newly returned to the island, the ones from Miami, and California, and Texas. The ones who came in vuelos de La Comunidad, in search of brothers and sisters, mothers and fathers left behind. With the smell of new rubber, and deodorant, and face powder clinging to their skin.

Elio could always tell who had come back to visit the island from abroad and who had never left the island. It was like what happened to Berto at the end of the block. Half his face collapsed after a stroke. Except, with these stayed-for-good Cubans, it was the whole face, not just one side. Perhaps it was the sun, but perhaps it was something else, like something in the water.

"I won't leave Cuba," he said, quickly offering her a corner of the tablecloth. She whispered something. Elio wanted to quiet her, he couldn't bear the sight of her falling apart right in front of him. He dried her eyes, her nose, her mouth. Brushed her hair away from her face. She rested her head gently on his chest, bursting into tears again.

CHAPTER 16

"THE SEA!" he told Sally. "I have to swim in the sea. A lake won't do, Sally-girl, no matter how grand. I need the complete, deep, blue sea. All of it! El profundo mar azul and the white powdery sand. Now, you don't have that here, do you? You got the beach, sure, but not the powdery sand. Arena blanca, like talcum powder. Sol bueno, y mar de espuma. Nope, you can't say that about Chicago."

"Ricky Perez, they spoiled you rotten in Cuba," she said.

It was April 3, 1980. They were in the corner booth at Daley's on Sixty-Third Street and Sally was midway through her second ice cream and pie. How she managed to stay as thin as she was, only she knew. Perhaps it was all that head banging to Pink Floyd in the bathroom while getting ready to tend bar at Jay's on Rush Street, where she made Moscow mules and served martinis from a proper highball glass to tipsy conventioneers and native Chicagoans on their way back from a show. Or maybe it was her morning dance routines to Richard Simmons, in leopard-print tights and pink leg warmers she'd knitted herself while watching *Dallas* on TV. Sally was a character, a real Americana. Made of beef jerky and bourbon, with a side of pie à la mode.

"Yes, yes," Ricky said. "The beach is my people's idea of paradise. Our beaches *are* paradise. Los Americanos fail to appreciate the perfection that lies at the heart of una buena playa."

"We know good playas too," Sally said. "How about the beaches in Miami? Are those *good* playas?"

"Miami's practically Cuba, Sally, so it doesn't count."

"I love your logic, darling," she said. "Frankly, you're probably right. Lake Michigan, though," she smirked, "now those are beaches."

"Ay, Sally…how can you respect a beach that doesn't have arena blanca?"

Poor girl, Ricky thought. She'd never been to a real beach in her life. Lake Michigan wasn't the worst he'd seen, that was true. But it wasn't Cuba. Let's face it, it was America's good old college try at a freshwater Varadero, a nearly unending beach that looked like Cuba on days when Ricky's melancholy forced him to squint in the daylight. The lake was clean and blue, but unlike Cuba's warm beaches, it was unpleasantly cool, with water temperatures in the sixties. Sometimes, however, and from his vantage point, it looked just like the ocean, feeding him memories of an island, a sea, and a feeling of being landlocked, the acute longing to leave.

"Maybe we should go to Miami…" she said.

Ricky rose from his spot on the booth and pulled Sally up by the hand to stand with him. "Sally-girl," he said. "I think you got yourself a traveling partner."

And that's how, months later, he and Sally ended up at the Flamingo Motel in South Beach—a beach as close to Cuba's as any he'd ever seen. She slurring about daiquiris and white sand dunes, and he waiting for a shrimp boat to take him back to Cuba.

It had been almost a month since a mob of people broke into the Peruvian embassy in Havana—10,800 people to be exact. It was the summer of 1980 and the height of the Mariel boatlift. Thousands of Cubans had abandoned their homes, family, friends, lovers, and possessions to climb into a boat and sail to the United States, Yuma. El norte, like a star, summoning an exodus *en masse*. A one-way journey whose irreversible consequences would be felt for decades to come. Ricky didn't believe in fate, but he had to admit that showing up in Florida was, well, a strange coincidence. At least that's what he told Sally. Not only did she agree, but she also let him borrow the two thousand he was missing out of the five thousand dollars it cost him to rent a private boat with a captain. Sally was good people. Really good people. And, given her savings, she was an even better bartender.

It was morning in Key West, the primary departure and arrival point for the exile boats making the trip to Mariel and back. He'd left Sally sleeping off a hangover in South Beach and he'd reached the Keys by sunlight. Due to all sorts of engine problems, though, he'd changed boats three times. For safety reasons, they'd had to wait for the right moment to leave. Time seemed to drag. Now, finally, they were on their way.

"Do you see those boats?" the captain said. "They're going to Cuba. It's like the Wild West out there—never seen so many Cubans on the water."

"Most of us," Ricky said, "haven't set foot in Cuba in over twenty years."

"Sounds hard," the captain said.

"You can't imagine," Ricky said. "We'll get him out, though. There isn't a Cuban in Cuba who doesn't want to be rescued." He hoped his encounter with his son would be the chance at reconciliation he'd long awaited. But he had so many questions. How would his son react? Was there any love left in him that might lead him to move past their estrangement and to react lovingly? One thing was certain: this trip would be one for the books—the dizzying union of the real and the imagined.

"You'd be surprised," the captain said. "Some people'd rather stay put." Wearing blue overalls and smiling in the faint, morning sunlight, he poured gasoline from a jerry can into a decrepit fuel fill. He made Ricky feel *mostly* unsure of himself.

Sooner than Ricky expected, the captain puttered the boat over crumbling whitewash, then higher swells. He opened his throttle, pushing them even faster over the waves, up and down. The whole boat thrummed with noise from the engine.

Ricky's vision blurred the sunlit deck and the rail, but he could see them, hundreds of boats, like a stampede. All those Cuban exiles going back where they'd come from fifteen, twenty years earlier. He was lucky; besides the captain, he was the only passenger on this boat. From what he could see, that wasn't the case for most passengers that day.

Once in the open sea, they spent more and more time in the air between each wave. Ricky Perez thought he would lose his gut in a bout of gagging. He was lying on the cool damp floor of the *Miss Juddy,* trying to figure out just exactly what he'd say to Elio. As confident as he was that Elio would forgive him, there was nothing more *taxing* than being abandoned by your father—even he knew that. But, he, Ricky Perez, was a businessman and Cuba, since 1959, had simply been *bad* business. After all these years, Elio would have to know that.

He closed his eyes and thought of Elio. He'd get Elio out—that was certain; he owed him that.

Up and down, and faster over the swells, the hull slapped and pulled Ricky out of his daydreaming. He struggled to lift himself off the deck floor and look over the rail. The boat bounced and swayed. The captain motioned for Ricky to sit back down. "Hold on to the rail!" he shouted. "And sit the fuck down!"

Ricky held on to the rail with one tight-knuckled hand, just as he was told, but the boat flew over another swell, propelling him into the air. "Fuck!" He shouted, dropping onto the deck like a leaf.

Not soon enough, the Port of Mariel reared up against the sky. He wasn't prepared. His breathing came fast. He wanted forward momentum, composure, fulfillment, redemption, logic. But instead the buzzing of a gathering panic swirled inside of him—and, suddenly, his eyes filled with tears. Returns are never easy, he thought, no matter how much you wanted to leave in the first place.

CHAPTER 17

ELIO WAS AT THE DYE HOUSE when he heard the call over the loudspeaker. "Duty calls, compañeros." He'd been tipping dyestuff into mixing barrels since 6:00 a.m. It was now 10:00 a.m. and he was covered in purple powder from head to toe. If he could have dug out an escape tunnel just then, he would have. But where in hell would he escape? He had no choice but to hide in a goddamn water closet again.

He opened the bathroom door, avoiding the small mirror above the sink. He wondered whose house it was his coworkers would march toward and who would be the poor bastard they'd take by surprise. This was the reality that he didn't want to face. Behind the appearance of so many years, without realizing it, everyone had changed. It wasn't just his face, or Maria's. Everyone was now someone else.

Elio gripped a paper bag in his hand and climbed onto the toilet seat, a foot on each side of the cracked toilet bowl. As soon as he steadied himself, he pulled out a dog-eared book from a paper bag. *The Count of Monte Cristo,* the gold embossed letters on the tattered cover read. It was the second time that week he'd refused to board the bus, hiding instead in the bathroom stall—reading a bit until he couldn't take the heat any

longer and it was safe to go. He was eager to finish the book and, at this
rate, and with the increasing number of rallies per week, he'd be done in
no time.

The human herd on the bus that afternoon would come from schools,
and jobs, and housework in buses, on foot, and on rickety bicycles.
Wielding bats, bottles, lengths of rusty pipe, chains, and anything else
they'd found along the way. Then windows would shatter and they'd
break in, dragging bodies out through front doors and broken glass,
over cracked sidewalks, and in and out of potholes. Tearing flesh and
breaking bones, as they harassed and tormented the poor bastards who,
having nothing else to hope for, opted to leave. Someone somewhere, he
knew, would hang themselves. Animals, he thought. Neighbor against
neighbor—it was criminal, that's what it was. The island, he knew then,
had turned against itself.

He crouched, keeping his head out of sight and waiting for the
stragglers on foot, the ones who had missed the bus, to run out of the
building and head to the park to join the others. He tried to read, but it
was hotter than a pig's ass in the stall. Were he to stay in there longer than
necessary, his heart would send smoke signals to his temples and panic
would take over. Poor bastards. Had someone warned them?

He could hear a rush of water, something like a steady flow coming
from somewhere inside the toilet bowl. The little maneuver inside the
tank must have been broken. But, for a second, Elio imagined something
else: It was a clear day, with air temperatures in the high eighties. He was
in Baracoa, near the bend, and about fifteen feet from shore. It came up
fast from deep down in the water. Its high dorsal fin parted the blue sea in
two like some strange Moses.

Elio lay on an inner tube, his right arm gently circling to counter the
action of the tide. Without warning, his paddling arm was seized. It was a

huge shark, approximately ten feet in length. Elio struck him with his left arm, but the shark seized that one too, tearing at his elbow. The weight of the giant fish knocked him into the water. For a moment, the shark loosened its grip and re-submerged. Elio swam away desperately but the fish went after him, seizing him again. This time, it had him by the leg, just above the knee.

The toilet's tank let out a metallic sound. Elio stared at his arms, and rubbed his thigh. His heart rate had risen and he was short on breath. At least the goddamn fish had left his testicle alone this time, he thought, shifting his weight on the seat. There was no way in hell he was ever going back into the ocean. He knew better now.

Hours later, Elio turned onto his street. It had just started to rain. He passed the turbina and saw the house of Elsa La Gorda and her daughter, Silvi. He could only guess, given the broken shutters and the cracked egg on the walls, that Silvi, just as she'd always told Elsa she would, was leaving for good. He was dismayed. It was Elsa's house the mob had marched toward. Doing what they always did. Sticking long metal rods through the shutters, breaking eggs and smashing tomatoes against the door and onto the porch. Tearing flesh with purple-polished finger nails. Spewing insults and slogans at the house like it'd been the house that threatened to leave.

Later, those same people who marched on Elsa's house—her neighbors, her coworkers, perhaps even her friends—would pretend that nothing had happened. Like the whole town didn't turn against her. Everyone would go back home, banking hard on the government bonus can of Vita Nuova they'd receive for turning on their neighbor.

Maria was already in bed when Elio came home but she'd left him a small pot of black beans on the stove. Elio reheated the beans, and listened to the latest radio reports of the Mariel boatlift—it was gaining strength.

Elio thought about Silvi, waiting for her turn to climb on the boat. Leaving for good, and changing Elsa's life forever. Hell, if anyone knew about that, it was he. Hadn't his own father's leaving changed his life forever?

As for the rest—and even as they, too, waited for their chance to leave—they did what they were told: spied on their neighbors, took notice of their ins and outs, showed up unannounced to take count of every container, appliance, radio, bicycle, and flashlight in the house so that, if one went missing, they'd be ready to take a leap of faith and call it in. Because there was nothing like having nothing to make people fight tooth and nail, to rat people out, to defile someone's good reputation, to ruin someone for good.

Elio was pleased to see that Maria had left him rice too. He heaped both rice and beans on a plate and ate standing up. Taking no pleasure in knowing that, if no one in Bauta had an egg to fry that afternoon, it was because they'd all been cracked against La Gorda's door. The value of it all had been lost to him when he saw the eggs on the walls of the house. But—at that moment, at least—he never once wished he could join them. He'd stay put. He might as well have been allergic to eggs and seawater.

Just as he was getting into bed toward 10:00 p.m., the phone made an odd sound. Not its typical ring, but loud enough that Maria turned over on the mattress and faced the wall. It took him a minute to trace the sound to the phone in the living room. At first he thought it must be broken because he heard something like a death rattle. Then a long, empty pause. "Operator, please hold," the voice said. Another pause. Then "Ricky here," the receiver finally said. The words echoed Ricky *heeere* in Elio's ear. His knees buckled and he coiled the sticky cord around a wrist, as if to steady himself. He said nothing. "Ricky here," he heard again. "I'm in Mariel with a shrimp—" Before the voice could finish, Elio pulled back on his arm so hard the cable snapped off and dangled from his wrist. He knew the word *boat* would follow. What a joke, he told Maria that night. Doesn't the guy know I won't get in the water?

No, of course he wouldn't know.

He never heard back—and he figured he wasn't going to. But he wished he'd had the balls to say something. If he had, it would have gone something like this:

"Who's Ricky? You mean, Ricky Lopez? Ricky Lopez, my biological father?" Not that he'd ever had another one. "Wait, so where are you? Mariel, you say? You're in the Port of Mariel with a rented shrimp boat? And who the hell gives a flying fuck?"

"I'm sorry," he'd have heard him sob. "I'm sorry." He didn't know who was more pathetic, his father and his apology, or him for hanging up.

"You're selfish," Maria told him the following morning. She was pulling a bedsheet over the edge of the bed.

"You're a funny woman," Elio said, sitting on the edge of the bare mattress. "You swore to your grandmother once that you'd never leave this place."

"I wish I'd never told you about that conversation. Why couldn't you talk to him? He wouldn't be calling if he wasn't planning on helping us. You're an arrogant son of a bitch, you know that? It's your father." Sheets flapping in the air like a bullfighter's red cape.

"That's not a father," he said.

"And how would you know? Tell me that—how the hell would you know?"

Elio waved off her words. "Look," he said. "If it gets really bad here, we'll leave." But he didn't mean it. He wished he could vanish. So he did the next closest thing—he walked out of the house, slamming the door behind him. Outside, two stray dogs, startled by the noise, ran in opposite directions.

Although neither Elio nor Maria told anybody about the phone call or the resentment that followed, Elio caught people on the street, at work, at la bodega looking at him in strange ways. They might not have known the specific details—who and when and what and all those things that didn't really matter—but they knew something. Enough to make him suspect. Enough to make him feel that his own neighbors—official and unofficial sentinels for the state—were watching him, knowing him in ways that only he could know himself.

He distrusted the inflection in their voices whenever they asked him how he was or where he was off to. He was aware of them beside him wherever he went, whatever he did. Listening in on his most private thoughts, jotting things down. Like Elsa, he wasn't going to get off that easy. Although only Silvi managed to leave, Elsa paid with three more rallies. It didn't matter that she was still there. Leaving was a family affair, so she was guilty by association. Everyone paid—whether they left or stayed. Elio knew they wouldn't relent until they heard him confess. Until they ruined him for good. Whatever else would happen from that moment forward, he knew he would never be alone—not really. Not in the way that people are alone with their thoughts.

CHAPTER 18

BY THE END of the summer, more than 70,000 Cubans had left the island through Mariel Harbor. Now if Elio passed by someone's house, he couldn't help but wonder who was missing. And who, among the thousands of Cubans who had left, would never return. He remembered Pepe asking him once if he thought it'd all be worth it. Elio didn't have an answer—how the hell would he know? All he knew was that he wasn't going anywhere, at least not any time soon.

It was a Thursday, the last week of September. Elio'd come back from work early on account of yet another repudiation rally. This time, though, he hadn't hidden in the bathroom, deciding instead to sneak out through a back door, hitch a ride with a produce truck, and surprise Maria. The day was clear, bright, and not as hot as usual. It was the kind of day when one could forgive almost anything. It had been nearly a month since his father's phone call and, although Maria had asked him more than once to try to make contact, she quickly learned to let him be.

When he plodded through the door, Maria was sitting on the checkered tile, sawing off the tips of her tennis shoes. "What?" she said, looking up at him. "My toes need to breathe." With sunburnt cheeks, tousled blonde hair, and one leg folded under her butt, she seemed to Elio like a seafaring goddess.

"Well," he said, kissing her damp mane, "are you surprised I'm home early?"

"Not surprised, thankful." She grinned. "Now you can fix the iron."

"In that case," he said, "I'll need your eyebrow tweezers." He was in such a good mood that afternoon that he met Maria's request with gusto. After all, he loved to be needed.

Finding the iron on the kitchen table near a small stack of his Lee pitusas, he sat down and started unscrewing the soleplate with the tip of a knife. He'd managed to loosen one screw but a second, smaller screw remained. He waited a few seconds for Maria to get the tweezers, then realized it'd be quicker to work with the knife. Meanwhile, Maria walked into the bedroom and began rooting about in her purse.

"Alright," Elio said toward the bedroom. "You can forget about the hair plucker. I've moved on to the second screw."

He was sweating heavily and his wrist was twitchy from each half turn of the knife, the tip of which he'd bent on his first try. Just as he was about to pull out the screw, he heard what might have been a bus outside. He gripped the knife a little tighter, but went on working, hoping the vehicle would continue on and turn at the end of the street, or stop at someone else's house. But then it became clear that the bus had made a full stop, right on his street and way too close to his house. His hand jerked. Both knife and screw flew into the air. His good mood was gone. His heart beat in a panic. He ran into the living room and quickly closed and bolted the shutters. Staring at his front door, he didn't know whether to call out to Maria or open the door and face them.

With the shutters closed, he couldn't see them. But he could hear them. A swoosh-swoosh-swoosh, a slurring, a kind of loud, continuous humming. Shouting that grew louder and louder until it reached his front door. It was another rally, recoño. In the past, they'd marched on Rogelio's house, on Irma's, on Raulito's, and, of course, on Elsa's. This time, however, they were here for him. There were too many incidents stacked against him. His lack of participation at rallies, his dad's phone call, and his dad's arrival at the Port of Mariel had marked him—turned him and Maria into lumpen, undesirables, people who'd betrayed the Revolution.

Elio started toward the bedroom to warn Maria to hide. Then he heard one of them call out, "Gusano!" The voice was unfamiliar. Elio didn't much care if they called him a traitor, or scum, or whatever else they came up with. But a worm? A goddamn worm? Sons of bitches, he thought. All for a fucking phone call? He wasn't leaving. *They* weren't leaving. The mob banged, and chanted, and rattled the shutters. There must have been over one hundred people on the porch, even school children. He could hear their louder, higher-pitched voices.

Elio rushed to the bedroom. "Maria," he whispered from the doorway. "They're here, they're outside." The voices on the porch rose and fell. But they didn't stop. He thought to grab Maria, then make it out to the lagoon through the back door. If they followed the water's edge, they could reach the turbina in no time. "Maria," he whispered.

"I'm here," Elio heard her say, finally. She had covered her head with a pillow and was hiding under the bed. Elio could feel dread rising in his chest, then anger. He had never seen her so scared.

"Pepe's not coming by today, is he?" she asked, sticking her head out from under the bed. Elio felt his blood pumping in his temples. Were Pepe to show up now, he'd make a scene, demand explanations, and they'd beat him to a pulp.

"I don't know," he said, crouching next to her.

"Here," she said. "Take a Chiclet."

"Where did you get that? What the hell is a Chiclet going to do for us?"

"Just chew it," she whispered. "It's like an aspirin. Fina's daughter sent it to her in an envelope. She can't chew gum, on account of her dental bridge, so she gave it to me," Maria said. She didn't shed a single tear, but kept her eyes fixed on him.

Before Elio could answer, he heard a loud cracking sound. He cast a glance over his shoulder. They'd pried open the shutters. Then more cracking, smashing, shattering. Crawling to the bedroom door, he looked out to the living room. A long, metal rod inserted through broken slats, scoured his living room. Everything they owned had been strewn on the floor—their wedding picture, their television, Maria's old books.

What horrified Elio the most was the coordination. They were zombies. Yes, it was like a zombie outbreak. A mindless, undead horde of people he'd known all his life. Weren't these his neighbors, coworkers, and childhood friends? These were days, Elio thought, when everyone looked in the mirror and saw two faces staring back at them. They were sad days, repinga.

He asked Maria what she wanted him to do. She looked straight at him. "Hit them as hard as you can," she said. Her eyes were red, and Elio thought they would explode or burst into tears. He looked at her for a moment to see if he understood. She nodded.

Picking up the half-gutted iron along the way, he walked into the living room. He didn't know what the hell he was going to do. They must have heard him walking around close to the front door or seen him through the shutters because, right then, their shouting stopped. He walked up to the front door, opened it, and stepped out on the porch. Suddenly, everyone faced him. One long moment passed. Then together, as if on signal, they were on him.

Elio gripped the iron in his hand, but before he could use it to defend himself, a brick hit him in the face, and he was kneed between the legs. He swung the iron in the air. He heard a thud. "You're shit!" someone yelled. "Gusano!" Elio retreated, and closed his eyes. He touched his forehead, which was bleeding. He felt like he would pass out. So dizzy he thought he would puke. His head feeling like his brain had been torn out of him. Just as he was about to tumble forward, Maria opened the door. "Get the hell away from my house! Perros!" she shouted. She'd brought him back from the dead. Then blows came from everywhere at once.

Some days later, while Elio was still at work, Maria walked to the back yard carrying her small collection of books. Her hands were bruised, and her face had a few small scratches. Worse than that, she felt shaken and angry. She wanted to erase any trace of the existence of books in her life. Books, as far as she was concerned, had brought her nothing but heartache, espejismos, and desires she'd never fulfill. The repudiation rally the day before had taught her as much. There was no room on the island for dreaming. No room for *Madame Bovary* and Sears catalogues. No room for books.

She set the books down on the concrete floor and made a small pyre with them. Then she doused them with luz brillante, and set them on fire. She watched her precious books as they burned themselves out. When she thought there's was nothing else to burn, she remembered Elio's counterfeit Lee jeans. She walked back in the house and found the small stack on the table, where it'd been the day before. She carried the jeans into the yard and threw them on the fire.

When it was all done, the yard was a cloud of smoke and the smell of burnt fabric and paper choked the air. Maria swept the remnants up with a broom—leaving no trace of books—or dreams—in her house.

CHAPTER 19

"WE HAVE TO LEAVE," Maria said. "We have no choice now."

She was sitting at the kitchen table, when Elio walked in the house. He had set off from the factory, keeping up a fast pace, wanting to get home as soon as possible. He took a moment to flick the shutters closed, then joined Maria at the table. Since the incident with the brick two weeks earlier, he'd had a daily migraine. His heart was beating fast but when he spoke his voice was quiet.

"We're staying. I don't care what they call us."

"When did you decide this?" Maria asked him.

"Yesterday, today, tomorrow," Elio said.

Maria had stayed home from work that day. There was yet another repudiation rally planned for that afternoon—so she faked a head cold. She'd told Elio that morning that she simply couldn't bear to be part of it—not after what they'd done to them, and to poor Elsa, and to so many other people they knew. Elio had agreed wholeheartedly. He, too, refused to participate in what had become yet another repressive measure on the island, yet another way—along with surveillance, short-term arbitrary detentions, forced labor, official and unofficial warnings, removal from homes and jobs, and, perhaps worst of all, forced exile—of keeping them stuck in a goddamn barrel. Most people didn't leave because they wanted to; they left because they had to. Plus, not showing up to work, or abandoning work completely—due to a lack of incentive and the shortage of absolutely everything, including toilet paper—had become a major problem. He figured, and hoped, she wouldn't be missed.

Maria touched a fingertip to her lips. Two weeks after the rally, her knuckles were still bruised.

"Don't worry," he said, avoiding looking at her hands. "It's just a little adventure. It's like your grandmother going to live in Cabañas, except we're not going anywhere. We're staying put. Everything will be back to normal before you know it—you'll see."

"No!" she shouted. "It's not at all like going to Cabañas. My grandmother had most of her life behind her. We have most of ours ahead of us. I have most of mine ahead of me. There's still time, Elio. Your dad's in Chicago…he could—"

"Leave my dad out of this. In over twenty years, he's called once."

"He's all we have, damn it. I'm scared they'll march on the house again. Next time, maybe we won't be so lucky."

Elio saw genuine distress in her face. "We'll manage," he said. "If you love me, you won't bring it up again. This is the place that birthed us, Maria. No other place will do." A long silence spread out across the whole room.

"What are you hiding?" Maria finally said, pointing to the hand he'd kept under the table all this time.

Elio was thankful that she'd suddenly changed the topic. The whole thing depressed him. He wasn't ready to accept a game that everyone, including Maria, seemed to think he, too, had to play.

He grabbed the brand new book on his lap. Placing it in front of her, he confessed, "I stole it for you." The words stretched a taut wire between them.

"Have you lost your mind? Any reason in particular you want to go to prison?"

"At least I'd go to prison for something worthwhile, for making you happy...for making myself happy. Don't we have the right to decide our own happiness, goddamnit?"

"Couldn't you think of something else to make me happy? I send you for bread and you come back with *Don Quixote?* I've already read it, anyway," she said, turning her eyes away.

"I know," Elio said. "I thought you'd want to read it again. You know, to remember old times." Elio knew Maria well and knew that, in spite of her concern and her frustration, the sight of a brand new copy of Cervantes's magnum opus made her heart beat a little faster. It was *Don Quixote,* for God's sake, not *Diary of a Nurse* by Corín Tellado.

"What am I supposed to think except that you've lost your common sense? Are you trying to give them more reasons to come after you? To add the word *thief* to the many names they've already called you?" she said. "Damn it. If I hadn't interfered, they would have beaten you to a pulp. Are you hoping for another rally? Or worse, another beating?" She took inventory of the room and shook her head. "Look at this place. You'd think you'd be more interested in improving our lives."

Hadn't she always loved *Don Quixote?* Perhaps if he'd brought her *Camille: The Lady of the Camellias* or *Fortunata and Jacinta,* he thought, she'd be more forgiving. But nothing could have washed, dried, and folded the chaos of their house. Not books, not miracles, not Elio. Because of neglect due to a lack of paint, varnish, and drywall, coupled with their own dwindling motivation, the house was in a state of absolute deterioration. Slabs of plaster hung from walls by a thread, termites gnawed on the entrails of tables and chairs, a mold-speckled bedspread covered a mold-speckled bed.

Elio shrugged at the book in his hands. "The bread was gone," he said. "Anyway, need I remind you that man cannot live on bread alone? Aren't we all supposed to be big readers on this island? Wasn't that what they were doing when they went into the mountains with paper and pencil in hand? Weren't they teaching us all to read? Well, why can't I read now?"

Unable to let it go, she said, "There's nothing worthwhile about books, Elio—that much I know. Next time you want to steal something, steal something we can actually use, like food, or toilet paper."

Elio looked at the small, empty bookcase in a corner of the living room. "If there were anything else to steal, Maria, I would have taken it already. You shouldn't have gotten rid of your books. Who does that?"

"*I* do that," she said. "*I* get rid of books." She pointed at herself with an index finger. "Do you think there's a point in reading *anything*, after what they've done to us? No books in this house. I don't want to see another book again as long as I live on this goddamn island. What do books have to do with leaky refrigerators and power outages? I'm not interested. Get rid of it." Elio took heart in knowing that the rest of his books were hidden from Maria's reach.

"Your grandma would be proud." He looked at the empty spot on the table where his Lee *pitusas* should have been. Maria had gotten rid of the jeans too, for fear they'd come back to search the house.

"My grandma's six feet underground. Let's leave my grandma out of this. Pepe came looking for you," she said and moseyed toward the kitchen. Elio's eyes followed her as she turned a corner and disappeared behind a wall. He loved her. He may never get his Schwinn, but he had her—and she was and would always be the best thing about the island.

"And? Talk, woman. Finish what you started," he said, gripping the book close to his chest.

"And he wants you to meet him at the park in an hour."

"What the hell does he want now?" Elio said, low enough to escape Maria's sharp ears.

He shuffled his flip-flops toward a window and let himself free fall into a chair. He stared at the book in his hands and let it rest on his lap. He'd be the first one to read it. Maria was right, though. He could go to prison for stealing a book—but not because stealing was a punishable crime, but because stealing a book suggested an even greater offense: the free pursuit of ideas. After the mob had marched on their house once, he was certain they'd come back, in one way or another. They were watching him for signs of dissent, waiting for him to make the wrong move— monitoring his movements, contacts, telephone calls, and correspondence. They were trapping him in place.

It was all too bad, he thought, fingering the scar the flying brick had left on his temple. He wasn't surprised she'd rejected the book—he couldn't blame her. Books were dreams, he thought, and there was very little room to dream on their island anymore. Nonetheless, he loved to remember that he'd be almost illiterate, if it weren't for her.

Elio slowly settled into the chair. Thoughts of Maria's youthful drives fell on him like snowflakes—but he brushed them off and opened the book. Pulled back the first page a little to detach it from the rest. Yup, a virgin book. The first text published by the Revolution, with an impressive run of one hundred thousand copies. One of the many triumphs of the revolutionary process.

Elio had stolen the book because there was nothing else to steal—and because he simply refused to give the librarian the satisfaction of checking it out the old-fashioned way. "Anything pique your interest today?" she'd ask him, lifting her brown nose from the daily gazette or flapping her jowls over a sluggish Rolodex. "Nope. Not today," he'd say. He'd already stolen *The Count of Monte Cristo, Twenty Thousand Leagues under the Sea,* and *The Black Corsair.* If not these, then he would have ended up with yet another rancid edition of *The Old Man and the Sea* pulling on his armpit hairs as he left the library. He was neither a fisherman nor did he want to be. Hell, after the shark attack, who'd wanna get back in the water, with or without Hemingway? Though, at this rate, he would have read the whole nineteenth century by the end of the year.

Truth be told, he'd loved Monte Cristo. The guy committed a prison break after fourteen years of being jailed on an island, changed his name, and became a member of society with a spotless reputation. What was not to like about the guy? Elio loved the book so much, he might make it a point to read *The Three Musketeers,* too.

He flicked the book shut. He'd get to it later. He'd need to find a place to read it first. A special book required a special place. Plus, he'd be screwed if Pepe caught him with a book. The guy was allergic to words, let alone ones that might turn into sentences and run for hundreds of pages, only to be continued in *Part II.* He sauntered over to a futon. Tucked the book under the pencil-thin mattress, already bulging near the edge with the rest of his loot. "I'll be back later," he shouted into the hallway, and walked out the door.

CHAPTER 20

THIS IS THE CLOSEST I've been to Jesus in the last twelve years, Elio thought, standing at the threshold leading to the vestibule. He turned the knob. The door gave a wail of complaint as he peered inside, waited, and finally stepped in. The dark, empty pews appeared and the afternoon silence deepened all the way to the cross above the altar. He wiped his sweaty forehead with the back of one hand, holding the paper bag containing the book in the other. Due to government restrictions, few people went to church anymore even if, privately, they were the unwavering devotees of a motley crew of saints. So, if he wanted to be left alone to read, the church was the place to be.

"Anybody here?" he asked toward the altar. Then he listened. As far as he could tell, the church was completely empty. There was nothing but the deaf and blind Jesus nailed to the wall. Out of habit, he crossed himself. Turned around and looked up toward the balcony. He stared at the stained-glass windows, the saints perched and frozen on wooden stands, the marble table at the top of the altar. All those eyes. There was a familiar smell, but he wasn't quite sure what it was—incense? Perhaps just mold. A sharp tickling sensation came at his temples.

He made his way to the door leading to the bell tower. As he took the knob in his left hand, his right gripped the bag a little tighter. He felt like a thief. That's what he was, in any case. What could they do to him? Accuse him of reading too much? Hadn't that been the purpose of the literacy campaign? Of the National Printing Office? Hadn't they succeeded? Almost one million Cubans had learned to read and write. But he, Elio Perez, owed them nothing. He'd learned to read and write long before the Conrado Benítez Brigade hymn became a top-forty hit on radio and television. Yes, he owed them nothing.

He opened the door and stared at the inch-wide crack, sensing what seemed like infinite space opening out beyond. The narrow staircase spiraled up before him. He waited until the vertigo passed, then started the climb. Suppose he couldn't come back down? Suppose he got stuck midway? Nobody knew he was there. He'd gone back home to fetch the book without Maria noticing; and, more importantly, even if she'd noticed, she wouldn't have known where to look for him.

He went up a few steps and reached back to close the door behind him, turning the knob once or twice, in case he screwed up and locked himself in.

The light meandered all the way down through the small opening that led to the bell tower. He'd have to crawl in and settle next to the bell, but it'd be worth it. He frowned at the high steps ahead of him but made his way up holding on to the wall. Then, finally, with a heartening thrill, he made out the small, square opening and part of the bell. He forced his torso through and, with some effort, hauled in the rest of his body.

A feeling of sublime overwhelm washed over him when he found himself inside the bell tower. The bell hung motionless beside him. Perhaps, because he knew he shouldn't, he suddenly felt a need to pull on the ropes and make it toll. He tried to unlock his shoulder from its place near the opening's frame. Tried to move his legs, but there wasn't enough space for them to stretch out or bend back. Fuck! His heartbeat climbed to his temples. He was trapped. Drops of sweat rolled down his back. He panicked, and muscled forward, grabbing one of the ropes to use as leverage to pull himself out. But it didn't work, and the bell tolled once. He made frantic efforts to free his legs from beneath him and to calm his breathing. *Repinga, I'm gonna get caught.*

He looked out toward the rooftops, then down to the park, waiting to catch his breath. How strange was Bauta from a bird's-eye view? And yet, it was the sudden re-encounter with something or someone long forgotten, but whose form or face he couldn't place in any particular context. He only knew it felt at once both familiar and uncomfortable. He was, and was not, part of that aimless beehive below, part of the gossip and din of small-town life. He had been born there. He'd spent his childhood in and out of those streets. He knew every nook, every crevice, every short cut. But he'd been singled out, turned into a stranger, an undesirable, a traitor—made to pay for his father's decision to come for him, even when he, Elio Perez, hadn't left the island. Because leaving was deemed to be contagious or a family affair, passed down from parent to child, like eye color or the color of one's skin.

Below him, on the street, frazzled mothers swished polyester miniskirts with crumpled plastic bags in one hand and a sniffling child by the other; whistle-blowers panned out the scene; young men leaned tan bodies against storefronts, scheming, stealing, bored out of their minds— pathetic men, like him. All of them, sending clouds of dust into the air with each shuffle of their feet.

He suddenly felt the need to escape, not only from the bell tower, but from the whole neighborhood, the whole island. But where the hell would he go? Not only was he scared shitless of the water, he refused to run away like his father—or to disappear like his mother. If he stayed, he'd have to face life on an island that had stopped being a revolutionary paradise decades ago. If he left, if he could leave, where would he go? Everywhere was paradise from above, hell below. Elio set the book down. He pulled hard on the rope again until it tensed enough, then he raised himself a few inches from the platform, spun around, and faced the opening. He'd set himself free. Now he'd have to turn around again to make it through the hole and descend the stairs. He didn't think about the book once. It was only when he'd reached the final step that he knew he'd left it in the bell tower.

All right, Elio thought, I'll come back for it tomorrow. But he hadn't walked more than two blocks from the church when it happened.

"Hey," she shouted. Her voice, a little breathless, came from somewhere behind him. Elio lengthened his steps. "Elio!" He heard again the inflections of the voice, and felt a touch on his shoulder. He turned his head, a dizzying movement in the sunlight, and met a pair of eyes. In her gaze, Elio saw nothing close to compassion. Had they not belonged to Mirta the Librarian, he would have found intelligence and beauty in them. "I think you forgot something," she said.

Elio stopped cold. She stood there, *Don Quixote* like a dead marlin in her hands. Elio knew he'd been caught. There'd be no way out of this one. Fuck.

"I was praying alone, as I tend to do these days, when I heard a sound," she said. "And there you were, opening the door to the campanario. I asked myself, why would Elio, who hasn't stepped foot inside the church in decades, be in the bell tower? So I had to go up and see. And there it was, one of our most cherished editions. When were you planning on bringing it back?" She held up the book for Elio to take a good look.

He swallowed. Coño, she was like a regular private eye. Could she be anymore obnoxious? "I must have gotten distracted and walked out with it," he said. "I had every intention of checking it out."

"Why, you're off the hook then," she said in a pleasant voice, though her smile seemed unpleasant. "Funny. I don't think you've ever checked out a book."

Elio worked to recall any book he had ever checked out. Nothing. He didn't mind stealing them. He preferred stealing them.

"You're right," he said. "I've never checked out anything. Glad you found it, Mirta," he said finally. "I was wondering where I'd left it. I swear I was planning on taking it back to you this week—"

"Save it, Elio. You should be ashamed of yourself. And please don't swear. We're less than two blocks away from the church."

"I know, I know," he said. "I should have been more careful. Let's walk back, and you can write today's date on the little card—"

Jesus Christ, how had she climbed those steps so fast? Where had she been hiding? Behind the pulpit? Elio'd known Mirta since they'd sat side by side in a dingy classroom at Bauta's Perfecto Lacoste Elementary School and she picked her mocos and stuck them underneath her desk. She'd never been fast at anything in her life, except reading—and he respected her for that. But truth be told, she'd always been a real pain in the ass.

"You're out of your mind if you think I won't report this. You might as well go home and get the rest of them. I estimate you've taken at least twenty-five books. Don't you think I've suspected for weeks? I just wanted to see how far you'd go. You thought I was stupid, that I wasn't going to catch on until you emptied out the whole library, didn't you?" she said, going blotchy all over her face. Elio knew that could only mean one thing: she was pissed.

The police station was open and empty. Elio was asked to take a seat. He scanned the shelves full of folders and papers looking for something to fix his eyes on. But nothing stuck. When the officer asked Mirta if he was dangerous, should he be handcuffed, Mirta said no need. "He's dangerous all right," she added, "but not that kind of dangerous."

All Elio was worried about now was Maria. How the hell would she react? She'd warned him so many times—all this crap for what? For some ball-sucking, stupid-ass books?

Because there was nothing else going on in town, this would be the event of the year. The block party nobody would miss, the offense, the crime everyone would remember. And you know what, he wasn't going to give up so easily. He was fucking bored, that's what he was. Just like he was bored at school. Nobody fucking cared that he was bored then or bored now. Bored out of his goddamn mind.

"Look," the young officer told him. "Your wife's got two hours to get here. Not here in two hours, I'm sending you to sleep on a cot for the next seven days, and then a judge'll decide what to do with your old ass."

When you're twenty and some, Elio thought, everybody else seems old. "She'll be here," Elio said. But the truth was that he wasn't so sure—who knows, she might have decided to teach him a lesson. She'd be furious—no doubt about that. "Don't people make you want to give up?" he asked the cop, with more than books on his mind.

The cop frowned. This kid is young, too young, Elio thought. Even a little too handsome.

"I have no idea what you're talking about. Listen old horse, if I didn't know people your age can do some crazy shit, you'd be in handcuffs right about now."

"Look," Elio said. "Nothing's happened here. It's a huge misunderstanding, you know." The bright fluorescent lights made him blink.

A few minutes later, he found himself standing against a wall and being photographed first straight on, then in profile. His fingers, stained as they still were from purple dye stuff at the textilera, were rolled one by one across a piece of cardboard. "Incredible, right?" the young man said. "On top of everything else, we're also out of fingerprint cards. Your fingerprints aren't already in the system, are they?"

"No," Elio said. "They're not."

"Okay," the young man said. His attention, however, seemed divided between Elio and two teenage boys who played *silently* at stomping on each other's shoes. Elio surmised the duo may have been called in for vagrancy, a serious offense for adult men on the island and punishable by house arrest—or worse—internment in forced labor camps. It was possible the two boys would get away with a warning this time, though.

The boys laughed and shouted, "You got caught, comemierda!" as the young cop led Elio to the Bauta police department's only cell, which was small and way too bright and damn hot. There was a copper-stained, long-necked sink and an equally stained toilet in the corner. Elio dreaded to think what he'd do, if he felt the sudden urge to go to the bathroom.

"I thought you said you'd call my wife," he said, raising his voice just enough for the young man to hear him. "How long am I staying in here?" People had been put away for years for so much less. He'd heard stories of inmates abused by other inmates and, worse, by prison guards. Poor people, he'd thought. He shuddered at the thought of becoming one of them.

"Give me a minute," the young man said, and disappeared behind a wall.

No one said anything else until outside the sky darkened and he heard Maria's voice. Elio's mouth was dry by then. But he felt huge relief when the young man opened the cell and let him out.

Maria waited in the reception area. She looked at him as if she were trying to read his mind. But there was nothing there. His mind was as blank as a sheet of paper. He felt a little tired, even. The wrinkles on his face deeper, somehow. He noticed that the two boys were no longer there. By now, he'd changed his mind—he hoped those two little pricks got what they deserved.

"Elio," Maria sighed. "Again? Is it that hard to control yourself?"

Elio looked at her, incredulous. "Do you *believe* that?"

"No need to be ashamed, dear. You just need treatment, you know. A good therapist to help you deal with your kleptomania—which is, after all, a mental health disorder."

In Elio's head, Houdini had just made it out of the straitjacket. Kleptomania, yes. Maria had saved the day.

Maria took a good look at Elio, then turned to face the young cop, filling her lungs with air. "I thought you knew," she said. "He's a kleptomaniac."

"A what?"

"You know, he's sick. He can't help it."

"Lady, the guy's taken over twenty-five books in the last three months. Are you saying he's crazy?"

"Kleptomaniacs are not exactly crazy...I wouldn't say that, but—"

Elio looked at Maria, stupefied. She was going too far, just as the consequences of his own stupidity could go too far. In any case, nothing could outweigh the joy he felt at having Maria always by his side. If he'd ever questioned why he loved her so, now he knew the answer.

"It's not his fault. Is that what you're saying?" the young man said.

"That's what I'm saying," Maria whispered. "It's...outside of his control."

"How can I help?" the young man said.

"Well, you can start by letting him go home. I'll make sure he gets, you know, professional help. This has gone on too long—he knows that now." She patted Elio on the shoulder.

It was a grand performance, which Elio decided to support by looking more and more dejected as she spoke. Boy, was he proud of her.

The young man handed her a sheet of paper. She sat on a bench, next to Elio. The back of an elbow pressing down on his upper thigh a little too hard as she filled in the form. "He wants to change," she said to the young man. "That's a good start."

Elio remained quiet, as if quiet revealed more about the fragile state of his mind than words ever would.

A few minutes later Maria handing the young man the sheet and he, in turn, held the door open for them.

By the time Maria and Elio headed home, a fair number of people in Bauta seemed to know that Elio'd spent the afternoon at the police station. Needless to say, the walk home wasn't pleasant. Small crowds at various corners stopped talking to watch him saunter by, or worse, to witness him being dragged by Maria as if he were some kind of Mazorra patient let out for an afternoon stroll. The last thing he thought when leaving home for work that morning was that things would turn out this way.

So they pretended that it was a case of kleptomania, that he didn't really mean it, that he couldn't help himself. But that wasn't true. When he stole the books, he meant it. Because, after all, these obsessions of his were needed distractions, all ways of escaping what he needed to do, but couldn't.

"You actually think that stealing a book is such a horrible deed?" he said, avoiding looking at her. The night was warm, muggy, but Elio felt a chill of real fear. They walked together, side by side, as they'd walked so many times before—only this time, it was different. He'd done something that, as petty as it might seem, could end up having real consequences for them both. At best, and as far as a hierarchy of punishable crimes was concerned, he would be guilty of the crime of not doing very much. At worst, it would be one more mark on the growing list of crimes they seemed to have against him.

"That's not the problem, Elio," Maria said. "Just because you think that something shouldn't be a crime doesn't mean you should take it upon yourself to change the way things are."

"The way things are—what *is* the way things are?" he said.

"Not now, Elio—please."

Elio nodded without a word. He still wasn't looking at her.

Smelling the jasmine-scented air, he smiled to himself. He had the crazed urge to take off in the opposite direction, toward Havana. No, not toward Havana, but toward the limits of the island, to Malecón, specifically. Because the island began and ended at Malecón. He was trapped like a fish in a barrel, he thought. He could do it. He could leave.

"I can leave as soon as you want me to get out," he said. He glanced about him, at the people walking past them on the sidewalk, the one or two bicycles squeaking by.

"Oh," Maria said. "I think it's too late for that. How would we leave now—by helicopter? You should've thought about that when your dad was here, at the Port of Mariel, sitting in a shrimp boat waiting to take us back to Miami, then Chicago, then—" She raised her voice. "I'm delighted, actually, that you finally realize that we should leave. But I think it's too late now."

He looked at her with dry-eyed conviction. "I guess you think I'm a coward, that I can't make decisions for myself. Is that what you think? That I'm afraid of starting over, of becoming my father, of going back in the water…"

She didn't answer. Instead, she looked down. Then, changing her mind, as if helpless not to, she said, "You *are* a coward."

CHAPTER 21

ELIO JINGLED POCKET CHANGE as he walked through the door.
Afraid to give off the wrong signals, he debated scratching his jaw.
Whether to scratch his scalp and his forearm. He took a seat. Crossed and
uncrossed his arms, beads of sweat mirroring sunlight on his forehead.

"It was a bad choice," he finally said, anxious to get the whole thing
over with.

"It sure was." The man behind the desk smiled. The two halves of
his mouth never quite matched. "And let me say that you are one lucky
son of a bitch to have gotten off so easy." He leaned against a large desk
covered in papers, behind which was a large bookcase filled with books.

There was a silence. Elio leaned back against the chair and shifted his
weight. The therapist circled a wedding band around a hairy finger.

Elio's head rattled like a box of marbles. He composed what he
thought would be seen as a smile. Then turned this way and that slightly,
sort of directing the expression to every object in the room.

The therapist's eyebrows rose to meet three wrinkles on his forehead.

Elio stroked the hairs on his forearm. Sharp beams of light bent over
papers on the desk, one beam resembling a broken spear. The other...

who the hell knew?

"Are you all right?" the therapist asked, turning to face Elio. "You seem to…well, grimace. Are you in pain?"

"I'm as right as…" Elio smiled, soothing the air with a casual hand. "It's nothing."

The therapist stared carefully into Elio's eyes. Elio did the safe thing, relaxing every muscle in his face.

Another silence began, thickening the air of the room. Dust teetered in the sunlight—all around and over the desk like nerve endings.

The therapist leaned back against the chair, spread his legs and pressed against the armrests. "The issues we're facing with regard to you involve some serious accusations. Would you know what I'm talking about?"

"I think I do," Elio said. He knew the therapist might be referring to more than just the stolen books. It was that running list Elio was sure they kept on him. The one that included his dad coming to the Port of Mariel, and Elio's refusal to participate in those horrible repudiation rallies, of which he and Maria had also been victims.

"You think or you do?"

"I do."

He leaned forward, his lips drawn back from his teeth in what Elio perceived as smugness. He glanced down at sets of reports within the trench his arms had made. "Anything else?"

"I stole a few books."

"A few books? You nearly put the Library of Bauta out of business." He looked closely at his papers. "Let's see. You left three unopened copies of *Das Kapital,* one of *The Old Man and the Sea,* one Corín Tellado, one Nicolás Guillén, twenty *History Will Absolve Me,* two Amado Nervo volumes, and a number of European classics in the adult section; in the children's section, *Elpidio Valdés, Babar the Elephant,* and Enyd Blyton."

Elio thought that the therapist wasn't too far from the truth. Not only was printing paper on the island practically non-existent—along with toilet paper, film rolls, chocolates, gelatin, sugar, and so many other things Elio forgot to count—but there was also the added insult of censorship in a country that had taught its people to read. So many books had been banned in the last years that, without the books he had stolen, there wouldn't be much left in the Library of Bauta.

"Thanks to the Revolution," Elio said, "I love to read."

"You seem to prefer foreign authors to our own native traditions,"

"The library didn't seem to have any of those," Elio said.

"I see."

"Are you selling the books?"

"No," Elio said. He held tight to the sides of his chair, but said nothing else for fear of incriminating himself further.

"Let me explain. Your behavior is quite a bit more unusual than we're comfortable with. There's a kind of…how shall I say, incongruity between you and our revolutionary goals. That sends up a red flag of potential concern during our evaluation process. Should we be concerned? We… how shall I say, invite you to explain the appearance of incongruity."

The window gave nothing more than a cracked sidewalk with heat-shimmers over it.

"Then there's before us the matter of your work assessment. Less than stellar." Now he showed broad expanses of red gums. "What I'm saying is that from a strictly psychological standpoint, there are problems. The first thing we need is for you to admit that there's a problem. Assuming these past incidents are accurate reflectors of truancy and alienation from our social standards," he said, still looking at the reports before him as if they were chess pieces, "I venture to say that this doesn't look good for you." He looked at Elio. "Well, what do you have to say?"

Panic at being misunderstood rose in Elio's chest. His heart banged against his rib cage. "You promised to get me through this," he finally said. "My wife is counting on it."

"Well," the therapist said. "I did promise Maria to take special care of your case…you know, Maria and I were classmates in elementary school. She always struck me as someone who was loyal. To her friends, in particular, but I venture to say, even to her country—although I'm not really sure how she might have changed over all these years. I think it might be good, now that you're here, if you were clearer about *your* loyalties. You know what I mean? With a Yanqui for a father, your performance at work, and your recent behavior, we're starting to question your loyalties. What side are you on?"

"I don't keep contact with my father."

"It would be a shame if you did," he said. "Your father's in Yanquiland. Think of all the people on this island, protected for so long from Yanqui trash. Exposure could lead to contamination, and contamination could lead to chaos. You must promise to do your part, of course. The first step toward rehabilitation is admitting that you have done something wrong."

Elio understood that point of view, albeit with some difficulty. But he decided to lead off with a crime he didn't commit. After all, the therapist seemed to be expecting a confession. He would give him that. "I admit that by keeping contact with my father, by avoiding my civic duties, and by stealing literature I have put in danger the ideological safety of my fellow comrades," he finally said.

"You're not just telling me what I want to hear, are you?"

"Of course not."

"That's a start. I'll just write here that we'll meet weekly. Instead of writing *dissident,* or *degenerate,* I'll write *patient.* How's that? You got the books?"

Elio tried to hide his relief by nodding casually. "Every single one," he said, picking up the paper bag on the floor. Twenty-five books in total. All in the bag, except for *Quixote,* which Mirta had taken with her.

"Good, good, good," the therapist said. His shoe nudged the bag under his desk. "Very well, then. I think we're done here."

And so ended Elio's first therapy session. What was he supposed to admit? That leaving the island had crossed his mind once or twice? That stealing was wrong? That reading was a crime? That stealing books from a local library nobody ever set foot in was antirevolutionary? Didn't those books belong to the people and wasn't he, after all, people? He was tired of everyone always sniffing around for a trace of ideological impropriety. Fuck them, he thought. Fuck them and their beady eyes peering through half-closed shutters. Fuck them all.

That night Elio and Maria walked side by side. They crossed Avenida José Martí toward the ice cream parlor and Elio weaved his fingers in and out of hers. It was Thursday, and nearby were mostly gaunt, shirtless boys playing a game of marbles. Laughing and cussing in voices full of adolescent husk, or breath, or both.

They made the line and ordered what there was: vanilla.

Maria adjusted her bra strap with one hand. "Let's sit down," she said. Elio turned his head toward a table.

"How was—well, you know?" Maria asked after easing her body into a chair.

"It was good. I got it all out," Elio hastened to say.

"Oh, that's great!"

"Yeah, nice guy," he said, his spoon piercing the ball of ice cream right down the middle.

"I thought you'd like him."

"I did. You like him too. Don't you?"

"Sure. If I didn't, I wouldn't have—"

"Wouldn't have what?"

"Elio, I wouldn't have asked for his help. What the hell is wrong with you?"

"With me? What the hell is wrong with you? How the hell did you think it'd be a good idea to get this type involved?"

"What type? He's an old friend, Elio. That's it."

"That's it, ha?"

"Yeah, that's it."

He seemed to have forgotten how proud he'd been of her performance at the station. How magically she'd taken a rabbit out of her hat and made the whole thing go away, at least temporarily. Maria remained quite still. Staring at drops of melted ice cream on the table. Not knowing how to start.

"Aren't you going to eat that?" she said, pointing to Elio's ice cream, a ball floating like a broken island in vanilla soup.

"Nah," he said. "It isn't chocolate."

"I'll have it, then," she said, with more ice cream than mouth.

CHAPTER 22

BY NOW, Elio'd made it back to the therapist enough times to realize that guy didn't know the first thing about psychology. Hell, had he at least known about body language, he would have refrained from touching his crotch so many times in the forty-five minutes they spent together that Elio thought the guy had genital crabs. Not that he cared, but the whole thing was unsettling, to say the least. Elio often stared out the window, or settled his line of sight on stacks of books and papers on the floor, just to keep his eyes from tripping over this type's pants.

One day, the idiot asked him about water. Did he have an opinion about it?

"Sure," Elio said. "Water's good, isn't it?"

"And how do you feel about water here?"

"Here?" Elio said, holding his chin in the curve between his thumb and his index finger.

"Yeah, here. Water."

Elio was starting to suspect a setup. He'd almost forgotten why he was there, so caught up had he been in talking about his life, even if he'd made most of it up, including his contact with his father. What the hell was he supposed to say? That the water here was infested with sharks? That it was contaminated? That if he'd caught hepatitis twice and had so many stripes on his liver that it looked like a zebra, it was because of the water here? That his mother'd drunk three times her size in water and died?

"What else?"

This guy was starting to piss him off. "What else? What else?" Elio said, scratching the side of his mouth to bid for time.

"Is this a difficult question for you?" asked the therapist, leaning back in his chair.

Elio leaned back in his chair too, and laughed. "How difficult can water be? We get thirsty and we drink water. We're dirty and we take a shower. That's not so hard. Water's easy." This fucking idiot was not going to let him go until he fucking told him what he wanted to know.

"Look," he said. "You've been coming here for weeks now. I think we understand each other, don't we? The total length of your time here depends on whether or not we understand each other."

"Sure," Elio said. "I have a job to do. I am here to continue to admit to my revolutionary shortcomings and to be reeducated in the ways of civic propriety and ideological choices."

"That's right. I also made a promise to your wife. We were to identify the symptoms and provide a cure. Our weekly meetings and your admissions are the cure."

What the fuck? Was this guy for real? What promise was he talking about? How well did Maria know this guy, anyway?

"Yeah," Elio said. "She told me. You know, the thing is that I've told you everything there's to know. I got nothing else, man. I'm emptied out."

"I actually think you're holding back. Why is that?"

"That's all I have, I'm telling you."

"None of my business—is that it? Is that what you want to say? Well, the thing is that it is my business. You see, I got a file here that says that you have a record of unusual relations, contacts going back to at least 1959."

Here we go, Elio thought. They weren't going to let him live it down. Goddamn 1959. He didn't fucking leave! His father left alone! He wasn't his father. He was here, wasn't he? Shit, he might as well have left—a lot of difference his choices had made. Elio heard a murmur coming from behind the door, then he heard something else, the scraping of a chair on tile. Who the hell else was listening to their conversation? Had there been somebody sitting right outside the door? Was there a tape recorder somewhere in a drawer? Behind a book? In the fucking trash can? Elio imagined a rope tightening around his neck. The room suddenly got cold, real cold. Snow cold. He had to get the fuck out of there, or he was going to pass out.

Part 4

Until We're Fish

Bauta, 1994

CHAPTER 23

IT WAS SEPTEMBER 3, 1994. About a month earlier, an announcement had been made that those who wanted to leave the island would be allowed to do so in any way they could. For the first time since Mariel, thousands took to the sea. Clambering onto small boats, homemade rafts, inner tubes, refurbished vehicles, and anything that floated including— some people swore—repurposed Chinese bicycles.

Elio was afraid he would end up old, pitied, and derided in places like Austin, Tucson, Tampa, Los Angeles, or Chicago—or worse, in Miami, shopping at places like Los Chinos and roasting pork out of a goddamn box, like so many people he knew. This, at bottom, was his fear. He wanted to be elsewhere, but he saw no way to get there. No money to speak of and, because asking for help from his dad was out of the question, he had no one abroad to reach out to.

Once in a while he found himself hoping that aliens would abduct him, even though he didn't believe in them. At least it would be a change. But it wasn't just he who felt that way. It was like a plague—a pestilence that had overtaken everyone, much as the euphoria of the early years had overtaken them. There were symptoms, too.

Only porches away Eloisa's *How are joos* and *Thanks Gods* erupted like fever boils in the afternoon heat. Not far from her, Francisco and Lydia, the couple who'd moved to Bauta from Pinar del Rio a year earlier, called to and answered each other shouting every conceivable American profanity: *fuck here,* when Francisco actually meant *come here,* and *fucking light,* when the lights went out. Lydia's favorites, in turn, seemed to be *bitch, cunt,* and *dick,* which she used indiscriminately to address both the local members of the ever-decrepit Committee of Revolutionary Defense and her next-door neighbor. Their swearing became so excessive that even Pepe, walking by on his way to Elio's, was always frightened. Sometimes the carryings-on really became alarmingly loud. Francisco screaming out "Go ahead, kill me! Anything is better than this!" and Lydia, "Lárgate, and ojalá you get your huevos chewed off by sharks, descarao!"

Perhaps even more ubiquitous were the televisions in every house, pulsating the metallic sounds of American action films like a chronic migraine, accompanied by rapid weight loss, restlessness, and pain for which no other cause could be diagnosed. It was, everyone conceded, a period marked by especially extenuating circumstances.

Maria, too, moving fast toward another world and all she didn't yet know, was almost sick with both dread and longing. Over the last fourteen years, she and Elio had managed to put so many things behind them—repudiation rallies, Elio's book theft, and his father's erratic phone calls. Where they couldn't move on, they'd understood long ago, it was possible to make allowances. Even Elio's yearly check-ins with the therapist had become part of an uncomfortable but familiar routine. Nonetheless, and given the state of affairs on the island, most days Maria felt spent.

On this day, she was exhausted and hungry. She'd been hoping to just slide into her chair at the telefónica unnoticed, but it would be impossible—everyone was there. They might have been too caught up in the business of cables to comment, but they certainly weren't too busy to notice her. Some stared over their lenses, so that Maria felt that she was being detected by four eyes, instead of two. Others looked at her intently, over the length of her body, as if searching for something on her face and on her clothes, especially on her clothes. Eyes that were dark and blue and green and hazel watched her with suspicion. "Ah, aló, *good morneen, ebreebothee!*" she said in English, as she walked by them. Maria knew what they were looking for. They looked for whatever they always looked for on this island when people decided to look: a sign of foreignness, of material evidence of contact with someone from abroad. When they found nothing, they went back to plugging and unplugging and they left her alone. In any case, after years of playing hooky recurrently and unbelievable excuses, it was as if they'd all agreed to meet there. The truth was that, like everyone else, she no longer cared whether she was late or not, whether she lost her job or not.

Maria could hear the phone console ringing as she slid into her chair—nearly missing its bottom. Without a word, she yanked the cables from the board.

At the next station, Nena pressed her chin to her neck and stared at Maria over chipped tortoise rims. "What are you doing?" she asked. She talked around the chewing gum in her mouth.

"I'm giving people the chance to call back—that's what I'm doing," Maria said, her eyes on the board, as cables piled on the console. She was pulling the plug on the town's lifeline, at least temporarily.

She'd been pulling and plugging cords around the clock at a four-position manual board for decades. If she felt like *only* pulling them out now, then that's what she was going to do. Pull and plug, a technique most telephone companies had abandoned by the 1950s. But on this

island, she was still pulling and plugging. She could have done away with
the old board years ago—found a different job. Though, most days, she
felt useful. Even when things got rough, she helped people find each
other. A brother in Chickaloon, Alaska, hoping to reconnect with a sister
in Bejucal when dengue-infected mosquitoes sank their mouthparts into
people's necks. A recent divorcee in San Francisco calling in on an old
elementary school flame after some light tremors had knocked down a
vase from New Guinea. Someone in Delhi responding to a newspaper ad
advertising young Cuban brides. And then there was Miami—so many
calls from Miami you'd think an alarm had gone off. Bleep-bleep-bleep-
bleep: break-ups, deaths, births, and cancer all came through her cables.

It was she who held people's lives between finger and thumb. She
who made reconciliations possible, who facilitated money transactions,
reunited old lovers, and encouraged arguments and mistrust. But it
went beyond that—because sometimes she listened in. Not to whole
conversations, but to snippets. Then she'd pass the time wishing it
was she whose voice reverberated through the cables like some rickety
rollercoaster.

The calls that day had been mostly uneventful. Then, in the late
afternoon, Pepe's voice came through her cable. "Oye," he shouted, "tell
Elio to meet me at the park tonight!" Despite her many gentle indications
over the years that he could speak at a normal volume, Pepe was still
convinced he needed to belt out his words loud enough to be heard
through her cables. "I'll let him know!" she shouted back. She unplugged
his line and rubbed her abused ear for a moment, then began working
to connect the next call, a long-distance exchange. It was a call from
Chicago. Her heart started to beat faster. Suddenly, she remembered the
promise she'd made to her grandmother—a promise she never intended
to keep. She was once again reminded of her childhood dreams, of snowy

landscapes, and lights, so many lights. Only lights, as far as she could see. She couldn't recall why she started dreaming of Chicago in the first place. Perhaps it was that crunch-crunch-crunch of snow she'd heard amplified in old American films that made Chicago better than Hollywood, better than Miami. Or, perhaps it was her darling Sears, the magic and glitter of which she could still remember. She could hardly have known what life had been like in Chicago for Elio's father. One could only guess.

Snow, white like talcum powder. Like a *luxurious* blanket over everything, just as she'd seen on TV. How she wished for it today. She wanted to complain to Nena about the heat but she wouldn't have known what to say: so much of it had become vapid and predictable. Just as she was about to pick up a blinking line, Nena wistfully alluded to lunch, trying to get her attention by miming peeling and devouring a banana.

"Operator—Bauta," Maria finally exhaled into the mouth of the receiver.

"Aló Aló! Aló? Ricky Perez here!" the voice said.

Maria froze for a moment. She thought she should say something. Something straightforward, *like we need you to help us.* She took a deep breath, then hesitated. And, finally, just when she thought she'd get the words out, she simply lacked the courage. "Where to?" she said. There was a nervous urgency to her voice that she tried to contain by putting her hand on the mouthpiece and catching her breath away from it; Nena took the action for an invitation.

"You can tell me, you know," Nena whispered. "There's no shame in it. Is it Elio?" Her elbow nudged Maria near a rib.

"It's not about that," Maria interrupted, a finger only seconds away from another red button. Since the rally, she knew better than to let her guard down at work. "I gotta get this," she said.

Maria had received a few phone calls in her time that surprised the fuck out of her, but this one—this one, she never expected.

Every few years she'd think of the city. She was in love from afar with this Chicago. The thought moved like one big muscle through her mind, shoving everything else out of the way with a kind of animal grace. She had started dreaming on the day Elio showed her the postcard, or was it earlier? She was in love with Chicago from afar—even as cities like Miami, LA, New Jersey, New York, Paris, Madrid, and Barcelona had ruined the island for whole generations. Over centuries, Cubans had looked about themselves and seen value only in what was foreign, what was outside of themselves. "Yes, it must be true," they told themselves, "Paris, Madrid, and Barcelona must be better than this small island. Miami, LA, New Jersey, New York, and Chicago must all be better than this." There was confirmation of it all around them, in t-shirt logos and canned food items, movies and phone calls. Long-distance phone calls. Everyone waited for them, putting up with echoes and cut-off conversations. Long-distance phone calls had replaced cassettes and letters laced with starched and ironed dollar bills, 18k-gold chains as fine as thread. She had no relatives abroad, so she had to make do with other people's conversations in code.

Again and again Chicago had appeared in the margins of her life, without influencing in the least its basic text. Lately, though, she thought of it more and more. Thoughts illuminated by movie marquees, hotel signs, and all that snow. But, though leaving seemed possible once again, Elio wasn't going anywhere. He was staying put, wasting motion as if it would go on forever, as if to spin one's wheels was to go somewhere.

She'd have to tell him. But what would she say? Your father called. He said nothing. *Aló, Aló! Aló?* Ricky Perez here! Then a dark void and the sudden click of a cut line. Was it snowing there? It couldn't be— it was summer there too. This disrespect for human connection, the misconnection, the miscommunication, the mistrust. She'd heard it all. All of this got passed on like a genetic disease or some great family dysfunction. Passed down like an heirloom, like some goddamn curse.

She'd tell Elio that night. Right after she told him that Pepe wanted to talk to him. No, she'd tell him before mentioning Pepe. That way, in case he needed someone to talk to about it beside her, he and Pepe could talk. She'd make coffee and ask him to sit down. No, she'd tell him she wanted ice cream and they'd sit at Bauta's modest Coppelia. That wouldn't work either—too many ears. Where? Poor Elio. She'd be happy to tell him that she'd heard from his father again, to persuade him, finally, that he should make an effort to reconnect, and perhaps his father might help them leave the island, and perhaps even get as far as Chicago. But she couldn't tell him. Not now. Not after the books, and the therapist, and everything else that had to do with a father who abandoned his son, and a son who refused to forgive his father. Who knows what he would do? He was fragile now, like a broken limb. *Her* broken limb. She'd have to build him back up, piece by piece. Mend all the tears.

Hours later, Maria sat at her kitchen table with a bowl of gofio and a charred piece of toast in front of her. The smell of burnt bread scented the whole house. Elio sat across from her and watched as she parted the mealy lump into two with the end of her spoon and slid the bowl toward him.

"Have you heard?" she said, waving the spoon in front of his face.

Elio looked into the bowl and took the spoon from Maria's hand. "What?" he said. "That gofio is just another word for shit?"

"Very funny," she said, her teeth speckled with breadcrumbs.

Elio was pleased to see that he could still make her laugh. He cleared from his throat what sounded like a fist-sized wad of grain. "That more people have left today than any other day in the last few weeks?" he said, with difficulty.

"Yeah, that."

"Not sure what's so special about today, though," Elio said.

"Sometimes people reach their limit at once."

"What would you have me do about it? We're not leaving—can't we talk about something else?"

Maria seemed stricken by those words and lowered her eyes. He shrugged, sat wordless with the bowl of gofio in front of him. He saw in her face genuine distress.

"Pepe needs to talk to you," she finally said. As always, she had no choice but to change the conversation.

Elio was totally lost. "What?"

"You heard me—what's the matter with you?" Her gaze blinked about the room. Messy, hot, dark, poorly laid out, and full of somber, worn furnishings that barely reflected any light coming in through the shutters; walls marked with water stains from yearly floods, and a few yellowed photographs reminding her that time had and would continue to pass.

"Don't tell me, he's leaving?" Elio didn't even realize that he'd said that aloud until Maria said, "Rumors are that everyone leaves sooner or later."

"Not everyone," Elio said, already nearing the front door.

Leaving the house, Elio walked straight to the park. No detours. Not even to drink some of Elsa La Gorda's coffee-infused laxative from a dented tin can. Tonight he wanted to know just what it was Pepe had up his sleeve.

He found him slouching on a rusty swing, his calloused feet buried in the sand like bashful armadillos.

"Is that the best you can do? Bury your feet in the sand? You look like a damn fool."

Pepe wiggled his toes until they cleared through the sand. "I got a job for you," he said, squinting up at his friend through the yellow light from the light post.

"Whose job?"

Immediately, Pepe went into lockdown mode. "Eli, brother, I'm not at liberty to discuss the details, man."

Elio didn't like being called Eli—only his mother had done that. "Leave Eli out of this—he's got nothing to do with it. Why would I agree to anything without the details? That's how we got here, you know."

Pepe clenched his teeth. "Because you got nothing else going on, goddamnit. Because how in repinga do you think you're going to take care of Maria, let alone yourself? Didn't you hear? Didn't the radio and the TV remind you, over and over again? This is a 'Special Period in Times of Peace,' my brother. And, in the meantime, we starve. You got your dick in your hand and you're too stupid to know it."

"Listen to me," Elio said, his heart pounding so hard that he could hear its pulse in every word. "Taking care of Maria is my job, not yours. You want to take care of someone, go right ahead. Don't think you're going to do it on my back."

"You're a goddamn fool," Pepe said. "It'd be a huge step up. You'd be managing—keeping the order, if you will. Making sure people don't get out of line, that sort of thing. Vigilancia type of shit. You get me? The job comes with perks, crap you could use, or sell, or trade—whatever the fuck you wanna do with it. Mostly, personal hygiene products—soaps, razor blades, deodorants, shampoos, toothpaste and toothbrushes, shit like that," he said, then waited. "Then, there's the Chinese bike, of course."

"There's a bike?" Elio said, unable to hide his surprise.

"Ahora sí te interesa, desgraciao? Yes, Sunday Bonus bikes…Forevers and Flying Pigeons. Is that a yes, or what?"

Perhaps it was because he knew just what "Maria button" to press. Perhaps it was because he couldn't stand the thought—not even for a second—that Maria would think him a weakling, a mistake. That she'd think she'd ended up with the wrong guy. Perhaps because he was in *no* position to turn down the perks—*especially* not the bike. For those reasons, and for those reasons alone, he decided to take the offer and make the best of it.

"Fuck you, man. What the hell do I have to do?" Elio finally said. After all, if taking the job meant that he could improve Maria's life, *and his,* it would all be worth it. Plus, if he had to live in a state of permanent vigilance, where everyone had to know who everyone else was, what they devoted themselves to, who they met with, and what activities they took part in, then it was to his advantage that *he* be the one doing the vigilance. Isn't that what the therapist meant when he talked to him about the tremendous power of reconciliation? Of replacing apathy and dejection with passion and commitment? "Intention is not enough," he'd told him. "You *must* be able to show, with concrete actions, that you're ready to enter into a new relationship with the state." Plus, Elio thought, there was a bike on the horizon—albeit a Chinese Forever or Flying Pigeon, but a bike, nonetheless.

"There you go, I knew you'd come around," Pepe said, rising from the swing and slapping Elio on the shoulder so hard that Elio nearly fell sideways into the sand.

"Now what?" Elio said, stretching the kinks out of his own feet.

"Now, you show up on Monday."

"Just like that."

"It's that easy."

CHAPTER 24

RICKY PEREZ WASN'T AFRAID to die, but he was hoping for enough time to put his affairs in order. In the thirty-plus years since he'd left Cuba, it never once occurred to him to return for good. But now, things were different. *He* was different.

He'd survived so many things over the years: the 1962 holdup outside Olive Burger that nearly killed him and left poor Sally pistol-whipped and unconscious by the side of the road; and the car accident on the way to Philadelphia in 1978, a broken femur and a sonofabitch concussion that nearly took his hearing on one side; the 1985 break-in at Frank & Dino's Deli in Buffalo Grove, another near miss that left him half maimed; then, there was the fatty liver in 1991 and his LDL in 1992, high enough to scare anyone into veganism. But if Ricky Perez had learned anything in this country, it was that you may survive everything else, but you won't survive stage four prostate cancer.

If he were to try to call again, what would he say? Hi, it's Ricky Perez, I'm your father, and I'm dying. He wouldn't get anything out, except *Ricky Perez, here*. He was *here*, in Chicago, exactly where he had been all these years.

In the last fifteen years, he'd largely managed to push Elio out of his mind, except for a few wild moments, but then cancer hit him like a ton of bricks and he could think of nothing else but hearing his son's voice. He spent many waking hours and a good number of sleeping ones regretting the lost opportunity of reconnecting with his son. He would have gladly given up everything he owned—his little apartment in Back of the Yards, his excellent book collection on the Strasberg method, and every last cent he'd saved over the years while mopping the floors in the old Woods Theater building. He'd even have given up Sally—for the chance to see his son again.

Ricky felt unending shame when he thought about Elio, partly due to the guilt his son had encouraged in him over the years, for abandoning his mother, for abandoning him, hell, for not getting him that damn Schwinn he'd promised him once. The shame, however, was most piercing, most agonizing, when Ricky revisited what he considered his fundamental flaw: abandoning his wife and his only child to the absurdity of an island that, like him, had failed them. He had tried to get him out, though. Hadn't he? Didn't that count for something?

Ricky looked out his window toward Lake Michigan. As always, the water was calm, mocking the agitation he felt inside. He was weary of the excuses he'd made for doing what no father worthy of being called a father should ever do, the never-ending justifications that choked him como una soga alrededor del cuello. What would he say to his son if they ever met again? Would he dare call him son, or use his first name? Or would they immediately resort to insults and blows? What would they have in common anymore besides abandonment and fear?

CHAPTER 25

MONDAY CAME. As usual, Pepe waited for Elio at the water tank. In daylight, with the sun pouring down on potholes and deep cracks in what was left of the sidewalks, the town's character revealed itself. It was an ordinary place, a town for nobodies, marred in absurd ways by second-story constructions and last year's satellite dishes. Pepe shook his head. "Mira eso," he said. "All's gone down to shit."

"Was there ever a time it wasn't shit?" Elio said eventually.

"Oye, you're in a mood de pinga. Pull it together, brother. You're not exactly a model worker. This is big time for you, so—"

"I got it. Let's walk," Elio said, as if turning the only method of transportation available into a choice would somehow make their journey worthwhile. They'd spent years walking to Cayo de la Rosa and back.

"No point waiting for Godot," Pepe said, low enough that only Elio could have heard him. "See, I'm reading too," he chuckled. "I got it, brother,"

"Ha," Elio said, squeezing his friend's shoulder. "Sometimes you surprise the fuck out me."

"I'm full of surprises."

"You sure are."

But the most surprising thing that day and in weeks to come was the way Elio'd managed to bend himself like dough around everyone he came into contact with. If he'd learned anything that week and in the following months, it was that he was pliable. Malleable in a way he never thought was in him. Demanding patience and sacrifice from people who'd had it up the wazoo with patience and sacrifice. It was courageous—that's exactly what it was. A hell of a lot more action than he'd seen in years. Perhaps, had his mom seen him now, she'd have chosen to stay.

The job that Pepe got him was well on its way. In the weeks to come, if menganito mentioned volunteer work, he'd be the first one to raise his hand. If fulanito brought up the question of productivity, he'd have his tricolored graphs ready for close inspection. Hell, he even looked forward to those goddamn Red Sundays he'd avoided until now. He was determined to get a goddamn Chinese bike out of it.

Often enough, he struck out into the back rooms with a clipboard to catch someone chatting up the day or bending over a duffle bag of black market merchandise: lubricants, lighters, old eyeglasses, bags of cotton balls, syringes of various sizes—even tampons in pink plastic wraps. The worst came when he got a load of a kneeling Celia, Head of Quality and Vigilancia, blowing the headlights out of Pepe in a corner near the men's stalls. Celia, who'd come from Oriente at the beginning of the year, was— as of the last few months—Pepe's regular habit, along with smoking, bullshitting, and trash-talking. Elio would have no choice but to give all of them a warning and ban Pepe's access to the back room.

"What the hell, man?" Pepe shouted. One hand pushing down on Celia's head, the other waving him back. "Get a life!"

He had a life. Didn't he? Get a life—as if it were that easy, he thought, walking back to where he'd come from. How long had it been since he'd looked between his legs to find Maria's mouth pulling on his pito like a suction cup? Way longer than he'd ever admit—much less to Pepe. That's it, he thought. He'd break the drought that night. He was nearly over fifty, not dead.

That afternoon he hurried home. Cornhusks paved the way from the front door to the kitchen, where Maria frolicked from counter to stove, as if carried by an invisible chariot. *"Hi, darleeng,"* she said, in English. *"Hao war joo?"* She was all laughter, all smiles.

He pulled up behind her like a revved up engine. *"Hello, Darlene,"* he said, in yet another version of Maria's *hello, darling*. "What may I ask are we having for dinner?"

"Well," Maria said. "By the look of cornhusks, one could venture, say, tamales. But they cut the gas, so I'd say some version of gofio and day-old bread."

"Oh," he said. "Whatever you make will be ambrosia to me."

"Ay, Elio. Sometimes you say such things..."

"I sure do. You know what? Things are changing. Things are changing. As a matter of fact," he said. "I brought you something." He pulled out a small bundle wrapped in rice paper. "I think you're gonna like it."

"What is it?" Maria said.

"You'll see."

Maria took the package and unwrapped it. Inside was a small purple soap. She lifted it to her nose. "Umm," she said. "Lavender! How long has it been since I smelled anything like this?"

"Too long," Elio said.

"You were right," she said, kissing Elio on the cheek, "things *are* changing."

That night they slept like husband and wife. Hell, they romped like husband and wife. Maria riding on handlebars. Maria backward and sideways. Maria, arms outstretched, tensed calves, knees bent down La Loma de Pita. Maria with the scent of lavender soap on her skin.

Elio knew exactly what they were celebrating, but he preferred to think that Maria was less about the unforeseen advantages of his new job and more about the way his one-and-only boxers stuck to his ass in the semi-darkness. It was easier to believe that nothing had changed and that she loved him the way she always had. After all, he was thinking mostly of her when he accepted the job.

A week later, when word got around that he'd been promoted to a more advantageous position, he was all anybody in town could talk about. Sometimes in the evening people came by to see what he'd been up to. Knowingly assuming that his new position afforded him surplus amenities—soaps, deodorants, razors and shaving creams, shampoos and conditioners, plus—they came in ones, twos, and threes, mostly to complain about the absence of red meat or to ask Maria about his whereabouts. They always stayed longer than they had to, as if his company had suddenly become their small investment, a nest egg of sorts. They were there and then gone, but they always left a taste of dog shit in his mouth. Even the ones he'd known all his life—especially those.

CHAPTER 26

WHEN ELIO'S NEIGHBORS realized he had nothing to offer in the way of tangible benefits, they went away. He couldn't blame them for trying. They, too, hoped for ways of staying, sometimes. Given recent directives, though, everyone who wanted to leave could do so, and would do so, in any way they could. In Bauta, it seemed as though aliens snatched people right out of their beds, so many had awakened to find a missing son or daughter, a husband or wife gone for good. People went missing every day. Some eventually turned up ninety miles away, with their feet wet or dry. Others never turned up, except to wash ashore on some local beach.

But Elio still hoped that staying was possible. Surely there were other joys the island could provide, weren't there? The island still had its natural beauty—its green valleys and its mountains, its Pico Turquino and, even if he himself could no longer enjoy it, there was the powdery white sand and the cerulean sea.

Perhaps he'd been on the wrong side of history all along—or he had refused to take sides at a time when taking sides had been of the utmost importance. In any case, and because he had nothing else to feel proud about, he delighted in knowing that his performance at the textilera was nothing short of stellar. At this rate he wouldn't only get the Chinese bike, but a pressure cooker and refrigerator to boot. So far, he'd gotten scented soaps from Canada and a small bag with deodorant, toothpaste, a travel-size bottle of shampoo, and a pack of razor blades, which Maria immediately traded for two onions and a bag of black beans. Hell, who knows what else they'd give him in return for all he'd done. He devoted himself to monitoring any and all activity at the textilera, looking for signs of dissent and waning political loyalty. Although, for moral reasons, he didn't dare turn anyone in, he banned Pepe from the storage room and insisted on dissuading other culprits from continuing with unauthorized activities—which could be anything from selling homemade yogurt at lunch time, to trading black market goods, to collecting empty lighters for resale, to criticizing the regime out loud and while in the presence of others.

In other words, he reestablished order. He was damn happy about it all. He felt people respected him, too. Where once he took extra steps to go unnoticed, now he was the proud owner of a strut that nobody could take away from him. Things had taken a turn for the better and there was nowhere else he wanted to be.

Finally, he'd arrived. Maria would have no choice but to be proud of him, and she'd understand why, now, they wouldn't have a reason to want to leave. He was determined to guide the textilera into better days, one small nudge at a time. One person at a time. All he had to do was follow his gut and he'd know the words to use, just the right amount of firm, just the right number of warnings, just the right moment to say Hey buddy, Hey lady, job well done. God only knows no one had done that for him. He'd be benevolent, too. Like a great king or emperor. You know, the kind that grants pardon right before the head's due to roll.

It was nearly 11:00 a.m. and Elio was in his office at the textilera. He had just stood back to admire two neatly stacked piles of folders on his desk with "Quality Control" written on top when Pepe walked through the door.

"So, what's on your mind now, caballo?" Pepe said, slapping a shoulder blade.

Elio turned around, startled. "Eh," he said. "What's the matter with you?"

"Taken a plunge into the sea, have you? With all the sharks, and crabs, and little fishes…"

"You wish," Elio said. "I'm here to stay."

"Gone off the deep end…like the time that shark had you by the balls—scared the piss out of you, remember?"

"What the hell is wrong with you?" Elio asked. "If I gave a damn about that, I'd have to punch you."

"Are you a man or a whale? A whale or a shrimp? Wait, you're a shark—that's it. A great white shark, like in *Jaws*. Remember the first time you saw *Jaws*? Man, you almost shit in your pants…I've never seen such a wuss—wait, I have. Yes, I remember. I remember that you cried like a little bitch when they'd told you you'd lost a ball," Pepe clowned. "Man, were you a sorry-ass whining little prick then. Hell, you're a sorry-ass whining little prick now. Look at you, you're pitiful, viejo. If I didn't know you so well, I'd think you were taking this whole friggin' thing a little too seriously."

"You're in an awfully good mood," Elio said, unwilling to let pass whatever had gotten into Pepe that morning.

"Hey, is it my fault women want me and men wanna be me?" He laughed, pulling on his crotch like his balls had suddenly doubled in size.

"Why are you making fun of me?" Elio asked.

Pepe leaned against the doorframe, put a cigarette in his mouth and lit it. "Why does it bother you?"

"It doesn't." He made toward the door, but Pepe stopped him.

Elio pulled his shoulders straight. Sucked in his gut in a kind of self-conscious effort to pull himself together. He had to put a stop to him, he thought—he was beginning to imagine that Pepe wasn't who he thought he was. Had the island somehow changed who Pepe was? Perhaps the transformation happened slowly, as if resting several times on the way. On each landing, something had been stripped away: the heart here, the soul there, until there was someone Elio didn't recognize standing in front of him. He was a stranger, with an enormous face gazing at him, mocking him from a place Elio wished had never existed.

Outside, clouds and tree trunks and rooftops were lead gray. No shadows, just long spaces of mute and motionless gray. A lone kite, high on the side of the building, spiraled down and onto an adjacent lot. Yes, Elio thought, it must have been the weather. It must have put him in a bad mood. The Pepe he knew would have never said those things.

"Something's off with you right now," Elio said.

"You fucking banned me from the storage room, you little shit," Pepe said, dropping his cigarette to the ground and stamping it out.

"I was doing my job," Elio said. "As a matter of fact, I was supposed to freakin' turn you in, and I didn't."

"Oh, I see," Pepe said. "I'm now supposed to be grateful that you spared me. Give me a fucking break. This job's gone to your goddamn head."

"You're out of line," Elio said. He started to walk away.

"That's right, squirm away like you always do."

Elio did just that—his workday was over, anyway. He'd strained to avoid punching the guy right on the nose. The pressure on his chest was evidence of that. He decided that he wouldn't make an issue of it. But there was an issue—that was clear. He tried hard not to let Pepe know that his words had felt a little too much like jabs. He was trying so hard, but somehow was failing. No matter what he said, he was always the loser.

CHAPTER 27

FOR DAYS, ELIO kept thinking about Pepe. Maybe what struck him most was that, after all these years, Pepe didn't know him at all. Hadn't he, Elio, taken risks, trounced the times, outsailed the storm? The shark didn't kill him. And he'd even won the girl.

On his way home from work, he rambled through the neighborhood, past the old theater and the ice cream parlor, past the park and the church. Perhaps more than ever, he noticed everything flaking, peeling, even leaning in ways auguring collapse. All of Bauta faded into a watery gray. He hoped to run into Pepe. He'd avoided him at work, needing time to fume about what he'd said. Because words had always had a particular claim on Elio, he was determined to have a word or two with his friend that afternoon.

He crossed the Carretera Central; there were hardly any cars passing. One disappeared into the distance; another was approaching slowly. A needling feeling made him slow his pace until the car passed. He suddenly thought with a shudder that, although there were probably several reasons why an unknown car might approach him, there was also a chance that someone was following him. That his never-ending sessions with the therapist, in an addition to his recent efforts at the textilera, had not been enough to erase his past offenses. He circled the park several times, sitting down occasionally to think about what had actually happened between Pepe and him, not knowing if he should go home or wait around for his friend to show up. He didn't see Pepe anywhere. Eventually, he gave up, turned around, and headed home.

CHAPTER 28

RED SUNDAYS CAME and went. Elio dove headfirst into work and into the deepest, most remote region between Maria's thighs. He forgot all about strange cars on the road, and all about Pepe. But he couldn't forget about Red Sunday bonuses. In fact, Red Sunday bonuses were largely responsible for his great mood. They were the ultimate reward to those who'd given up leisure time to rally, to commemorate revolutionary events, to cut sugarcane, and anything else requiring consistent and enthusiastic mobilization of the masses. Leaps of faith, Maria called it.

Chinese bikes were the ultimate Red Sunday bonus, and Elio was determined to get one. So far, besides the scented soaps from Canada, deodorant, toothpaste, shampoo, and razor blades, he had received a "Thank You" plaque and a telescoping frame air pump from Korea for the Chinese bicycle he had yet to get.

It was the last Sunday of the month and Elio was informed, finally, that he'd been nominated to receive a Flying Pigeon. That bike, together with the Forever, had become the epitome of Chinese entrepreneurship on the island and—besides feet and the occasional lift—sometimes the only method of transportation. The meeting was taking place on the opposite side of the square. Feeling certain today was the day his efforts at the textilera would be rewarded, Elio left the main building by the side door and walked across the courtyard. It was well past lunchtime when he entered the room and took the first seat available, across from Pepe and close enough to Celia that he could eavesdrop. She was having an unofficial, half-whispered conversation with Isabelita, secretary of the textilera and Pepe's old girlfriend. "How are things, Isa?" asked Celia. Isabelita complained that secretarial work for the textilera was too much for her alone, and that there was no help from anywhere because nobody observed the obligations of filling out orders and approvals and other pertinent paperwork; these were dumped on her desk instead, with the expectation she would complete them herself, or ignore the need for them completely. "Don't worry, Isa, I'll make sure everyone knows they have to complete their own paperwork, I promise you," Celia said.

Isabelita begged Celia, who seemed to be her friend but who also happened to be her boss, not to do that. But the latter was not listening anymore, nor did she seem to have a sympathetic ear, even for a friend. Her attention had gone to Pepe, who ogled at her from across the room.

One by one, those who participated in Red Sunday activities and were eligible for Red Sunday bonuses came in and either took a seat or stood in the back of the room. When Celia found there were enough people present, she called for silence and opened the meeting with a short introductory speech. After condemning the inefficiency of the former Red Sunday Committee, she proposed nominating candidates for the election of a new committee, then went on to other matters. Finishing that, Celia passed the list to Isabelita, who proceeded to read off the names of candidates nominated for Sunday bonuses. Elio's heart beat a little faster when he heard his name. Then, finally, the two sole recipients of the much-coveted Chinese bikes. Elio held his breath. "And the Flying

Pigeons go to…"

"Well, so that's that, comrades," Celia said. "Let's speak frankly. For our two honorees, job well done. The Revolution thanks you. As for the rest, the Revolution believes in you. You'll have to try even harder next time."

Her words were followed by a round of applause, shouts of "We shall win!" and smiles. Elio did not speak, and did not smile. He looked around the room. He could see that Pepe was uneasy, tapping his fingers on the table. But he'd said nothing. No support from Pepe, not even a "Hey, let's reconsider" or a "Let's take a closer look at the facts." Instead, Pepe picked his nails with the torn edge of a cigarette carton and gawked at Celia from across a table. This time, her mouth was closed. From the opposite side of the room though, Isabelita locked eyes with Elio. She seemed sorry—Elio appreciated that.

Where the hell did these "revolution" mongers get off robbing him of what should have been his Chinese bike? What had *he* gotten for his efforts? They were all such goddamn phonies. Is this what they called a "revolution?" Well if that was a revolution they could all shove it. He wanted none of it. He believed in love and friendship, but Pepe had let him down—especially, Pepe.

There was a little more talk, with less and less observable coherence, with no rhyme or reason. About thirty minutes later the meeting was closed. They went off, one by one, with everything except a sense of satisfaction. The two honorees rode their Flying Pigeons home.

The following Monday after work, Sunday bonuses behind them, Elio and Pepe hitchhiked in the back of a pickup truck on its way home to Bauta. Although they'd both managed to act as though everything was normal, this was the first time they'd hitched a ride together in a while. Pepe stretched out on the truck bed and Elio pressed his back against the driver's cabin. Bouncing over potholes and gravel roads, they were nailed down by silence and the smells of wet grass and hot manure. The road looked as if no one had traveled on it in days, months, years.

They drove past high stacks of sugarcane, grazing cows, and roadside billboards. The truck moved fast, nearly missing puddles and all manner of roadside distractions. Nearly missing a forty-year friendship. But now, even as they rode home together, Elio no longer saw the point of being around people who were clearly set on behaving as if he hadn't taken his job seriously in the first place. The whole thing had been a fucking mistake.

He felt stupid for even wanting a bike. If his hard work was to go unrewarded, why the hell even bother? He could've just as well continued mixing dye in a bucket for the rest of his life, and saved his goddamn energy for something worthwhile.

The truck wheels went on. Pepe kept playing lizard in the sun.

"Why didn't you tell me I wouldn't get a goddamn bike?" Elio finally said.

Pepe shrugged. "You're acting like I promised you a bike."

Elio shook his head. "So nobody—like nobody—thinks this is wrong? Not even you? Repinga—"

Pepe's face was suddenly close to Elio's. He said, "What the fuck is your problem? Why can't you fucking figure it out? Why the hell do you think you got passed up? You don't know how to play the fucking game."

"I'm just saying you should have warned me." Elio's face turned red.

"You know, Celia's right. You're an idiot—you weren't meant to take it seriously. Jesus Christ, you were supposed to turn a blind eye."

"Oh, so turns out you're listening to your day-time whore?"

"Look, there was nothing I could have done about it."

"How about backing me up? You're a fucking coward—"

"And look who fucking suddenly found his missing ball. I'm against the wall, carajo—can't you fucking see that you're fucking it all up with your goddamn sudden fealty?"

Elio felt confused. Suddenly, he wasn't sure about anything. He should have never trusted Pepe—never.

Pepe shook his head. "You took it seriously, Elio. You fucked it all up, man."

The following Monday—perhaps out of some unspoken commitment—they walked to work, side by side. No words, just steps followed by another step, then another. Once again Elio had that strange feeling that he was being followed. He looked down at the road, back to where they had come from, and all around. But he never saw anyone. Pepe smoked, looked at stray dogs and at the pyramids of trash that marked the boundaries between one neighborhood and the next. Elio looked up at a billboard along the side of the road, at least once—more to feign disinterest in his companion than anything else.

About three blocks from the textilera, Pepe explained that he'd prefer to arrive separately, as Celia was afraid that Elio's overly enthusiastic attitude would jeopardize Pepe's good name at work. She didn't want to deal with interrogations, he said. Elio was a little stung but, trying to mimic Pepe's nonchalance, said sure. He'd planned to pick up Maria's blood pressure medication first at the pharmacy, so why not take their separate ways right then and there. Pepe shook his head as he walked away.

It turned out that Maria's prescription wasn't ready so Elio made his way back sooner than anticipated. About a block or so from the textilera was Celia's house, right along the main road—and just as fragile and dilapidated as the rest of the houses there. The further away from Havana, the worse the situation got. He could only imagine what it was like in Oriente—no wonder Celia'd made her way to Bauta.

Just as he came up to the house, he saw them. He took a few steps back, landing right behind a fence. He sighed, rolling his eyes. Sure enough, Pepe and Celia stood near the front door. Although it looked like a fairly normal meeting, Elio understood it as evidence that Pepe was spending way more time with Celia than with anyone else he'd ever shacked up with in the past. To Elio, that could only mean trouble to come.

Pepe and Celia were always working and never working—that is, they were always in some compromising position when they weren't otherwise pretending to work. Groping each other under a table, or necking in the supply room, or whatever else they did.

For Pepe and Celia there was no division between labor and pleasure—and it was not because they found pleasure in labor, but because they pretended to labor while they sought their pleasure. How could Pepe get away with it without making a single enemy? The whole thing made Elio intensely suspicious, and even a little jealous; they seemed too open, and generous—even in love—although, to tell the truth, Pepe very recently hadn't been acting too "generously" toward Elio.

Elio kept walking, though he feared that in a future not too far away, Pepe would end up doing shit for Celia that he'd never have done for himself.

After lunch, when Celia—lips swollen—came into his office to request the day's reports, Elio finally lost it.

"Quality reports ready?" she asked.

Elio said nothing. He watched the wobbly rotation of a floor fan and, finding it difficult to breathe, he opened the top button of his shirt. Then out of nowhere, as if descending from the ceiling, the right words came to him.

"Here's what I do with your stupid shit," he said, shouting his words through a curtain of spit and sending a pile of folders on his desk flying through the air.

"What the fuck," Celia yelled, "do you think you're doing?"

"I shit on your papers and your time cards and on all the shit in this factory…that's what I'm doing. You didn't even have the freakin' decency to announce the winners yourself. You had Isabelita do it?"

"Look, it's not my fault you didn't get the stupid Chinese bike!" she said. "Everyone voted."

"I shit on the bike too," Elio said. "And see," he added, crumpling up a stack of papers, "I wipe my ass with it all."

Perhaps Elio could have made his point more delicately, but he had never been good at delicacy or diplomacy, or at anything that required more restraint than he had energy for. The truth was that Celia and Pepe should have stood up for him. They should have said something, and they didn't. It wasn't about the bike. It was about their loyalty.

"Well," Celia said, her small body stretched to the limits to block the door. "You're writing a formal resignation. How do you like them mangoes?"

"Fuck you, your family in Oriente, and your stupid job. Move the fuck out of the way, Celia."

"You touch me and I swear to God I'll jab you with the first sharp object I get my hands on."

"Get out of my way, repinga."

Then Pepe, whose work room was close by and who must have heard them arguing, appeared in the doorway. "Let me talk to him, Celia," he said. "He's just stressed out. Go tally up some numbers and blow some nicotine." Pepe's arm bent around the woman's waist, and she moved to let him in.

"Fuck you too, Pepe," she said, waving a middle finger in the air as she swayed her hips past him, and made her way out the door.

"C'mon, brother. What's with all the drama? Over a goddamn bike from Hong Kong?"

"It's not the bike, goddamn it. It's about you—about our goddamn friendship. After all these years, I expected more from you. I needed you to back me up, que te comportaras como un jodío amigo."

"You're gonna lose your job, Elio. You're this close to getting your ass written up. I'm gonna have to bang the black beans out of Celia for this one. She's getting old as fuck. It's not easy."

"You're an asshole," Elio said, leaning against his empty desk, feeling wiped out.

"You're a lucky motherfucker, you know that? C'mon, let's go. If we hurry, we'll make the last fifteen minutes of the rally…no one will ever know about your hissy fit."

"It's the middle of the work day, Pepe," Elio said.

"Yup, and no better time to show you care. If you don't show up to the rally, you won't have a work day to come back to," he said. "See how that works? You gotta play the game, mi hermano," he said, as he lit a cigarette.

The mass of bodies became denser, the voices louder, as Elio and Pepe approached the outdoor gathering. Cuban flags, and hundreds of clamoring hands waved in the air. It was hot and the light was intense. The sour smell of sweat rolled through the crowd, ever more acrid and unbearable the deeper inward they moved. Elio squinted at the crowd as they got closer. Temporary wooden bleachers and crates filled with tomatoes had been set out; the whole space was already occupied to the last inch. People were still eating from cardboard boxes, bellowing that "It does not matter how small you are if you have faith and a plan of action," and "Until victory, always." Everyone repeated these and other such mantras, meant to dissipate hunger spasms, in exchange for fresh fruit and a drink that wasn't water.

When the crowd began to lurch toward cans of warm soda, Pepe and Elio, who were thirsty as fuck, joined them. The goal, always, was to get closer to either drink or food. They barely spoke as they walked; the tumult and the constant "Don't push," and "Wait your turn," and "Don't fuck with me," to get past some bottleneck or other made any chitchat impossible. Sometimes Pepe had to grab hard onto Elio's arm to prevent them from being separated by the crowd; other times it was Elio who had to hold firmly onto Pepe's shoulder to stop him from being swallowed up by the hungry mob. For seconds at a time, Elio could make out Pepe's voice in the crowd. "Me cago en diez!" and "Fuck the tomatoes!" Pepe shouted. Then the insatiable horde wolfed down his voice.

It took them a while to get to the front. And, although they missed the warm sodas entirely, they arrived just in time for someone to climb down a wooden platform and hand them each a box of tomatoes. "Where the hell have you two been?" the man said. He stuttered, so it was more like "Where the hell have you-you-you two been?" which, in any case, was appropriate, as they were so many *you's* hoping for a box of tomatoes that day.

"Don't be a comemierda, brother. We were the first ones on scene. Good tomatoes, wouldn't you say, Elio?" Pepe said, nudging his friend in the ribs.

"And you are?" Elio said.

"Roberto Salas, District Rally Coordinator and Bauta's new

bodeguero," he said, stretching out a sweaty hand. He wore a gray Fila t-shirt and worn Levi jeans; even then, he looked serious, stiff, and extremely thin with a short forehead and bushy eyebrows. He also looked like a real asshole.

Elio let the hand hang in the air. "Good tomato," he finally said, holding out the bruised fruit instead. He tried hard to sound natural. As far as he knew, he wasn't under current suspicion for anything, but the guy, everyone knew, wasn't just handing out tomatoes at the rally. Roberto Salas was not only District Rally Coordinator and Bauta's new bodeguero. He also happened to be its latest whistle-blower. He was CDR Captain and that, as everyone knew, meant one thing: he was dangerous—which was why Elio couldn't help but find his choice in clothes somewhat *contradictory* since, as CDR Captain, it was Roberto Salas's civic duty to crush the meekest expression of Yankee love.

CDRs or Committees for the Defense of the Revolution were a system of collective revolutionary vigilance meant to conduct intensive monitoring of every neighborhood on the island. As captain, Roberto Salas devoted himself to knowing the whereabouts of everyone in Bauta. In fact, it wouldn't have surprised Elio one bit if Roberto Salas himself had been the driver of the car following him weeks earlier. It was *his* business to know who his neighbors met with, what they devoted themselves to, where they went or had just arrived from and, last but not least, what activities they took part in. In other words, Roberto Salas carried out neighborhood activities whose number-one purpose was to maintain tight surveillance of suspected government opponents; non-participation could and would be suspect.

Not that attendance meant you were a committed revolutionary. At this point in the revolutionary timeline, most people, Elio included, were not there out of deep commitment to a cause long forgotten. They were there because they had no choice, because the incentive to show up that afternoon was the promise of tomatoes, cans of warm sodas they perhaps never got to drink, and a cardboard box of food they didn't arrive in time to receive.

"My brother here was saying that if it weren't for these rallies and food they provide, his wife would have killed him by now," Pepe said, giving Roberto an affectionate pat on the back and talking way too much—enough to make Elio uncomfortable.

"Is that so?" Roberto said.

"Well, you know women…they worry about food and—" Shouts, cheering, and applause at the appearance of more boxes of tomatoes on the stage forced Elio to raise his voice. Painfully aware that language could and would betray him, if given a chance, Elio relied on vague, half-phrases—not clear, not direct. The language of the people. In turn, Roberto seemed to rely on vague half-phrases—as many as he could muster.

"What's there to worry about?" Roberto's sideglance fell on Elio. "It's all here, isn't it? Paradise…We're there, co-comrade—we just have to-to keep on getting there."

"Well said," Pepe added, looking down at the box of tomatoes cradled in his arms. "This deal's over. We gotta head back."

"You take care of yourself, Elio. You look, you know, worn out. It's not good to look worn out, you get what I'm saying?" Roberto patted Elio's back with greater force than Elio would have hoped for, as if responding to Pepe's pat a few seconds earlier. Roberto Salas's unexpected familiarity alerted Elio that both he and Pepe should tread carefully from that point forward.

"Nothing a nap won't fix, right?" Pepe said, resting a hand on Elio's shoulder and squeezing.

Later, at the park, Elio sat on a bench looking down at the ground. He had been born on that soil, he thought. Yet, he felt out of place and waited for Bauta to reabsorb him somehow. He was too much of a coward to defend what was rightfully his: a sense of belonging to the place where he was born. When they'd marched on his house, they'd taken *that* away from him. He was being torn apart by opposing sides, by divided allegiances: there was Maria, insisting again that they leave, and then his loyalties and fears insisting that he stay. He wished, more than anything, that he could reconcile the two sides—somewhere in between would be the perfect landing.

As a produce truck doubling as a bus passed, Elio held his breath until its exhaust spread out into the air, then dissipated. A line of people across the street moved or seemed to move quickly—more so than usual. He remained there for hours, until the last person disappeared from view. Then he got up.

Walking home, he summed up the last days into something comprehensible. He concluded that anything could and would happen in a day, if only he, Elio Perez, could see in it all a glimmer of possibility.

CHAPTER 29

"IF THEY WON'T GIVE me a goddamn bike," Elio told Maria the
following Saturday, "I'll build one myself."

"Ahora sí," she said, taking a bite out of a juicy tomato. "You know
what the problem is…we should have left this goddamn island years ago.
Each time we had a chance, you decided to stay. And when you stay, you
gotta learn to roll with the system, lean into it. *You know what I mean?"*
She said the last phrase entirely in English and tomato. "Look at Pepe,
he's maybe as two-faced and slimy as a mango pit, as far as I'm concerned.
Tall, wide, hairy, and not very deep, but he knows how to work the
system. You gotta work the system, Elio."

"Yeah, maybe that's it," he said through sagging lips. If he told Maria
just *how* Pepe worked the system, and that the system's name was Celia,
he might as well kiss Pepe goodbye. She wouldn't have it. It'd be her or
Pepe, she'd say. Pepe was a fucking coward, anyway.

"Try a little harder, you know. Put more shoulder into it, more stamina."

"Woman," he said. "The little stamina I got left, I use to make our
ends meet." He laughed, although as far as he was concerned, his mind
was made up. "It's easy for you…all you gotta do is answer a goddamn

phone all day. Connect. Disconnect. Connect. Disconnect. Show up to one or two rallies per month—"

"You know it's never as simple as one or two rallies per month. And believe me, it's not that easy to plop your ass on a chair for hours with your ear pegged to a receiver. You have no idea the kind of calls…Let's just say it's not the life of a prairie dog at the zoo."

Elio smiled. The life of a prairie dog at the zoo. Which zoo? The one in Havana? As far as he remembered those poor rodents—that's what they were, weren't they?—had probably died already.

"Well, it's news to me. You're not exactly a talker, you know. You come home and stay shut up in your own world—not a word about your day. I don't know who called or who stopped calling."

"Oh," she said. "You're right…because Elio Perez is a talker. He loves to share. The only conversation you have any more is with your books. And, even then, you're the only one doing the talking."

"What the hell is that supposed to mean?" Elio said. He wished Maria appreciated him a little more, that she knew better than to voice any disagreements or discomfort with him at a moment when he was trying to figure out just how the hell to motivate himself to continue that charade of everyday life on the island. Because, since the incident with the Chinese bike, he wasn't really sure he had the energy to continue trying—and that was the goddamn truth.

"It means that you're no one to demand anything from me," she said.

Maria loved to be cryptic sometimes. Sometimes just straight out indecipherable. This was her way lately of taking small, piercing jabs at him. Short-tempered, shut up in her own world like a sheep. Not that she was dumb. She wasn't—not at all. She was one of the most intelligent women he'd ever met. She just wasn't there most of the time anymore—at least not there, there. Not where he wanted her to be. And he didn't even know where that was now. He wasn't sure what he'd done, either.

Perhaps he hadn't lived up to her expectations. Hell, he hadn't lived up to his own.

The next day, he read the headlines from *Granma:* COMMANDER IN CHIEF FIDEL CASTRO ANNOUCES MORE SPECIAL MEASURES FOR THE COUNTRY'S ECONOMIC SITUATION and WE WILL OVERCOME ALL OBSTACLES AND INTERFERENCE and THE COUNTRY'S BASIC ACTIVITIES AND SERVICES WILL NOT BE ABANDONED. It was almost too much to think about, all the intended and unintended consequences that befell an island in the death throes of revolution. And what could *he* do about it? The more he read about special measures, obstacles, and abandonment, the more he thought about how they had robbed him of his chance to finally get a bike, even if it was a damn Chinese bike. They—colleagues, friends, people he'd pissed with into the bushes behind the church, the ones he'd known all his life. Not even Pepe had stood up for him. Fuck Pepe.

He read past the first paragraphs under COMMANDER IN CHIEF FIDEL CASTRO VISITS NEW YORK, then lost interest. Turning page after page until coming to a headline: MAN BUIILDS HIS OWN CAR IN HAVANA. Panic had him by the neck. His muscles tensed up one by one. Sweat pooled in his pores. At the same time he'd stop producing saliva and couldn't swallow. He didn't need to read any further. He tossed the newspaper on the couch and left the house. Maria had gone out to perform her cleaning duties at Fina's and wouldn't be back for at least a few hours.

Thirty minutes later, Elio walked through the front door carrying a hoard of rusty pipes and bicycle parts. A fusion of American and Soviet antiquities that had finally met their day. Everything he'd need was there, though: a set of dented pedals, handlebars, a couple of chains, a metal seat with the springs still attached, a set of tires.

He pushed all the furniture to one side of the room, making space for scrap metal and that old welding gun he'd once used to fake his Lee pitusas. If there was one thing he'd learned from his dad—hell, one of the few things he learned from his dad—it was to tinker.

Elio only vaguely remembered his father's face. A father who did not care for him or, as he'd once put it, "his attitude," one bit. In any case, Elio couldn't help but think of him now with something close to tenderness—after all, he was the only father he'd ever had. If he knew how to use a welding gun at all, it was *because* of his father. "Welding," his father had told him once, "is a skill that takes *years* to perfect. But you gotta choose the right rod. End up with the wrong rod and you shorten the lifespan of your engine. You know what I mean?" Elio had never perfected the skill, nor did he ever have a choice when it came to rods, but that welding tip was one of the few things his father had left him. Instead of making him feel closer to his father, however, the memory had the opposite effect. It reminded Elio of all the tangible and intangible things that had been denied to him through no fault of his own.

As soon as he realized what he was feeling, he brushed it off. "Solavaya," he said out loud. His father had promised him something and failed to deliver: a Panther II. And even now, with a gut that rose above his belt buckle like a watermelon, Elio remembered that Schwinn. Red, like a goddamn apple. With its sleek frame and its new trimline tank. A real gem, not like those Soviet bikes that fell apart the second you decided to pedal off into the sunset. Or like the Chinese bikes, with their poor assembly, lack of lights, and faulty brakes.

He was determined to tinker with the scrap until it became something. Then they'd all envy him and his invention and wished they'd been as resourceful, as inventive, he thought, his face hardening.

Drawn by a subtle force, Elio set idea to paper. He'd need to let the thing manifest in front of him first, then pull each piece together, as if gathered by an invisible string. Make the pieces twirl, leap, somersault into the air before knocking into each other and converging to become the thing he imagined. He wasn't an artist—he couldn't paint to save his life, not even a wall. But he could sketch enough to get the job done. And that's all that was required.

Emerging from the pile of scrap metal, he found it was fully night, the air fanning a kind of cool optimism and something else, something perhaps like the unexpected feeling of snow. He only knew the bluish tint outlining snowy landscapes from illustrations, the grayish, slush-covered sidewalks of an American postcard.

CHAPTER 30

ON HIS EIGHTEENTH birthday, and only months after he'd found his mother's lifeless body, Elio'd received a postcard from his father. On one side, Chicago's skyscrapers rising up from winter slush into dull, gray skies. On the other, his father's even-handed script: *Hello from Chicago!* He hadn't heard from his father in five years. The last time he'd seen him, he was walking out the door. His shirtless back floating past the threshold and onto the sunlit porch.

Sometimes Elio imagined himself escaping small-town life like his father; but in his mind he was a fish falling through the drain. Growing bigger and bigger until his fins got caught in the rusty, calcified stalactites and stalagmites of pipes underneath the town. Then squeezing himself through, all the way to the bay, to grow to enormous size. He imagined himself somewhere beyond the island, swimming toward the windy city, Chicago. Or, perhaps, he'd returned to settle somewhere underneath the island, appearing and disappearing in lakes and riverbeds, responsible for whirlpools and sinkholes.

Awareness of the giant fish would seep into the island's red earth like rain, entering sugarcane roots and mango and papaya trees, thinning the consistency of the viscous chirimoya fruit and thickening the milk of coconuts. Inflecting new rhythms on the rise and fall of tides. Entering its cities' eclectic architecture, and altering traffic patterns. The island becoming an organism, constituting itself in relation to a threat whose heart beat right beneath it. A sea monster with a heart so large its regular beating would bring about tsunamis, reverse the course of wind currents, raise or lower blood pressures. And then every bus stop, every market and paladar, every porch and living room, rooftop satellite, hand-me-down cell phone and flash drive buzzing with good news: another island rising, another island founding itself, not like a copy of the other one, but like its undecipherable, master translation.

With a father gone and a mother dead, Elio'd had a chance to restart his life on his own terms alone. But now he was nearing fifty, and somehow life hadn't started. Only Maria made sense. She'd been there for him, always. His heart swooned and, although he knew how impossible it was, he heard snow falling onto sidewalks right outside his window. Covering rooftops, cars, fields. Blocking porches and barn doors, and smothering animals from one end of the island to the other. Snow from as far away as Chicago falling right outside his window. •

CHAPTER 31

A BLIZZARD WAS RAGING outside, as Ricky Perez stood by his front window to watch the air stiffen with snow through a near-frosted glass pane. Beyond his window sill, the pavement had disappeared under a thick, white cushion. The snow fell more and more heavily, and it was getting dark. The streets were almost empty. It was a Saturday, and those who'd been unlucky enough to be caught in the blizzard fled into the side streets or took refuge inside shops and restaurants. He'd been waiting for Sally since the morning, but when the blizzard broke—suddenly, like a cold shiver—he'd given up. He passed the time eating Maruchan ramen noodles from Jewels, and watching Ricky Ricardo on TV. He might have thought it was the coldest day ever in Chicago, but he knew better. He'd been there long enough to know that the temperature could drop to a numbing twenty-one degrees below zero faster than he could shout *I'm Cuban!* And how does a Cuban, bred on mangoes, scorching heat, and white sand beaches brave the storm? He stays put, and reimagines Chicago in the sun.

Ricky cast his eyes over to a small picture frame hanging on the wall. A mustached man, dressed in light summer clothing, Panama hat with a snap brim shaped like a fedora and a narrow black hatband, stands beside a scrawny boy in short-trouser pants, suspenders, and a flat, light-colored ivy hat. Behind them, the Avenue of Flags. Ricky looked closely at the picture, remembering the warmth of the midday sunlight on his bare arms, and the blinding sunrays all around, casting giant shadows off the flags at the open-air exhibition sites.

It was 1933, and the height of the Great Depression. He, Ricky Perez, held his father's hand and strolled through the grand Avenue of Flags at Chicago's "A Century of Progress" World Fair. This was the city's second fair, held on Northerly Island, in the Burnham Park/Harbor area, just southeast of the main downtown district. All Ricky had to do was close his eyes and he could hear it all, now in Dolby Stereo:

LADIES AND GENTLEMEN, CHICAGOANS, WORLD FOLK, HERE WE ARE, AT CHICAGO'S WORLD-FAMED "CENTURY OF PROGRESS," A SPECTACULAR FAIR THAT WAS STARTED FROM A BEAM OF LIGHT FROM THE STAR ARCTURUS. PEOPLE FROM ALL OVER THE WORLD HAVE COME TO SEE ITS MAGIC AND ITS MARVELS. NO LESS THAN TWENTY-TWO MILLION OF YOU COME SWARMING INTO THIS COLOSSAL SHOW TO WITNESS THE BRILLIANT HANDIWORK OF ITS MODERN UNPARALLELED INGENUITY. HERE IS THE FAMOUS AVENUE OF FLAGS, A BEAUTIFUL FLAG-BEDECKED BOULEVARD FILLED WITH AN ENDLESS STREAM OF PLEASURE SEEKERS, IN GAY ATTIRE, FULL OF THE HOLIDAY MOOD, KEYING THEIR SPIRITS TO THE GLITTER AND SPARKLE OF THEIR SURROUNDINGS, EAGER PARTICIPANTS IN THE SWEET GLORY OF A SHOW UNMATCHED IN THE ANNALS OF FAIR MAKING!

"Only in el norte. Right, Ricky?" His father had asked, squeezing his hand. "These Americans are something else! Money's freedom, Ricky. The only real freedom there is. El norte has always been our north star. Cubans were born looking north."

That had been it. All Ricky'd had to do then was look up at the fair's giant Ferris wheel and know that this was the place everyone should go. He had been dream-bitten, and his appetite for American streets, department stores, and skyscrapers with their slants of light and sparkling glass windows was insatiable. It had been a yearning to be surrounded by norteamericanos. It may even have been a need to lose himself in their company, to start over.

But Ricky'd never had any money to speak of. In fact, one of his greatest regrets was not being able to help Elio like he'd always wanted to, like his son deserved. The lottery was no good. No large sum of money ever made its way to him, even when Walter Mercado came on the Spanish channel and said, "Libra, today the sun enters dramatically in your sign. This is your time, and these are your lucky numbers. Don't let them go to waste, Libra." Ricky'd stared at his TV as the numbers popped up on the screen, one by one: 11-64-22-3-42-37. But, although he'd spent his last fifty dollars on tickets, not a single number came up—not a single one.

During the first years in the Heart of America, he'd been forced to juggle several jobs: short-order cook, security guard, and janitor, to name a few. He'd ended up with the janitor job because, well, they kept him; and also because at least he was cleaning a theater and not some grimy subway bathroom. In any case, he'd sent Elio money. Not a lot—what he could manage, damn it. Did anyone ever write back to ask where all the money was coming from? He sent money, even when he'd been wary of sending money directly to Elio's address, for fear that the envelope would be opened and the sum, however small, confiscated. But, he didn't know anybody who could, perhaps as a favor, perhaps for a small fee, take it to Cuba for him. It wasn't as though Chicago were Miami, where everybody was Cuban, along with the crackers, the coffee, and the cat. He was ashamed and regretted that he hadn't been able to do more. But he did what he could, carajo!—he thought. He sent the money any way he could.

He looked out his window again. For a moment, he imagined that a bright sun had thawed and melted all the snow on the street. Ricky felt as if he, too, were melting in the sunlight.

CHAPTER 32

IT HAD BEEN seven years since she had heard from Ricky Perez while she worked for the telephone company. That Maria mistrusted his voice on the other end of the line didn't surprise her. She'd been taught to mistrust like she'd been taught to say thank you. "You cannot trust these people," her grandmother repeated—often enough that Maria committed it to heart like a childhood poem. *Who these people were,* Maria wasn't quite sure. Who? The people who left? The ones leaving? The ones who would leave? Who were these people? These people looked so much like her that it was difficult to make distinctions. Was Elio one of *these* people? Was she?

"Ricky Perez here!" the voice said. Maria held the telephone receiver in a death grip. She hesitated. "Aló?" the voice said. Her heart beat fast. She wondered if she should ask Ricky for help. "Aló? Is anyone there?" the voice spoke again. But she remained quite still. Then, unable to get a word out, she hung up. She paced the floor of her living room, reflecting that if she had the answer to her questions, if she were a bit more trustful, more courageous, then she would know what to do. She left the house, taking her worries with her. The night was star-studded and cool, as she walked up to the door in the dark. "Fina," she shouted from the porch, "are you in here?" She heard Fina's *yes, come inside.* Maria pushed the door slowly with an open hand just in time to see Fina sitting in a rocking chair in the living room, wiping her eyes with a handkerchief, and holding a buttered piece of bread in her hand.

"Come, sit down here," the old woman said, pointing to a chair next to her. She tried to tuck her handkerchief inside her bra in such a rush that Maria could still see the little bulk sticking out from her collar.

"I need your advice about something important," Maria said.

"I didn't recognize your voice, hija," Fina said, latching her free hand to the back of Maria's head and pulling her close. She kissed her forehead the way she'd always done, as if Maria were still a child. Her lips were greasy from the butter.

"Ay hija, is everything okay? I've known you all your life—isn't that so?"

"Since I had use of reason, Fina..."

"That's right. It's hard to trust people, dear..." Fina's white head bent down toward her lap, then rose to watch Maria for a little too long. Her eyes blinking as she searched Maria's face like she was trying to guess what her next words should sound like, before taking a bite out of the bread again. Fina inhaled, and let a piece of bread slip from her hand onto the floor.

"Oh!" she said, attempting to pick it up. "My grip is not what it used to be."

"Please, don't trouble yourself. I'll get it," Maria said and did so.

Maria had dragged her irritation about Ricky Perez's phone call all the way to Fina's house. She was hoping to get on with it and tell Fina about it. Perhaps the old woman could inspire in her the courage she needed to call him back and ask for his help. At Fina's, possibly because it wasn't her own home, Maria felt she could say almost anything.

The old woman's house was old and cold, but also well kept. At night, kerosene lamps lit the living room while the rest of the neighborhood endured the blackouts with ill-natured raillery and gossip. During the day, two large fans cooled the living room so that, according to the neighborhood gossip, Fina's house was the coolest, freshest house in all of Bauta. It was, according to Maria, *the right way to say fabulous.*

"I just need a little piece of advice—" Maria started to say.

"Is that so?" Fina looked at her, rather disconcerted.

But Maria couldn't reply because—to her astonishment—Fina went straight on to talk about something entirely different. During the next hour, Maria didn't get a chance to talk to Fina about the phone call, for the old woman overwhelmed her with as many wants as Maria had questions. Fina wanted her to mop the floor, dust the shutters, make new curtains, mend the mosquito nets, wash her clothes and hang them out back to dry. She wanted so many things, and promised so many others, it was hard for Maria to be patient and listen to her. At some point, she gave up entirely on getting the advice she needed. "What exactly are you asking me to do?" Maria said. Fina didn't clarify it for her, but changed the course of the conversation to territory that, at first, seemed completely unrelated.

"Your name must appear on the rations booklet, dear," the old woman whispered, "for five years." She tossed her words out casually, as though this was the sort of thing she told Maria every day. Fina didn't need to say anything else, though. Maria understood. What Fina was proposing was an exchange. Maria would clean Fina's house, in exchange for the house at the end of five years, or upon Fina's death, whichever came first. Five years of indentured servitude. At the end, however, Fina's house could be hers.

The conversation didn't go on very long because Fina brought up Benito, her late husband, and Maria's patience wasn't as developed a virtue as she would have wanted it to be. Yes, it's hard, she'd tell Fina. Forty-five years is a long time. No, I wouldn't trust his family in Miami, either. Sure, it's understandable—all of it. By Fina's account, Benito's family in Coral Gables wanted their house back, and they'd stop at nothing to get it. Along with terry cotton towels from the J. C. Penney in Coconut Grove, sugary treats from those dollar stores meant only for tourists, and housedresses from Ñooo! ¡Qué Barato in Hialeah!, Fina commonly received one or two letters a month from Benito's family. Each letter echoed the one before: *Dear Tía Fina... We have no problems of conscience reclaiming what our uncle worked for...and Dear Tía...They don't have the right to give away anybody's property...*and *I was only five, but I had the feeling we weren't going back any time soon...*and even *That house means everything to us."*

Likewise feigning nonchalance, Maria told Fina she was flattered, then said she had to talk it over with Elio. She wouldn't need to remind her that foreigners had little claim on her house, even if those foreigners were family and lived ninety miles away.

Maria's mind was made up, though. She had no intention of being Fina's night maid. But a house was a huge thing, and she couldn't help but feel tempted. After all, Fina's house was *fabulous,* she thought, making herself laugh. She could see her snobbish grandmother rolling her eyes so far into her head that she'd flip backward in her grave. "What's so great about Fina's house? It's just big," she remembered her grandmother saying. But, there were so many details that made Fina's house a great house—for starters, it wasn't Maria's house.

"I trust you," were Fina's last words. Maria had the feeling she really meant it, but when she shut the door, she heard Fina sobbing. Maria thought to open the door again, letting instead this soft moment nestle in Fina's heart.

She weighed the pros and cons, and by the time she walked down the block to her own house, dusty bread in one hand, she'd changed her mind. She turned right back around, like someone who suddenly discovered they'd forgotten their luggage at the train station. While at first she dragged her flip-flops against the asphalt, sidestepping cracks along the way, she soon found herself almost skipping. It was as if she was standing on the sheer edge of something and all she'd have to do was jump for things to change. Who knows, perhaps staying wouldn't be the end of a road, after all.

She went to the old woman's door. Once she was certain that Fina was no longer crying, she walked in. "I'll do it," Maria told her.

She'd say nothing of it to anybody. Just like she kept the phone calls from Elio, she'd keep this, too. Because there was no need for him to know everything. Hadn't she always told him everything? Well, she had secrets now.

CHAPTER 33

IF HE COULDN'T have the Schwinn of his dreams, or its second-rate Chinese version, then the tallest bicycle would do. He, Elio Perez, was designer and builder of the tallest bicycle in Bauta—hell, probably the tallest bicycle on the island. "If you fly high, no one can touch you," his father had told him once. Well, he'd be flying high now. Holy, holy Lord! He'd be the envy of the town, rolling in style, riding high, flying high, loving life. He'd be the Orville Wright of Bauta, except on a bike—a very *tall* bike.

He stared at the thing in awe. The seat rose at least five feet from the floor. Only Frankenstein had been capable of more. He couldn't have been more proud. He even puffed his chest a little, like some young rooster. Hell, this was worthy of a world record. How the hell he had managed to weld together so many rusty parts, to get the chain back onto the mangled teeth, and bang the hell out of the dents on the metal, he wasn't sure. There was the field research, of course, and the interviewing, and the sketching—and, mostly, a whole lot of working out the kinks in his head.

"Feast your eyes on this," he told Pepe later that afternoon, opening the front door and pulling his hands away from his friend's eyes. Despite having had plenty of opportunities, Pepe had yet to apologize for not having helped him get the Chinese bike. Elio hoped that by inviting him over, he'd given Pepe one last chance to say he was sorry.

"Stop fucking around, brother. Guinness world records, Elio? What the fuck, repinga…I swear if I didn't know you any better, I'd think you'd caught dementia," Pepe inhaled and exhaled smoke.

What else could he expect from Pepe? Praise? At least he'd shown up—that was something.

"Dementia isn't syphilis, Pepe. I can't catch it," Elio said, feigning a smile.

"You don't need that shit, brother. You can have my bike."

Too late, Elio thought. "Now you're the one eating shit—keep it," he said. "I don't need your rusty, one-pedal piece of crap. Not when I have this beauty."

Elio didn't want to be the one to bring up the Chinese bike again. Or to continue demanding an answer from Pepe, a satisfactory explanation for Pepe's lack of support, for his not knowing how to be a real friend, for his cruel teasing. Perhaps offering Elio his bike was Pepe's apology, a gesture meant to rectify the consequences of his behavior. After all, Elio had never heard Pepe apologize to anyone except Maria and, even then, Elio'd been surprised. In any case, that had happened nearly fifteen years ago during Mariel—it shouldn't even count.

When Maria walked in an hour later, her reaction had been no different from her reaction each time during the past several days. She'd come into the house to find him tinkering with the bike—except it wasn't dementia she'd suggested. It was something worse.

Elio'd never seen her like that. She grabbed his arms and shook him; she couldn't even speak at first. "Is that what you've ended up with?" she said. "Are you purposely trying to ruin our marriage?"

Pepe turned to Elio. "You gotta listen to what your beautiful wife's trying to tell you, brother," he said.

"At last," Maria said, looking at Elio, but gesturing toward Pepe, "someone's taking my side in this house." Her voice didn't rise as it had minutes before, but was subdued, as if weighed down by Pepe's words.

Over the years, Maria had often been Elio's partner in crime, not his adversary. But Elio now felt like he could talk till he was blue in the face and she wouldn't really understand what having that bike, *at last,* felt like. Although she had clearly been furious, Elio now noted a difference in her face, an unspecifiable radiance. Then *she* struck him as a little changed. Pepe hadn't moved from his spot on the armchair near the window. And yet, he too looked different. Amid the chaos, the countless newspapers stacked one on top of the other risking collapse, and old clothes in ramshackle piles on the verge of toppling over; amid the shapeless mess of pots and pans, and bread crumbs rounding half-filled cups of coffee like makeshift necklaces, Pepe seemed confident—and almost hopeful. It was as though he and Maria were connected by a single promising thread.

"It's a bike. My bike. My Schwinn. I finished it," Elio said.

"I see," she said, calmly, taking a seat and looking first at Pepe, then up at Elio. "What are you planning on doing with it, exactly?"

Elio realized the transformation must have taken place somewhere between the time Maria walked through the door and the moment Pepe came out in her defense. The relative strangeness of Maria's exchange with Pepe had invaded the house as well. Now the typically dark living room seemed brighter, but also artificial and, worse, temporary. What were they playing at?

"Well, I was thinking I'll ride it," Elio said. "Being that it's a bike and all, that's the first thing that occurred to me. Riding a bike is like riding a bike. You know, you never forget." He couldn't get over the fact that Pepe had managed to calm Maria down and he hadn't. And what the hell was that all about? He imagined his mother's trembling hand reaching out toward the glass of water, perhaps in the swoon of being called out of this world.

"Please don't be angry with me," he sighed. "I couldn't take it if you were angry with me." *He was destroying their marriage?* Maria had behaved as though the bike were a malicious impulse at best and, at worst, a rejection of her.

"I'm tired of all of this," she said. Her arms pointed around their living room, everywhere at once, it seemed. She sounded angry still, and thwarted, and also helpless.

In a few days, fearful of what the neighbors would think, Maria demanded he tear the bike down. It took him some time to adjust to the idea, then it took him and Pepe just as long to break it down as it'd taken *him* to build it. Perhaps even more. It broke his heart to pull apart what he'd so lovingly, so carefully put together.

The wheels came off first, then the chain, and the pedals. At last came the handlebars, the extra-large grille, and the seat. Then there was everything else—all the screws, and washers, and bolts. When they were done, a pile of metal bones took up the center of the living room. Pepe mangled his fingers on the chain and shouted more repingas and recontrapingas than Elio was able to keep track of. As a result, Elio didn't take his eyes off him the entire time. Maria seemed unusually polite and buoyant, making coffee at least twice and showing her teeth way too much when Pepe noted her good spirits.

That night, before she left for Fina's house, Maria made a point of scorning him yet again. The bike, by then already in fragments, took a whole corner of the living room.

"Whatever made you waste your time with that pile of rust," she said. "You should give it up. It's just not possible. It will only make you unhappy."

She looked exhausted and Elio didn't know what to say. He lay in bed on his back, in his tattered boxer shorts, enduring her words, the damp heat, and the mosquito bites. If he didn't know any better, he would have thought that she was purposely trying to hurt him.

"I'm leaving for Fina's house," she finally said. "I'll be back later."

Elio didn't answer. He felt bitter. He let her walk away and was relieved when the door slammed behind her.

His mind was running a monologue. In a few days, it would be as though nothing had happened. I'm going to get a life. Any life. I will it. I have to will my life into being. The refrigerator makes its nocturnal sound and it's like whooping cough, repeatedly thawing and reforming the ice that clings to the freezer bin and drips into a puddle in the kitchen. Even that damn General Electric from God-only-knows-what decade couldn't pull it together. Why should I?

He twisted in bed, his arguments only noise that kept him from decent sleep. This was an island. He was trapped, goddamn it. Trapped. Nothing gave way. But he believed that he could change the things that seemed to resist change the most. Because he willed it. Because he desired it. Goddamn it—if he wanted a bike, why couldn't he have it? Not getting the bike, yet again, made him hungry. It was the kind of hunger he'd often felt in his youth. The kind of hunger that had once propelled him toward Maria. But now, it wasn't just Maria. And it wasn't just the bike. He wanted all of life. Everything. Every little crumb of it, every sliver, every morsel. If not, what good was an island? Because otherwise nothing made sense. Not even Maria.

He didn't want comfort, coño. He wanted miracles, goodness, and freedom. God, in whatever way it, he, she came. At whatever hour to take his breath away, to smite his heart with all that fathomless beauty. Horizons that receded the further he stretched his hands to grasp them, the further he spiraled into the abyss.

CHAPTER 34

WHEN MARIA WAS a little girl she rushed into everything. Typewriters and sewing machines propelled her forward. Life was in books, in imaginary landscapes. She swooned at shapes in the clouds, at rain falling onto asphalt, at her own body. She looked out to her lagoon and saw such different things. Heard music in the chirping of crickets and fireflies. But at some point, she woke up and life no longer had that special hurry. Perhaps that was old age, perhaps it was something else. Just like her body no longer remembered that fucking was good. Real good. That an orgasm was like a warm gushing of stars.

She no longer dreamed. And if she did, she didn't remember. Just like she didn't remember her keys, or her wallet sometimes. Because she'd lost desire, along with her good looks, and her dreams, and her books, and everything else. Life broke her. Not in a big way. But one hairline fracture at a time.

She sometimes fancied herself without Elio. On that day she fantasized about, she was truly herself. She imagined that she walked out the door. That she got on a plane and never came back. But it was useless. Because at her age, without children, without any skills other than connecting and disconnecting telephone cables, what could she do? Had technology outside the island moved on without her? Were there women plugging and unplugging day in and day out in Chicago, or New York, or LA? Where would she go? It had been a hundred years on an island and nothing had changed. Not much, not really. People were born, then they left or died, which was to say the same thing.

Sitting on the edge of her bed, she remembered all those people who'd left never to be heard from again. People like Nélida, and Martica, and so many others that she'd lost count. She tried to smile in an effort to console herself, but she just couldn't. Because when people left, she thought, they rarely ever remembered those they'd left behind. Just like she wouldn't remember any of it if she left. She'd lose that, too. They all lived on an island and it was not meant that they should travel far. It was not meant that they should dream, not even a little. Because dreaming clogged the brain with muck. Yes, that was old age—wasn't it? Youth's leftover green muck?

But when she thought about leaving Elio, she thought of wild flowers in Viñales, of stolen mangoes so fragrant she could have bathed in their juice, of those powder-blue clouds in the sky, and of her books. Her beautiful books, the ones she had long since discarded, with their equally beautiful heroines. Poor Emma, she thought. She'd tried so desperately to find out exactly the meaning of *bliss,* and passion, and ecstasy—words that had seemed so beautiful in books. Maria could see her, waving her down as she turned a corner and walked away. And she could see Elio, too. Small and skinny, like a twig. He'd always loved her more—and who could resist that?

CHAPTER 35

"I DWELL IN POSSIBILITY," said Elio, as he walked into the house. Newspaper in hand, he bore the look of someone who'd seen a truth unravel before his very eyes.

It had been at least a week since he and Maria had squabbled over his stupid bike and, although he was still plenty upset about it, more than anything he wanted to make life right again.

"Oh, Jesus Christ, here we go!" Maria said. Her face hidden by a pyramid of cornhusks. Propelled by the blades of a nearby fan, they soared through the air like kites and trailed off onto the kitchen floor. Each time she was lucky enough to make tamales, Maria would purposely place the fan close to the cornhusks. "I love to watch them take off," she'd tell Elio. "At least *they* get to go somewhere." In spite of the nuisance, Elio knew better than to move the fan.

"What's the matter, my pragmatic Penelope?" Elio asked. "Can't you see that possibility has now entered the room?" Elio brushed the cornhusks aside, and set the newspaper on the table. Leaned in and kissed Maria on the forehead.

"It's you. You have entered the room. Jesus Christ, you haven't been stealing books again—have you? Is this the *possibility* you've been talking about?" She shook her head and dropped her shoulders. Little drops of sweat quivered on her upper lip, and she brushed them off with the back of her hand.

"One could call it reading, my young kitchen mouse! While you perspire, my overactive sweat gland, I inspire. See the difference?"

"I'm tired, Elio—not now, please." She grabbed another piece of corn from a bucket. Ripped off the husk.

"Has my trotting centaur been handling too much lately? Let me help you—"

It took Maria a few seconds to reply. He hoped his odd little words full of love and mystique were having an appeasing effect on her.

"Your trotting centaur has been trotting all over town trying to figure out how the hell we are going to manage to eat," she said.

"Oh," said Elio, "I taste a liquor never brewed—come sit on me, my wild cactus." He slapped his thighs and called her to him.

She chuckled. "Have you been drinking? When are you going to grow up?"

From Maria's reaction, Elio deduced that he'd managed to erase the incident with the bike from her mind and that she wasn't entirely displeased with his attempt at making up. After all, he was measuring his words so they might express precisely the genuine passion for life she so deserved. Centaurs, odysseys, and liquors never brewed, he hoped, would have the cumulative effect of bringing Maria back into the realm of those who still believed in dreams.

"I'm working on it," he said.

"On what? What are you working on now?"

"Leave that to me, my little vermin—you'll see. Elio will surprise you." By the time he was done with his grand performance, neither he nor Maria remembered the bike—or the squabble over it.

Maria was right, Elio had found the trail back to Cervantes. It was all about *Don Quixote* then—the rest was a blur, even Maria. This time, though, he didn't have to steal it. At the end of that summer of 1980, before she left for Opa-locka on a bowrider and for reasons Elio couldn't figure out, Mirta El Moco, Bauta's librarian, had a change of heart. She'd stolen the book back and given it to Elio. "Here," she'd said, "a goodbye present." To Elio, Mirta's gesture was simply one of the great ironies that kept his beloved island afloat.

That "Night of Cervantes," as Elio liked to call it, Maria slept soundly under the mosquito net while he embarked on his first sally. He read all night, turning to one side, then the other—his body restless, his muscles twitching, as if they, too, heard the call.

Reading *Quixote* was like a slight twinge, that—as he kept thinking about it, long after the page was done and the book was set aside—became an unbearable pain, even—why the hell not—a certain kind of joy. Because the more he tried to wrap his head around it, the more he understood the knight's journey. It was the human spirit, Elio thought, that propelled Quixote forward. A force that spoke through him, but wasn't him.

To Elio, Cervantes was a prophet. It was as if he'd looked right into the Spaniard's preternatural eyes and known it all. The worst of it was that he couldn't talk to anybody about it. Sure, *Don Quixote* was a masterpiece and read the world over, but who the hell on an island where other matters—like eating—pressed, would care about an old guy on a horse galloping across the plains of La Mancha? Elio was so confused about it all; he didn't know where La Mancha began and the island ended. La Mancha, the stain, the scribble, the green muck on it all. It was as if someone had purposefully spilled ink on some fundamental truth—what was it, damn it?

He felt sorry for the old knight too. So sorry that he was certain there couldn't have been a reader in the world who felt as sorry as he did. Who understood *DQ* as much as he did, as painfully as he did? Nobody, that's who.

CHAPTER 36

IT WAS NOVEMBER, and the downpours of early fall seemed to be behind them. After stopping at the bodega for her ration of milk and loaf of bread, Maria arrived home from work that day to an empty house. Elio was nowhere to be found. She wasn't sure where he'd gone, or why, or what time he'd be back. That morning he had left for work as usual, but she had noticed that he was fidgety. She tried to ask him about it, but he brushed it off and blamed it on the thirty-year-old mattress. Too thin to let me fall asleep, he said. But she knew there must have been something else. He was quieter than most mornings.

Imagining that Elio would turn up sooner or later, sometime after dinner, Maria walked to Fina's house in the dark. She knocked, but no one responded. Using the key the old woman had given her days earlier, she let herself in. Fina was nowhere around, but she'd left the lights on and a note on the kitchen counter: *Gone to study the Bible in Punta Brava.* Maria rolled her eyes, and threw away the note.

She fastened a red scarf to her head and looked around. There was little to do, really. Dust a bit, mop the floor, tidy up the kitchen, starch and iron the old woman's handkerchiefs and pillowcases, and wipe down picture frames. On most days of chores, Maria tended to Fina's house with Fina sitting close by talking up a storm. It was as though the old woman only really wanted her companionship and nothing else.

She'd been considerate enough to write her a note, Maria thought. Notes were wonderful when they were full of answers such as "Be back after lunch," and "Closed until further notice"; or, better yet, like the ones she often found on her table at the telephone company: "No point coming to work tomorrow, we're all staying home," or the note about her annoying boss, "Yenisleydis's a rat." Fina's note, she thought, had in it nothing she wanted or needed to know. And because it left her with as many questions as she already had when she walked through the door, she almost wished there had been no note at all.

It was fall but nothing at Fina's house that night gave away the season. In keeping with weather patterns for that time of year, it was sunny and the temperature was a comfortable 76 degrees; nothing on the island could have warned her that winter was only months away. Sweating, Maria nudged the day's crumbs on the kitchen table toward a cupped hand. She thought of Chicago. According to her old Sears catalogue, now *that* was a fall that mattered. Fall was *Save on thousands of seasonable needs* and *more than a thousand price cuts.* In the pages of the catalogue, yellow, orange, and red leaves piled up along city and country roads, or blew in the wind. Seasons in Chicago, she was convinced, made a dent in people's souls—or better yet, mirrored people's souls.

Here the island of eternal summers, except for the occasional winter chill that often required nothing more than an old sweater, denied any possibility of change. Perhaps this was why life seemed to move slowly, because it wasn't working itself up to some ultimate transformation. Life on the island moved at the speed of a turtle. A hundred-year-old turtle, she thought, pinching the sagging skin on her neck between her index finger and thumb.

She'd been cleaning Fina's house for a few months now. She'd grown accustomed to the beautiful bidet, with its silver faucet, the Sevrès porcelain tea sets, the silverware, the *terry cotton* towels, and the RCA Victor gramophone—with all her records: Benny Moré, and Rolandito La Serie, and Lecuona, and Perez Prado, and Been Crosbee, Luis Armstron, Ella Fitzgeral...And *of course* Beelee Holeethay. It was all *so fabulous, so number-one*—how could she not be *one hundred percent* in love with it? Fina was easy, a good woman at heart. Maria hoped that all her hard work would one day pay off. Perhaps Fina would leave for Coral Gables before the five years ended, and she and Elio would move into her house sooner. Their lives would change then. Falling houses brought people down. Maria had given up on her own house a long time ago.

All she needed to do was to put more shoulder into it, tend to Fina more. If she got really lucky, the old woman would take pity on her. Because deep inside, Maria was afraid Fina had made a promise she wouldn't be able to keep. Perhaps Maria was being too gullible and shouldn't rely on an old woman's promise. If Fina's family in South Florida ever decided to claim ownership of the house, blood would be thicker than water. And Maria would never get the house. Although Fina was full of good intentions, Maria would be no match for family trauma spanning over thirty years.

A few hours later, Fina returned and Maria went home. When she walked into her own house, she found Elio sitting at the kitchen table, a finger in a bucket petting an oversized red goldfish.

"Isn't he beautiful?" he asked, taking Maria's hand and crouching next to the bucket. "Isn't he perfect?"

"How do you know it's a he, Elio? Maybe it's a she and now you're confusing it."

"Ay, Maria, you'll never understand."

At this point, she didn't need to understand. She was so used to Elio's quirks that she no longer found them strange. Although he was becoming quirkier, harder to figure out than when he was younger. Perhaps that's what men did as they got older—they simply became stranger and stranger, until one day you could no longer recognize them. She needed to concentrate her attention on the issue at hand: getting Fina's house. But as far as understanding Elio, she needed nothing to do with that.

That night Elio stayed up until dawn, finishing the last chapters of *Don Quixote.* He'd waited for hours for Maria to fall asleep. When she finally did, he slid out of bed, and tiptoed into the living room. He pulled the book out from beneath a clump of newspapers, and sat down to read. In the bucket, close by, the red goldfish opened and closed his mouth near the water's surface.

Over the years, Elio had been accused of being everything from dreamer, to coward, to gusano, to crazy, to thief, and so many other things he hadn't cared to keep track. But no one had ever accused him of loving Maria too much. So, when near dawn he finally reached the hendecasyllabic verses that conclude *Don Quixote, Part I,* something in him stirred. He felt vindicated. Reaching the first line, he looked down at the fish.

"See," he whispered, pointing at the page. "It's all right here, little fellow. But you already knew that, didn't you?" Elio made sure to read quietly, but he read anyway:

"She, whose full features may be here descried,
High-bosomed, with a bearing of disdain,

Is Dulcinea, she for whom in vain
The great Don Quixote of La Mancha sighed.
For her, Toboso's queen, from side to side
He traversed the grim sierra, the Champaign
Of Aranjuez, and Montiel's famous plain:
On Rocinante oft a weary ride.
Malignant planets, cruel destiny,
Pursued them both, the fair Manchegan dame,
And the unconquered star of chivalry.
Nor youth nor beauty saved her from the claim
Of death; he paid love's bitter penalty,
And left the marble to preserve his name."

"Ha," he said to the fish, "that Don Quixote knew one thing: love. Love that was always at a distance." He could follow the game or ignore it, Elio thought, but it wasn't just a pastime. It was a battle to the death. What a sad bastard. So sad it almost broke Elio's heart. If Elio didn't know any better, he would have thought Don Quixote lived on an island, too.

CHAPTER 37

ELIO HAD MOST certainly experienced more comfortable nights than
those he spent with Don Quixote, lying on his stomach and fending off
mosquitoes somewhere in La Mancha. But he had learned valuable lessons
in the process. One, he hated mosquitoes. Two, given the size of his gut,
in spite of the famine, he had no business lying on it—it was simply too
damn uncomfortable. Three, previously stolen books were almost always
a good read, for various reasons. Four, he wasn't as much of a coward as
he'd thought he was. In fact, every attempt he'd made to improve his and
Maria's condition, every effort at creating something for him had been an
act of courage. The Lee pitusas, the new job—all of it. Even reading he'd
done for Maria. And finally five, perhaps the most important one: if given
the chance, people could surprise you. It was this last one that came to
Elio's mind when, nearing the end of the fall, he found Pepe weeping in
the storage room at the textilera.

Pepe was crouched down, with his back against the wall. His face in
the palms of his hands.

Men crying were a peculiar thing, Elio thought. It was neither pitiful
nor heroic, but somewhere in between. Elio had never cried much, and he

sure as hell never imagined Pepe ever had. So when he came near him and tried to speak, he choked on his words a little.

"What's the matter?" he said, working his tongue around a dry mouth.

"You wouldn't fucking get it, repinga," Pepe said. His hands were shaking so much now his words came out almost in Morse code.

Elio took a look around to avoid Pepe's eyes. He heard the hiss of nearby machinery join his friend's gurgled sobs in some sort of unfortunate symphony. He noticed a little plastic bag with pills near Pepe's shoes. Jesus Christ…diazepam?

"Okay, get up," Elio finally said. "Get up, c'mon—what the hell's gotten into you?" He gripped Pepe's arm to pull him up, but his friend flicked him away.

"Leave me the fuck alone, Elio—you can walk this one away."

"What the hell are you talking about? What's the matter? Is it your mom?"

"My mom's fine. She's in a fucking nursing home in Tampa. It's not my fucking mom. Get a clue, repinga—it's Celia."

"Okay, get up," Elio whispered. "Get up, coño, before somebody comes in here and catches you sobbing like a goddamn willow. Gimme that," Elio said, snatching the bag of diazepam from the floor and stuffing it into his pants pocket.

Pepe stood up. His face was swollen, his eyes smaller than usual. From skipping out on work now and then to shoot the breeze at the beach, Elio expected. Sudden bursts of anger over the smallest turd on his shoe, he expected. But crying in the storage room over a woman who gave him weekly blow jobs against the wall in the courtyard, Elio did not expect. This was a new one—and it was a good one, too. It was the one he couldn't wrap his bald head around. Elio could only imagine that, in spite of the casualness with which Pepe had gone about his relationship with Celia, the guy had ended up fucking it all up and falling in love.

"Let's take a walk. C'mon," Elio patted his friend's back so gently that Pepe turned to look at him.

"I'm not a goddamn invalid, you know. Don't worry, I wasn't planning to overdose on diazepam. It was for my nerves. Elsa La Gorda gave it to me this morning—she thought it'd help."

"Elsa knew about this and *I* fucking didn't? You're starting to piss me off, you know that. Can you just tell me what the hell happened? Wait, let me guess, she's leaving for Tampa and you can't live without her." Elio said, mockingly.

"Shut the fuck up or I'm gonna have to break your head in two," Pepe interrupted him before he could say another word.

"Okay, look—just come out with it."

"Celia left last night."

"Jesus Christ."

"Yup—gone to Tampa on some rickety raft with a refrigerator engine and an old propeller. Fuck—she's gonna get torn up by the sharks, man." The sobbing started again. This time he hid his face in his shirt collar.

"Did you love that woman?" Elio's body shook. He couldn't help but imagine a shark circling Celia's raft, tipping it over. Then a great splash.

Pepe looked frantically in his pockets for a cigarette. When he finally found one, he lit it, and took a puff.

"You're an idiot," he said, letting out smoke through his nose. He seemed suddenly recovered.

Sounds came from everywhere at once: the clattering and whooshing of machines, the whistling of valves, and voices barking out orders with sharp determination, as though the world was about to end, not only for Pepe—but for everyone.

"Look, I'm trying to understand here, but you're not giving me much to go on, you know," Elio said.

Pepe's crying was lovely, in a way. It somehow made him much more likable. Elio needed that. He needed to feel that Pepe, at least once, was less equipped to deal with life than he was. He wasn't happy for his friend's current misery. No, of course not. He was relieved. Relieved that it hadn't been him crying in front of Pepe. Of course, according to Pepe, he already had.

"I've known it was coming for a long time," Pepe said. "But I wasn't as ready as I thought I'd be."

There Elio learned that he'd misunderstood the whole thing. It hadn't been the weather. It wasn't he who triggered Pepe's strange mood nearly a month earlier when Pepe called him so many names. Names like "shrimp" and "little bitch who'd lost a ball" and "sorry-ass whining little prick." He almost wanted to use Celia's leaving to explain Pepe's betrayal about the Chinese bicycle, but there was nothing that would excuse that. Not even that it was 1994 and people did what they had to do to survive.

That afternoon, as Pepe cried over a woman who'd left him high and cold for a better life in Tampa, Elio learned of the kinds of subcutaneous connections people make when pummeled by life's miseries. He learned from Pepe that, on the island, diazepam was a one-in-all cure, after trabajitos and inner tubes floating to Miami. He learned that Pepe was human. And he learned that the sadder and stranger the reality around him, the less waterproof it was and the worse he felt, the more he thought about his father. He learned that the only thing that truly frightened him was water, because it was all around him—the most frightening of all knowledge. Most importantly, he learned that Pepe had a certain kind of troubled heart that neither Cervantes, nor diazepam, nor he—Elio— had anticipated.

"Someone's put a hex on me," Pepe finally said, taking a puff on his cigarette. "Sprinkled day-old piss on my door or frozen the shit out of me."

"Listen, you're either gonna make it through her leaving with a clenched heart or you won't. But you gotta pull it together."

"I just have to wait," Pepe said, contemplating the end of his burning cigarette.

"Wait for what?"

"Wait. I have to figure this shit out, repinga. I can't just let it all end like this."

CHAPTER 38

PEPE DIDN'T DREAM of Chicago. He dreamt of Tampa and its
stainless-steel minarets. Its Riverwalk and sparkling beaches, its sprawling
urban centers and pot-bellied retirees strolling endless golf courses year-
round while chomping on three-inch steaks and fries and slurping mojitos
to waterfront views and bay breezes. Ybor City, Tampa *Baai*. Cuba City,
the mecca of the world. The Al-Andalús of the New World, Celia told
him once. Cubans, Sicilians, Germans, Romanians, and Jews. Tampa,
because it was the crossroads to Cuba. Land in Tampa, party in Ybor City,
and catch a ferry to Havana. The whole thing had sounded strange to
Pepe, so he'd pressed Celia to clarify and she'd said, "Don't tampa with the
blues in Tampa," which was a great thing because Pepe'd always, *always*
loved the blues.

How the hell she'd make it to Tampa Bay on a raft, Pepe couldn't
fathom. He also couldn't fathom what he'd do, if he ever made it there.
Before leaving, Celia'd told him that he could be a lector in a cigar store,
even if he'd never been a reader—they were all full of Cubans from
Artemisa, she'd say, who also didn't like to read. "They roll Dominican
cigars, mi amor, made from tobacco grown from Cuban seed," she'd say.

Celia was crazy, una loca, arrebatá. Pepe didn't know a lot of things, but he knew tobacco changed its flavor based on the place it had grown. A Cuban seed planted anywhere else would not taste identical to the one planted in Cuba—it was as simple as that. But Celia didn't know what she was saying. Plus, she was leaving, and Pepe hadn't wanted to break her heart. He missed her, cojones. He missed her more than she ever knew. "The Cuban sandwich, Pepe, was invented in Tampa," she'd say. "José Martí has his own park, cariño. Tampa's the place to be."

And she would cook for him, she'd said. And they'd eat and eat and eat, and they'd go shopping and he would mow the lawn and paint the house once a year, and they'd have all the things that they'd never had in their lives. And they'd make love and protect each other and there would be goodness and trust and quiet between them, and so much love. Yes, so much love. But she was gone.

What was he supposed to do now, swim all the way to Tampa?

CHAPTER 39

THE SAME YEAR Celia left, a man accused Pepe of treason. Elio did not know the man very well. He was short, with limbs that swung way too far from his body when he walked. And a glistening forehead that—when he stuttered, which he most certainly did when pressed for information— dropped beads of sweat onto a thin upper lip. Had Elio allowed himself to muse deeply, he would have called him disturbing or disturbed. But the man was none of those things. He was a whistle-blower, and that was the worst thing anybody could be.

Nobody knew where he'd come from, although some thought he was from the neighboring towns of Punta Brava or Bejucal. What he was doing in Bauta, Elio could only speculate. Some said he'd been a chemistry teacher, until an explosion nearly killed one of his students. He'd survived, but had been left with the ga-ga-ga. Others swore they'd seen him before, but couldn't remember where. And then there were those who said he'd been an artist at the San Alejandro Academy, but had been kicked out in the 70s for God knows what and forced to rehabilitate by cutting sugarcane.

There were lots of things Elio didn't know. But he was certain this guy was dripping in bullshit. Couldn't they tell he was robbing them blind one black bean at a time? The man had taken over the bodega a year earlier and, since then, he'd ratted out half of Bauta. The other half had joined him. He was both a thief *and* a whistle-blower—the guy was metralla.

"Look," Elio'd told Maria over coffee, banging his nearly empty cup on the table. "I gotta talk to Pepe. Celia's leaving has made him vulnerable to suspicion. They'll accuse him of whatever they want."

"Don't talk to him here. And don't even think of doing it at work."

"In Caimito?"

"Why there?" she said, dabbing spilled coffee grounds with the end of the tablecloth. "It's at least thirty minutes away."

"Well, it's not Bauta. There won't be anyone around to pry into our conversation. It's about privacy, Maria," he said. "When Pepe comes for me on his way to work, tell him to meet me in Caimito."

"Where exactly in Caimito?" she furrowed her forehead.

"The Cave of Paredones. You know, the one with the petroglyphs and the idols."

"Good idea," Maria said, getting up to close the shutters to prevent Elio's voice from seeping out to the street. "Does Pepe know you've got his bike? How's he supposed to get there?"

"Well, I didn't steal it, if that's what you mean. He left it here last night, so I plan on using it. As far as getting there, he'll figure it out."

Elio'd thought it strange that Pepe would have opted to walk home the night before—after all, his bike was in relatively good condition. But Elio hadn't had the chance to question Pepe's reasoning, as Pepe'd walked out and Elio didn't notice until later that his friend had left the bike behind.

Buoyed by a sense of honesty and justice, and perhaps even keen to leave Bauta behind for at least a couple of hours, Elio planned to leave the next morning for the Cave of Paredones. It was a Sunday, and he had pressing matters—like Pepe—to tend to. As far as he knew, Roberto Salas hadn't denounced Pepe yet, but given the guy's reputation for being an SOB, Elio was sure he would, in due time. He wanted to warn Pepe. He didn't want that no-good piece of shit to take Pepe by surprise.

"We gotta figure this thing out, Pepe and me," he'd told Maria. "If we don't, they'll make Pepe's life a living hell, then ours. We'd be guilty by association, yet again." It was 5:30 a.m. and the sun was beginning to raise its hot head above the roofs. Maria was making coffee on the stovetop and burning bread on a small frying pan. The smoke shrouded the kitchen and rippled through the rest of the house.

"Where are you going this early?" she asked, smoke tearing up her eyes.

"I gotta meet Pepe, remember?…Something's burning in there," he chuckled.

"I like my toast charred…and, yes, I remember."

"I'll be back later," Elio said, running in quickly to kiss her temple. She shook it off.

Elio knew she was upset about the bike. She couldn't stand the fact that he'd have to take anything from Pepe. Plus, if Pepe *had* a bike it was because he'd been doing the funky chicken with nearly every woman at the textilera—married, single, or divorced. But she didn't know Pepe like he did. She didn't know that behind all those repingas and chest hair was a beating heart making do with what little life had given him. Plus, he owed Pepe his life. The one working ball he'd wrestled away from that shark decades ago was still swinging because of Pepe.

Pepe's bike leaned against a wall in the living room. It was old and rusty, a Soviet-made MB3, with back-pedal brakes, and handlebars shorn of handgrips. Not the kind of bike Elio had always imagined himself riding down La Loma de Pita, but it was a bike—and it worked.

Maria banged pots and pans against the counter in the kitchen as he readjusted the bike's blackened chain, wiped his hands on a rag, and opened the front door. He steered the bike through the threshold. Hands gripping the handlebars, he swung one leg over the dented metal seat and adjusted his crotch. It'd be a bumpy ride all the way to Caimito so he might as well protect his unfortunate crotch as best he could. One leg on the floor, the other one on what was left of the pedal, he pushed forward until he made it out to the porch and onto the sidewalk. It had been decades since he'd ridden a bike. Shit, he hadn't even been able to ride the one he built before Maria'd made him tear it down.

The street was empty, although that meant nothing—there was always someone peering behind shutters. Elio wanted to avoid being seen at all costs. He was hoping to turn Caimito's Cave of Paredones into a place he could use to talk to Pepe openly about the possible denunciation, without the need to whisper or close the shutters. He hoped that together he and Pepe could come up with a preemptive plan to stop the denunciation in its tracks. The cave, with its natural skylight and mysterious drawings, was a place he'd visited with his father once or twice before. Elio thought he remembered it well. He needed to protect it.

Lately Elio'd noticed more vigilance and he'd learned to recognize who was watching and when: someone's grandmother, at once both fragile and threatening, with her seemingly innocent requests for a pinch of salt or a tablespoon of sugar, concealed the real reason she'd knocked on your door: to take a quick inventory of all that was inside; underweight middle-age women on a diet of gofio and sugary water who stood around gossiping only feet from your porch or who followed closely behind as you walked down the street; or strange cars that slowed down next to you or parked behind a sign as you passed by.

Elio'd done his best to ignore the people and the cars, often changing his route or crossing over to the opposite sidewalk when he spotted them. Sometimes, to avoid having to walk past or approach them directly, he would pretend to be distracted by stray dogs on the street or by the sound of sputtering engines on main roads. Other times they were impossible to avoid because he ran into them unexpectedly with no opportunity to change direction, so ubiquitous was their presence in his life, and in the life of the island.

Right when he was about to pedal off, someone stepped onto a porch directly across from him. On the other side of the street, Teresa, his decrepit neighbor, threw her matutine bucket of urine on the tile. He'd timed it wrong, or she was late. Hair like a tousled crane, naked under a mostly see-through white gown, she was more like a character from a horror movie than a woman. Every morning without fail, right before sunrise, she came out with a bucket of her fresh unnameable. A surefire way to ward off the evil eye. Jesus Christ—hadn't she heard of an onyx?

She wasn't harmless, either. Had a tongue as long and venomous as a serpent. He raised the obligatory hand in her general direction and took off down the street. If he was lucky, Teresa'd be too freaking fogged up by the steam of her own piss to remember she ever saw him. Though he surmised that his fumbling about with the bike on the porch, and his departure at the crack of dawn when the rest of Bauta was sleeping, might in fact dog-ear the moment in time for her. More from instinct than reason, she must have thought that his rushing about and *his* general state of vigilance, as far as she could see from across the street, was worthy of suspicion. Elio wondered how many of the people walking about, the people peering through their semi-closed shutters, were whistle-blowers. More than he cared to know, he guessed.

He passed the water tank, made a right at the corner, and pedaled as swiftly as potholes allowed toward the Carretera Central. He avoided the bodega completely. The trip would be easy. He'd reach the Farm El Pilar and, from there, the town of Anafe. Caimito would be right around the corner.

It took Elio an eternity to pedal Pepe's rickety Russian bike from Bauta to what some called the *curba asesina*. The bike was truly a near-lethal combination of shoddy engineering and obligatory overuse. He had to work so hard to keep the bike steady on the road that his arms were cramping up and his legs were starting to buckle. It was miles beyond the last intersection where he would turn left and head south. This last turn, the one before venturing closer to Caimito, was in yet another rural community with houses so fragile the sight of a whirlwind would have been enough to send them spinning through the air. Truly, there was Havana and nothing else. Beyond it, all was country. And even then, if it weren't for Vedado, Havana was just as provincial as the rest of the island.

It was about 6:15 a.m. when he reached Caimito. Thick shrubs prevented him from riding the bike to the cave. He had to dismount and walk the rest of the way. Large, rounded mogotes rose like sleeping giants a mile or so from the road. Linked, mossy hills with steep, nearly vertical walls were surrounded by flat land. He pressed the bike through the dry, prickling shrubs until he reached his destination.

It was still early morning and, thanks to the cave's natural skylight, there was enough light beyond the entrance that Elio could easily see where he was going. Nonetheless, and anticipating greater darkness as he moved beyond the main chamber, he took out a lighter and walked in as far as he could. The air inside was cool. He panned a flickering flame across the wall, thinking of the first time he'd visited the caves with his father. "This is something magical," his dad had told him. "This is Cuba's past. When Cuba was taína, and its people called it cubanacán, jardín o tierra labrada." Just as Elio remembered, there were five petroglyphs: an almost life-size naked woman, a dog, a seat or bench, and a snake. There were four idols, each carved on a stalagmite, out of which two had always stood out to Elio: the first one was a human-looking idol about a foot and a half high; the second one, two feet in height, he'd never been able to make out. This last one had no human-like body details, but it displayed a head with a double-sided face, front and back—there it is, he laughed, a two-faced monster. It was believed that while the drawings were probably already there before Colón's arrival on the island, African slaves, who used the caves for religious ceremonies, were responsible for the idols.

As he moved the flame closer, something else caught his attention. Above the snake was what looked like a scratching or the markings of an irregular circle.

He moved the little flame closer to the wall. He couldn't believe his eyes. The snake was there, but so were the round markings, right above it. What the hell was that? Had he discovered something new? Elio imagined himself poised behind a podium in one of the biggest halls at the University of Havana:

"Compañeros," he'd say, "I've made a great discovery. Underneath the great plain that takes you through karst country south of the province of Havana, there are numerous caves whose galleries extend approximately 2,000 feet long until they are lost in a lake water table. Formerly known as Cueva de San Antonio, the cave mouths or entries are located very close to the road that joins Ceiba del Agua with Alquízar. On one of their walls, there lies what to the untrained eye looks like mere markings, but are in fact, and upon closer and expert examination…"

A tall, thin gentleman in the audience suddenly interrupts his speech: "Have you seen the fish?" the gentleman asks, a scraggly beard quivering as he speaks. "Can you grasp its length and breadth?"

"Indeed!" Elio exclaims, puffing up his chest toward an audience of bald academics from all dusty corners of the world, "a giant fish swimming in a vast ocean—so big that when an aboriginal hand attempted to draw it on the cave's wall, it could do nothing more than scratch one uppermost scale. To speak of the markings on the cave's wall, ladies and gentlemen, is to speak of a scale, but also to recognize a cipher, and a universal truth."

Only now did he realize the meaning of all that water. He wasn't stuck in a bucket, was he? There was water. Water all around. All he had to do was find his way back to it. This was huge. In his mind, at least, everything made sense.

He felt in his throat a kind of vibration, rippling to other parts of his body. First to his shoulders, followed by his heart muscle that spasmed, then remained quite still; then to the pit of his stomach, his groin, his thighs, his kneecaps that rattled like tin pans, and all the way to the tip of his toes. It simply felt like he'd actually found something worth escaping for, a kind of destination. What he had before his eyes could be something. It had to be something. He needed it to be.

If he never missed having a camera before, he missed it now. How he wished he could take a picture of the wall. Maria wouldn't believe him without it. Why hadn't Elio ever noticed the markings before? Everyone knew about the drawings, but the markings? Pepe wouldn't believe him, either. He'd need to see it with his own eyes. In a few hours, though, he would.

Elio wanted to touch the markings, but stopped himself for fear of smearing or erasing them. Fuck, this was something really special, he thought. Something like a sign. Like the goddamn sign he'd been waiting for. He walked out of the cave into the sunlight. Nobody would believe him. Or worse, nobody would care.

He waited around for hours, but Pepe never made it. Elio concluded perhaps he'd overestimated Pepe's ability to find a ride to Caimito. After all, with gasoline ever scarcer on the island, transportation had become a real goddamn challenge. At first, Elio didn't worry about his friend, but soon he began to imagine a second scenario. What if they'd caught him making some kind of shady deal with a tourist, like buying foreign merchandise, or exchanging dollars? Elio thought about tourists then, how ugly they were. How rancid they smelled, like spoiled canned goods. He'd rather starve than transact with any of them, because they never came to really enjoy, to really understand. They came to stare at the fish bowl. To walk around snapping pictures of old cars, and old furniture, and old buildings. Turning poverty and hunger and decades of deterioration into panoramic views, coffee table books, and beautiful postcards.

An hour passed, then two. There was no sign of Pepe. Elio passed the time sleeping, exploring adjacent chambers, then sleeping again. Although hungry at first, he gradually forgot about the pangs in his stomach, so accustomed was he to going without food these days. In any case, if he was hungry, so were the nearly eleven million Cubans living on the island, the thought of whom made him feel like he wasn't alone, after all. By 5:00 p.m. it was clear Pepe wasn't coming. Me cago en su madre, Elio thought. Something better have happened to him.

Elio left the cave, pedaling swiftly all the way back to Bauta. The late-afternoon sun turned billboards and roadside towns into a mirage. Uphill, he stood on the pedals and gripped the handlebars. On the way down, he let go of the handlebars completely, grunting once or twice when the smell of manure from the Farm Villa Paz irritated his nostrils.

He felt both strained about Pepe and also excited about what he'd found on the cave's wall. His only regret: no one else had been there to see it. When he passed a motorbike or two, he waved with both hands in the air. "Eh, compay!" he shouted.

He made it to the giant, metallic tank at the end of the block, panting from both excitement and exhaustion. His legs weren't what they used to be and his thigh muscles spasmed a little. "Eh!" he heard somebody shout, from inside the bodega, "How was Caimito?" Fuck.

Jesus Christ. It was Roberto Salas, el bodeguero. How the hell did he know Elio had been in Caimito?

CHAPTER 40

"OYE, REPINGA, where the hell were you yesterday?" Pepe whispered in his ear the following day. He slapped Elio's back so hard, he knocked the air out of him. "What's going on? Stepping out on Maria in the middle of the day or what?"

They were in one of the break rooms at the textilera, amid the continuous ripple of the long ply-frames, the rhythm of hopping bobbins and revolving cards, the grinding sound of the looms, the heat, and the terrible ventilation.

"Or what," Elio said, raising his voice just enough for Pepe to make out his answer. "Do you know that I waited for you for at least four hours?"

"So, I kept you waiting? What am I now, your girlfriend?" Pepe said, his eyes fixed on the tip of his cigarette.

Elio wished he could tell Pepe about the cave markings, but he understood that the conversation would go nowhere. "We gotta talk," he whispered, turning on a small fan near his feet. The sound of his voice mingled with the sound of the fan blades and the labored rhythm of the machines that spilled vapor and lint everywhere. With ears trained like his own, however, Pepe heard him without difficulty.

"Alright, alright," Pepe hushed. "How was I supposed to get there? By motorized pinga? You had my goddamn bike. I want it back, by the way. I gotta be frank, compañero, people are starting to wonder where the fuck you were," he said, more smoke than words.

"Yeah, I know. And don't worry, I brought your bike with me. You can have your second-hand piece of junk today," Elio said. "We need to talk."

The smell of chlorine in the air was stronger than usual and it made Elio want to gag.

"I know we need to talk, repinga. My mind's a little tied up with Celia right now. Fuck. What the hell am I supposed to do, brother? Here," he said, reaching in his shirt pocket and pulling out a cigarette, "have a smoke and calm the fuck down."

Elio ignored the offer. "You're supposed to mourn Celia, at least."

"Very funny."

"Funny, yes," Elio said.

"Listen, brother," Pepe whispered, throwing his arm over Elio's shoulders. "I settled a big debt with some Italian guy yesterday—"

"Is that where you were?" Elio said, looking around quickly in the direction of the door to see if there was anyone around who might be listening. Elio could hear enough voices nearby to make him uncomfortable about discussing at the textilera anything having to do with tourists and dollars.

"Yeah, on my lunch break…you ask too many questions," Pepe said, slipping an envelope into Elio's hand. "This is for you, so you can get the hell out. The situation here's only gonna get worse, mi hermano."

Elio opened the envelope. Inside it, a crisp one-hundred-dollar bill. Somehow, the situation had reversed, and it was Pepe helping him, not he warning Pepe.

"Where the hell did you get this? I can't take it, Pepe." Elio pushed the envelope to Pepe's chest.

"Celia sent it to me. It's for you—I won't need it."

"Celia or your mom?"

"What are you talking about? My mom's in a home. Don't you think that if my mom had a wad of cash lying around she would have sent it to me already? Find a way to get out," he said, shoving the envelope in Elio's hand. "Do it, cojones."

"Alright, alright," Elio said. "I'll keep it."

Next Saturday, Elio was back in the cave. He'd brought some provisions this time: a small canteen with water, some day-old bread with something like mayonnaise, a box of matches, and a magnifying glass. None of which he'd use. All he really needed was time to think. If he told Pepe now, he'd think he'd lost his mind. If he told Maria—he couldn't tell Maria. Not yet. What would he tell her, anyway? That he'd found some indigenous scribbling on the wall of some cave and that he was sure it was the sign he'd been waiting for? That, yes, water would be the only way out of the island? But that everyone had understood it all wrong?

In the days that followed, Elio couldn't shake off the giant fish. Something told him that if he could figure out how to get back in the water, everything would change. But if he hadn't been so wrapped up in his own goddamn life, he would have known that everything was changing already.

CHAPTER 41

ABOUT A WEEK after his last trip to the caves of Caimito, Elio walked into the therapist's office. He was due for a yearly checkup. This time, however, Roberto Salas, the man Elio suspected would likely denounce Pepe, was in the room—along with his bushy eyebrows and Fila t-shirt.

"What the hell is this?" Elio shouted.

"Take a seat, Elio," the therapist said.

"What the hell is *he* doing here?"

"He's come across some issues we can't easily ignore." His face turned to Roberto Salas sitting to his right. "Tell him, compañero."

"The-the," Roberto Salas stuttered, "the thing is that-that I caught you in the Cave of Paredones."

"And?" That fucking rat. Elio sat down. His spine stiff, erect against the back of the chair. He couldn't believe his ears. No wonder the guy had questioned him on his way back from the cave. He must have been following him all along. Unfortunately, Elio hadn't been aware of anyone; perhaps his concern for Pepe had kept him so engrossed that, if there had been someone following him, he simply hadn't noticed.

"And he believes that you were defacing a national treasure."

"Look," Elio said, breathing from his belly to regain composure. "I was—"

"The truth is we've had enough, Elio. This whole thing has gone too far, you know what I mean? Too far."

Elio's face tensed up. The stale cigar smoke in the room dried out his throat. He remained silent.

"Look, I caught you s-s-scratching out those drawings on the wall," he puffed out his words like smoke.

"They're not drawings," Elio said. Idiot. "They're—"

"What should you care what's on those walls? Since when were you appointed historian?"

This guy was a ñame.

"I think what the compañero means," the therapist said, "is that you are not authorized to go where you're not supposed to without official permission—otherwise, we might be inclined to consider it trespassing."

"And what places would those be, exactly?" Elio said, this time unable to keep his mouth zipped up.

"Here's the thing. We're willing to forget the whole thing, on one condition."

"What condition is that?"

"Tell us what Pepe Fernández is up to."

Elio's blood went cold. It was just as he'd suspected all along.

"Where's Pepe?" were the only words he could muster. Elio was afraid Pepe could have been detained for one of those petty crimes they considered counterrevolutionary or simply outside the party line—like buying meat in the black market, or growing a pig in your backyard, or dealing with tourists. Without the right to legal counsel, wherever Pepe was, he'd be staying there for some time.

"We were hoping that you could tell us that. He didn't show up to work today. Did you know that?"

"Ah, he's probably—you know—shacking up with someone or other. The guy's a tiger, you know."

"Nah, we think it's something else," the therapist said.

"Like what?"

"Again, we were hoping that *you* could tell us."

"Well, I can't."

"We think you can. We think that you are just the person to tell us."

What they were asking him to do was unthinkable. What was it that they thought Pepe was doing anyway? Did they think he was plotting to leave? Was leaving even a crime anymore? Elio stayed quiet.

"Listen, repinga," the therapist said, his fist striking the wooden desk in front of him. "You either do as you're told, or it's gonna get real ugly for you. How ugly is really up to you. Talk to your wife. You have a couple of days to mull it over," he concluded with a smile.

The therapist then offered him a cigar, and Elio did the unthinkable and waved it away. Then, "No," Elio said, squeezing the therapist's hand a little too tight. No to the cigar—and no to everything else. "I don't need a day to think it over. I don't have to talk to my wife. I know right now, and the answer's no, goddamn it. No."

Elio couldn't sleep that night. He went looking for Pepe, but couldn't find him anywhere. He walked all the way to the Cubalina and knocked on Isabelita's door, but she hadn't seen Pepe either. By the time he got home, it was around midnight. Maria was sitting at the table, a cup of water shaking in her hands.

"Elio," she said, "sit down."

"What the hell is going on?"

"Sit down, please," she said. Small, red eyes fixed on his.

"Tell me what's going on, carajo. What the hell's going on here?"

"It's Pepe," she said, swirling the water in the cup.

That night, between the time Elio left the therapist's office and the time he'd walked through the door, Pepe had drowned. They'd found him on Baracoa Beach washed up on shore, as naked as the day he was born—the sea had swallowed him up and spit him out.

"Where's his body? Where's his body, repinga?"

"He's gone, Elio."

"The guy was a swimmer. They killed him, carajo."

"Who? Nobody killed him, Elio."

"I want to see the body—it's gotta be someone else." He was about to walk out of the house to go to the morgue when he fixed his eyes on a corner of the room. "What the hell is that doing here?" he said.

"The fish? The fish you brought here?"

"Yes, the goddamn fish." He walked up to a bucket, lifted it up in the air, and threw it against a wall. The fish flew out with a gush of water and landed with an almost inaudible thud on the tile floor. Elio shut his eyes. He couldn't make himself look at the fish. An empty feeling slowly widened in the pit of his stomach. His belly sunk in. Something like a cold void was sucking the air out of him. And yet, he couldn't bear the weight of his own body.

"What the hell are you doing?" Maria exclaimed. She ran over to the fish, scooped it up in her hands, then tossed it in her cup of water. "There," she said. It took the fish only seconds to recover. Then it swam in circles inside the tin cup.

Maria walked back toward Elio and took his hand, pulling him gently in the direction of the kitchen table. "You've lost it, Elio," she said. "Please sit down, there's nothing you can do. It's done."

Elio let Maria push him down onto a chair. He sobbed onto clenched fists.

"Look," Maria said, pointing at the wall near the front door. "I found it there when I walked in from work."

His head still held up by clenched fists, Elio turned his eyes toward the door. Leaning against the wall was Pepe's bike.

CHAPTER 42

IT WAS ISABELITA, Pepe's old girlfriend, who took care of everything. Because Pepe had no family left on the island, and because Maria had threatened she'd leave him if he showed up at the morgue and made a scene or otherwise interfered in the arrangements, Elio stayed put and waited for the funeral. When the day came, Maria had something for him to wear.

"It needs some letting out of the hems and a little starch," Maria said, holding up a blue and white sailor suit like a peace offering.

Elio looked up gloomily from his morning coffee, then back down. "Don't tell me—it was Benito's," he said into the cup. Benito, Fina's late husband, had been a persnickety old man and a religious zealot who spent his evenings pacing his living room murmuring prayers and counting rosary beads with clammy hands. Elio wanted nothing to do with his suit.

Maria's eyes widened. "How did you know that? It's nice—I think it's worth a go. It'll do you some good to get out of those ratty shorts for once."

"The hell I'm going to put on Benito's old getup—" Elio said.

"What did Benito ever do to you?" Maria took the pantleg close to her mouth and bit on a loose, grayish thread. She pulled with her teeth, and the piece of thread slid out from the fabric. "See, it's easy," she said through clenched teeth. "We'll just iron out the hemline and it's done."

Hot air pooled around Elio's temples. He'd had it up the wazoo with hand-me-down suits and people's old shoes. Hard to believe it, yes—but he still had some dignity. "I'm putting my foot down. I'm not wearing that old man's suit—that's that."

"You're putting your foot down, really? Please, that's all we need now, for you to decide to put your foot down. Someone's died, damn it. This is what you have to wear, Elio Perez. And that's that," she said, her eyes tearing up. She slumped her body on a chair and sobbed. The suit martyred like a national hero on her lap. They remained silent for a few seconds, tensely looking each other in the eye.

"Don't cry, please. Okay, look—okay," he said, soaking up the coffee with the frayed end of a rag. "I'll wear the goddamn suit, if it matters so much." Elio started sweating profusely, as if a water pipe had busted inside him. Beads of sweat slid down his face, neck, and back. "I'll put it on," he said again. "Just don't cry, please." It never occurred to him that Maria's tears might have had nothing to do with the suit.

"Where are my hairpins?" she said between sobs, running anxious fingers through her hair as if feeling for nits.

"Look in your bra." He laughed, hoping to lighten the moment enough to stop her from crying.

"They're not there," she said. She stood up, put the suit down on the chair, and walked to the bathroom.

"You don't need hairpins—you look fine with your hair down."

"Don't tell me what I need, Elio—I know damn well what I need," she shouted back from the bathroom. Her voice already hoarse from crying.

He looked at her, but didn't respond. Instead, he patted his damp, shaved face with the dry end of the rag and lifted his arms to air-dry his armpits. Not even today could he get a break, he thought. Then he reached into his shorts pocket for the little bag with diazepam.

Maria gazed at her face in the small mirror above the bathroom sink. She didn't like what she saw.

She grabbed a wet hairpin from a soap dish and dried it with a small rag. Then, she gathered a few gray strands toward the hot heft of her head, leaving some wisps to fall limply around cheekbones. She liked that—more youthful. For once she wished to hear somebody say Maria, you're so beautiful. Life was hard for her now. Maria had been so smart once she could have been anything—anything at all. "I want to be something great," she'd told her grandmother once. Her grandmother had shrugged. "Women don't need to be great," she'd said. "They just need to be. Stay put. Silence is a virtue, and so is patience."

Her grandmother was a woman who shut her eyes at night and disappeared. A woman who made do. "That's what being a woman is about," Maria could hear her saying. "Being a woman is about sacrifice, about living for your husband, and your children, and your grandchildren. It's about putting yourself last, so that everything and everyone around you can grow." Maria had stopped listening then—her grandmother was so often wrong. The face in the mirror, wrinkled and withered, looked so much like her grandmother who had been gone for years. Maria knew it was inevitable that, with each passing day, they'd look more and more alike. Yup, that was her grandmother.

Lifting her shirt, she scooped out one breast from her bra, then the other. They were long, sad, and unimportant, she thought. An enlarged pink areola topped each one like a kippah. Each small nipple a reminder that she'd never breastfed. If at the very least her breasts had kept their shape—even *they* reminded her of her grandmother's. Five years ago, she'd found her first gray pubic hair: a milestone, younger, more evolved women would have told her. Well, *she* refused to let it be, and yanked it—and sure enough, bent on vengeance, it multiplied.

She shoved her breasts back into the bra cups and pulled down her shirt. Maybe it made her younger that she still cared about her breasts all that much. Her eyes gazed again at those other eyes in the mirror. They were blue, too. She laughed. Well, there's *that* at least, she thought. She felt a motionless heaviness inside of her that held her in place. She didn't want to attend Pepe's funeral. But she would be there, and when the time came to throw a handful of earth onto his grave, he would be dead, and it wouldn't matter what she looked like.

Looking a long while at a face that was and was not her, for a few seconds, she succumbed to her earlier dream. The most destructive of all dreams: life beyond the island. Chicago.

It was a dream fed by frustration, disillusion, and discontent. A dream she'd first glimpsed in the pages of a Sears fall catalogue, and that, even then, she regarded as the greatest of all dreams—equating it with virtue, and intelligence, and physical beauty. There, en ese norte de todos los nortes, the eyes and lips wrapped themselves around kinder words; and bodies leaned and hooked and probed into each other, making love at odd hours; and machines did what only men could do here, with calloused hands and by force. There, death was death, not exile, not forgetting. There, she'd heard, there was snow, as white and cold and pure as anything she'd ever seen or felt. There, drowning was something that happened in the movies. If she could only discover the secret of *there,* she could harness it here. Trap it in a glass jar, like a firefly.

To hell with it all, she thought, fixing her hair up like she'd seen in that same fall catalogue so many years before. As far as updos went, that was one of her favorites. A part on the side, with hairpins holding up the whole deal. She looked just like herself. Well, *almost* just like. She opened the faucet and splashed her face with water. She felt calmer now, refreshed, which was truly an accomplishment, given Pepe's death along with the island's current circumstances. All of a sudden, people who already had nothing had even less. No gas, no electricity, no water, no soap, no clothes, no food, no nothing. Perhaps all one could do now was look in the mirror and know that there was someone still there to look back. And that had to be something.

An afternoon thunderstorm erupted on the way to the funeral house. To Elio it was fitting—a sign of defeat on Pepe's part, he concluded. If Pepe could have had it his way, the sun would have been at its highest on the day of the funeral. Right above Bauta like a reading lamp—except he wouldn't have been reading. He would have been screwing the living lights out of Celia.

They huddled under one small umbrella—two consecutive broken rods—so that heavy raindrops pelting the canopy plunged from the droopy edge and cascaded onto Elio's forearm like a waterfall, drenching Benito's already mangy suit. The rain whooshed, pushed, and gushed over everything with torrential force. Elio looked to Maria's shoes, a pair of old moccasins with missing tips. Exposed to the elements, her toes huddled together into an irregular triangular shape, stuck out, and touched the wet pavement whenever she pressed on. She pushed Elio right and left when there were puddles ahead. He could see them, he just didn't care to avoid them. What's more, it made him feel light and at ease in a queer way whenever his shoe plunged into one, splattering Maria's legs.

Even though Maria had kept her promise and let the hems out, the pants came up to Elio's bony ankles. With no socks to speak of, his bare feet squished inside his shoes. He was starting to feel woozy, and everything seemed to slow down. Blinking through a curtain of rain in front of him that now fell ever so slowly, he handed Maria the umbrella and reached out a hand. It all came to a standstill.

"Are you okay?" Maria asked, steadying the umbrella.

"I'm not feeling well." He closed his eyes for a moment, tuned to the quivering of his eyelids underneath the umbrella. That damn diazepam was playing a number on him. He should have taken one, not two— what the hell was he thinking? One foot before the other, he tightroped his way onward. He thought of the markings on the cave's wall. There was something to that. It was the realization that, like the markings, life was multiform and multiple and utterly incomprehensible. It wasn't a fixed point on the horizon, but a scribble we were meant to decipher. A book that took the form, the color, and the tone of the reader. A fish, impossible to grasp, because it's always, always slipping away. He was glad he never had the chance to tell Pepe about it. What did Pepe know about markings, and fish, and everything else that drove Elio crazy each time he went into that cave to stare at a goddamn wall?

But he, Elio Perez, was made of a different mettle entirely. He, *a kind of Cuban Quixote, trudging through a flooded Sierra Morena, with Dulcinea by the hand. Thrusting into the air with his lance. Rocinante and Sancho doggy-paddling up ahead on their way to the Island of Barataria.* "Master," *Sancho calling to him somewhere in the horizon.* "You kept your promise! I see the island—I see it!"

Elio's head swooned with Sancho's every word. "I see it too—yes, I see it," he mumbled. *He pulled Dulcinea closer to him, and thrust his lance forward again. "Do not flee, cowards and vile creatures, for it's just one knight attacking you!"*

"What in God's name is wrong with you? We're not there yet," Maria said, taking hold of the umbrella again. It had tipped forward so far and no longer served its purpose.

Elio felt dizzy, sleepy, and confused. He wished he could put his head down on something. Benito's suit, now soaking wet, clung to his body. It made him feel heavy and clumsy.

Maria was silent, again—she must have been boycotting the rain, he thought. Because perhaps rain on the day of a funeral was too much to bear. Because rain on the day of a friend's last day above ground meant much more than on any other day.

They reached the park. Bauta's bell tower, the same one he'd once climbed to and where he'd once forgotten his *Don Quixote,* loomed above them. To Elio, it seemed to spin in all directions, like a mad weathercock, or blades on a windmill. He wished the bells were tolling now. If there was a time for tolling, it was today. The park was empty, but Elio imagined people hiding in bushes, behind benches, atop the high branches of trees. There were others, too—he just couldn't see them. They were there to keep tabs on his whereabouts, to make a record of his every move. They were there to remind him that just as the therapist had predicted, things would get worse for him from that point forward.

They passed the Carretera Central, la de la Rosa, the one that led to El Cayo. A few people watched the rain from their porches. They smoked and talked in low voices, but stopped to watch Elio and Maria drift by. At the corner, the old Bar de Enrique, now the pizzeria, was closed for the day. A wet paper, hanging by a corner on the door, alerted that it would reopen after the funeral.

Daria's Funeral Home stood between the large wooden gate to the

Baya de Gallos and Sira and Francisco's house. The gate opened to a long passage, and concluded in a large, quadrangular patio that Basilio used for cockfights. How Sira allowed such gruesome battles in her own backyard, Elio couldn't fathom. She'd been everyone's preschool teacher, including his. A damn good one. Didn't make them like that anymore. The only one who'd ever understood him, really. Through a haze, he remembered Francisquito, Carlito, and Ilda, now somewhere in Miami. Everyone gone. Why they didn't have funerals for them too, he couldn't understand. He hadn't seen or heard from them since 1982—as far as he knew, they had also drowned.

Across from the funeral home was Antonio Guerra's old home. Antonio was gone, too. This time, though, not to Miami, but to a place Elio wasn't sure existed—much less for suicides. He'd been a music teacher at La Escuela de Berto, and Pepe's elementary school friend. But because Antonio gave up, and because he didn't leave a note behind, Pepe, who'd never really been the grudge-holding type, refused to forgive him.

"I need to get my face wet," Elio finally told Maria, sticking his head out of the umbrella, and letting the raindrops cascade down his cheeks. He wiped his face with a sleeve. It made him feel better.

"Have you been drinking, Elio Perez?" She turned Elio's face toward her with a wet hand.

"Yes, whiskey—lots of it," he said with a chuckle.

"This is not the time for jokes, you know that?" She looked straight ahead. "Try to not be yourself when we get there, okay?"

"I'll do my best." He slumped his shoulders and pulled down on Benito's pants. They were so far up his shins now, he might as well have been wearing Bermuda shorts.

By the time they reached the funeral home, Elio's muscles were twitching, and his breathing was shallow.

The two large entrance doors were closed. Sheltered by the roof's overhang, Maria closed the umbrella, and shook it. A lot of good it'd done them—they were soaked. Benito's suit had been through the ringer, and Elio's shoes spurted out water with each step he took. Maria's gray skirt clung to her thighs, her beige slip sticking out on one side, like a saggy tongue.

"You're scaring me," Maria said. "Let me fix you a little. I think you were right, this suit's too small for you." She pulled down on his wet sleeves, and patted down the hair around his bald spot. "I love you, okay?" she said, as if she needed to hear herself say it out loud.

"I know. I'm just not feeling well."

She pushed on the handle and opened one of the doors. Elio paused to let her go in first, but she pushed a soft elbow into his ribs, and he went in ahead of her. Closing the door behind them, the rain seemed to stop. Cigar smoke and incense in the room turned his stomach. People who'd known Pepe for years packed the room. Elio and Maria looked around for a place to sit. There were a few empty seats in the last row. Excusing themselves, they sidled sideways down the row and into their seats. They ended up staring at the backs of heads and a giant wooden cross hanging on the wall at the end of the aisle, between two small wreaths of white carnations and yellow paper flowers, each with a purple bow at the center. In the middle was Pepe's open casket, toward which a long ribbon of folks scuffled their way.

"Not even flowers," Maria said. She set the umbrella beside her and tucked the slip in under her skirt with nervous fingers. She was right, there were very few flowers. Besides the wreaths, there were a few roses in purple plastic vases, but no carnations. "Some," Elio said.

"They're probably plastic."

No sooner had they sat down than Elio started fidgeting in his seat. He didn't want to be there. He'd been wrong—he didn't want to see Pepe's body. Or to be reminded of his mother's own dead body. To know what Pepe looked like dead, all he had to do was close his eyes and remember his mother, and he didn't want to do that. Not now, not there, and not with all these people around.

"What's the matter now?" Maria said.

"I can't take this kind of thing. I'm leaving."

"You sit your ass down, Elio Perez. Sit your ass down, or I'll nail it down to the chair for you."

Elio stared at Maria. But, instead of saying anything, he stayed put. It was impossible to fight everyone at once, and much less Maria. A cramp tightened his chest, and he felt dizzy again. His hands were clammy and shaky.

"I don't feel good," he told her. But she looked straight ahead and listened intently to the service. She had tears in her eyes. Did Maria still have feelings for Pepe? Elio thought, then decided it'd be best to let it go.

After the service, Isabelita came up to them, a mustache of perspiration glistening on her upper lip. Circles of sweat dampening the underarms of her brown shirt—low cut enough that when she leaned over to kiss him, Elio turned his eyes away to avoid seeing into her bra.

"You have to see him," she said, large silver hoops dangling near her neck. *"Dale,* c'mon." Pulling on their hands like a tug-of-war. "He's so handsome. Mimi went all out with his face—doesn't look swollen at all, you know."

"Who talks like that?" Elio whispered into Maria's ear. She pretended not to hear him, giving up instead to Isabelita's pull and sitting closer to the edge of her seat, which wouldn't help her much, Elio thought—she would still be sitting in the back row.

A small crowd gathered around Pepe's coffin at the end of the room. Everyone crying, hugging, leaning on each other's shoulders for support. Everyone was there, even the bodeguero. Descarao, Elio thought.

Goddamn hypocrites, they turn him in one day, and mourn him the next.

As Elio might have expected, there were lots of women. Some sat in corners smoking in silence, or rummaged for handkerchiefs in their own or other women's purses, or doubled over with sobs. In fact, there were more women than men—that was certain. Then it suddenly occurred to him that nobody had thought of telling Celia.

"Nobody's called Celia," Elio said. "Pepe would have wanted that."

Maria shrugged. "Not my place to call anybody," she said.

Elio let it go. Maria might have been right; it wasn't her place to call. Perhaps a friend of Celia had called already. In any case, Pepe would have wanted somebody to tell her. Elio had called Pepe's mother in Tampa, which had been hard enough. Not only had the poor woman not seen her son in nearly thirty-five years, now she'd never see him again.

"I did. I called her—her sister gave me her number," Isabelita said, giving Maria a side glance and lifting her chin to the ceiling. Growing taller momentarily. "We're too far from the coffin. To get a good look at him, you gotta get closer."

Maria stood up and Elio followed her. Holding on to Maria's hand, he felt queasy again. His palm, as cold and clammy as a frog's back against her warm skin. Isabelita led them through the crowd, pushing, elbowing, and nudging until they were right in front of the coffin.

"Ta-rá!" she said, her arms opened wide in the air like she'd just nailed a difficult landing. "Doesn't he look fabulous?" She shook Maria's shoulders. But Maria didn't respond. She stared at Pepe's face, her eyes welling up with tears.

From Isabelita's words alone, Elio concluded that Celia had been the wrong woman to fall in love with.

Women gathered around him, dark eyes lined in black, circling his body like moths around a light bulb. There was pointing at his face. "The makeup artist did a damn good job hiding the pockmarks," some said. Or, "Take a look at his hair—nice, right?" Isabelita combed it herself." Others, the older ones, perked up their breasts before coming closer, as if Pepe could appreciate their immeasurable fullness from his coffin. They marveled at the breadth and width of his chest, his large hands, the girth of his thighs. Spellbound by his mouth-watering, jaw-dropping bulge. Isabelita even said that she'd never seen a more beautiful drowned man than Pepe—and God only knew she'd seen many. Elio moved to the side to get out of the way of the women.

"I can't take this," Maria said, her hand over her mouth. She sobbed, "I have to go, Elio—I don't want to see this." Shoving her way past the crowd, Maria edged back to the entrance, forgetting to take her umbrella. Within seconds, she was gone. She'd disappeared behind the door.

Perhaps Maria had noticed Pepe's cracked lips underneath the pinkish lip gloss, or the sloppy stitching beneath it, or his fingers stiff as paddleboards against his thighs.

Elio didn't attempt to register what had just taken place. His eyes followed Maria's path through the crowd. Isabelita walked after her.

"Oye, compadre, glad you showed up—what's with the little sailor suit?" someone close by said. Was it Pepe? "You okay, man?" He should sit down. Elio swooned. He couldn't identify a single voice. He heard a saxophone belt out a familiar whining—Charlie Parker, perhaps? Or something else entirely. Maybe this was what happened when a man approached death, a kind of dizziness. Elio straightened his spine to steady himself and fixed his eyes on Pepe.

"You're a son of a bitch, you know that," he said to Pepe's corpse. "A real son of a bitch. First you go and betray me, then you drown yourself to avoid an apology. You have some balls, Pepe Fernández."

"Elio," Isabelita whispered. Her warm breath blooming in his ear.

"People can hear you—they're gonna end up asking you to leave. Pay your respects and go."

"I can't stand being in here another minute." Elio turned away from the coffin. He couldn't make out her face. There were so many faces around him. He imagined himself in one of those paintings where one face merges into another, then another. All he had to do was squint, and they would all vanish. He felt his vision drifting away.

"So why the hell are you here?" Her breath heated up his ear. He swayed. She tried to steady him by the shoulders, but his legs buckled under him, and he fell on the floor with a thud. On his side, like a capsized blue and white sailing boat.

CHAPTER 43

A SOFT RAIN fell as Maria walked home from the funeral. She'd left her broken umbrella behind, but she didn't want to go back—not today, at least. If she got lucky, it would still be there tomorrow. Today she wished she could leave it *all* behind.

She didn't mind the rain so much now, but she understood the deceptively harmless nature of a drizzle. In the long run, drizzles were responsible for more head colds and chills than any other type of rain. Trickles, dribbles, drips—with or without the sun, they all wore down the rock, eventually. She understood that.

Her joints were stiff and thunderclouds still darkened the sky, and Pepe—well, Pepe was dead. Without preamble, she started to cry. There's more to come, she thought. She wanted to grieve in private, to cry in the rare quiet of an empty house. Mourn because there was little else to do, little else to make time go faster. Or to slow it down enough to jump off the spinning platform. Jesus bendito, she didn't even know what it was she wanted.

A few nights before Pepe's funeral, Fina hadn't seemed to be her old lively self and had complained to Maria about it during bath time. She'd confessed that she rarely dropped by her old friends' anymore for the latest news from Miami or a small bowl of sweet potato pudding. She'd given up on her knitting and macramés. She was losing her eyesight, too. Maria had looked at the old woman and seen someone fragile and susceptible to the slightest pressure.

"You know," the old woman said. "Benito was never the love of my life." She was barefoot, in a flowered housedress, with her back to Maria.

Maria took a moment before answering. "Would you ever have left him?" she said.

"Never. You hear me—never. Getting married is like reading a book. You choose the book, you open it, and you read to the end—whether you like the story or not. It's about commitment. You have to see the story to the end."

Maria remained quiet. Yes, to the end, she thought. The old woman was right, Elio was the book she'd chosen to read some thirty years ago. In fact, he was the only book she knew now, and books had a way of becoming you, she thought. Elio was a part of her. Whether he'd been the wrong choice, whether she'd misunderstood the story, it didn't really matter now.

Maria grabbed a towel and handed it to the old woman. Fina used it to cover herself after undressing and climbing into the tub. Holding the towel over her private parts, the old woman seemed to Maria a vision of middle-class propriety. Her white hair was tied in a high bun in the back and bobby pins kept the side strands from falling on her face.

Perhaps noticing Maria looking at her, Fina said, "If Benito could see me now, he wouldn't recognize me."

"Don't say that, Fina." Maria shook her head. "I was just thinking how young you look, how proper."

The old woman didn't answer, instead letting out a fart, which seemed to take even her by surprise. "I'm sorry, hija. Qué pena," the old woman rushed to say. "I don't know how—"

"Ay, Fina. It's not a big deal. You're at your house." But Fina was red in the face and Maria felt sorry for her. "If everything was as harmless as a fart, por Dios, we'd all be so much happier," Maria continued, tipping a bucket of warm water over Fina's shoulders. The water ran down the old woman's front and back, and between her butt cheeks. Fina smiled and, as if hoping to end the affair on a high note, she let out a gurgling pluma.

Both women had a good laugh then. But poor Fina, Maria thought. The old woman had no choice but to resign herself to the small indignities of old age.

"I'm really fed up," Fina said, as if reading Maria's mind. "Tired of living in this world."

"You're gonna stick around to be a hundred, Fina," Maria said, patting the old woman's body with yet another new towel. "I wouldn't worry about that just yet."

"That would be awful, mija. I'm just waiting now. You don't know what comfort it is to know that it won't be long. My body won't move the way I want it to anymore. As you heard, it has a mind of its own." She laughed again.

"I'm almost there, too," Maria had said.

She thought about Fina's words a while longer. Marriage, according to the old woman, seemed to require a sense of duty, enduring commitment, and unflinching sacrifice. Never mind love or passion or happiness. One had to read the story to the end. Maria's spirits had been so low on the way home all she could do was drag her shoes on the pavement, and hope the rest of her body would follow. Pepe's death had frightened and confused her. Clearly not only had Pepe run out of time, but Elio and she too were closer to old age than either one of them might want to admit.

Starting over, anywhere, wouldn't be easy. Had Pepe understood that? His drowning had been an act of desperation, hadn't it? What else? Isabelita seemed to understand that—why didn't Elio? Why didn't anybody else?

Secretly, perhaps—and in spite of her sadness that day—Maria hoped Fina's house would settle her and Elio's life for good, and that was reason enough to laugh—or, at least, to do something other than cry. She was ready to replace her old dream of Chicago's city lights and snow-covered streets for the new dream of a house, *living luxury,* with *exciting new colors,* and *glamour, and style*—and she did so with a fast-beating heart. She had no reason to tell Elio now about his father's phone call. She and Elio might stay on the island after all.

Back from the funeral and in her own living room again, Maria let herself collapse into an armchair. "Sit down, Maria," she said to the walls of her tumbledown home, as if giving herself permission to do just that. Her stiff joints thanked her. She laughed, then sobbed. Because she didn't have the faintest idea what she should do next, she walked to the bucket in a corner of the room and peered inside. Looking at that poor fish tracing circles in the water, she felt strangely mingled feelings of sadness and joy. She determined then that whatever she did from that point forward, she'd forgive herself for it.

She took off her sopping shirt and bra and slipped into a housedress. She was wringing the shirt in the kitchen sink when Elio and Isabelita clomped through the door.

"Oye, mamita, we almost lost another one today," Isabelita said. She held Elio by the hand. He had a small cut near his right temple and looked out of sorts.

"What happened?" Maria said, running to greet them. Her hair, still wet, clung to her temples in gray and blond wisps. The hairpin now hanging from a loose strand.

"What happened?—niña, por tu vida, he dropped like a dead fish right in front of Pepe, like he was ready to take a leave himself. He scared the shit out of me. ¡Por tu madre, qué susto!"

"Let's sit him down. Sit down, Elio—c'mon." Maria took Elio's hand and led him to the bedroom. She helped him into bed and propped him up against the headboard with what few pillows they owned.

"Is it an embolism? A heart attack? What the hell is going on?" She tried to speak softly, slowly—in case his processing wasn't all there and he wasn't able to grasp the meaning of her words. Plus, in case it was serious, what good would it do to alarm him? She checked his face for paralysis, his mouth for droopiness. But other than the cut, he looked okay.

"Nah, boba, I just—I took some diazepam this morning." The clarity of his words surprised her, and so did the mention of diazepam.

"Diazepam? Where did you get that from?"

"I took it from Pepe the last time I saw him."

"Ay mi madre, that's mismito what killed him!" Isabelita said. She'd followed Maria and Elio into the bedroom and stood at the door, a hand over her mouth. "How could you let him, Elio. How could you?" she cried.

"It's not like I killed him," Elio said, pressing down on the cut to prevent the blood from spreading. He seemed confused.

"Don't stress him out, Isabelita." Maria's hand rose to a halt in the air. "I know you didn't kill him, Elio."

"Why would he do this?" the woman asked, pulling a box of Populares from her purse with trembling fingers.

Maria felt ashamed. She'd been so selfish, so totally dismissive of Elio's feelings, of what he must have been going through himself after Pepe's death.

"Outside, Isabelita. Vamos," Maria said, then turning to kiss around the cut on her husband's temple, "Close your eyes, Elio. You'll feel much better." Elio did as he was told and leaned his head back into the pillow,

278 SUSANNAH R. DRISSI

falling asleep so fast Maria almost thought to check his breathing. It wasn't until she left the room and closed the door that she thought about her own heartbreak.

On the porch, she took a cigarette from Isabelita's box. Lit it. She hadn't smoked in decades. It felt so good—why the hell did she ever stop smoking? Yes, lung cancer—but wasn't she going to die anyway? Hadn't her grandfather smoked until the day he died and was probably still lighting up in his grave? It felt so damn good to smoke.

While Isabelita was already half through hers, Maria held her cigarette at arm's length, the gray smoke swirling up into the air. It was a goddamn conspiracy, she thought. Lung cancer, my ass—they'd schemed to take away from women one of the few joys they'd still had. Isabelita coughed once or twice, but Maria ignored her. "Look," she finally said, cigarette dangling from the side of her mouth like a new permanent fixture. "Let's calm down—I'm sure there's a good explanation for the diazepam."

"Like what?" Isabelita gaped. "The guy was a damn good swimmer, Maria—everyone knows that."

"Oye, chica, I'm trying to get to the bottom of it too—" she said, her eyes tearing up. "Right now, nothing about Pepe makes sense."

Isabelita suddenly realized Maria was heartbroken about Pepe's death. "What's the matter with you?" Isabelita asked, offering Maria a second cigarette. "You'd think it was Elio who drowned."

CHAPTER 44

THE NEXT EVENING, feeling tired, old, and sad, Maria walked to Fina's house. She hoped to find solace in the dutiful mopping of the old woman's floor, perhaps even a bit of quiet and a moment of peace. Exhaustion, and sadness over Pepe's death, had sent Elio to sleep early. Maria had no need to rush. But midway between her house and Fina's, a few people had gathered in clumps on someone's porch, giving Maria a good-enough reason to quicken her step. But it was useless. It was as if they'd been waiting for her to step outside.

"It's nice to see you out here," someone sprang to her side. "We'd thought you'd be, you know—"

"No, I don't know," Maria said.

"Well, it's all so sad."

"It was sudden," Maria told them, tapping a foot on the pavement.

"But you must have known something was up, didn't you?" they insisted. Digging, always digging for more, Maria thought.

"Not a thing," she said. The night was fresh, and the hum of other conversations floated through the air. But her mind, far from listening in to someone else's evening chatter, was alert to what was happening to her.

She guessed that this interruption was something they had planned in advance—perhaps they had even been waiting for her every night, until they finally had her.

"Humpf!" they snorted. "That man was such a good swimmer. So strange the whole thing."

"Accidents happen." Maria shrugged.

"We didn't see you at the cemetery. Where did you go?"

Maria didn't answer. She leaned forward to scratch a mosquito bite on her leg. "I have to get going. Elio's expecting me back soon," she said.

"Espérate, niña." One of them grasped her forearm. "So when are you and Elio leaving?"

Maria was tempted to jerk her arm and set it free, but she thought better of it.

"Why are you asking?" she said calmly. Didn't they know by now that they weren't going anywhere? Hadn't they learned that it was never up to them?

When she finally came up to Fina's house, she saw the front door open. A couple—foreigners, judging from their rain boots—stood on the threshold. Maria felt pure dread. She knew what they'd come for. It didn't much matter if they could or could not succeed. It was enough that they'd try.

"It's only fair," she heard the woman say. "We're supporting you, and maintaining this place." Though from a distance the young woman appeared ready to cross the threshold and walk into the house, Fina never stepped back, establishing a kind of invisible barrier between them. Maria knew who the young woman was—she'd heard her voice in her receiver before. Not often enough, if Fina had it her way. She was slim, and Maria knew she was probably in her late thirties at most—by the way her back made out a tense arch, and her butt still held up the seat of her white jeans against the pull of gravity.

In spite of herself, Maria resented this new enthusiasm that second-generation Cuban Americans, who'd never set foot on the island before, now seemed to feel for their only remaining Cuban relative and her house. Because poverty was charming and tin cups were quaint. Because old refrigerators, and old cars, and old everything were vintage, and hip. Because there were hidden treasures in every house, and because, according to them, Cubans in Cuba were just too stupid to know that the table crumbling away with comején in the kitchen was really a very valuable antique.

"It's only fair," the man next to the young woman added. He was more or less the height of his companion, but wider. Probably from guanábana shakes from El Palacio de los Jugos on Fortieth Street and heaping plates of rice and beans in La Calle Ocho, the most Cuban of all Cuban streets in Miami—from what Maria'd heard gushing out of phone cables.

"I see," was Fina's only retort.

Fina's house was lovely at night—especially at night. How majestic it looked, with its wraparound porch and pointed ironwork, sticking out of its surroundings like a wild orchid. Maria reasoned that it would be nice for Elio and her to stay in the neighborhood. After all, people forget, and why shouldn't she and Elio forget about the repudiation rallies, and the peering through shutters, and the gossip, too? But she knew exactly what Elio would say, "What neighborhood?" She'd tell him then that it wouldn't be so bad and that, in the past, people forgot quickly. She would then wait for his nod, though she would already know the answer. She'd insist that it would be nice to come home for once to a house whose walls didn't peel. Where there were rocking chairs both on the porch and in the living room, and where the fan would be better too, and so would the refrigerator. But Elio would shrug his shoulders and say that those things had nothing to do with forgetting, much less to do with the neighborhood. Nice beds, fans, and rocking chairs couldn't bring back his peace of mind, his right to be—and they certainly couldn't bring back Pepe. And the neighborhood was no longer a neighborhood the day it became a surveillance post, he'd tell her. And he'd probably be right. "I don't want to be forced to move," he'd conclude. And she'd have to comply.

An awkward silence followed the brief exchange between the old woman and her visitors.

Maria stood by, quite still, wanting desperately to remind them that it was she who'd been caring for Fina and her house for almost a year. She, who bathed, and fed Fina most nights, and cleaned her toilet bowl with ammonia, the fumes nearly singeing her eyelashes and peeling off the skin from her face—all in return for Fina's house. But she thought better of it.

She slowed her steps and waited in the dark, half afraid they'd turn around and see her—or worse, hear the squishy sound of her shoes. Half hoping they'd catch her, and she'd be forced to talk. She expected Fina to make an impassioned pitch for doing whatever the hell she wanted with the house. But it was the man who spoke up. "Don't decide now," he went on to say, as if anticipating what Fina's snap decision might be. "Think about it, sleep on it—"

"Yes, good idea," the young woman interrupted, her elbow nudging his arm. "Just think about it, and we'll be back soon."

There was another awkward silence and Maria took that as a clue to walk past them without being noticed. She made it all the way to the very corner of Fina's house, where she remained, hidden by the darkness, a pile of junk, and the neighborhood's water turbine, whose failing rotor made it possible for her to eavesdrop on their conversation. A few children bounced a ball around across the street. Had they seen what she'd seen? Had they seen her seeing what she saw, eavesdropping? She wished Fina's answer had been an adamant *no*. But beyond what she expected, she was furious with herself for even thinking what she was thinking. They were the rightful heirs, weren't they? The son and daughter of her only sister? The babies, toddlers, pimply adolescents, and graduates in all of her crocheted picture frames. However, surely they knew, just as much as Maria, that foreigners couldn't own property on the island—whether or not they were the rightful heirs. Fina's assent was merely a gesture.

By the time the visitors left and Maria entered Fina's house, the old woman was waiting for her in an old nylon duster, holding a plastic container of talcum powder in her hands. Beneath the duster her legs were pale and thin—but also what Maria considered *American,* meaning long. Had Maria thought to squint or stand at a certain distance from the old woman, Fina would have looked to her like an old Sears ad from the mature ladies' section—growing old and ever more graceful with each succeeding Sears decade.

"I'll need help again, dear," Fina said, raising the container in the air. Loose powder blew in all directions, and an unexpected freshness filled the room. "Baby powder, hija. I can't survive the heat without it," the old woman said.

"No one can." Maria smiled, remembering how she'd always loved baby powder on her damp skin.

Puffs of fragrant snow, she thought, as she followed Fina into the bathroom and steered her into the shower area. "Tell me when you're ready," Maria said, turning her back to the old woman.

She wondered just then if Fina would ever bring up the visitors. She wanted to stretch the conversation long enough to give the old woman a chance to tell her about it.

"Well, there's nothing you can do about the heat," Fina said, gesturing for Maria to pour the tepid water over her.

"You're right." Maria feigned a smile. "There's not much one can do."

Maria handed Fina a sliver of soap. When the old woman finished washing herself, Maria poured the water over her again, at intervals this time.

"You know—" Fina paused, grabbing the towel from Maria's hands and wrapping it around herself. She stared at Maria for a few seconds. "I just remembered there was something I wanted to ask you," she said.

"Of course, ask away." Maria hoped this would be the question she'd been waiting for.

"How are you doing, mija? Still upset about Pepe? How did he die?" Fina changed the conversation the way old people often did, abruptly. As if suddenly the phone had rung and she'd had to respond to someone else, elsewhere.

"I don't want to talk about that." Maria said. "I don't think I can just yet." Her mood had changed considerably after arriving at Fina's house, but not enough for her to want to talk about Pepe, and not enough to forget that she was hoping for a different question entirely.

Maria slept at Fina's that night, just as she'd done several times before in the last few months. She loved Fina's house, no doubt about that. There were no squabbles over stolen books, or giant bikes, or whatever else Elio set his mind on. No holes in the roof, and no sad fish in a bucket to either feed or ignore. The refrigerator actually stayed stocked with food, and its grunting was minimal. How Fina did it, Maria didn't know. Even the old woman's fan was better than Maria's—for one, it was brand new.

Fina made no mention of her visitors that night. But in the morning, just as Maria was about to leave, the old woman made a request. Could Maria hide some papers—anywhere, just not in Fina's house? Maria was puzzled.

"Mija," the old woman said. "Just hide them under your sink, or in your mattress, or freeze them. Do whatever you think is right—I just don't want the papers here when they come back."

"Can't you just say *no?*" Maria knew then the old woman must have seen her passing by the day before.

"*No* is something I was never taught to say, mija. It's better this way."

That morning, Maria took home Fina's deed papers, tucking them neatly inside a newspaper. She walked into the bedroom to check on Elio. He was still asleep.

In the kitchen, she sat down on a small bench near the counter and read the fine print. Over and over, as if with each reading, an answer to the question of staying versus leaving would surface. She put the papers in the freezer, newspaper and all. Her heart lifted, the warmth of those papers in her hands was enough to thaw any cold. But she couldn't hold back her tears. Because, in spite of it all, that old woman intended to do right by her. Thinking about it, she realized her grandmother had been wrong. Yes, there were those people, but there were also other people who surprised the hell out of you. She touched her damp face. She was still there. On the island, where nothing was truly yours, and where there was no state recognition of property, Fina's deed papers held no real power Maria could think of, but they meant something to her, and certainly to Fina.

CHAPTER 45

THE UMBRELLA was right where she'd left it the day of the funeral. This told her that there was now a larger supply of umbrellas than there had been at any other time in the recent history of Bauta—had there not, the umbrella would have been gone—with or without the mediation of a dead body in the funeral home.

Just as she was about to walk out the door, a woman's voice called out to her, "Maria, espérame—hold on!" Then the quick snapping of chancletas against tile, and Isabelita made her way through a back door. "Ah, it's good to see you, vieja," she said, catching her breath. Maria kissed her cheek. Isabelita's face was puffy and sweaty. She held a cigarette in one hand, and some sort of paper bag hung from the other. She had on the same brown shirt she wore to the funeral, but her earrings were different. These weren't hoops, but little Cuban flags hanging from a red plastic bead—the kind sold only to tourists near the cathedral in La Habana.

"Do you work here?" Maria asked, surprised to see Isabelita at the funeral home in the middle of the afternoon.

"Nah," Isabelita said. "I got the key, though. I help clean up sometimes, you know? Not that I like hanging around dead people or anything like that. I just…I feel bad for them."

"For whom?" Maria asked.

"What do you mean *for whom?* For dead people, vieja. Death is brutal—lonely as hell. Today I'm here *strictly* on business, though. But, do sit down."

"I don't have much time, Isabelita."

"Déjate deso, and sit down."

Maria took a seat, and Isabelita sat next to her. "Are you still down in the dumps?" she asked. The flags billowing near her neck.

"Well—you know it takes time." Maria was determined not to say anything else.

"Don't I know it," Isabelita said, looking around. "Nothing like a funeral home to remind you que la vida es un suspiro. One day you're walking around making plans, and before you can even…you're gone… here, take a look." She showed Maria the contents of the paper bag she'd set next to her feet. Maria peeked inside the bag. A framed black and white picture of Pepe on a rock in Pinar del Río, two white candles, an old toothbrush, and a dried-out mango pit.

"A mango pit and a toothbrush?" Maria asked. She could explain everything else, but she wasn't sure about the combination of these items in any Santería ritual she'd ever witnessed.

"Pepe liked mangoes, and the toothbrush—" She laughed through a cloud of smoke. "Well, he'll need to brush his teeth right after, won't he?"

Maria laughed, too. "Coño, vieja, but couldn't you find him one that doesn't look like you fished it out of the gutter?"

"You gotta improvise, niña—I can only do so much." Suddenly she was in tears. But then, who wouldn't get weepy these days—there was so much going on, or nothing at all—perhaps that's why people always went around laughing to the brink of tears. From despair to near hilarity. Maria touched Isabelita's shoulder, then made the universal sign for a cigarette.

"What's wrong, you can tell me," Maria asked, striking a match. She had taken up smoking since Pepe's death. Somehow, what she'd never done or cared to do when she was younger, had become indispensable. It made her feel a little reckless, a little free. She was looking up at the ceiling. The rain had left bubbles on the paint, and there was a plastic bag near the center, haphazardly covering what was probably a hole.

"Never mind that," Isabelita said, swatting her hand in the direction of the ceiling. "My brother Manolito fell through while patching up some leaks before Pepe's funeral. He's fine, like a cat—landed on his feet." She lit another cigarette. Maria waited for her to speak again. She knew there was more. "Pepe was a good man, whatever anyone thinks," Isabelita finally said. Inhaled, then exhaled. "But he would have been happier with someone else, that's all." There was a pause.

"And you?" Maria prodded.

"Niña, I haven't been with Pepe for years. Since I was a kid, vaya. I'm no good at picking men, you know. And I'm a real maniac when it comes to relationships, too. Muchacha, I dive in, como una loca, vaya. I lose it—I'm all heart," she said, tapping on her chest. "What about you—are you happy?"

Maria took a deep breath. Why was this woman she hardly knew confiding in her, asking her questions? Instead of answering, Maria moved closer to the edge of her seat, and pointed her cigarette toward the hole in the ceiling. "You see that hole?" she said. "Well, it's kind of like that." But if she had a hole in her heart, she wasn't about to tell Isabelita his name.

"You don't have to tell me. To a good listener," Isabelita said, "a few words suffice." Her words betraying a kind of insight Maria wanted more than anything to ignore.

"So, what's all that stuff for?" Maria said, hoping to take the conversation in a different direction. She pointed at the paper bag on Isabelita's lap.

Isabelita's right leg, crossed over her left knee, swung back and forth like a tilted pendulum.

"Don't mind the leg," she said, catching Maria's half smile. "It's got a mind of its own."

Maria didn't know why she liked Isabelita so much, but she did. She was one of those women you want to be friends with. She only wished she'd met her sooner. They would have been good friends, she thought. "Sorry," Maria said. "Just thinking that if you kicked your leg any higher you might fall off your chair." They laughed.

"Seriously, you know—I'm just making sure he makes it there safely."

"There? To Tampa?"

"No, vieja. There, there. The light, el más allá—paradise."

"Ay, Isabelita—you believe in that?"

"Not really. But it's better than doing nothing, right?"

"I guess I should—"

"Maybe this can help," Isabelita said, handing her one of the candles in the bag. "Look, it's not a lot, but it's something. Go home and light it. You'll see—it'll make you feel better. If anything, you have a candle to fend off the spooks when the lights go out again."

"Are you married, Isabelita?" Maria asked, matching Isabelita's earlier question with one of her own.

"Nah, never did find a good match. Pepe came close, though. But we were way too young. Babies, you know?"

"Sure," Maria said. "Pepe was—well, he wasn't the marrying type."

"Oh, but he was the marrying type. He was—it's just that the one he wanted to marry turned around and married someone else."

Maria thought perhaps if Isabelita repeated it, then the words would somehow change. "What?" She felt herself falling from a rooftop onto the street below. She shook. "What was it that you said?"

"I thought you should know…the guy still cared." Her face suddenly serious, she looked at Maria as if they were friends—perhaps they were.

"How do you know he still cared?"

"That doesn't really matter, does it?"

"It matters, Isabelita. It matters a whole lot. Who the hell says something like that after someone's drowned? What about Celia?"

"Forget about Celia. Celia was a…passing ship in the night. I'm telling you all this because there's nothing worse than going through life not knowing. I tell you, so that you know. There's nothing you can do about that now, but guess what?—you can do a lot of other things. I loved that man once, a very long time ago, but I got on with my life. Use the candle I gave you. Say goodbye. Move on. Sayonara, Pepe, and anyone else who doesn't make you happy. Because you deserve to be happy, don't you? Well, I do too. So I'm gonna go home and light the candle I just stole, and wait. When I'm sure he's crossed over, my job will be done. I owe him that."

CHAPTER 46

DAYS LATER, ELIO found Isabelita rummaging through a box of papers in the supply room. "I have to give you something," he whispered. He pulled her by the hand toward the back of the room where they couldn't be seen from the door, and closed the door behind him. "Here." He handed her a folded one-hundred-dollar bill. "He left you this." Surely, Isabelita needed it more than Maria and he did. In any case, he had never meant to keep it.

Isabelita fell silent for a couple of seconds. She wiped small drops of sweat on her forehead with the back of her hand, and adjusted a ponytail that could barely restrain her mass of dark hair. She seemed overwhelmed. "I need it for food," she said finally, taking the money and tucking it inside her bra. "So I'm gonna take your word for it."

Elio laughed. "I'm glad, Isa."

He had no intention of telling her the truth, nor did he feel like inventing an awkward lie. At any rate, there was no point in telling her what she already knew.

That night Elio biked to Pepe's house in El Belica, a nearby neighborhood whose distinguishing characteristic was newer homes, flanked by generous side yards. Since Pepe'd been spending more and more time at Celia's, Elio hadn't been there in months; and with Maria performing her routine mopping of Fina's floor, there was no better time. The bike ride took him less than ten minutes, not counting the time he spent veering right or left to avoid potholes.

He passed the back entrance to the church and made his way down Loinaz del Castillo. The scent of jasmine and galán de noche infused the air with a kind of optimism, and he pedaled as fast as his legs allowed. Not too many people out that night. But Elio was sure someone was still watching him. He could feel their eyes on him, and their breath on the back of his neck as he pedaled on in the dark, but he no longer cared. Not much, anyway. The part of him that still cared, though, couldn't help but remember Roberto Salas and the therapist's threat. Things would get worse for him. They'd gone after Pepe. And they'd gone after *him* before— they would do it again. Perhaps not that night. But on a night when he least expected it.

The air was hot, and everything around him was motionless. Suddenly weighed down by sad presentiments, and by a bitterness that rivaled all the bitterness of a sea that was never too far away from him, Elio came up to the dusty road that led to El Belica. The road extended downward a long way to an enormous ceiba, and no further. To the right, the Cemetery of Bauta, an aboveground city of the dead whose mausoleums smelled of mildew and dead flowers—it wasn't a smell most people recognized. You had to have been to a cemetery many times to detect it—one of the reasons he'd never returned, and one of the reasons why it was timely that he passed out at Pepe's funeral when he did. A good excuse to get out of throwing a handful of dirt into a hole in the ground. But he was returning to El Belica with distinct memories of a place that had been, for a while, a second home—or, perhaps, his only home.

The town was a product of the 1950s and had been named after Belica, an old woman, whose house had been the only one there for many years. No buildings, no shops, no water pipes or homes, and just a handful of people. Back then, the house had been painted a light green, covered in wood planks, and fixed so close to the ground that it seemed only natural that the road ended at its doorstep. To its left, cherry trees. To its right, a wide road leading to the ranch. Out back, a solitary grain mill, a lone Don Quixote. Time had spared its sails, but nothing else.

When Elio finally arrived at Pepe's house, he got off his bike, which he walked into the front garden and parked on the dark porch, tucked away from the street light. He looked up to the rooftop and his mind slowly drifted to that afternoon, nearly thirty-five years earlier, when they'd ended up on the roof, drinking Cuba Libres, and listening to Charlie Parker. Cuba libre, Elio said to himself. He was just about to repeat the words a second time, for his dead friend, for Pepe, when the sound of footsteps brought him back. Once again he couldn't help but think that he'd been followed, and that things would, in fact, continue to get worse for him.

Reaching Pepe's door, in semi-darkness, Elio hoped that once inside the house he'd find the note he was looking for. Painfully aware that he might be watched, he prodded one end of Maria's tweezers into the keyhole, shaking it around to find the lever. It didn't work. Then again. This time, he heard a click. He crept into a dark living room, careful to lock the door behind him. He set down the bag with Maria's quinqué on the tiled floor. If she didn't kill him for bending her only tweezers out of shape, she'd skin him for taking the quinqué. Either way, he'd be in hot water.

He dug in a pocket for a box of matches, and pulled out a match. Then he struck it once against the side of the box. It worked the first time. By the door, Pepe had the old Vittorio record player, with that little white dog Elio always wished was his in real life. Nailed on the right wall was the Rocky Balboa poster Pepe'd loved so much. Elio's mind replayed that afternoon on the rooftop again. Pepe shouting out "I am!" to the whole neighborhood, his bare feet so close to the rooftop's edge that Elio kept his face turned the other way, for fear that his friend might actually jump. Then Pepe strutted around, continuing his Rocky impersonation. His mouth like a buñuelo, his eyes half closed, "You know Elio, the world ain't all sunshine and rainbows. It's a very mean and nasty place." They always had a laugh.

Next to the Rocky poster was a small painting of a red bird perched on a branch. Near them, but closer to the front window, a 1962 almanac with Ben Bella's long face was fixed to the wall with black electrician tape on all four corners. Together, they had a surreal effect that made Elio chuckle.

The house was in a state of semi-abandonment. Two green patio chairs from the 50s and a small wooden coffee table took center stage in the living room. On the coffee table, empty cans of Vita Nuova passed for ashtrays, stuffed to the brim with brownish cigarette butts that had been doused with beer and now gave off a bitter stink. If there had been a note, however, he would have left it there.

The phone was on the floor, flanked on one side by the rusty leg of a chair. Elio imagined Pepe, legs up on the coffee table, smoking up a storm while waiting for his mother's monthly call from a hospice somewhere in Tampa. All was a little dusty, but neat. Elio wondered why no one had come to clean out the house by now, and who would get the house next. He wished he could take the record player and the Charlie Parker albums, but thought better of it. It'd be one more thing he'd have to answer for, and God only knew who watched him at that very moment. Every step, a consequence, Elio thought.

He drifted through the room, moving the quinqué around—trying not to miss a thing. Leaning against a wall was a box of dyestuff there was no doubt Pepe'd taken from the textilera. There was no note there, though—and not much of anything else. The kitchen was no different. A few pots and pans on the counter, a wooden table, and in a cupboard, a bag of rice and five aluminum tumblers in different colors. Elio had always loved those. They reminded him of Christmas ornaments in storefronts in Havana.

In the bathroom, torn newspaper squares hung from the usual nail on the wall. A razor, brush, and sliver of soap had been neatly placed inside a tattered *Romeo y Julieta* box. Then there was the medicine cabinet. Elio pulled hard on the mirror to pry open its door. Inside, nothing but an old toothbrush and a bar of deodorant, the kind they gave out for Sunday bonuses. In the bedroom, Elio rummaged through Pepe's drawers. He opened one, two, three drawers. In the first one, Pepe's old military ID and a small silver metal of some sort, perhaps his late dad's?

He was looking for a suicide note, but there was none to be found. The second and third drawers were full of black and white family photos from before and after the triumph of the Revolution. Some in better condition than others, and all held together in bunches and secured with rubber bands. He pulled out a cluster of crumpled-up handkerchiefs with Pepe's initials embroidered on them. Nothing remotely resembling a note.

What he saw when he opened the fourth and final drawer, though, stunned him. It was a picture of Maria on her fifteenth birthday. Elio gazed at it for a short while. Maria, hands behind her back, in a white, satin gown. Quickly, he turned the picture over. Just as he thought, the rest of the story. It was Maria's handwriting. Flowing words that rose and fell, tilting this way and that in a kind of graphic waltz. "To my Pepe, on my fifteenth birthday." *"My* Pepe?" Elio read out loud. What did she mean? The words seemed to move then, and he felt dizzy. Maria had danced with Elio at her quinces, how could she have given a photograph to Pepe? Pepe himself had encouraged him to pursue Maria, and Maria had sworn there had never been anything between them. Had she lied to him all these years?

The night was hot. Elio threw his head back and stretched out his legs. He removed his shirt and flung it down beside him, then loosened his belt. He needed to breathe. He wished he had a glass of water. Or, better yet, a cold beer. How long had it been since he'd had a beer? Years? He stared at the trembling picture in his hand, turning it to one side. Then, the other. His eyes strained. "My Pepe." He supposed a good observer would have noticed what he himself had missed. Jesus, he thought, I must have been blind.

CHAPTER 47

IN THE WEEKS that followed, and just as the therapist promised, everything got worse for Elio. He was demoted at work, and went back to dying fabric. It was natural selection in practice. Since he wasn't the type who got rewarded for volunteering his body on weekends, and because he'd refused to play their game and become the neighborhood's whistle-blower, he'd been selected to go back to the barrel of dye he'd come from—that's all. He didn't mind much anymore, though.

Maria acted as if she'd never had anything to hide. Because he didn't know how to broach the subject—and because, even if he did, he probably wouldn't—he took to visiting the cave more and more. Sitting with a lighter close to the cave's wall and staring at the markings until he thought they became something. Entering a trance, where the edges and seams of everything became painfully clear. Because on an island, there are only seams and edges, limits. Anyone could make a mistake, as long as they knew their limits—even Maria. Perhaps it wasn't wise then, politically speaking, for him to ignore the limits and visit the cave without an official permission—especially when the therapist had forewarned him that it would be considered trespassing. But he wasn't planning on asking for permission. He wasn't a researcher, or a tour guide, or anyone of any status to whom the state would grant permission to visit that cave, or any other cave, for that matter. He was following his instincts, and his instincts told him not to ask for permission.

Sometimes he was certain he heard his father's voice bouncing off the cave walls and stiffening the air. "I learned what it meant to be a man when I left," the voice hovered above him. Its tone was acidic, though it changed as soon as Elio recognized it as some kind of genetic predisposition for discontent. Elio traced it back to himself. Then it became more melodious, like a kind of singing, when it seemed to pick up on Elio's resentment and said, "When the time comes, you'll hear the call, too." Its disconnection from the environment was absolute. It floated from chamber to chamber until Elio could no longer make out the words, though he knew they were there.

Alone in the cave Elio felt the deepest disappointment, the most profound sadness. Pepe was dead—was that even possible? He wished he could see him. Just one more time, for old time's sake. Because although he knew he was dead, sometimes not to see him was to imagine him somewhere else, like Tampa, Ybor City, Cuba City. Anywhere, but dead. To leave or to die—there was very little difference between the two, as far as Elio could tell.

Hadn't people left never to be seen again—and they weren't dead, were they? Or, it was all a lie, and they were just five feet under, rotting in a ditch somewhere—frozen, their jaws tight shut, stiff forever in some shoulder to shoulder arrangement, like sardines.

"Leaving wasn't for you, Pepe," Elio said to his gone friend in the dark, this time daring to touch the markings, but doing so cautiously, softly, in a kind of circular motion, so that to trace the thing was to follow the Fibonacci pattern of a fingerprint. Elio looked at his index finger for signs of residue, but there was nothing. It didn't rub off, he thought. It was there to stay.

Though there were examples of people who left and came back, there were many more who were never seen again. The whole leaving and returning was meagerly documented on either side, Elio thought, and ultimately clotted by a strange reticence.

While it was clear that lots of people cared if Pepe had drowned, his death was the kind of thing the state and its henchmen and women would use as example: "Middle-aged man drowns attempting to swim from Baracoa all the way to Tampa Bay." Idiot, he could hear them say.

Elio fixed his eyes on the cave walls and, as on a Cinerama movie screen, he imagined Pepe returning.

One evening, a man he wouldn't recognize would make straight for him and lock him in a powerful embrace. The features would pull together slowly. But by the time he grinned, Elio had figured it out. This was no dead man. No stranger. It was Pepe, his childhood friend.

"Look at this guy," Pepe says.

"How the hell are you, caballo?"

"What have you been doing with yourself, repinga?"

"Not a pot to piss in, but can't complain, you know. Putting up with this island, and the island putting up with me—you know how it goes."

"Coño, man—I've missed you, compadre." He stared at Elio, as if it was Elio who'd changed. But Elio hadn't changed much. In fact, if he had, it would have gone better for him. But he refused to change. Changing was like giving up entirely. So he remained the same: stuck.

They embraced again. This time Pepe squeezed him so hard Elio felt his chest fold closed like a book. His eyes flashed, like fireflies in the lunar setting of his face. Elio couldn't believe it was him, after all this time. And yet it was Pepe—it could only have been Pepe. A grin, like an anchor, right below that unmistakable nose.

Pepe had a life in Tampa with Celia, even a kid. He pulled out his phone, and showed Elio a couple of pictures. The kid got his nose and Celia's heavy-lidded eyes. "The little bastard likes to tinker with his bike," Pepe says. "Just like you."

"So tell me, brother, what's it like in Tampa?" Elio asked.

Now Pepe said things like "you'd flip if you knew" and "if you could get out of here, you'd see." And then they sat down at Bauta's Coppelia and talked. Twenty years of catching up to do, and Coppelia only served vanilla. "It's not easy, Elio," he continued to say.

"Yeah, everyone says that. It's not Bauta, brother." Elio took a spoonful of ice cream to his mouth and leaned back. The cave's cold wall sent a chill up his spine, and just like that, Pepe left for good. Poof, gone. Elio strained his eyes in the dark, hoping to find him again. But he was nowhere.

The big-nosed kid Elio had known long before that fateful day at the beach was afraid of nothing—not even drowning. Pepe wasn't afraid of the water, not like he was. Elio was terrified of the water, of its unpredictability, of its depths. He looked at his hands and flapped them in the darkness—how he wished they could have been fins.

By the time he stepped outside, it was already too dark. And the heat, even after sunset, still felt like a brick to the face—it was both painful and disorienting. With Pepe gone, everything felt a little emptier, the void always greater. Elio simply didn't know what to do with himself.

There was something about it all, he thought, that no longer seemed worth the effort. But the mind finds a way in the dark more than it does in sunlight. It was no surprise, then, that stepping out of the dark cave into Caimito's dark brush land, he found himself with the sudden thought: what if he could sacrifice his life for his hopes, dreams, and aspirations for another, alternate life? But he had only begun to probe at the answer when he sensed someone or something looking at him. He sprang around. Small eyes, blinking and green, looked right at him. A cocuyo. Elio laughed.

One Saturday afternoon, though, just as he was nearing the top of the Loma de Pita on Pepe's bike, the breeze ruffling against his skin, it happened. Two men on bicycles turned the corner near the end of the hill at Farm Villa Paz, came to a halt, and waited for him to pass. Elio pedaled faster, leaving them behind. He resisted the urge to look back, but the squeaking of tires against gravel was a surefire sign they followed closely behind.

The main road between Caimito and Bauta was a single lane in both directions for several miles. Convinced the two were government lackeys, Elio tried to pedal faster, but got stuck behind a slowpoke truck full of chickens. In any case, had he tried to go faster, Pepe's old bike would have just spit out its chains or popped out a tire, leaving him stranded.

"Hey," he heard one of the men call out. "Stop, cojones." If he stopped, Elio knew he wouldn't come out of it in one piece.

"Que pare tu madre, hijoeputa," Elio said, his words getting lost in the chicken truck's cloud of exhaust fumes and flying gravel. As if responding to his words, the driver revved up the engine. Elio blinked through air-bound dust. Coughing, he pedaled on. His thigh muscles burned, and his right knee popped each time he pushed down on the pedal.

The clink-clonk of the bikes behind him was closer now. All he'd have to do was make it to the entrance of the town. They wouldn't dare touch him in public. "Oye, compañero—where do you—think you're going?" the words pelted Elio's back. But this time he heard the breathless gasps.

He knew their lungs couldn't take another mile.

So he lifted his butt off the seat, and pushed harder on the pedals. So hard that at times he thought that while veering to the right, he'd lose control of the bike and end up head first in a ditch—or worse—straight into a small pool of cow shit. He pedaled like mad, and whistled, because in these kinds of situations whistling was the antidote to fear.

By the time he reached the park, though, the clink-clonk was gone. Elio was convinced he'd left them behind. Dragging his feet on the pavement, he came to a halt. He needed to rest. He thought he'd won, but then a hand shot out from somewhere and pushed him. "Qué cojones? Did you think your shitty, one-pedal bike would save you?" Elio tried to catch himself from falling, steering the bike into balance.

Someone pushed him again. This time, Elio fell to the right.

The bike toppled over in the opposite direction. Elio heard a loud crash, but he wasn't sure if it was his head or the bike against the pavement. His body turned heavy, and he could taste tar on his tongue. The playground, the church, and La Glorieta spun around him. He couldn't make the spinning slow down enough to figure out where he was in relation to his assailants. Judging from the blows, they seemed to be nowhere and everywhere at once.

Just as he was about to push himself up, a foot came from the pavement and kicked him in the face. "Crazy as shit," he heard a second man say. "Watch your goddamn step."

The next thing Elio knew, the men pulled him to his feet, tearing his one and only undershirt…Elio heard the slight rasp of material ripping. "Let me live in peace! Goddamn it!" Elio shouted. "This guy's a nut," he heard one say. For a second, he fluttered his lids and moved his fists about. But soon the pavement slid out from under him, and then everything turned quite still—except for a kind of dark buzzing in his ears. With his eyes and mouth slightly open, he seemed a fish that, having washed ashore, lies quite still and alert, sorely aware of its gills.

Elio was agitated, and could still taste the strange mix of blood and newly laid tar. With a black eye and swollen face, he slouched into an armchair, letting Maria dab his injured eye with chamomile tea. Pepe's bike leaned against a wall near the front door. At least they'd left the bike alone, he thought. At least they'd taken it out on him and not on his dead friend's bike.

"Well, whoever they were, they left you looking like a blowfish…Jesus Christ, Elio—what did you do?" Maria said, as she continued to tend to Elio's wounds.

"What do you mean what did I do? How the hell should I know?"

"I told you to be careful? What were you thinking? All those stolen books, Elio? Didn't they warn you about trespassing?"

He sensed her losing faith in him. "It's not like I'm selling the goddamn books to tourists, like lots of people do. You know the library's almost empty, right? If anything, I'm saving the stupid books. And as far as the cave, I don't give a damn about what they think is or is not trespassing. You think I'm crazy too?"

"I didn't say that—"

"What did you say, then?"

"I simply meant that things have gotten out of control around here."

"Things have been out of control around here for a long time," he said, raising his voice.

Maria made a shush-finger. "We should have left years ago, damn it. It's too damn late now—you know that, right? Too damn late."

"Leaving's got nothing to do with this. I was being fucking followed—you know what that feels like?" He looked at her unblinking, hoping she understood exactly how he felt.

"You need to calm down. Lay low and stop your antics."

"Do you know that your idiot psychologist and that other piece of shit bodeguero wanted me to turn Pepe in? That I went back to dying fabric?"

"What does Pepe have to do with anything?"

"They caught him in something, Maria. What, exactly, I don't know. But whatever it was he was doing, they got wind of it. Celia had something to do with it, that's for sure. She tied him up in some goddamn knot, lo amarró—that's what it was."

"Please don't start with your theories of ill-doing, hexes, and evil eyes."

"That's right, it's a goddamn evil eye—a big, mean one. If not how the hell do you figure that a swimmer like Pepe drowned?"

"He overdosed on diazepam, Elio. Even Isabelita thinks so," Maria said.

"Ahora sí the world's gone feet up. Look, I don't know why or how, but they killed him. I knew Pepe, and he would have never, *ever,* done something like that. If they're fucking capable of beating me up in broad daylight, and in the middle of the park, they're capable of much worse. Can't you get that?"

"What's the problem with saying that your Pepe had enough?"

"*My* Pepe? I simply don't believe it," Elio said, painfully recalling Maria's inscription, "To my Pepe," on the back on the photograph he found at Pepe's house. He knew the truth about her relationship with Pepe, but he'd never admit it to her or anyone—not even to himself. His heart beat fast. He knew once he admitted it out loud, he couldn't take it back. Then, he said, "Because the whole thing about leaving or staying is that they're permanent, irrevocable choices. Pepe chose to leave, and now it's final—he's gone. Or worse, he's dead."

She nodded, lingering as if she had something else to say, but said nothing.

CHAPTER 48

"MANOLITO, CHICO—don't do this to me." Somewhere in La
Cubalina, Isabelita gave Manolito a restless glance. A small spray bottle in
her hand squirted water on his hair. They were out back in the yard, next
to a giant avocado tree. Isabelita couldn't fathom cutting hair anywhere
else. The avocado was something special. It knew its stuff, she always
thought. It was a vegetable dressed as a fruit, and she liked that.

"Paris is where it's at, mi hermana," Manolito said. The back of his
head turned to Isabelita's scissors.

"Prepárate," she said. "I'm giving you the cut of your life. Longish all
around, and longerish on the back. Didn't Brad Pitt have a cut just like it
in that film?" She tapped her head with the scissors. "What was the name
of that film with Brad Pitt? Manolito, coño, I can't remember...the one
with the car."

"The one where the two women drive off a cliff? The one we watched
with La Gorda's VCR?"

"Ay, solavaya," she said, her scissored hand in the air, flicking death
away. "That one."

"Telma and Luis," Manolito said.

"That's it!" The snapping blades of her scissors nearly missing the top bend of Manolito's ear.

"Coño Isabelita, concéntrate, vieja. You almost took my ear off," he said, shielding his right ear from Isabelita's tonsorial sword.

"This isn't easy, my brother. Your hair is not exactly Brad Pitt's, okay?"

There was a subtle wave to Manolito's hair—but truly, so much more manageable than anything else she'd been dealing with lately, which usually involved no shampoo (because there was none), no soft tresses (no conditioners or relaxers, either), and lice colonies to boot (an island-wide epidemic). But if she told him his hair was soft, with or without a decent shampoo, it'd go straight to his head—and who could stand him then?

"And you're not Vidal Sasón, vieja. Just finish up, so I can get the hell out of this chair. My back's cramping up already." He shifted his weight, and Isabelita saw no choice but to tap his head with the stiff end of her hand.

She went on shearing, clipping, and evening out the ends of Manolito's hair. Gold iguanas hung from her earlobes, as she darted from one end of the chair to the other. She circled Manolito and leapt back to gain perspective on the job.

"Wherever we go, it has to be near the beach," she said, suddenly.

"Because you've never been to Paris. Remember Antonio and Lula?"

"The one with the lame foot?"

"Yup, cojones. They're in Paris, lame foot and all—*C'est la vie,* vieja. We gotta get the fuck out of here. There's nothing here, mi hermana."

"Ay, mi hermano, I don't know. Any reason in particular you want Paris?"

"It's freaking cold in Chicago, did you know that?"

"Cold? Ay, no." She frowned. "And Paris?"

"Beaches galore. Antonio told Cuqui that he swims in the Seine at least once a day."

"And the bread?"

"All you can eat."

"I don't know, Mano, Paris is far. Anyway, you can't freaking float all the way there, you know. Mami and Papi *are not* in Paris."

"I know—It's something to think about, I guess."

"Don't think about it for *too* long—Niño, I'm getting older by the minute." She turned, taking in his warm eyes, his high cheekbones, his clean-shaven face. She had been just a girl when he was born. Fifteen years they'd lived together in Oriente, until Isabelita came back to Bauta. She hoped that, being closer to Havana, she'd get a full load of clients, perform a number of tricky perms, y rayitos, lots of rayitos, with impeccable skill; and she would prosper, damn it. For once, she'd finish each day with her feet up, un cigarro, and a highbolito in her hand. Club Tropicana all the way, right in her back yard. Because if the economy was bad in La Habana, it was caquita in Santiago, and the rest of the east. But her clientele never materialized, so when a job at the textilera became available, she took it. She'd been in Bauta for four years, when Manolito decided to join her. And so now every week they headed out to Baracoa, or La Habana. They talked. They talked a lot. Isabelita knew he was never going to change his mind about Paris.

After the Maleconazo riots earlier that year, Manolito wasn't the same. He came back from Havana a different person. He walked in through the front door shouting "Liberté!" as if she, too, was holding him back. Freedom? Isabelita wasn't sure what that was. She'd grown up with the Revolution, and she only knew repression, scarcity, and conformity. Everyone was leaving, Manolito had told her, and why shouldn't they leave too? Because life could throw some shit your way, and if you weren't ready to pick up and start up, you were gonna get left behind to turn out the lights. Mami and Papi were in Miami—it had to be Miami. So close to Cuba she could backstroke and wash up in Baracoa in a day's time, if she wanted to. How come no one ever thought to build a bridge from Miami to Cuba? Oye, they'd thought of so many things—why not that? She pursed her lips. Miami.

She had saved the one hundred dollars Elio gave her. It wasn't much, but it was something. Enough for supplies and whatever else Manolito came up with. She loved that kid.

Isabelita teared up just thinking about those one hundred dollars. She suspected Pepe didn't mean for her and Manolito to end up with them, but she missed him, anyway—even if he'd never really missed her. Though she'd moved on a long time ago, she regretted not getting the chance to tell him. But who the hell knew he was gonna end up drowned and washed up on the beach?

One thing was certain, she was totally and irrevocably ready to start over. Ready to see Mami and Papi, after all these years. She missed them, carajo. She missed their caritas. Maybe they all could get an apartment near Miami-Dade College—everybody went there, didn't they? Then she could go to school. Wait, she'd need a job first. She'd clean rich Cuban women's houses. Or pump gasoline into rich Cuban women's Mercedes. Or she could up-do rich Cuban women's hair, or give them highlights. Do their nails, do their husbands. No, not that. She wasn't a homewrecker. In any case, once in Miami, the possibilities were endless. But it was sad, wasn't it? She might be half starving and half losing her mind, but she still had some dignity left.

What was certain was that neither Paris nor any other city Manolito could come up with would ever compare to Miami. Because everybody said Miami was the Cuba that Cuba should have been. What Cuba was that, she thought? Perhaps if the whole island hadn't left for Miami, maybe Cuba would have been what it should have been, and it wouldn't have needed Miami for any of it.

"Oye, are you done yet—or did you leave me bald?" Manolito turned sideways to look at her.

"Ay," she replied, realizing that it'd been minutes since she'd last said a word. "I was at a Gloria Estefan concert."

"Dale with the same song—feet on the ground, Isabelita. We gotta figure out how the hell we're gonna leave this treasure island first."

"I know, Puki—just taking a flight, with a layover at Calle Ocho. Oye, what a pepillo!" She said, her hand flopping in the air like it'd caught on fire. "Go to the bathroom and take a look. Brad Pitt would be jealous."

"Pepillo? Where the hell did you get that word from? Nobody talks like that anymore."

Then she looked over at him, tipped back her head, and laughed.

"Jesú Cristo, papito. You look like a movie star!" Isabelita told Manolito, who was on his way toward the door.

"*Je t'aime,* mi hermana. Mua! *Jooar noomber juan,*" he added in English, as he entered the house.

Isabelita swept her small patch of concrete floor. "Pelos be gone!" she said. The avocado tree cast a light, breezy shadow over her. She had learned—from decades of gossip, photographs, letters, cassettes, flash drives, and paquetes—that anything was possible in Miami. Because Miami was more Cuban than anything else, and because to be Cuban in Miami was better than to be Cuban in Cuba, and better (much better) than being Cuban anywhere else. Who knows, maybe she could be a gardener or a florist in Coconut Grove, care for people's yards, and show up at funerals, weddings, and baptisms in Coral Gables with bouquets

in her hands. Talk to their orchids and Casablanca lilies, like they were
her own. "Ay, mimi, you look so pretty today," and "What an inteligente
flower," and "Aren't you all ready to pintar the town red?" she could
hear herself saying. No carnations, carnations were not a thing there.
All summer long she'd watch their plants, singing to them, if she had
to. They'd take off to Punta Cana, or San Juan, or both, and they'd leave
her the key to the beach house, so pleased were they with the way their
flowers grew. She'd let herself in, test the soil and water the orchids, and
sleep in their bed, and eat their Manchego cheese. If Cuqui's cousin,
Nena, had done it, why couldn't she? Or maybe, she'd start cutting hair in
Hialeah, and move her way up to South Beach, for real. Like she meant it.
Like she'd been trained in cutting hair. After all, hadn't cutting hair gotten
her this far?

Then it occurred to her that she wasn't thinking big enough. Word
would get around that she was doing a hell of a job, and it would
eventually reach…yes, Andy Garcia's ears. Now you're talking, Isabelita,
she said to herself. This is something you could sink your teeth into. God
knows she wouldn't mind Andy Garcia one bit.

Some weeks later, while Andy (she'd call him that) was away, his wife
would have friends over for a poolside brunch. Isabelita wouldn't have to
hide to listen—water would carry sound like Maria's phone cables. She'd
be in view, ravishing in white capris, and scantily clad in one of those crop
tops, with a knot above the belly button.

The women would look around the garden and see her trimming rose
bushes, and they'd say, "Look at those roses, as big as plates—is she the
one who does your garden?" Then they'd point at Isabelita, because she
was in view, in case they cared to look. The women would turn to the wife
and say, "When you're ready to let go, we'll scoop her up in a heartbeat."
The wife would say, "No way, she's priceless," and right away she'd walk

over, as if to stake her claim, offering Isabelita more pay, and a personal assistant's job inside their Miami palace—right next to Julio Iglesias's, and across the street from Gloria Estefan's. And when Gloria came to visit and offered her a job, Andy's wife would say, "Fair is fair," and Isabelita would leave in a flash. Because God only knew she loved Andy, but who could say *no* to Gloria.

The most important thing is that she'd have no regrets. She'd let her unbridled determination prevail. Because when it came to unbridled, and determination, no one could compete with Isabelita.

CHAPTER 49

HER EARS STILL RINGING with Isabelita's words from a few days earlier, Maria sat on Fina's front porch staring out into the darkness. The lights had gone out again and the air was fresh. The sky was covered with stars—ice-blue stars hanging high and out of reach.

She took in a long breath, filling and expanding her lungs, letting the air out with a sigh of resignation. In the street crickets played sweet music. There were no shouting neighbors. No televisions, or radios sounding off the daily news. No rain pelting down on leaky roofs. No barking dogs like sentinels at the end of the road. No squeaky wheels, or sputtering engines, or children marching on their way to school. Maria reflected that it would soon be morning and that light, with its usual magic, would return all to its proper place. The coffee would brew, the sun would come up, and Elio would come home. In the darkness, all was misplaced and out of reach— in the light, something miraculous happened, and all was made anew.

"Oap!" she exclaimed, shaking her whole body in a spasm, as if waking from a dream. They had it in for her, these mosquitoes. "Here they are! A whole black cloud of them!" she whispered, not wanting to wake up Fina. They were everywhere, the little vampires. They meant to suck the life out of her, one sting at a time. They had her legs and arms covered with bright red welts, like she'd been the victim of a goddamn plague. "The lights go out, and they think it's a carnival." Maria swung a roll of tattered paper around at them.

With each passing day at Fina's house, Maria felt less and less like returning to hers. The more time she spent at Fina's, the more comforting and familiar she found the old woman's trinkets, pots, pans, and picture frames. By contrast, her own house grew smaller, dirtier, more disorderly. She'd simply grown accustomed to the better life, she'd say, laughing to herself whenever she thought of it.

Elio was more and more distant. He'd lost some weight, too. Even his gut—unyielding as it was to daily bowls of gruel—had come down a bit. They just couldn't move on. Pepe had been in every photograph, every birthday—every forgotten wedding anniversary. He was yet another irreparable tear they could neither mend nor talk about. Because without Pepe there wouldn't have been a marriage at all. And yet, here they were. With Pepe drowned, so was their marriage. She never knew what took place, exactly. She had been in Cabañas at the time of Elio's accident at the beach. By the time she returned, weeks later, she saw Pepe knocking on Elio's door. They would become the best of friends in no time, and Pepe would never look at her again.

Five years later, buoyed by a sense of duty, Maria's grandmother began cutting the first lines of her granddaughter's wedding dress. Because, she said, "Elio's broken. He will never leave you." What her grandmother never considered—the thing that never crossed her mind—is that one day Maria might just want to leave him.

At Fina's, she felt safe. It was the home she'd never had with Elio.

"Maria!" a voice called from somewhere inside the house.

"I'm coming. I'm here, Fina. Don't panic—I'm here!" Maria rose from the rocker, startled.

"Hurry, Maria—I'm dreaming again," the voice insisted.

Maria set the newspaper down on the bottom of the porch, swatting a few mosquitoes with her bare hands.

"Goddamn these creatures, they wanna eat me alive! I'm coming, Fina. Don't panic!"

She walked inside the house, tapping the cool black and white tiles with her naked feet, and stretching her arms far in front of her to clear the way. A few candles flickered here and there.

"Maria! Hurry up, Maria!" The piteous sounds were heard again.

"I'm here, Fina. I'm here," Maria answered, walking slowly toward the voice.

Once in the bedroom, she lifted the mosquito net and sat on the edge of the bed. Fina was drenched in sweat. "I'm here, Fina. I'm here now," Maria repeated, holding Fina's hands.

"Feel my heart. It's Benito, he spoke to me." She clenched Maria's hands and held them to her chest, which heaved painfully.

"No, chica. It's nothing, just a dream," Maria said, gently untangling her hands from the old woman's tight grip and patting her softly on the head, as if she were a child. "It's ok. What did he want?"

"He wants me to make my will," she said. Her eyes fixed on Maria's.

"A will?" Maria, wrinkling her eyes together until they became two blue dots in the darkness, looked at the old woman's face.

"I need my papers back, dear."

Maria understood who'd won the battle, at last. But because Fina couldn't bring herself to tell her, it was Benito who'd brought the very news Maria had been waiting for, with the conclusion she'd dreaded. "I'm so sorry, my dear," Josefina told her. "Benito says the house should go to my niece and nephew, whether or not the state agrees." Maria would never get Fina's house. The old woman was taking the papers back and her family, the young man and woman of the picture frames, had been declared—once and for all—the rightful heirs.

That night, sitting at her kitchen table, resting her face on the palms of her hands, she dreamt as Fina had done, but with eyes wide open. She found her purse and pulled out the candle Isabelita had given her, wedged it in a crevice on the table, and lit it. What should she do now, she thought. Pray? She was worn out by sadness and effort and failure, by the debilitating realization that yet another dream hadn't borne fruit. It was a blow as painful as it was unexpected.

Suddenly, it all came out, along with the tears. How she'd still pondered her feelings for Pepe all those years. How she speculated whether there was anything she could have done to change the outcome of her life. How she loved Elio, too. And why the hell not? Why couldn't she love two people at once? Because Elio had been the love of her life, too—but differently, somehow. Elio had always been her only child, and what kind of a mother abandons her firstborn? Fina's house had been the one thing that could have changed her life. The one thing that would have made her stay. Staying and leaving were both irreversible choices— Elio was right. But she didn't need Elio to know, as she'd always known, that either choice was final. As long as Elio didn't know about the house, leaving was a possibility of life; and Chicago, a letting go, where dreams were puffs of snow over rooftops. She had yet to tell Elio about his father's phone call, but she would soon.

She stared at the flickering candle flame and thought of Isabelita. What would she say to it? What words would Isabelita use to let it all go?

CHAPTER 50

SOMETIME AROUND 1:00 a.m., Elio threw his clothes on his bedroom floor and got into bed. He fell into a deep, warm sleep. Afraid the two men would return for him while he slept, he'd spent the last few days in the caves of Caimito. He'd come back home too worried and tired for restful sleep. It took a while for his body to stop shaking, for the burning in his thighs to dissipate, for his heart to wrestle down its jumping out of its cage. He woke up later, hearing what he thought were shouts right outside the front door. What the hell was going on? He peered through the shutters. Nothing. It was dark then, and he was glad.

As soon as he turned away from the shutters, he heard the clattering of pots and pans in the kitchen. It was Maria. Where had she been all night? He'd been here. He wormed back into bed, and waited.

Tin mugs clanked against each other and against the porcelain of the sink. Water gushed from the faucet and then choked in rusty pipes shuddering beneath him. Her footsteps came closer. Seconds later his side of the mattress sank with the weight of one tottering knee, then another. She climbed over him to her spot against the wall. Once under the sheets, she turned over. He feigned sleep, but his heart beat faster and faster. Then he couldn't hold back, "Were you at Fina's?" She didn't move. He shook her foot through the sheets. Nothing. He could tell she was breathing a little faster now—the sheets rose and fell, rose and fell to meet her breathing. But she didn't answer. If she'd decided to stop talking to him, he knew it'd be days before he'd hear her voice again.

In bed, so close to Maria, all the days seemed the same, the way people you meet are all the same until you get a little closer. Days spanning all the years of his life. A closer look revealed so many things. Like the man with a broad smile and slicked dark hair, who could have been a movie star, had turned out to be his father. The lady with arms crossed and hair rollers falling from her head, was not some random woman he didn't know, but his mother.

He must have dozed off, because when he awoke it was morning. Rain pelted the roof, and the black and white television was on. Maria was gone again. He watched television until his pupils burned. Time fell off in black and white segments. Then he got up to get something to eat. It was hot in the kitchen in spite of the rain. Saturday, and everyone was out doing something, even Maria. He warmed up some milk and poured it into the coffee she'd left for him. He'd try talking to her again, as soon as she came home.

He drank the coffee standing up and tore at the remains of a piece of bread, then went back to the television. Just as the great Pedro Infante, mustached and dark-eyed, belted his soulful croon in *Pepe El Toro,* he heard Maria's voice on the porch. He peered through the shutters. Maria, Isabelita, and a man Elio seemed to recognize were talking. For a moment, Elio thought it was Pepe, and the thought alone stunned him.

"Not as far as I can tell," the man said. He was young, tall, and shirtless. Elio moved even closer to the shutters, rubbing his eyes as they adjusted to the porch light and the image once again came into focus. Yes, there he was: young, unruffled, and charming as hell.

Because it couldn't be Pepe, Elio concluded that he was just tired, and that he simply needed to rest, that whatever he thought he was seeing was nothing more than the work of heartbreak and grief. He must have just seen him before. But, in the dim light of the porch, he couldn't place him.

"Are you sure?" Isabelita said. Are you sure he's this or that, she might have been saying. Was she talking about Elio?

"Not so sure…but we can think about that later," the man said, his hand on Maria's bare shoulder.

Elio's eyes went wide with surprise—genuine surprise—because he never thought he would have to guess what his wife was doing with a younger man, especially a man Elio might have known. And even if he had no idea why they were together, Elio couldn't help but feel shaken and hurt by what he saw.

"Anything else?" Maria looked at Isabelita first, then at the man.

"There's one thing—" Before the man could finish, Elio flicked the shutters close. He'd seen and heard enough.

The possibility of Maria being unfaithful made him feel sick to his stomach. He couldn't make heads or tails of what he'd seen. Worse yet, that guy had a haircut Elio thought made him look too much like Che Guevara, or a Beatle. He'd groped Maria's shoulder like he was testing an avocado for ripeness. He was younger, though—much younger. Is that what she was into now? Was that what it'd come to? Elio wanted to run out and say hi to Isabelita, to interrupt their conversation, but he thought better of it. He had to get away. He could face anything else, but not this. He'd leave Maria a note and pretend he never saw or heard a thing. He'd say he'd come home later—gone fishing with Pepe, he'd say. Yes, fishing in the rain with a dead friend. It was raining—wasn't it?

He sat down on the bed wondering if this was the moment when

Maria would leave him for another man.

By the time he made it out the back door, the rain had gone. The
air wasn't even slightly brisk. He yanked a pair of wet shorts from the
clothesline, snapping pins off across the yard. Shorts in hand, and
shirtless, he climbed onto old cement sacks heaped against a corner, then
jumped over the wall. Overgrown reeds and grass, along with an empty
can of Vita Nuova tomato sauce and a few moldy cornhusks, cushioned
his landing. He followed the edge of the old lagoon, sidestepping a
bullfrog along the way to the turbina. It was almost noon.

"Should we go our separate ways?" he imagined Maria proposing. "Is
that what you want?" he'd ask.

"Well, do you have a better idea?"

He was out of ideas. "Give me time," he'd say.

"I've given you years, Elio."

They'd both look elsewhere. As irrational as it may have been, he'd
gleaned from the brief exchange he'd witnessed that Maria was ready to
leave him. She may not have been ready to leave Cuba, but she was ready
to leave *him*.

People ambled on the sidewalk. Some held bags under their arms,
others dragged crying children, like wet mops, back home from the park.
And still others teetered rocking chairs on wet porches—counting puddles
on the street.

A few houses down, Teresa, the crow from across the street, leaned
over a three-foot wall and fixed her wild eyes on him. He pretended not to
see her—whatever strength he'd had now seeping out onto the sidewalk.
Over the edge and into the gutter. Would the two men who'd followed
him and beaten him come after him again? It was now his turn to follow.
Now his turn to listen in, to pry, to investigate the affair further.

Crossing the street toward Bauta's Coppelia, he saw them again. This time the young man held Maria's hand and Isabelita walked beside them. His blood pressure must have gone up right then and there because his face was hot and his head was throbbing. Pepe would have known what to do.

Maria looked put together—not her usual Saturday housedress, but shirt and skirt. And she'd added highlights to her hair—or was it just the sun? What was she doing? When had this happened? Who was this son of a bitch moving in on Maria like Elio didn't exist, and what did Isabelita have to do with it?

"Where the fuck have you been?" he could hear Pepe saying. He wished for the familiar voice, followed by a life-saving slap on the back. "Don't look back. Let's get the fuck out of here."

"You know about it?"

"Let's just walk."

Elio let Pepe's memory usher him away from Coppelia as if into a better seat at the movies.

"What the fuck, brother? You snapped." Pepe's voice went on, making circles around him—trapping him in place.

"You think Maria's got a lover?"

"Nah, that Rocky Balboa look-alike? She's got eyes only for you, brother?"

"I fucked up."

"You can say that, again."

Weeks went by waiting for Maria to bring up the meeting with Isabelita and the Rocky Balboa look-alike. If there was nothing going on, why wouldn't she tell him about it? He was having bad days again, and long nights. At work only Isabelita talked to him. He wanted to ask her about the meeting, but each time he tried, he felt sick to his stomach, a pain above his belly that grew sharper the closer he came to saying something. It was as though the words, like rocks, were lodged inside his throat, refusing to come out. Everyone else treated him like he'd been contaminated with the kind of morbidity and sense of foreboding that can only be brought by the death of a good friend. They seemed to be following the same impulse that kept him from going near the water all those years: they were afraid. Terrified they'd end up like Pepe, drowned and washed up on a local beach.

Maria was cold and silent, like a tomb. He wanted to corner her into saying something but each time he saw a chance opening up, she scurried out the door on her way to Fina's house. He didn't hear or see anything again, but he couldn't get the picture of her and the other man out of his mind. One night, while they ate in silence, his patience ran out.

"What the hell is going on around here?" He raised a spoon dripping with chickpea soup.

She hesitated, then started to say, "Isabelita—," but quickly changed her mind and blurted, "Your father called." Her spoon made circles in the soup.

He didn't say anything for a while. The words seemed to belong to ages ago. He'd imagined so many things, but not this. Though he noticed the deliberate change of subject, what she revealed upset him way too much to let it go. With exasperation, with disappointment, he said, "I can't waste time thinking about my father when there are other more important things for me to think about."

Maria stiffened. "Look," she said, "maybe it's something you have to deal with." She clasped her spoonful of chickpea soup sideways, letting it drip back into the bowl. "Just call the man and see what he wants. You owe him that much." Her voice was calm. She waited, wiping clean the bean residue on the edge of her bowl with the tip of her index finger.

"Perhaps I could call him. I could explain the situation..." she said finally.

"Don't even think about picking up that phone. I don't owe him squat."

In over fifteen years, this was his father's second call. By always refusing to find out what the calls were really about, Elio had turned each one of them into a pointless gesture.

"Jesus, you need to call him, Elio. I want to leave," Maria said. "Otherwise..." She'd told Elio the same thing soon after they married. "Bound, gagged, or blindfolded, I'll leave," she'd told him. But this time, Elio noticed a firmness in her voice. The opening to an ultimatum, which terrified him.

They argued all night about his father. Though there were plenty of silences, plenty of gaps and fissures in their words, he couldn't bring himself to mention what he'd seen. He'd been so riled up by the phone call that he couldn't ask again. Each time he thought of it, he stalled. He didn't want to be accused of eavesdropping. Didn't want to know what she didn't want him to know, what nobody should know about a wife. He gleaned that if he said anything else that night, she'd pack up and leave.

CHAPTER 51

MANOLITO CAME UP with the plan a few days after talking with Isabelita and Maria. Isabelita was in, but Maria had yet to make up her mind; he wasn't about to worry about that. All he cared about was putting his goddamn plan in action, so he talked to a buddy about it, a mechanic. The guy thought it was nuts, but Manolito knew it could work. It was a great idea. His viejo's 1959 Buick converted into a boat, with a propeller hidden underneath so he could still move the car around if he needed to. No one would notice the damn thing. Styrofoam injected into some of the parts, so the old Buick could float—and that's that. Nothing too complicated. Way safer than a rickety raft, roomier than an inner tube, and a hell of a lot more pimped up than an actual boat. Tinker here and there, and Booya!—they've got themselves a boat. How they'd managed to keep the goddamn car was something of a miracle.

At first the idea scared Isabelita, but then what else would they do? What options did they have? The parts weren't easy to find—what was, right? Once focused, though, he couldn't think about anything else. Soon he had a propeller, enough cans of Styrofoam to open up at least a kiosk, gas, and provisions. Powdered milk, water, and the last surviving cans of Russian meat. Everything came from the black market, where else? Isabelita was going on and on about how dangerous it was, and how scared shitless she was. It was an interesting thing, sibling relationships—he loved her a lot, but she drove him fucking insane.

He'd never leave her behind, though. They'd spent time apart before, when he was younger and his parents split up for good. One in Oriente and one in Pinar del Río—the further apart the better, or they'd have stabbed each other to death with insults. Manolito went with Mami, and Isabelita with Papi. But Mami and Papi didn't stay away from each other for too long—at the end of the month, they were back at it again, pisando like rabbits. It was a miracle there were only two of them, and not a herd.

Manolito'd come back to Bauta when he turned twenty and he'd been living with Isabelita ever since. When Mami and Papi found a way to leave, they left. Never did manage to get Isabelita and Manolito out, though. Finally they had a solid chance of making it to Miami in one piece, of reuniting with Mami and Papi after all these years—so yeah, Manolito was a little obsessed.

CHAPTER 52

IN THE WEEKS that followed, Elio found himself preoccupied with other matters. The cave didn't feel like it used to and was beginning to stifle him. He'd spent hours staring at the markings, unraveling them with dark, dilated pupils, letting them spring back into place when his eyes started to twitch and then turning in for the night, in a fetal position cocooned in the dark, his back against the cave's wall. He started to think that whatever he'd seen in the cave, whatever good news he'd learned from the saddest of all knight-errants, he'd need to share. He'd have no choice but to let people in on the secret.

Maria was still giving him the cold shoulder about Ricky's phone call, but he'd found a way to put up with the silence. He wanted to wear her down with tolerance and trust, but she was slipping away. His feelings about his marriage, what it signified, and how to save it might have been misplaced. There was something else—something unspeakable, something lacking all possibility of intelligible speech that bugged the shit out of him. But Elio couldn't leave her—not before she'd left him. The most awful thing, according to Elio, was not that Maria could be cheating on him, but that he, over the years, and in one way or another, had cheated *her.* Nothing could have been simpler than that small but undeniable truth that weighed upon his heart with dark foreboding.

Maria was a strange bird. She had neither the pleasant poise of the pheasant nor the proud elegance of the eagle. She was more of the tropical variety: boisterous and temperamental. When happiest, her tread was like the skim of a bird that had not quite settled on its branch. When sad, she sniffled. But she was happy, mostly—wasn't she? As long as she could cut the tip of her shoes to let her toes wiggle and breathe, she'd say she was fine. It was those small pleasures that made life on the island bearable, she'd tell him.

She didn't complain much, either. Happy to nearly blow up the house with an old pressure cooker in an effort to tenderize the toughest piece of beef. Celebratory when corn came to town and she'd make up her mind to spend the next few days yanking the golden hair from poor, unsuspecting yellow husks, and then throwing them in bunches onto the floor. Elio remembered the air of the nearby fan and chuckled. Husks soaring through the air, like a flock of yellow kites. Elio loved everything about her. But she'd started to lose her patience, even with him.

CHAPTER 53

ISABELITA LIVED ON 147th Street, close enough from Maria's house that the walk might have taken another woman at least a quarter of an hour. But it took Maria much less. She walked past the park, then crossed at the next corner. She turned right at the hair salon then, a few blocks down, she made a left at the shoe repair. There she stopped and glanced down, as if she'd dropped something. Down, then back. Nobody was following her. A very thin woman laboring up a ladder to her rooftop, a bag in one hand bending her sideways; a boy in a Ninja Turtle costume and roller blades clinging to the grille of a bike. Two old porch barracudas each clinging to a glass of sugar water while rocking themselves to sleep.

On this Sunday morning, Maria kept her head down. Eyes barely a few steps beyond the tips of her toes. If asked, she would only say that she was pressed for time. She walked along the sidewalk, avoiding uneven asphalt for fear of turning an ankle. It wasn't yet 2:00 p.m. when Isabelita's porch came into view. Painted in screaming yellow, the house wasn't easy to miss. It was in the worst condition, too—perhaps in even worse condition than Maria's, and that was a lot to say. Because it was the last one on the block, and because there was nowhere else to dump all the trash, the little house seemed to tilt to one side, pushed by the conical pile of trash leaning against it. The front door was open slightly, perhaps anticipating an afternoon breeze. Old cracks lifted what was left of the sidewalk toward the sky and two full-grown malanga plants greeted Maria's steps, like premeditated acts of faith. Even in December, long slants of sunlight fell across the porch.

When Maria came closer to the door, her stomach roiled. It wasn't hunger—she knew that feeling well. It was something else. Something, she thought, like jumping out from the open door of a moving train. It was reckless, that's what it was. And she wasn't exactly sure what she was doing there. She only knew she'd run out of patience. But there were choices in life you couldn't take back: this would be one of them.

A shirtless Manolito opened the door. "Finally," he said, "you're here." Seeing her, he seemed genuinely moved. He spread his arms wide, wanting to embrace her, and would have if she hadn't stopped him by holding him gently by the arm. In any case, this was the third time they'd closed a physical gap between them. Each time, Maria's heart pounded in her throat, so hard she felt it fleeing away from her.

He observed her carefully, affectionately. "Really, I'm so happy you're here," he repeated, following her inside the house. His voice was soothing, convincing from the start. She was at once reminded of how handsome he was, and how much she'd once loved a swimmer's muscular chest. Something about him drew her in, unsettled her. Manolito was tall, and she wasn't used to looking up at men—not men like him, anyway. She didn't think of Elio as short, he just wasn't that kind of tall.

Manolito was handsome, too. Despite Elio's green eyes and the generally attractive shape of his face, Maria had never heard anyone describe him as handsome, or attractive, or even masculine, though over the years she'd found him to be all of those things. But now, even Elio's eyes didn't look right. And his arms and legs appeared shorter, his body longer. The last of his hair falling out into clumps onto the bathroom sink.

"But don't just stand there," Manolito said. "C'mon in."

Maria stepped into the living room. The air was thickened by the smell of something resembling burned sofrito and the chooka-chooka-chooka of a pressure cooker. "Is Isabelita here?" she asked.

"Yeah, she's in the kitchen…Isabelita, Maria's here!" he shouted toward somewhere inside the house. He was still taking her in. "You walked?"

"Coño, Manolito," she said. "How else could I have gotten here? It's only a few blocks and—"

"A bicitaxi, vieja—Isabelita, she's here!" he called for a second time. Maria's face was damp with sweat. She fished a handkerchief out of her purse, wiped her forehead. Isabelita stepped into the living room looking just as frazzled and damp as Maria. Her hair was up in a haphazard bun that left loose curls sticking to both sides of her face. Buttoned incorrectly, her shirt neglected an extra button at the bottom.

"Ignore the house," she said, shaking her head. "Manolito's a pig— and I just don't have the energy."

"Look who's talking!" Like a melody, Manolito's voice trailed in from the kitchen. "I'm the maid around here."

"Of course he'd say that, fresco." Isabelita threw her hands in the air, shook her head again, and sighed.

Maria tried not to notice the orderly state of the living room, but she couldn't help it. It was perfectly clean and organized. Not an ashtray or a picture frame that didn't already belong on the round coffee table in the middle of the living room. There were no spills or sticky spots on the tiled floors. No messes to either tend to or ignore.

Every single object, every piece of furniture, had been set about with such deliberate care that she found it almost unsettling. What had she expected—her own house? Isabelita's house looked the way a proper home should look; it was *one hundred percent good housekeeping*. If it unsettled her so much, though, why hadn't she ever bothered to do the same for her house? But hers was chaos of a different kind—wiping, and sweeping, and hiding things away wouldn't have solved her problem.

"Niña, sit down, for God's sake. You're not gonna get any taller." Isabelita said. Maria laughed. She sat down on a small, green sofa. Isabelita sat down beside her. A radio came on at top volume and the sound of timba filled the room.

"Isabelita," Manolito shouted from the kitchen. His voice broke through the singer's voice. "They're playing your song."

"That's not my song, song, song," Isabelita sang back. She scooted over a few inches to sit even closer to Maria. "Okay," she said, her voice cracking into a whisper. Her hands grasped Maria's face, redirecting her eyes away from the kitchen. "Get ready whatever papers you'll need to take with you. Put them in a plastic bag to avoid them getting wet. Don't bring anything else. Manolito and I will bring water and something to eat. We'll leave before sunrise. Nothing to do right now, me oyes? Be patient and wait. When it's right, I'll come and get you. You get it?" Her dark eyes as big and round as a pair of plump prunes.

Maria's body swayed. She felt sick and Isabelita clasped her hands. "Niña, you look like you're dancing, but you're as cold as a frog. Manolito!" she shouted, fanning Maria with an open hand. "The lemonade, for God's sake—this woman's about to pass out, if she doesn't drink something fast."

Maria was cold, then hot. Then cold again. When Manolito brought her lemonade in an old mayonnaise jar, she smiled up at him. Then suddenly aware of the stains on her teeth, she stopped. What the hell had gotten into her? The kid could be her son. He had to be at least nineteen years younger than Isabelita, and Isabelita was at least six years younger than her. That made him about twenty-five years old, give or take a chest hair or two.

"Look," Manolito said, crouching down near Maria's knees, then holding on to an armrest for balance. "The thing is, we have to be real quiet if we're gonna make it. You can't start blabbing it to everybody. I warned Isabelita—if I hear a peep from anyone about this, I'm sailing solo. You hear me, Isabelita?" His words came out firm against the sounds of timba. The realization that this time she might be leaving the island was dizzying. Maria heard Manolito's words in Morse code, or as in one of those bad telephone connections she'd had no choice but to unplug over the years: *Look–Real–Make–Sailing–Me.*

"I'm sitting right here, Manolito—coño, stop being such a goddamn pest." She heard Isabelita say, as if coming up from a dream. "Get lost, go on. I gotta talk to her alone."

Here–Dream–Lost–Go–Alone.

CHAPTER 54

ONE NIGHT WHILE Maria slept, Elio took off to El Salao on Pepe's bike. He pedaled fast, hoping nobody would stop him. Nobody did. Not even Teresa was out at that time. It was just half past one on a Sunday night, and the streets were deserted. Once or twice he saw the flickering lights of a television through half-closed shutters, but all was dark and still otherwise. He was so impressed by how calm the night was, and so afraid it could all change rapidly, that as soon as he reached the end of the block, he decided not to pedal too fast. If he had, the tires squeaking against the ground alone might have given him away.

At the beach, he lifted the bicycle across the sand and trudged toward the shore. When he came to a tree, he leaned the bicycle against it. The swoosh-swoosh of the waves and the smell of saltwater in the air sent a chill up his spine. His skin was moist with ocean spray, so close was he to the water now. But he couldn't turn around. Pepe was right, he had to grow some balls, or at least grow back the one he'd missed all these years.

"Today," he said toward the swelling waves. Then he took off his tank top and shorts, and waded into the water. It was warm, warmer than he remembered it. Repinga, perhaps this was why sharks loved these waters.

His legs shook a little, but every new step was easier than the last. Hell, at this pace, he'd be diving off the pier in no time. If only now he decided to let it all go, all he'd have to do was float away from the shore. He looked up at the sky, a star-studded universe. Lovely, cojones!—especially at night. Though far too big for such a small town, for such a small island. And yet, he knew he was not alone. There were others looking at the stars, in nearby islands–in Haiti and Dominican Republic, in Puerto Rico, and in Jamaica. Beautiful Jamaica, as he'd heard his dad call it once. It pained Elio to think of them all, the Greater Antilles, and he felt sick to his stomach. What had gone wrong? Why were these islands so poor and devastated, so heartbroken and beautiful?

That night he walked in as far as his waist but, although he had planned to go all the way with it, he changed his mind right then and there. A few feet farther in, and completely oblivious to him, a silver marlin leaped out the water, made an arch in the air, and dove back in. Elio knew the difference between marlins and sharks, but he was as scared as pinga—he couldn't help it.

In the nights to follow, though, he returned again and again to El Salao. Until the bottom of his feet became reacquainted with broken shells and uvas caletas. Until he had no choice but to thrust his body forward, extend his arms in front of him, and swim.

Diving into the Caribbean at night, naked as daylight, swimming as far into the ocean as his lungs could take him, he felt at ease. It was all those dark silhouettes moving freely in the water that caught his attention. He was transfixed: the effortless meandering of the creatures just above the ocean floor was the very expression of divine release. And so, like everyone before him who ever found himself in the presence of the divine, Elio sought to make it his. Sinking his head and torso into the water first, then letting his lower body follow, he sought to dive deeper, much deeper,

until his fingertips touched the ocean floor. It was like melding his mind
with another mind, like fusing to a kind of sublime emotion.

It was like floating in and out of different selves. The thrill of it
electrified him, priming him for the reception of a new truth. The sea like
a central commandment he only now understood, agitating his spirit with
awe and delight. Like never before, he sensed he was going somewhere.
Leaping up and into the water like some goddamn Flipper one night,
he thought of swimming away. Where would he go? The Pacific Coast,
perhaps? Fiji? Anywhere but here.

Then thoughts came to him. He thought of the brush pulling on his
mother's tangled dark hair. His father's back floating past the threshold.
Three Kings' Day and the rebels' black and white victory march into
Havana. Pepe, quiet and still at the funeral home. Then the photograph
of Maria's quince, with the handwritten note to Pepe who wasn't Pepe
then. He was a skinny kid with a heart as big as his nose. He was a strong
swimmer, yes. Elio'd heard him say once that he'd swum across the Gulf of
Batabanó to Isla de Pinos and back, in one afternoon.

"Muchacho," he'd say, "I went at it like a tiger. Leaping up to each
wave. I call it the ambush method." Elio knew he was lying, but he
found the stories amusing. They'd met in El Salao Beach, near the bend,
by El Pillo's old shack. They didn't become best friends until they found
themselves both in love with Maria, and then they felt an instant and
mutual sympathy—something like the stealth recognition that neither
would ever stand a chance.

It was back when Elio was Elio and Maria was a sun-kissed blonde
girl on a beach towel, learning English from a Sears catalogue. So much
had changed since then. They had both deceived him. But Maria, Maria
was breaking his heart.

A few days later he traded two cigarette cartons he'd taken from Pepe's house and a few bicycle parts for a net and primitive scuba gear. He began showing up at home with pails full of live fish. He had left the Cave of Paredones behind him and was entering into a new year. The Year of the Fish. The more he thought about the markings, the more he knew what it was he needed to do. Not even Maria could stop him.

"I don't know if I have enough oil to fry so much fish," Maria said, rushing forward to take the pail from Elio's hands. "But we can freeze the rest. Finally, fried fish!"

"They're not for eating, woman. They're for watching. They know what's coming."

"Let me remind you," she said. "Fish can neither think nor speak. I'm starting to think you've lost it. No, worse, I don't even know what to think. Look at you," she added. "You look like Captain Nemo. Hadn't you sworn off the beach?'

"A man can change his mind, can't he?" He could not tell what sentiment troubled Maria's words that day. All he knew was that he sensed in her reaction an irremediable frustration.

It was about this time that Elio started talking about torrential rains, about a great flood that would sink the whole island underwater and release them all, all except the fish—they were naturally free.

CHAPTER 55

IT WAS A SATURDAY afternoon, and Elio was riding back from El Salao Beach. The road home was mostly clear, except for an old Chevrolet every so often, or a newly-minted bicitaxi with two or more passengers taking a break by the side of the road. A few miles from home, as Elio struggled to pedal up hill, a green 1959 Buick sputtered near him. The driver revved up the engine and the car moved a few feet, sputtering a second time and coming to a thrust, then a halt. Elio's bike wobbled and stopped a few feet behind. The driver's door creaked and moaned and the driver slid out, turning toward him.

"Oye, brother. Give me a hand—this shit's gone up and died on me again," the driver said. Elio's eyes closed in on the face, which belonged to none other than the Pepe look-a-like he'd seen with Maria and Isabelita weeks earlier. It was the same goddamn kid. What were the odds? The hell if he was going to help this bastard out.

"Coño, Elio—are you gonna help me or what? I need a hand, repinga," he called out again. How did this guy know who he was? Elio's eyes trained on his face. There was something else, too. That repinga could have only one origin.

Elio's heart raced. His grip shook the handlebars. A sudden change of heart drove him to salvage something, he supposed. He got off the bike, and then leaned it against an electrical post.

"Get in the car," he told the kid. "You're lighter—I'll push."

"Coño, brother." A grin lit up the kid's face. "You got me good for a minute. I'm Manolito, by the way," he said, extending a hand. "I'm Isabelita's brother—the one who got you off the floor at Pepe's funeral, man—you don't remember a goddamn thing, do you? Mi hermano," he said, shaking Elio's hand for a second time. "I owe you one. I gotta pick up Isabelita and take her to Corralillo. You know how that is, brother…en la lucha siempre."

"That was you?" and "I'll push," were the only words Elio could muster. The diazepam had not only nearly knocked him out during Pepe's funeral, Elio thought, but it seemed to have also erased all recollection of ever meeting Manolito there. As far as Elio was concerned, the first time he'd seen the kid was in front of his house some weeks ago. If Elio was ready to help him now, it was because he was curious to find out who the hell this kid was, and what exactly he was doing with Maria.

Manolito looked around a couple of times before sliding into the driver's seat. He put the car in neutral and stuck his arm out of the window, giving Elio the go-ahead. Hands on the trunk, Elio took a deep breath and pushed.

"Push to the curb!" Manolito shouted from the driver's seat. But pushing a clunker midway up a hill, even if it was to the curb, Elio thought, wasn't easy. Nearing the edge of the road, the kid stuck his head out the window. "You alright back there?"

"I'm fine," Elio said. He could feel his cheeks reddening, and he was out of breath and sweating. Had he raised his hand to wave even once, the car would have rolled back and over him. Elio imagined the car sliding back down each time he pushed, and having to start all over. Wasn't that what his life had been like all these years?

He pushed without stopping until he reached the curb, his shoes sliding back twice on the gravel. As they neared the side of the road, Manolito steered to the right, giving Elio the chance to adjust his weight and push one last time.

While Elio pushed, Manolito very gently eased the car toward the green edge of a field and came to a full stop. Elio let his hands hang limp at his sides. Drenched in sweat, his tank top felt like a second skin. Just then, he remembered Pepe's bike. He turned around, searching for the pole at the bottom of the hill.

"You okay? I owe you one, man. My only other option would have been to let the car roll backward down the hill," Manolito said, springing out of the car with the agility his youth afforded, then padding Elio on the back. "You're sopping wet, old man. That was a workout de pinga. Coñó!"

"The bike's gone, goddamn it. Someone's taken it," Elio said, his eyes following the hill down to the lone pole at the base.

"A Chinese Flying Pigeon? You're better off—they're a piece of crap, if you ask me."

"No, not a Chinese bike. A dead friend's bike. My dead friend's bike, damn it."

"Pepe's bike?" Manolito asked. "Nice guy, I heard. I only met him once, you know?...And then at the funeral, of course. I mean...you know what I mean. Coño, man—what bad luck!"

Elio started to tear up, and he must have been doing a pretty shitty job of hiding it, because Manolito looked at him sympathetically. "You okay?"

Elio drew himself upright, his spine stiffening. "Ven acá, chico—what the hell were you doing with Maria the other day?"

"Where did *that* come from?" Manolito cocked his head to one side.

Elio scratched the back of his head—he was itching all over. His legs, and his arms, too—hell, even his butt crack itched. "Forget it. It's nothing you'd care about," he said, his hand waving his words away.

"It's not what you think—I know that much," Manolito said.

"Yeah, I know. You got a cigarette?"

"Nah, I don't touch the stuff. Gotta keep this body pure, mi hermano. That's not good for you, you know that—"

"I know that, too." Elio smiled. He didn't touch the stuff either, but Maria certainly seemed to lately. Whether it was Pepe's death, or something else, entirely, she had suddenly turned into a chimney. Now it was he who wanted to smoke. What was going on with her, anyway? He supposed it was a special time, when everything appeared to be held together by ingenuity and doggedness. But in fact, everything was falling apart. Perhaps nicotine and an empty cloud of smoke would have filled the space where so many things should have been.

"Then let me tell you something you already know," Manolito said. "The world ain't all sunshine and rainbows—"

"I know," Elio interrupted, with tears in his eyes. "It's a very mean and nasty place, and it don't care how tough you are, it will beat you to your knees and keep you there permanently if you let it."

"Are you gonna let it?" Manolito added. "'Cause I sure as fuck won't."

Elio smiled. "You're a regular Rocky Balboa."

"Estalón, 1976," Manolito said. "Doesn't get any better than that. I do a little bit of boxing myself—featherweight, you know?"

"You do?" Elio was amused, in spite of himself.

"Sure do." He shadowboxed in the air. "You see this scar?" he said, getting closer to Elio.

Elio spotted a small scar on Manolito's left cheekbone. "That's rough," he said. "He got you good."

"Oh, yeah," Manolito said. "I got distracted. Right hook, heavy as death, man. The guy blasted me out...I'm tired just thinking about it. I say we take five and sit by the side of the road. You know, take a whiff of cow dung and burn to a crisp under the sun."

They sat down, in silence. Legs extended in front of them toward the road. Manolito passed the time biting his cuticles and staring at the road. Elio piled loose gravel into a small heap between his legs. The sun hung right above them, its heat pelting down like some strange rain.

They remained silent for longer than Elio needed to fit the pieces together. Rocky Balboa, Elio thought, like father like son. Goddamn Pepe had gone and made a son with Isabelita. The same Isabelita he started messing around with right before Maria's quince. As a matter of fact, Elio remembered Pepe hadn't heard from Isabelita again until a few years ago when she came to work at the textilera. And the whole time the guy had no idea. If he had, he wouldn't have done what he did, Elio was certain. Hell, Pepe had never liked children much, but he would have liked this kid. He was Pepe, but better—without the kinks. As far as having something to do with Maria, though, there was evidence stacked against them that Elio couldn't simply ignore.

And that poor Isabelita...no, not poor, selfish. She'd come back to La Cubalina five years earlier, and in those five years she'd never once said a word of it to anybody. Perhaps that's what the damn conversation that night was all about. "Are you sure?" Isabelita had asked Maria. Are you sure we should tell him, she might have been saying. Was she talking about Manolito? She couldn't have been. Manolito had been there, standing right in front of both Isabelita and Maria. And, if Elio was sure of one thing, it was that Manolito had no idea that he was Pepe's son. Right when he was about to turn to Manolito and pry for an answer, he saw Isabelita walking up the hill, carrying a bucket in her hand.

It was a warm day, but with plenty of sea breeze. Along the road, the blaze of big green leaves of grass, every possible shade, flickered in the sun. His mind wasn't on Manolito and Isabelita any longer, or even on Maria. It had gone back to his stolen bike, Pepe's bike. Elio didn't even speculate about who could have taken it; and it would have been difficult to do so—it could have been anybody. A stolen bike on the island was as good as gone—there was no point looking for it. He was full of regret over his carelessness, wishing that the day would reassemble itself around him and that the bike would reappear, as if by magic. Pepe's bike, leaning against a pole, exactly where he'd left it.

Elio watched a blue and white Transtur Havana bus roll by. The bus honked at Isabelita and passed her, followed by a bicitaxi that hooted its horn as it slowly toddled up the hill. She cursed at them both with a stiff middle finger pointed to the sky. He saw her stop to catch her breath, then go on.

Manolito saw her, too. "Look who's here," he said, springing up from the grass. A step or two, and she was right in front of them. Elio stayed put, looking down toward the loose gravel he'd been heaping for the past fifteen minutes.

Isabelita set the bucket on the grass along with her purse, then sat down next to Elio. "Manolito, were you planning on picking me up, or what? I told you we have no water," she said. "Nothing, Not a drop, zilch. The well in Corralillo's empty."

Manolito's nostrils flared like a bull's. Nothing like anger and frustration to bring people's gene pool to the surface, Elio thought.

"No water, no light, no nothing." the kid said, looking at Elio and shaking his head. "This place's killing me, compadre."

"I need a ride to Mirta's house in Caimito. She's still got water at home."

"I know," Manolito said. "I was on my way to get you when the damn car stalled and refused to turn back on."

Instead of responding to Manolito's last words, Isabelita turned to look at Elio. "What are you doing here?" she said.

"Nothing much—just telling Rocky Balboa how lucky he is to have a *sister* like you."

"Go to hell."

"Calm down, vieja. The guy's messing with you—" Manolito's hand rubbed her shoulder.

Isabelita shrugged off Manolito's hand, and then turned to Elio. "I know what you're doing—and you better stay the hell out of it. Let's get this damn cafetera going again, Manolito. We get the water, then we drop off funny man here at home."

"Why don't we try that engine, again," Elio said. "You never know." Just as they were about to walk toward the car, they spotted a Lada coming up the hill. Elio recognized it instantly. It was the same car that had followed him weeks before Pepe's death.

"Now we're fucked, repinga," Manolito said.

"Nah, it's nothing. You got nothing, right?" Elio's chest rose and fell as he watched the Lada come up the hill.

"I'm not so sure." Manolito stood up taller, as if anticipating a future blow to the chest.

The car came to a halt right next to them. Elio recognized the passenger instantly. It was Roberto Salas, District Coordinator, CDR Captain, and Bauta's bodeguero. The driver, Elio had never seen before.

Isabelita hopped toward the car. Her arms outstretched for balance.

"I hurt my ankle," she said. "Twisted it in a pothole at the bottom of the hill. We're just waiting for the pain to go away a little."

Elio was thankful that Isabelita had come up with something to draw attention away from the fact that they'd been stopped on the side of the road long enough to look suspicious.

The driver got out of the car, strutted around, and peered inside Manolito's back window. The bodeguero remained in the passenger seat, one arm propped on the edge of his window. Elio and Manolito stayed put.

"You got anything on you?" the man finally asked Manolito.

"Like what?"

"You tell me."

"Look," Elio interrupted. "Bauta's out of water, again. We were just taking her to get some in Caimito when the car refused to start. You know how it is with these old cars. Tem-per-a-men-tal." He was hot in the face, and his heart beat faster now.

"Nobody asked you. Did you hear me ask you? Hey, Roberto, did you hear me ask this tipo here? I didn't. 'Cause I would have known if I had asked him something. What do you got in the trunk? Prop it open. Let me see what you *don't* have in there."

"Ay, what pain, mi madre. It's broken for sure." Isabelita gripped her ankle.

"Sit down, Mami. If it was broken, you'd be crying right about now. Open the door…what's his name?" the man said.

"Manolito," Isabelita said.

"Open the door for your—"

"Sister," Isabelita was quick to add.

"Open the door for your sister, Manolito," the man said.

Manolito fixed his eyes on Isabelita, then stared up and down the length of the man. "What the fuck do you care who she's to me?" he said, his chest suddenly larger, and his body taking up more space.

"Eh," he said. "Look who thinks he's got spurs, Roberto. Careful, papito. Mira—" he said, taking out a small ID card from a shirt pocket, "—state security. Open the trunk, repinga." He grew longer and wider right before Elio's eyes, like a great white. Elio urgently wanted to prevent Manolito from making any sudden moves. It occurred to him that, if Manolito were Pepe's son, then Elio would be forced to react in one of two ways: either by embracing the kid, or by pushing him away— and Elio would never push Pepe's son away. Confronted with fear and intimidation, Manolito might very well cow, or else be moved by the sudden need to break the guy's face.

To Elio's dismay, Manolito turned around, but something must have pulled him back. He turned again to face the back of the old Buick and did what he was told, which was, for Elio, a great relief.

"Manolito," Isabelita shouted from inside the car, "get me my old tennis shoes. These damn jellies are caked with mud."

Manolito popped open the trunk after tinkering with the blunt tip of a clothes hanger he pulled from under Isabelita's feet. The latch clicked, and he lifted the trunk. Standing a few feet away, Elio hoped there was nothing in it but Isabelita's shoes.

The tension built in Elio's chest, heartbeat giving way to heartbeat. The man eyed the trunk's interior from a short distance but, for some reason unknown to Elio, he didn't come right up to the trunk. He simply walked in a semicircle around Manolito, back and forth. Something in his movement again brought a shark to Elio's mind. He was unsettled. Isabelita sat in the car, her legs dangling out the open door. She held her head in her hand, and quietly began to cry.

Elio felt trapped, as stunned as if he'd stuck a wet finger inside an electrical outlet. If Manolito threw a punch, he thought, he'd take it as sign to join in and crush the man's skull against the ground. He didn't even know himself then or why he felt the way he did. But he felt sorry for Isabelita—and even more so for a fatherless Manolito. Sorry for his own mother lying in a casket, for his father, for Maria, and ultimately, for himself. Sorry enough that he was ready to pounce.

The man searched the trunk from back to front, reaching in all the way, until his hand touched the stiff surface of the back seat. He rummaged around every corner, every small crevice. Loosening and lifting the vinyl covering that had replaced the original upholstery. Nothing, except for a roll of old *Granma's,* a rusty jack, an empty twelve-gallon metal gas tank, and a few nails caught in a groove between the edge of the vinyl covering and the car's right-side panel. Not finding anything particularly incriminating, he slammed the trunk closed, then turned to Manolito, "And her tennis shoes?"

Manolito shrugged.

The sky seemed to darken rapidly. Minutes and heartbeats giving way to faster minutes and faster heartbeats, in a song and dance Elio knew well. And then, as suddenly as the men appeared, they left. Leaving them stock-still at the top of the Loma de Pita.

"How could such an ignoramus have a driver's license and a car, while I'm walking around with an empty bucket trying to get to Caimito under a scorching sun? You tell me, if that's fair. Anyway," Isabelita said, turning to Elio, "the most important question here is do you think they'll come back?" She was no longer holding her ankle. Her brown, inert legs hung off the side of the seat and toward the road.

Elio wished they could have waved down a car or a truck, but there were no vehicles on the road and the last bicitaxi they'd seen had passed nearly an hour ago.

"Not sure," he said, with a half smile. As far as he was concerned—and based on her most recent performance—if Isabelita ever decided to leave the island, she'd have a bright future in Hollywood.

"They're not coming back," Manolito said. "They didn't find what they were looking for."

"And what was that?" Elio said.

"Bueno, chico…truth be told—"

"Manolito," Isabelita interrupted, "let's try it, c'mon. Like Elio said, you never know."

Manolito shrugged. He no longer had a grin on his face. "It'd be nice to have a cigarette now, wouldn't it, old man?"

"It sure would," Elio said.

As if reading Elio's mind, Manolito took an invisible cigarette to his lips, inhaled, then exhaled. Then he flung the half-smoked, invisible bud near his feet. He stubbed it out. "There—I feel much better now." He shrugged. "Why the hell were they following *me?*"

Elio knew it wasn't Manolito they were following. They were following him.

"I can help you push, Elio." Isabelita said, sliding out of the seat, and stretching her torso from left to right. "I can do it. Just give me a second to pull it together."

Elio had been staring at her the entire time, hoping perhaps that his eyes could ask her what his tongue could not. But he didn't need to ask anymore. He'd read the answer in her eyes.

He was right, after a few tries, the engine sputtered, then rolled, as if changing its mind after all. "Get in, old man," Manolito told him. "I'll drop you off at home."

Elio resented being called an old man, but he figured it came from a good place.

"Sure thing," Elio said, and hopped in the car.

From the passenger seat, Elio scanned a motionless sea of grass. His bike was gone—Pepe's bike was gone.

Once he'd gotten over the initial surprise at discovering Manolito's relationship to Pepe, he wasted no time asking himself if it was worthwhile circling about matters that weren't any use. Nor did he want to know whether his suspicions about Maria and Manolito had any actual substance. There was no point in pushing Maria further away from him. He'd been trying to win her over all his life—he wasn't about to stop now. But he needed his life to have a real objective; if anything, Pepe's drowning had taught him that. Pepe may have died in the process, but he was going somewhere. Elio'd read *Quixote* like a Bible, finding in it new prescriptives for his life. He'd schlepped through dry brush in the murky sunshine to stare at markings on a wall. He'd scratched at them, hoping to cipher in them something like a revelation—and because he did it enough times, that's exactly what he'd found. And finally, when he thought all was lost, he'd found fish. In the pitiful itinerary that was his life, fish were a destination.

CHAPTER 56

ALTHOUGH ELIO COULDN'T manage to convince himself that there was nothing going on between Maria and Manolito, he decided to turn his attention to other things. Through losing Pepe he'd learned that it hurt to look for reasons. He waited for the unhappiness to become yet another discontent, yet another void in the pit of his stomach. It summed in the labor of every day: surviving food shortages, making the bed, helping Maria with the washing and drying of clothes, enduring the abuses of neighbors, and coming home to devote himself, more than ever, to his fish.

It was a Saturday, and Elio had been lying on a cot all afternoon in tattered trousers, when Maria walked in from the kitchen.

"Elio, you're destroying the only house we have," she said.

She seemed preoccupied. Elio could feel her worried gaze on him, but he wasn't entirely convinced that whatever she was feeling had anything to do with the house. The house was like it always had been, so there was nothing to worry about.

"Silence, Maria," he whispered through a hush finger, "I'm envisioning a different world."

"Look at this mess!"

Maria looked around the crowded living room. It was bursting with old bicycle tires heaped in piles, two open bags of cement, pieces of glass, green plastic tubes, fishnets, and pails of seawater and algae. "This place looks like a junkyard...look at all this water!" she said. A thin trail of water and sand had settled all along the narrow corridor that connected the living room with the kitchen. Maria wiggled her toes—they were full of sand. "Once again," she said, "you're wasting your time on something that won't remotely improve our lives. If anything, your fish are adding to the chaos we're already living in. At least, for a short time, I want to feel like we're prospering, like we have enough to go around. Can you bring something home that could make *that* happen? "Look at my feet...they're all wet!"

"Your feet are beautiful, Maria...wet or dry."

Elio laughed. He rose from the cot and shuffled toward the woman, pulling up his wet trousers as far as he could to cover an exposed brown belly. "Let me see those feet," he said, reaching for Maria's legs.

"Hands off," she said, and flicked his hands away. "Look at yourself, aren't you embarrassed, showing your belly and your breasts like that? You should be ashamed of yourself."

"Pure muscle," Elio said, hands cupping bags of flesh. "And this," he said, rubbing his belly in circular motions, "all your loving, Maria...all your loving."

Maria laughed, showing the brown stains on her teeth. She grabbed a few strands of hair that stuck to Elio's forehead, placed them in the middle of his bald head. "There. All better now. Now you can clean it all up."

"Nonsense," he said. "The fish are staying."

Maria shook her head at the fish tanks. "You've gone too far this time. Too far."

Elio chuckled. "I've read, Maria...we come from fish. You had flippers once. Like it or not."

"I've read too, Elio, and we come from Adam and Eve. Maybe you had flippers...look at yourself," she said, pointing at Elio's breasts. "I had two arms and two legs from the beginning. See?" She flapped her arms and kicked her legs until she felt tired. Then moseyed toward the kitchen, doing what she could to avoid the puddles.

She was making great efforts to hide from Elio and from herself the anxiety she felt. At every moment, she thought, soon, I'll be leaving, and I won't see him again. The best she could do was to continue in that marital up and down that they'd both grown so accustomed to over the years. And continue to keep secrets. At that moment, secrets were all she had.

She'd been married to the man for decades. She knew when to leave him alone. At first it was a fish in a bucket, and she tolerated that. She even grew to love the little bastard. Then it was two or three new fish tanks a week. Then suddenly their house became a goddamn aquarium of the Caribbean. Elio had been sucked into another world the way people get sucked into their television in science fiction movies; Maria couldn't tell where the cut in the film had taken place. Where it had all gone wrong. What he did in the living room all those hours, she called praying. "It's a prayer," she'd tell Fina. "You know how Elio is...some have God, Elio's got fish."

"All the same, dear," Fina would say.

Left to himself, Elio sank an index finger into a tank. "Just right," he said. His red fish dashed back and forth, its long, forked tail behind him. "There, there," Elio whispered. "You're not just any goldfish, are you? You

are a comet-tail goldfish. I know, I know. You're a big fish in a little pond.
A trailblazer. You're meant for bigger things."

Elio stood up. Reveled in the sight. All around him, fish tanks of all
shapes and sizes filled the otherwise modest living room. The old green
sofa, the two wooden chairs—one of which had a short leg and was
leveled by a phone book—had been moved to a corner of the room to
make space for the fish. It was here that Elio spent his days away from
work, staring into the big, dumb eyes of his fish. Waiting for something
extraordinary to happen. Waiting for the markings to unravel themselves
and give way to what he knew was there: meaning.

"Well," he said, making sure Maria could hear him from the kitchen,
"Prepare yourself for the worst: the flood is coming."

Maria had heard him say so many things over the years—so many
that all the fingers in her hands and all the fingers in Elio's hands were not
enough to keep track. But this time, there was something like a promise
in his words that made the little hairs on the back of her neck stand on
end. Elio had been partial to many things: fake pitusas, reading, and giant
bicycles, among many others. But he'd left them all behind sooner or later.
Maria could stand the quarreling over money, the Mao Zedong hairstyle,
and the various piles of unfinished projects in every corner of the house.
But there was something about the way those fish came in and took over
the house, something in the way Elio gazed into their eyes, something in
the way he stood at the center of all those fish tanks for hours that she
resented, loathed.

To her credit, Maria wasn't the only one to express contempt for Elio's
fish. Elio's new pastime had detractors at the textilera, too.

"The fish'll know," Abelardo, new Head of Production had overheard
Elio saying to someone in the courtyard after work, "and it will be
preceded by torrential rains." It was around that time that Abelardo
brought up the fish during a quality control meeting. "Ven acá, chico,
I've been hearing…you know, some rumors…people like to talk, you
know what I mean? What's going on with all those fish? Have you gone crazy
or what?"

"We are a little concerned about your present state of mind…"
Ramón Gómez, Chief Machine Operator, added. He had taken out a
stubby red pencil and clipboard and started to mark something on a piece
of paper.

"Look, compañeros," Elio said, "this is not a state matter. I still show
up at pep rallies, right? And you never hear me complain, do you? I gotta
tell you, if anyone is worried, that's me. The big one's coming and no one
seems to care."

"The big one? What the hell is that?" asked Abelardo. He patted Elio
on the back. Elio stared at him. Abelardo meant for him to shut up. But
how could he?—this was too important to let go.

"Go ahead," he said, "call me crazy. Hell, fire me, for all I care." And
that's just what they did.

At home, Elio attempted to make peace with Maria. "It's not a big
deal. You got the telephone company and there's the government aid.
We'll be fine."

"Look, Elio," she said, shaking her head. "You better start making
some money around here. We don't even have enough for an extra bar of
soap. I'm still making soap bars from leftover soap slivers, you know that?
If you like your fish so much, why don't you earn your keep and start
selling fish tanks. Cubans have a long-standing love affair with fish tanks
in their living rooms, haven't they?"

A week later, when Maria walked in from work, she could do no more than plop into a chair. In addition to the fish, the fish tanks, the pipes, the tires, and everything else that had already taken over her home, there was now a small crowd of people dashing about her living room. The fish tank business had taken off.

"I sold two six-by-fours to a restaurant near Bejucal, and three one-by-threes to Mayra Fernández. Only minutes before she closed me down," he whispered to Maria.

"What a hypocrite!" Maria told him. "She spent the 70s breaking windows and calling people gusanos and lumpen, and now she's buying fish tanks from you. Then she closes you down? You gotta have some balls."

"Don't get agitated," Elio said, his hands patting down the air. "You'll scare off my last customers."

"Who the hell's going to buy a bunch of makeshift aquariums? Elio, people are starving."

"Weren't aquariums your idea? Food's got nothing to do with it, Maria. Some people know that."

In the following weeks, Elio continued to sell his fish tanks, but kept under the radar. He found a distant cousin nearby willing to stash his materials and let Elio assemble them on his rooftop. One night, as Elio dove his head into an empty tank to install a couple of water pumps, the sky lit up. Seconds later, he heard what he thought was thunder. He looked around. The roof was a minefield of electricity cables, clandestine satellite dishes, and pigeons. Elio packed up. He took the stairs and when he reached the sidewalk, scuttled off toward home.

"This is it," Elio said, as he opened the front door and ran through the living room to check on the fish. "This is it!" he shouted. "Prepare yourself!"

Maria was sitting at the kitchen table sorting a pile of papers. Next to her, a small bowl of uncooked black beans. Surprised by Elio's sudden presence, she moved the bowl of beans closer to her, inadvertently knocking the papers off the table. For a moment, she stayed very still, then pretended it was nothing. She left the papers on the floor, and without even looking at them said, "Have you secured the windows? If so, go to sleep."

"O, Maria, faithless woman…" Elio said, walking toward her. He pulled a red bench up to the table and sat down next to her. The papers were only inches from his feet but he, too, decided to pretend he didn't see them. The light of the moon trickled in through the shutters. There was no place he'd rather be.

But, although the rain came crushing down with the strength and persistence of a deluge, the old lagoon behind Elio and Maria's house overflowed only a few feet above normal level.

Elio was crushed. "This is not what I envisioned," he said, staring at the muddy water that Maria vigorously swept with the frayed ends of a broom. "I imagined torrential rain that lasts days, weeks, months. Rain that floods our lagoons and our rivers. Rain that raises the tide. I wished for a flood of Biblical proportions. The kind that only we would survive. You know, I'd be Noah and you'd be…what was her name?"

"I have no idea. Forget about it," Maria told him, scuttling from one corner of the living room to the next, happy to be forcing the water out.

"The big one's coming. I know it," was Elio's only response. The flood he had in mind, the one that kept him up at night in puddles of sweat and anticipation, would be a great one. He was sure.

CHAPTER 57

FOR MARIA the days passed in an anxiety that, mixed with feelings of guilt, kept her from sleeping. Some nights she became alarmed in the middle of the night and turned to the empty spot on the bed where Elio should have been. She saw almost nothing of him for days at a time. It was hard to pinpoint the exact moment it happened, when even the sex stopped. He was distracted, disinterested. Sex, even bad sex, could have mitigated the food shortages and the blackouts, the boredom, could have given an impression of real life.

She continued to work for Fina, with as much dedication as she'd done at the beginning. But knowing full well she'd never get the house. That dream, like so many others, was done now. And she wished wholeheartedly that a kinder, softer, more innocent world would somehow reassemble itself around her, saving her from the self she'd become—so far was she from everything she ever dreamed.

All had been in vain, even the years she'd dedicated to Elio. A happy marriage, she now knew, depended on so many factors—so many details had to be in place. Although love need not be constant, she thought, commitment had to be. And perhaps she hadn't always been as committed as she should have been. She, too, didn't care for sex with Elio anymore. And why should she have been the one to make the effort? In the dark, all the reasons for unhappiness that she had prudently left nameless all those years got mixed up and were concentrated on Elio.

The moment to prove to herself that she was capable of making her own decisions was finally here. She thought of the promise she'd made to her grandmother decades earlier. She swore to God she'd never leave. But swearing to God was like wishing on birthday candles, or throwing coins into a pond, or playing the lottery. Those were empty gestures everyone knew would never alter the course of one's life. In the bedroom, she felt her heart ticking like a bomb set to explode at zero hour. If she stayed, it would happen—that was certain. She rummaged through a box of old papers with trembling fingers, thinking that were Elio to walk through the door at that instant, she'd change her mind, yet again. 3:00 a.m. sharp, Isabelita had told her. She had less than fifteen minutes to find what she was looking for.

Right when she was about to let it all go, her fingers found the small note, wrapped in red yarn that came to a bow, right at the middle. She had found it years earlier in one of Mima's books, months after she'd passed. Maria'd kept it for years and then one day she opened it. She then couldn't erase from her mind the markings she'd found inside.

It was 3:38 a.m. She waited.

Finally, when she'd almost given up hope, she heard the Buick's engine. Peering through shutters, she watched the car slow down, then come to a halt. She turned around to look at the fish one last time. Some lay still, playing dead in the water. Others nibbled at the mossy bottom of the aquarium. But the goldfish, Elio's favorite, swam in circles close to the glass—one circle smaller than the other, until he seemed to be chasing his own tail. She thought she understood then what Elio saw in him.

Then she hoped. She hoped her mind could fade into the past. She hoped that she could change it all somehow. Then she hoped again, but this time she hoped with all her heart for Elio's flood—for his sake, at least.

From a rear seat, she stared ahead into the middle distance. Her chest heaved. "Chicago?" she said. Isabelita and Manolito both looked back at her.

Maria stared back at them. "Just thinking out loud," she said.

"Niña, you scared the shit out of me! I thought you'd lost it for a minute there." Isabelita leaned over the front seat. "Here," she said, "take a Chiclet. If we can't smoke, we can chew."

"I can't turn down Chiclet," Maria smiled. She unwrapped the chewing gum, and popped the whole thing in her mouth.

The Buick bounced over soft mounds of sand. No clouds obscured the sky, and starlight fell upon the hood in huge cool puddles.

"Sit tight. We're going in the water," Manolito said, his lips scarcely moving as he spoke. "Can you swim?"

"Yes," Maria said in a flat voice. She looked at Manolito's eyes in the rearview mirror. She wanted to say more, but the words wouldn't come out.

"Well, then—" Manolito started to say.

Isabelita interrupted him. "Sure, she can swim," she said, "but she'd be grateful if she didn't have to, though. She's not Yuri Gagarin, Manolito. What kind of question is that, viejo? Just get us to Miami in one piece, okay?" Her voice trembled. Her right leg kept time against the dashboard like a metronome.

"Yuri Gagarin wasn't a swimmer, Isabelita. He was a fucking astronaut," Manolito said.

"At the rate we're going," Isabelita said, "we'll end up on the moon before I ever see Calle Ocho."

"Isabelita, you're too much," Maria said, with a half smile.

The Buick waddled on the shoreline, then thrust forward and stopped. Maria thought of Chicago's skyline, smoky with the vapor of spring-melted snow, glass like stardust frosting the horizon beyond her eyes.

"Qué pasa, Manolito?" She heard Isabelita's voice. Maria looked out toward the water. The dark waves deepened her uncertainty. What the hell was she thinking? Who was she kidding? There was no starting over. She thought of Elio walking into an empty house, probably hungry, or with some new harebrained idea—or both. Hadn't he loved her enough all these years? Hadn't he tried? What the hell was wrong with her? She knew better than to hold him responsible, didn't she? All he had done was try to change things. In his own way, yes—but he had tried.

Just as she was about to reach for the door handle, she felt water swoop beneath them, and the propeller turned on. "I can't swim," she said, leaning forward and whispering into Isabelita's shoulder.

"You won't need to, vieja. We'll make it, you'll see. Anyway, Manolito can swim for both of us. Isn't that true, Manolito?" Maria saw Manolito turn back and raise his eyebrows as if to say, I can't make promises now. She imagined Emma Bovary then, sitting next to her—her hands gripping the seat, terrified of nearing her own end.

Then about a mile from the shore, she saw it, a fin cutting water in two—like in the movies.

A quarter of a mile from the Buick, the night was just as cool. Dark, except for starlight, and a half-moon hanging high in the sky. Elio stood at the shoreline. His bare feet sank into the sand each time a wave broke and pulled back into the sea. He was close to the pier, near the bend. Right where it all started. This time, though, he was ready. He put on the goggles, spit into them, and adjusted the mouthpiece. His gums burned. He turned around, giving his back to the water, then began to plod his way in. Lifting up, then stepping back.

The fin cut the water in two. The shark was not an accident, Elio thought. It had come up from far across the bay looking for him. It, too, knew it was inevitable. Elio had never been so ready. Feet anchored in the sand, he steadied the spear above the water to a point in the distance, and waited. The fish swam fast toward him, just under the surface. The fin knifed through the water without wavering. Elio watched him come on. His head was clear and full of resolution. He knew what he had to do. He remembered the chop of teeth against his groin. Nerve endings as sharp as needles puncturing his spine, and Pepe's voice as distant as the stars, but just as ominous: "Swim, coño!"

When he was close, so close he thought he felt the shark's smooth hide glide against his wetsuit, he thrust the wooden spear into its side, twisting it right and left beyond the ribs, and into the fleshy middle. The fish pulled back, then thrust itself up vertically, like a man on the water, then plopped back in, the spear a perpendicular line between it and Elio's upper torso.

"Jesus Christ," he shouted to the fish. It rippled the bloody water. The bluish color was lost in the dark, but the sword-like bill was unmistakable. "You're a goddamn swordfish."

The fish thrust near him, the spear spinning in the water, like blades on a windmill each time the swordfish turned over on itself. Elio remembered reading once that fish couldn't feel pain, but when the fish turned once more, its head above the water, their eyes met. There was awareness in those eyes, fish eyes that paralyzed Elio. He had rendered the creature helpless.

From where he stood in the water, he saw nothing but sea and sky merging into one dark mass around and above him. He had the feeling of being trapped in a giant crystal globe, the limit of which he could touch, if only he reached out a hand to touch it. He felt defeated. He looked down at the fish, so close to him he could have cradled it in his arms. Swordfish were shaped like cigars, Elio thought. They didn't really taper out like many other game fish. Swordfish were pure muscle, and incredibly strong swimmers—but they weren't sharks.

The fish lay quietly for a while on the water's surface, then went down very slowly. When Elio was certain the fish was dead, it was as if he himself had died. As if he'd turned that spear against himself. He knew he'd been defeated and there was little to do but turn around and go home. Home to Maria, the only destination he'd ever had.

The breeze was fresh as Elio trudged his way back through the sand, hopeful that there was still the one thing that was possible. Because a man is never defeated, he thought. He can be destroyed, but not defeated.

CHAPTER 58

RICKY PEREZ TOOK OFF his clothes, and dove into the still, icy waters of Lake Michigan. He surfaced like an arrow, piercing the air straight up, grinning, like a Cheshire cat, splashing water like crazy. "Come on, prostate cancer. Take me! Me cago en ti y en toda tu prole, hijoeputa!" All around were tourists; many didn't seem to notice Ricky or the fact that, because she was rather inebriated and also because he didn't deserve what was happening to him, Sally egged him on from the shore: "I believe in you, Ricky Perez! I'm here for you, you old bastard! My bags may be packed, but I haven't left town!" High up was a frosty half-moon, casting virtually no light. Along the shore, small, college-radio crowds fisted beer cans around blue-red fire pits, and boomed The Jesus Lizard toward the water. "Go, Big Papa!" They shouted over the pseudo-industrial noise of their radios, at different intervals, so that Ricky felt the words pelting his skin—one after another.

Goddamnit, he was still breathing, wasn't he? Yes, he was still alive, y nadie, pero nadie, was going to nail the coffin on Ricky Perez just yet. He whipped the water with his fists, then jumped straight up as though he would reach the sky, landing on his back and sinking down, his mouth and eyes dripping water. Up again. Still beating, leaping, diving. Up again, and shouting, "You hear me, Willie Loman? Nothing's planted. I don't have a thing in the ground!"

From the shore, slurring, Sally shouted back at Ricky bits of lines she remembered from his show decades earlier: "Willie Loman had a good dream. You hear me, Ricky Perez? It's the only dream you can have—to come out number-one man. He fought it out here, and this is where you're gonna win it—for him. For Willie Loman." Sally stumbled out toward the water, cursing. "Son of a bitch, Ricky Perez. Come out this minute, or I'm coming in to get you."

"I love you, Sally Rogers! You and your American ways!" he said, coming up for air again. "And you're a Perez, through and through. You hear me, Elio, son of a bitch?" he shouted to the night sky.

Two hours later, and back at his little tenement in Back of the Yards, Ricky switched the phone from one ear to the other as he waited for Elio to respond. Yet however he held the phone, he felt horribly aware of his ears, burning against his head. "You're just like your mother. You reduce me to that one decision, that one inevitable decision." Ricky spit out the words into the receiver. "You think you have everyone figured out, but you don't. You're stubborn and unforgiving. I'm dying, goddamnit, and doesn't that mean anything?" He was painfully aware that there was no one on the other side to either reject his words or receive them.

He set the phone down and looked out his window toward the night sky. There it was: Arcturus, one of the brightest stars, light-years away, pegged against Chicago's night sky, like loose glitter on a giant crystal globe, the limit of which he, too, could touch, if only he'd reach out a hand to touch it.

CHAPTER 59

ELIO WALKED for a long time on his way home from the beach, his suit over one shoulder, fins and goggles in one hand, his body still wet. It was almost winter, and a cool breeze chilled his bones. He wanted to walk and tire himself out; perhaps then, he'd be able to sleep. In his first year of marriage, he'd had a hard time sleeping. He'd worried how Maria would react if, at some point, she discovered that he wasn't who he'd seemed to be. Worried about how they would survive the years to come. But, even then, they were young. The island was young, and anything was still possible.

Part of Elio thought he should have cautioned Maria, warned her that life wouldn't always go according to her wishes, if only to prepare her for the goddamn possibility of disappointment. Because if anyone knew about disappointment, it was him. But what right did he have to caution anyone, when he had been incapable of abandoning his own desires? He hadn't been any less practical than Maria when it came to whatever it was they wanted out of life—which, somehow, was also supposed to include their marriage. Nonetheless, he never cautioned himself against hope. After all, if he didn't have anything else, he had hope. And yet, mistaking the swordfish for a shark, and killing it, was only a reminder that he'd gotten it wrong one more time. Coño, what the hell had he done?—as if there weren't enough dead bodies floating around at the beach, he'd added one more. But this one was on him. *He* was responsible. In any case, it was done, and he tried not to be too anxious, tried to steady his breathing, tried to stop himself from making a bigger deal out of the whole thing.

He met almost no one on his way home, only a dog rooting its snout into a pile of trash. Looking at it, Elio had a sense of dissolving, as if he, that pile of trash, had suddenly been thrown about by the tide all night and now was floating without shape, on the crest of a wave. He had to tell Maria what happened. She'd know just what to say, just how to put him back together again.

By the time he reached his front door, his heart and mind had settled into a certain optimism. Yes, if anyone could put him back together, it was she. She'd be angry, sure. But, ultimately, she would understand. Life could often take an ironic turn, and she would get that. Yes, if anybody would get that, repinga, it would be her.

He opened the front door and threw his wet scuba gear into a corner. Anticipating Maria's warm body, he tiptoed into the dark bedroom, and slid into bed. They weren't getting along, and it'd been years since they fought openly, or given and received love in full measure; but it was comforting to lay next to her. As soon as he turned toward her usual spot against the wall, however, he realized she wasn't there yet.

"Goddamn it, Maria," he said, sitting up with such force that a mattress board snapped right beneath him and he sunk half way to the floor. Where the fuck had she gone now? It was nearly 6:00 a.m. and she wasn't home? Where the hell was she? He couldn't help but think of Manolito then. She would either be at Fina's, or with Manolito. Gone, like everyone else.

Climbing out from his sinkhole in the mattress, he made his way to the kitchen. She wouldn't be long, he was certain. He may as well make some of that watered-down shit they called coffee and wait up for her. He hoped she'd be back soon. He could scarcely endure the idea that she might be gone for good. The thought of losing her was a pain that he urgently wanted to be without. He didn't want ever to have to say *Maria has left me.*

For a long time, he made and unmade their bed, tidied the kitchen, changed the water in the aquariums. His agitation from earlier in the night returned and his heart raced. Maria, it was clear, wasn't coming back. He stared insistently at the door hoping that, wherever she was, she'd come to her senses and turn around. He moved closer to his goldfish and tried to catch his eye; perhaps he knew something. The poor bastard slept. In fact, at least right then, he looked dead, or otherwise unreachable. How Elio wished he'd been a fish then. Wouldn't life have been a hell of a lot easier? He felt so lonely. This was how it felt to live on this island. It was goddamn lonely, repinga.

It was several days before someone came to check on him. Who told him, how, or when, he couldn't remember. And it didn't really matter, did it? The only question that mattered, the only question that always mattered was Why? And nobody could answer that, except Maria. "Me cago en su madre, recoño," he'd said to whomever came to check on him. "She, too, didn't leave a note."

That night, or perhaps the night after that, he slept deeply, dreaming for the first time since Maria left. He swam through flooded sidewalks leaping in and out of the water, like a fish. It was as if not just the unknown but the unknowable was within his reach. No one knew who he was or where he'd come from. This was how it felt to be a fish, and it pleased him to think that there'd be no chance in hell he would bump into someone who might recognize him and call out his name. He could be whoever the hell he wanted to be. A fish—dumb, mute. But also free.

In the dream, he heard Maria mouthing, *I have to go away.* He dreamed of being taken to the Malecón in a barrel by both of them, Maria and Pepe. They left him thrashing on top of the seawall. His fins outstretched and his mouth agape. The old man, wrinkled and bearded, just as he'd been decades before, was there too. This time, he didn't try to stop him. "Take a goddamn leap!" he shouted. But just as he was ready to dive onto the rocks, Elio woke up, startled.

CHAPTER 60

WAITING FOR THE FLOOD without giving a thought to its consequences, Elio forgot to board up the windows and raise the mattress away from the reach of the water. He seemed purposely careless, leaving everything in the hands of some otherworldly force that even he had struggled to understand. He was right though, a big one was coming. On March 13, 1995, at approximately 6:00 p.m., about four months after Maria left, and approximately a year and one month since the last sorry excuse for a flood, Elio looked into his tanks. The fish were restless; they swam back and forth, hitting the glass and knocking each other out of the way like bumper cars.

Poor bastards, he thought. They're jammed into the tank like sardines.

At Maria's request, Elio had sold one of his last two tanks to Adelaida Murillo, Maria's old piano teacher and now Elio's replacement at the textilera.

"So," Elio protested then, "not only did she not teach you to play the piano, I must give her one of my tanks?"

"You are not giving it to her, Elio. You are selling it to her," Maria had said.

"Those fish are going to kill each other in there. Fish are not meant to live like that."

The only tank left was a beauty, though, and it had taken him days to make: five feet by three feet and three feet high, with thick black rubber from old bicycle tires for seams and a green mossy bottom crushed here and there by the weight of a giant conch shell. Elio got closer. His goldfish, now dead, floated on its side at the far end of the tank. The other fish had moved on quickly. Pushed their way from one side of the tank and back. Never making it past the glass. He leaned in and poked his finger in the water, tracing the fish's red tail. "Hi, little buddy," he said. "I let you down, didn't I? You had dreams, didn't you? I know, it's not easy to carry the weight of the world on your back, is it?" It crushes you, he thought.

He sighed and stepped back from the tank to turn his attention elsewhere. The sky had turned a dark gray, as if God had drawn a curtain to separate the island from the rest of the universe. "It's a hurricane with winds in the 200 kilometers," the radio had said. "It's gonna be an ugly one, folks." The windows and doors shook. Elio felt the house itself slipping off its foundation. For the first time, he was afraid. He thought that if Maria had been there, he would have sent her away. You'll be safe elsewhere, he would have told her.

Have you lost your mind? He'd hear her say. *I'm not leaving you.*

"You have to trust me, Americana," he said out loud. He imagined her smiling.

About a month after she left him, Maria had sent a postcard. *Wishing you were here,* it said. He *was* here. He'd been *here* all along. He hadn't been an asshole, recoño. If he could have, he would have given her the world. But he didn't know where *here* was or how the fuck to get there.

The windows rattled again. A flash of light. Elio turned his thoughts to the front door. He had spent so many months in solitude, going weeks without speaking to another human except to say *I'm fine* and *I haven't heard from her* and *Stop asking, repinga.* The possibility of someone now knocking at his door to warn him to evacuate filled him with a heavy dread.

Within twenty-four hours, the lagoon behind his house promised to overflow. Elio climbed on top of his refrigerator to watch the water rise and his walls turn green with frogs.

"Amazing," he said to himself, "so little and look how they stick to the walls. Look how they know that something big is coming." Outside, the wind growled like a rabid dog, throwing itself against windows and doors until, all at once, windows and doors opened. Rain and wind were upon him. The fish tanks toppled over. Elio watched as his fish swam away from their collapsing glass house and struggled to join the current. How different they were from each other. There were the blue and orange Angels and the Clownfaces; the Gobies; the gray and white Hamlets; the Butterfly fish; the blue Tangs with the lighter blue underbelly; the multicolored Basslets—he had plenty of those; and the Tank-Breds, striped in orange and white, and outlined in black. There were others that he couldn't identify by name, but whose colors seemed to multiply, making streamers and rainbows in the water as they swam away.

The old refrigerator shook beneath him and Elio struggled to hold on. He took off his shirt and threw it into the water. He tried to stand up, but his head struck the ceiling and forced him back down. He watched his life float past him: old, discolored toothbrushes, foreign magazines he'd once hidden under the mattress, Maria's old broom, his stolen copy of *Don Quixote*, and the red goldfish, on its way to a place Elio now forced himself to imagine.

The lights went out. Elio sat in the dark, high above the water. If he didn't jump into the water soon, he'd be swept away. He breathed deeply. His chest rose and fell with every breath, as the island buckled beneath him. "This is it," he said one more time, and then suddenly, just as he was about to dive into the water, he heard a voice: "Co-co-compañero, this is it. You either cu-cu-come out or we-we take you by force."

It was Roberto Salas, the bodeguero. Elio recognized his stutter, and it took him only a few seconds to respond. "By force," he said. "Take me by force."

"Swim, coño. Or this cou-could take hours. What's with all the goddamn drama?" Roberto said, pulling Elio down by a foot.

A second man stood next to Roberto. He was about Elio's age, with sideburns, and an overgrown mustache. Elio thought he looked like an American cowboy. The man stared at Elio, and said nothing. He seemed unconcerned by the water that came up to his chest, and continued to rise.

Elio didn't respond, letting his body topple into the water with a splash.

"Grab him, Agustino. He wants to play stiff," Roberto told the man. "Coño, viejo," he then said, looking straight at Elio. "Don't you think you're getting too old for this?"

"You know this guy, Roberto?" Agustino said.

"Yeah, he used to work at the textilera. Pull him up. He's, you know, a strange bird. But harmless."

Elio let the two men hook him under each arm and pull him through the water until they reached the sidewalk. His bare feet scraped against the raised cracks in the pavement. The world had gone in reverse, he thought. The ocean was here and the island out there. Somewhere else. Repinga, this was a world still inventing itself. Transforming itself, rising, submerging, and breaking apart. New bodies broke off from the mainland daily, drifting at sea, with or without a goddamn compass, with or without trade winds, with or without good-byes, carajo. Because people didn't even do that anymore.

You had to look with different eyes to see it. Not everyone could see it, but he could. Islands were meant to be left behind, and this one was no different. His itinerary was clear. He was leaving, but not for Miami, or Tampa, or Chicago, or anywhere else. He was going elsewhere.

"Walk, recoño. This isn't the French Riviera. We gotta go," one of the men said, thrusting him forward.

Elio remained quiet. It was as though his mouth had been shut tight on a wire. He went light in the head, but in a strange way, as if he were breathing differently, taking in more oxygen than usual. Suddenly, he felt himself being pulled by an invisible line and dragged again through the water. He made a wild, panic-stricken, jerking motion and the men lost their grip. Elio saw his chance, perhaps his last one, and he dove into the water.

He heard the men shouting in the distance, their voices muffled, rippling in the current. But he no longer recognized his name. He thought of reaching the Malecón, but he was set on a different destination entirely. *Swim, coño! Swim!* he could hear Pepe shouting. And so he did, he swam. He swam as far as his mind and the current could take him. He vanished without a trace, but someone, somewhere would need to look for him. He wished it were Maria. His was the place, he'd tell her, where everyone should go.

DISCUSSION QUESTIONS

1. Discuss the title, *Until We're Fish*. What does the author try to communicate? How do fish express the relationship between Cubans and the sea? How is water used to discuss dreams and personal freedom? What deeper meaning may water represent for those living on an island?

2. The novel opens with a quote from Dante Alighieri's *Vita Nuova:* "In my book of memory, in the early part where there is little to be read, there comes a chapter with the rubric: 'Here begins a new life.'" Discuss this statement as it applies to the "new life" Elio and Maria embark on, both in terms of the 1959 Cuban Revolution, and also in terms of their marriage.

3. How does the prologue, "Fish Eyes," contribute to the novel's overall mood and feel? How does the prologue amplify the meaning of Elio's journey? After reading the novel and returning to the prologue, what can we see that we couldn't see before?

4. Elio dreams of owning a red Schwinn bicycle. What role does the Schwinn play in the plot? How is it used symbolically in the story?

5. The novel is told from several different points of view: that of Elio, of Maria, and of others. How does Elio's understanding of himself differ from Maria's understanding of him?

6. What are the main differences between Elio and Pepe? Why is Maria drawn to each in different ways? How important is it for a couple to share similar goals? Is there a parallel between Maria and Elio's marriage and the 1959 Cuban Revolution? What is the author saying about the effects of the Cuban Revolution on individual lives?

7. Elio is determined to stay in Cuba. What does staying mean to Elio? How would you characterize Elio's relationship with Cuba?

8. According to Elio, "the island has turned against itself." What are some instances in the novel that support his statement?

9. Elio steals books, while Maria stops reading altogether. What is the role of books and reading in the novel? What might the author be suggesting by alluding to novels such as *Madame Bovary, The Count of Monte Cristo,* and others?

10. In reading the note on the back of a photograph meant for Pepe, Elio finds out that Maria had feelings for Pepe, even though Elio and Maria were courting at the time. Do you think it would have changed things between Maria and Elio if she had ever told him about her feelings for Pepe? How do you think she would have told him? Have you ever discovered news by reading something you shouldn't have?

11. Maria makes a great many sacrifices to support Elio. What does it mean to be a supportive wife or husband? Do you think Elio acts

selfishly? How do you support someone in something if it requires sacrificing so much for yourself? Is Maria's final choice justified?

12. Many artists, dreamers, adventurers, etc., take tremendous risks at the edge of their pursuits for numerous reasons. Do you think Elio is justified in his pursuit of his obsessions? Is it fair to Maria? At what point must one consider the needs of others more than one's own? How does fear influence—or skew—Elio's decision-making? Has fear ever prevented you from pursuing your interests?

13. What is the role of the therapist in the novel? What does the state of mental health in the novel reveal about life on the island? What does the state of mental health in the novel reveal about weathering defeat and finding joy in life?

14. What is the function of sex in the novel? How are sex and the Revolution intertwined, according to the author?

15. In what way are Elio and Pepe joined forever? What does it mean to owe your life to someone else?

16. American products and a concern for the American way of life are ubiquitous in the novel. What do you think the characters' special fondness for the United States suggests about Cuba's relationship with its northern neighbor?

17. What do we learn from Isabelita and Manolito about Cubans' knowledge of life beyond the island? What sets Isabelita apart from the other women in the book? In what ways is she innocent and naïve? In what way is she wise?

18. What does the therapist mean when he tells Elio: "Your behavior is quite a bit more unusual than we're comfortable with?" In this scene, "we" represents the state. Who else in the novel could be a substitute for the state?

19. How does the 1959 Cuban Revolution function as a character in the story?

20. What is the significance of Elio's visit to the Cave of Paredones? What is he hoping to find? What does he actually find? How does what Elio finds impact how he views the world?

21. Why do you think the author included a supernatural element in *Until We're Fish?* How does the presence of ghosts change Elio? What do they represent to him? Are readers meant to take the presence of the ghosts literally?

22. Whether it is excessive rain, oppressive heat, or devastating hurricanes, the weather is an important part of the story. How does the weather affect characters in the novel? What might the weather symbolize?

23. What are the men's attitudes toward women? Compare Ricky Perez's perception of American women to his perception of Cuban women. How do Cuban women in the novel defy Ricky's perception of them?

24. In the novel's carefully crafted structure, relationships and events build upon one another to culminate in an emotionally complex ending. What implications can we draw from Elio's return to the sea? What parallels are made and how do they help us understand Elio's journey? Can you think of other symbolic comparisons?

25. After everything that Elio has been through, the last words he hears are a passionate call to life: "Swim, coño! Swim!" Why do you think the author chose to end the novel on such an optimistic note? What are your thoughts about Elio's destination in the last chapter?

26. Though *Until We're Fish* is entirely a work of fiction, the author's firsthand experience of life in Cuba informs many of the events that take place in the novel. What did you know about the 1959 Cuban Revolution before reading *Until We're Fish?* Did the book challenge any preconceived ideas about life in Cuba?

ACKNOWLEDGMENTS

To Maria and Elio, whose presence in my life is inextricable from this story. To everyone at Propertius Press for making this such a warm and effortless publishing experience. I will forever be grateful. To my editors, Maya Rock, Nick O'Hara, and Faye Roberts, thank you for your invaluable guidance. To my artist, Lance Buckley, for the magnificent cover. To my creative director, Raven van den Bosch, for the beautiful interior.

I am indebted to authors and generous mentors Mona Simpson and Cristina García, for their early championing of this story. A heartfelt thanks must go to my amazing writers' group (Jennifer Hudak, Clarissa Goenawan, and Suchi Rudra), for their collective energy, talent, and support. Special thanks to Jonette Mauch and Christina Maria García for reading versions of this story at various points in the writing process. Thank you to my sister, Jacquelle Marie Rodríguez, for her brilliant observations, and to my brother, Bryan Rodríguez, for his keen philosophical insights on Elio's journey. I am grateful for the Department of English & Modern Languages at California State Polytechnic University, Pomona, for the time and resources to complete this novel. Thanks go to Gabriela Herrera Stern, Simona Livescu, and Magdalena Edwards for their steadfast belief in my capacity to tell stories.

I am also forever indebted to each member of my family there, here, and somewhere in between. Our shared memories, love, and bitterness for what we left behind helped shape this novel. To my mother and father, Aleida and Jesus, for showing me what love, courage, and resilience look like. All my love to my two beautiful daughters, Kamila Maia Drissi and Leila Nauelle Drissi, for your creative genius and untiring support. And to my husband, Karim Drissi, no amount of words can express my gratitude. Thank you for defending my dreams, always.

To the people of Bauta: May we heal and never again have to go through anything remotely like the things that happen in this book.

ABOUT THE AUTHOR

SUSANNAH RODRÍGUEZ DRISSI is an award-winning writer, translator, and scholar. Her poetry, prose, and academic papers have appeared in journals and anthologies such as *In Season: Stories of Discovery, Loss, Home, and Places in Between,* which won the 2018 Florida Book Award; the *Los Angeles Review of Books; Saw Palm; Literal Magazine; Diario de Cuba; SX Salon; Raising Mothers;* the *Acentos Review;* and *Cuba Counterpoints,* among many others. Her plays have been performed in Los Angeles and Miami, and she is currently at work on *Nocturno,* a musical. Rodríguez Drissi is the author of *The Latin Poet's Guide to the Cosmos* (Floricanto Press, 2019) and is on the faculty of the Writing Programs at the University of California, Los Angeles.

For memorable fiction, non-fiction, poetry, and prose,

Please visit Propertius Press on the web

www.propertiuspress.com

Made in the USA
Las Vegas, NV
02 February 2022

42853953R00224